A Game of Battleships

Also by Toby Frost:

Space Captain Smith
God Emperor of Didcot
Wrath of the Lemming Men

A Game of Battleships

Toby Frost

MYRMIDON

Myrmidon
Rotterdam House
116 Quayside
Newcastle upon Tyne
NE1 3DY

www.myrmidonbooks.com

Published by Myrmidon 2013

ISBN 978-1-905802-77-7

Set in 11/14pt Sabon by Falcon Oast Graphic Art Limited,
East Hoathly, East Sussex

Printed in the UK by CPI Group (UK) Ltd, Croydon, CRO 4YY

Contents

Prologue

The Fortress of Iron squatted on top of the mountain like a skull driven onto a spike. It was the shape of the ant-like head of Ghast Number One: its mouth a doorway big enough to fit a tank, the radio masts a pair of huge antennae rising above the gun emplacements that served it for eyes.

Praetorian assault-lieutenant 28935/H, Stormfist Legion, snarled into the polar wind as he lumbered across the snow. The cold stung his lattice of facial scars, but to flinch would have been to show weakness. And weakness, of course, deserved death.

Captain 948356/B awaited him at the doors to the citadel beside a writhing coil of bio-wire. As the lieutenant ran up, a succession of muffled explosions rippled from inside the fortress like great belches. The Earth-scum had laid plenty of bombs and the drone clearance teams were still finding them.

'*Ak nak!*' 28935/H bellowed. 'All hail mighty Number One!'

The captain nodded. He was slightly over half the praetorian's height. 'All hail our glorious leader. Are the humans dead yet?'

28935/H swallowed hard. 'Almost, Captain. We have them trapped in the Museum of Puny Human Artefacts. As soon as we gain access, they will be annihilated.'

948356/B shivered and pulled his leather coat tight around his meagre body. 'What are you waiting for? Lead me to them!'

They slogged their way across the compound. The museum loomed above them like a corrupted Greek temple. Huge pillars clustered around the doors. Above the entrance, a bas relief showed Number One stamping on the great buildings of Earth, his heel grinding the head of the Statue of Liberty to dust.

Ghasts swarmed around the building, flies on carrion. Trenchcoats and stercoria flapping, the ant-men rushed about yelling threats and orders to one another, pointing and saluting. One praetorian unit had shot its weakest member and, now that rigor mortis had set in, was using him as a battering ram against the service door.

'We have made all efforts to break into the museum,' 28935/H snarled. 'Superior Ghast construction hinders our efforts.'

'A feeble excuse,' the captain replied. His breath hissed into the cold air. 'Failure to crush these Earth-scum immediately will result in you being relocated to the delightful snow-capped mountains of the M'Lak Front!'

28935/H saluted very quickly. He could have easily pulled his master's head from its narrow shoulders but, without a command to do so, he was powerless. 'We shall double our efforts,' he promised, pulling his gun and shooting a minion to show that he meant it. He paused, and a rare moment of curiosity passed through his reinforced skull. 'Captain?'

'What?'

'Is it true that Isambard Smith is inside? *The* Isambard Smith? The one who assassinated indestructible Number Eight?'

948356/B ignored him.

'Because, I was thinking. . . Number Eight was genetically perfect – all the posters say so – and if you can kill something that's genetically perfect. . .'

'Lean forward.' The praetorian leaned. 'Bit closer. I can't reach.'

28935/H almost bent double. 'How is this, great one?'

'Perfect.' 948356/B slapped him across the jaw. 'Never think for yourself!' he shrieked. 'Now smash your way in and slaughter them!'

*

In the cool dark of the museum, under the glow of Florence Nightingale's lamp, Major Wainscott gathered his men. The Deepspace Operations Group loaded their weapons under an exhibit entitled *Puny Humans Tolerate Illness.*

'Pay close attention,' Wainscott said, stroking his beard. 'We've got two minutes at most before those ugly bastards bash their way inside. The charges are laid, but we need to get some distance. Smith, how's our transport?'

Isambard Smith took his mouth away from the siphon and said, 'Nearly done,' and got a spurt of petrol in the face for his trouble.

'Excellent. We'll go out guns blazing. Susan, you and the chaps'll be on top deck.'

His second in command pushed a fresh power-pack into the top of her beam gun. 'Right.'

'Now, where's that damned alien. . .?'

'Greetings!' Suruk the Slayer strolled out of the dark, past a model of *Louis Pasteur Failing To Develop A Deadly Viral Weapon*. Suruk opened his mandibles and smiled. 'Apologies for my lateness. I was distracted by *Feeble Bladed Weapons of the Stunted Himalayas*. I trust I have not missed any of the carnage?'

Smith spat out petrol and stood up. 'We're all set. Let's get loaded up. We've only got half an hour to meet up with the ship.'

'Well said,' Wainscott replied. 'Hop on, men! And hold on tight!'

*

Ghasts crowded around the front entrance. 'Obedience is strength!' a praetorian roared, and it ran head-first into the doors. 'Oof!' It staggered back, helmet ringing.

A second praetorian shoved it aside and charged the doors, snarling like a dog. 'Obedience is strength! Oof!'

Captain 948356/B smiled as he watched them. 'How ironic,' he mused, 'that the humans should die among the worthless clutter of their pathetic culture.'

'Culture?' snarled the lieutenant, cocking his gun. 'Where?'

948356/B smirked into the wind. 'And how very, very pleasing.'

The doors exploded. In the last half-second of his life,

948356/B saw something like a shining red cliff come roaring out of the museum in a howl of engines and twisting steel. He saw a window and a human face behind it, and realised that he was looking at Captain Isambard Smith – and then the bus hit him and he burst across the windscreen like an enormous fly.

The Routemaster ploughed through ranks of bellowing praetorians like a runaway juggernaut. Smith activated the windscreen wipers, and the blades threw gouts of purple alien slime across the snow. The horn tooted merrily and the storm-ants, unable to disobey their orders, rushed forward and were reduced to mush.

A Ghast threw itself at the bus, clinging on with all four arms. It headbutted the windscreen and smashed its helmet through the glass in four brutal blows. The alien thrust its face through the hole and tried to bite the steering wheel. 'Nutrition is victory!' it snarled. 'Eat the weak!'

Smith drew his .48 Civiliser, pushed it into the praetorian's nasal hole and blew its rudimentary brains out.

By God! thought Smith, as the bus bumped over a succession of bulbous steel helmets and bulging rear ends, sometimes duty was its own reward.

'All aboard, fools!' Suruk the Slayer bellowed from the far end of the bus. He snatched at coats and helmets as the vehicle drove through the Stormfist Legion, hauling the ant-men onto the running-board. The great sickle-shaped blade in his hand rose and fell and heads rolled against the base of the stairs before Suruk tossed the bodies back into the snow. 'No ticket? Then I shall conduct you to your doom!'

Upstairs, the five members of the Deepspace Operations

Group poured fire into the aliens. Susan swung the beam gun and praetorians fell apart as the laser touched them. The Ghasts ran after the bus, blazing away wildly, even trying to chew through the hubcaps as it sped past, but a combination of murderous gunfire and moral fibre drove them back.

The bus left its pursuers behind. No doubt the Ghasts would be calling up reinforcements but, for now, the way was clear. Smith switched on the radio. 'Claymore calling John Bull,' he barked into the intercom. 'Claymore calling John Bull. Come in, John Bull.'

A girl answered him. 'This is Claymore,' came the reply.

'No it isn't. *You're* John Bull. I'm Claymore.'

'You know,' Polly Carveth said, 'this would have been much easier if you'd let me choose my own callsign.'

'I've told you before, I get to choose the callsigns.' Smith swung the bus onto a narrow road. A notice in Ghastish threatened death. Most notices in Ghastish did that. He ran it over. '*I'm* the captain.'

'But why do I have to be crappy John Bull?'

'Because if I let you choose your own name you'd be Glitter Pony or some similar nonsense. This is a commando raid, not a gymkhana.'

'No I wouldn't. I'd be Polly Princess.'

'Damn it, Carveth, are you going to pick us up or not?'

'Keep your bulls on, Claymore! I'm on my way.'

The bus rumbled down the narrow roads towards the landing strip. Nothing followed it: Smith knew that, back at the fortress, the Ghasts would be readying their hover-tanks, calling up reinforcements to cut the humans off before they could escape the planet. Suruk chuckled.

Without any enemies to slay, the M'Lak was leaning out the doorway, tongue out, enjoying the falling snow.

The gunfire had stopped on the upper floor. Wainscott bounded down the stairs and stopped beside Smith's shoulder, rubbing his hands and smirking at the road ahead.

'Almost at safe distance,' he said.

'Good.' Smith consulted a diagram sellotaped to the dashboard. 'Listen, when we hit the fence it's going to get hotter than a Friday-night phaal. We'd better time this right.'

'Very true,' Wainscott said, rubbing his beard. Technically, he was in charge of the mission, but Smith knew that he was always willing to listen to reason in the field – in as much as he was capable of listening to reason at all. The fact that Wainscott was not yet nude apart from his gun and boots meant that the mission was going pretty well.

'Ready?' Smith said.

Wainscott glared over Smith's shoulder at the road ahead. 'Ready.' He turned and ran back upstairs. Suruk put the last of the severed heads into his bag and zipped it shut. Smith gunned the engines and the bus crawled downhill. The thrusters of dozens of hovertanks had turned the road into a frozen track as smooth and pale as milk. He hoped that the chains on the wheels would do the trick.

Nelson, the Deepspace Operations Group's technician, called down the stairwell: 'Enemy behind!'

Smith looked in the rear view mirror. Vehicles were pouring down the road, a black armoured snake. He accelerated. 'What's the range?' he called back.

'We're out of the blast range.' This was Wainscott. 'Let 'em have it, Nelson!'

Five miles away, the Fortress of Iron exploded. The huge skull on the hillside cracked and burst apart. Thunder rippled through the valley, knocking great sheets of snow from the hillsides. The steering wheel jerked in Smith's hands, and he wrestled them back on course.

'Boom!' Wainscott chortled.

'Very good!' Suruk exclaimed, as if at a joke. 'Very good indeed!'

The landing pad was up ahead. Smith saw rows of space-fighters parked behind an alien fence. 'Hold on,' he called, and he turned the wheel and drove straight through the bio-wire. The bus swung out, ploughing into a row of fighter-craft, smashing their tail-fins. Two Ghasts ran onto the far side of the landing pad, hauling a disruptor-cannon between them.

Gunfire clattered outside. A shot clipped the engine block and suddenly black smoke poured into the cabin. In the top right of the windscreen, next to several holes, a speck had appeared and was growing into Smith's battered space freighter, the *John Pym*.

'Our transport arrives!' Suruk announced.

Smith threw on the brakes, turning the bus side-on to the enemy. As he slipped from the driving seat, the windows burst in a roar of disruptor-fire. He crept down the length of the bus, boots crunching on shards of glass. A fresh burst of alien shooting slammed into the side, wrenching the metal.

'All change!' Smith called. 'The ship's here!'

'I think we may have angered them,' Suruk observed, as he picked up his bag of heads.

Wainscott glanced at Susan. 'All set?'

14

She nodded. 'I'll keep you covered. Craig, pop some fog out there!'

They ran out in a billowing wall of white smoke. The air was cold and smelt of burning. Susan levelled the beam gun and the laser arced out and cut down the Ghasts on the heavy disruptor. Two more ran in to take their place.

The *John Pym* dropped from the sky like a meteor – far too much like one for Smith's tastes. At a hundred feet up, Carveth clearly remembered the brakes and the engines roared as it slowed and turned, peeling the paint from the roof of the bus. Half a dozen praetorians ran to meet it.

The *John Pym* twisted mid-air and the great rusty boom of the tail hit the bus. It rocked and flopped onto its side, flattening six solider ants under several tons of steel.

The *Pym*'s landing legs hit the tarmac. The loading ramp dropped open, and the raiders rushed into the safety of the hold.

The soldiers ran through the hold and into the mess-room. Smith paused by the door, hand on the lever. 'Where's Wainscott?'

'Right here.' Wainscott looked back at the landing pad. It was littered with dead praetorians. He snorted. 'Elite shock troops my arse. Come on, chaps, let's get the kettle on!'

Smith braced himself as the *John Pym* tore off from the ground. He closed the mess door and walked into the corridor. He followed the Deepspace Operations Group into the kitchen, then wandered through to check on the rest of the crew.

Suruk was already in his room, making space for the new additions among the skulls on his mantelpiece. In the next cabin down, Rhianna Mitchell sat cross-legged on a pile of genuine Procturan crystal-cushions, a lopsided dreamcatcher hanging above her head. Smith wanted to kiss her hello, but it would be unwise to disturb her meditation. It was Rhianna's psychic ability that was keeping them off the Ghast radar.

He started to creep past. 'How'd it go, Isambard?' she asked, not opening her eyes.

'Pretty damned good, thanks. Want some tea?'

'Herbal?'

'Certainly not. I'll bring you one in.'

'Namaste, Isambard.'

'Carry on,' he said, and he strode into the cockpit.

Polly Carveth looked round from the pilot's seat. She wore her utility waistcoat and had rolled up the sleeves of her collarless shirt. The ship's emergency goggles looked enormous on her small face. 'Are we safe yet?' she asked.

'Nearly, Carveth.'

'Thank God for that. How was it?'

'Clockwork.'

She glanced at the console on her left. 'Uh-oh. We've got a pressure problem, boss.'

'Pressure? What's happened?'

'We've taken a leak. Either they've shot us or some lemon's not shut the back door properly.'

'I'll be back in a minute,' Smith replied. 'Carry on.'

He left the cockpit and headed down the corridor. Rhianna still sat in her trance, looking pretty and smelling herbal. The Deepspace Operations Group were pouring out the tea. Smith yanked the door open and stepped into the chill of the hold.

The air was thin: they were leaving the atmosphere behind. Smith crossed the hold, the wind howling around the open door, and reached out to the button.

A massive red shape rose up beside him.

28935/H had been hiding behind the packing crates: out of ammunition but too fanatical to retreat. The leather coat whipped around his bulging stercorium. Under the steel helmet, yellow eyes glared out of a face that was all scar tissue and fangs.

'I'll smash you!' he snarled. 'Smash you good.'

He lumbered forward and swung a huge pincer at his head. Smith ducked and slammed his fist into the beast's midriff, knocking him back.

'Die!' the praetorian grunted. 'Weaklings must die!'

28935/H charged. Smith darted aside, stamped into the side of the alien's knee and tripped the brute with its own momentum. He grabbed the back of the Ghast's helmet, hooked his fingers over the front, punched his right hand forward and yanked the left hand back. There was a sickening crack and the praetorian kicked, shivered and was still.

Smith gave the body a good shove and it flopped out of the back door. He watched it fall, the leather coat wrapped around it like a dead bat's wings. Then he closed the door.

On balance, it was probably time for a holiday.

27th of April, 1853.

Success!
   I am delighted to report that my first test subjects have returned apparently unharmed from their trip through the Breach. I purloined a rabbit from the Dean's vegetable garden and purchased a tom-cat from a travelling fellow, and on Saturday night I put them both through the gate-way. The rabbit seems entirely untroubled by the experience and indeed appears to want to return to the portal as quickly as possible. The tom-cat, although it has made itself scarce since its return, leaves me with the impression of being contented.
   But this is not enough. I am on the cusp of a discovery that will make me the toast of Oxford. If my research is to be concluded, I will need larger test subjects. I considered using an ape, but I suspect that its absence would be missed. I need a higher organism, but one that is generally neither seen nor heard. Wait a moment – how about a child?

Part One

The Big Bang

Isambard Smith leaned back in his chair, put his model kit down and turned to the girl in his bed. 'You know, Rhianna,' he declared, 'there are many spaceships in the British fleet, but I think this must be the finest.'

Rhianna looked around the room, taking in the ambiance of HMS *John Pym*: the exposed pipework, the slightly rusty bolts and the subtle, yet pervasive, smell of last night's dinner. 'Um, okay,' she replied, brushing a stray dreadlock out of her eyes.

'No, *this* ship,' Smith said. He held up the model kit. 'HMS *Valiant*, first of the Cerberus-class fast destroyer fleet. Do you know, it fires ten-pound railgun shells? Ten pounds! Imagine getting alongside Gertie and letting rip broadsides with a couple of those! Boom! No more war of aggression for you, you dirty moon-men!. . . Are you alright?'

He paused, model raised ready to swoop. Rhianna gave him a small smile. 'I'm fine.'

Smith lowered HMS Valiant. It was difficult having a girlfriend, especially a foreign vegan who disapproved of war. He had come to realise that girls were different from men and that he had to make allowances for that. If walking out with Rhianna had taught him anything, it was that women had to be treated with tact and respect. 'You look less than chipper, old girl,' he said. 'It's not a lady problem, is it?'

'No, Isambard. Don't you know what day it is?'

'Indeed I do. It's the day before the anniversary of the Battle of Agincourt.'

'It's three days before I have to go away. And I don't want to leave you, even though you are obsessed with battleships and high on glue fumes. I know we have to be apart, but still. . . I wish we didn't.'

'I know.' Fear rose inside Smith: she was going to make him talk about *feelings* again. For any decent Englishman there were only two kinds of feelings: righteous anger and quiet satisfaction. Anger was usually directed towards aliens, traitors, foreigners and Carveth, his pilot, android and alleged subordinate; satisfaction might be felt after thwarting invaders, thrashing tyrants, eating a pie or releasing wind. He was not certain he could produce the emotions Rhianna expected of him: after all what was one supposed to think of the sea-beams glittering on the shores of Orion beyond it all being quite nice – for abroad?

'I shall miss you too,' he said. And he would; he knew that for a fact. 'I like you very much.' It sounded feeble. 'I think you're super,' he added. She smiled at that, so he risked continuing to speak. 'When I first met you, I thought you were just some funny bird from New Francisco. But I've learned to appreciate you properly. There's so many facets about you that I like,' he added, making a rhetorical gesture towards some of the facets in

22

particular. 'You're nice, and you're pretty, and you like Pink Zepplin too.'

'I prefer the acoustic stuff.'

'I wish I knew where you were going,' he said.

'Me too,' she replied. 'But it's top secret. They need me to help research the Vorl.'

'I know. War effort and all that.'

She nodded. 'Just got to chill out and carry on.' Despite Rhianna having been born on the New Francisco orbital colony, Smith thought that she was picking up the language pretty well. He realised that they hadn't reached the end of the convoy run yet, and he was already missing her. Well, dammit, there was no point moping about like a sad-sack. They'd jolly well have some fun first, just as soon as he'd sorted out this model kit.

Rhianna stood up and picked up her skirt from the floor. 'Isambard, you look really stressed. Is there something wrong? Something you're not telling me?'

'Not really—'

'Have you glued HMS Valiant to your hand?'

'A little bit.'

At 3.25 Greenwich Mean Time, Captain Smith strode into the cramped cockpit of the *John Pym*. 'Status report, crew!' he ordered, dropping into his chair and picking glue off his hand. Gerald, the ship's hamster, scurried happily in his cage.

Polly Carveth consulted her notes. 'Status is bored and slightly nervous, captain. As you can see from the chart here. . .' She held up a battered Galactic Survey map. 'We've passed the system core and are now proceeding with the rest of the convoy to the Ravnavar system, where we will drop Rhianna off with the Service's contact there. Then we and the rest of the convoy will proceed to the outer rim, which in terms of our schedule puts us somewhere between mid-afternoon tea and having a little sleep.'

'Excellent plan. We'll need to get our energy up for late afternoon tea. Anything to report, Suruk?'

Suruk the Slayer stood by the wall, polishing some of the better pieces of his trophy collection. 'Only a disappointing absence of mayhem,' the alien replied, carefully brushing some dust from the bulbous skull of a black ripper. 'I fear that hand-to-hand combat is rather difficult to find in deep space.'

'In which case,' said Smith, 'you can help me with the crossword.' He rummaged about at the side of his seat and came up with a folded newspaper. 'Let's try three down. . . *Creature that hunts prey*. Seven letters.'

Suruk lowered the trophy-skull, opened his mandibles and made a thoughtful purring noise. 'Carnivore,' he said. 'Abbreviated.'

One of the instruments began to clatter rapidly. Smith glanced up, wondering what the device was for. The needles in two dials rolled upwards and a white tongue of tape began to rattle out of a slot under them as if the machine was jeering at his ignorance. 'Important thing happening, Carveth!' he called out, feeling that this sort of detail was best delegated.

She peered at the tape. 'It's a message from the tankers, boss. They say everything's fine.'

'Are you sure?' Smith asked.

Carveth shrugged. 'Well, depends on what you call fine. When you said we were taking a cruise across the galaxy I didn't realise we'd be escorting half a billion tons of explosive fuel.'

'Nonsense, Carveth. The convoy is fully automated. What could go wrong?'

'Well, what happens if one of the cooling computers packs up? Or what if your girlfriend gets off her face and throws one of her joints out of the porthole while it's still lit? I don't like it. I might as well have stayed at home and sat on a hand grenade.'

'Or the washing machine,' Suruk added helpfully. 'Do you remember that time when I walked in—'

'Shut up, Suruk,' Carveth said. 'Look out of the window.'

Smith leaned forward. 'Let him finish, Carveth. If there's a problem with the washing machine, I want to know. A good captain always—'

'No, look!' Carveth pointed to the window. 'What's that?'

Smith squinted at the windscreen. A small ball of light had appeared in the middle of it, growing steadily. 'I wouldn't worry,' he said. 'It's just the sun or something.'

'The sun tends to stay the same size,' Carveth said. She unfastened her seat belt and slipped under the dashboard. 'Tell me when it's gone, would you?'

Smith reached to the navigation console and took down the slide rule. 'Stop worrying, Carveth. It's way off. It won't reach us for at least a parsec.'

'Actually,' said the voice from below the dashboard, 'parsecs measure distance, not ti—'

The world exploded.

*　*　*

Smith opened his eyes. He was looking at the stellar chart attached to the ceiling. His chest felt heavy and breathing was difficult. Faces loomed in at him: Carveth, slightly grimy from her time under the dashboard, and Suruk, his mandibles parted in an enormous grin.

'What happened?' Smith asked.

'We got hit in a blastwave,' Carveth said. 'Systems are down to twenty-five percent. The main engine's on half power and we've lost part of the landing gear.'

'On the plus side,' Suruk added, 'we rode the sun.'

Smith hauled himself upright. Breathing became less difficult as Carveth lifted the hamster cage off his chest. 'What about Rhianna?' he asked.

'I'm here.' She stood in the doorway. A single droplet of blood ran down her forehead. She wiped it off and peered at her forefinger as if she'd never seen the stuff before. 'Are you okay?' she asked, stepping into the room.

Smith blinked. 'Nothing broken. But your head. . .'

Rhianna reached up to her scalp. There was a circular object wedged in her dreadlocks. She breathed in and yanked it free: it was a panmelodium music-disc, fallen from the shelf in her room. She looked at the title. '*Relaxing Moods*,' she said. Rhianna closed her eyes and the blood on her head dried. Suddenly, there was no cut at all. 'There.'

'Well then,' said Smith, 'everybody's fine. We can get back to escorting this con—'

Carveth raised a hand. 'Er, slight problem. There isn't a convoy any more.'

Smith rushed to the window. In the far distance, the remains of half a dozen robot tankers rolled slowly in the void. They looked like scraps of metal eggshell, spinning lazily from the force of the blast, their edges glowing as the remnants of the fuel cooked off.

'Good God!' Smith whispered. 'They've exploded. . . Carveth, this is a disaster.'

'You're telling me.'

'And it raises a single question. . .'

'Will they dock it from our wages?'

'Is this the work of the enemy? Can it be that even here, deep in the back end of space, we can still feel the insidious touch of the Ghast Empire? Is there no region so dark or obscure as to be safe from the vile probings of alien tyranny? Is this the main thrust of the attack or must we—'

'Basically, yes.' Carveth sat down and shook her head. 'I knew this was a bad idea. God, I've not seen such a horrible cock-up since Suruk tried to milk that bull on Ambridge Prime – hang on, there's something on the scanner—'

'Look!' Rhianna cried.

Space rippled in front of them. The stars flexed and bent as if painted onto stretching rubber: space seemed to pull back, then spit something out of itself before the *John Pym*. Cold blue lightning crackled over soot-encrusted steel. For a moment Smith saw the front of a spacecraft: bigger than the *Pym* and angled as if to ram it head-on; striped with red as though smeared in blood; spikes welded to the hull; chains thrashing between them in an electrical storm. The storm swelled, wrapping the hull of

27

the craft in crackling white lightning – and suddenly it was gone. Only space remained.

'Well, crikey!' said Smith. 'Did everyone see that, or am I just concussed again?'

'It was totally real,' Rhianna replied. 'Believe me, I know a hallucination when I see one. I mean, when I see something that isn't really there, I really know it's not real. If you see what I mean.'

Smith tried not to work it out. 'Well, at least nobody's hurt. Carveth, check the instruments!'

At the back of the room, Suruk rubbed his stomach. 'I feel uneasy,' he said. 'I am afraid that the impact may have triggered my reproductive cycle.'

Carveth moved towards the door, then looked back. 'What did you say?'

The alien grimaced. 'Most irksome. It seems that I am about to breed. I feel nauseous.'

'You're not the only one,' Carveth replied. 'The thought of you having babies. . .'

'Bucket, quick!' Suruk snarled.

Smith dropped down and grabbed the emergency flight recorder box. He tipped the emergency flight recorder out of the box, shoved it into Suruk's hands and darted back just in time for Suruk to be noisily and voluminously sick. They stood around him like murderers around the body of their victim, realising the enormity of the horror they faced.

'That,' Suruk announced, 'was most unpleasant.'

Rhianna was first to recover her composure. 'Well, that is wonderful news, Suruk. New life is always a cause for celebration. When are you due to, er, procreate?'

'About five seconds ago,' Suruk replied.

Carveth crept forward, one hand over her mouth. 'God, Suruk, you've been eating a hell of a lot of tapioca,' she said.

'That is not tapioca. Tapioca is unnatural.' Suruk straightened up. 'It is spawn.'

Smith stepped forward. It was all rather horrible: any proper spaceship, he reflected, would have had a trained medic or a mechanical nanny to deal with things like this. 'Right. Thanks for that, Suruk. Perhaps if you could remove your, er, substance, we can get back on with things. No doubt you're very pleased at having bred—'

'Not especially,' Suruk said.

'—but we do have to get back on with our mission. Even though all the ships we were escorting have exploded.'

'Wait,' Rhianna declared. She drew up to her full height in a soft hiss of tie-dyed fabric. 'I feel we should formally congratulate Suruk on his experience. After all, Isambard, children are our future—'

'What – *now*?' Face contorted with alarm, Smith stumbled back towards the door.

Carveth tugged his sleeve. 'She means mankind's future.'

'Oh, right!' Smith smoothed his uniform down. 'Right, yes, of course. Children – good idea for mankind. In general. Very true.'

Suruk flexed his mandibles. 'Excuse me, humans. Once you have finished gabbling about the sanctity of reproduction, do you have somewhere where I can dump this frogspawn, please?'

*

Like an explorer wading through jungle, Carveth shoved a roll of dangling tubes out of the way and pressed on into the heart of the engine room. Behind her, Suruk looked around with suspicion. The ship rumbled around them. The air smelt of burning.

'All this dust and questionable repair work,' he muttered. 'On my planet, an engine room would be very different. Less gaffer tape and more skulls.'

'It looked better before we were caught in a colossal explosion,' Carveth replied. Above her, one of the boilers vented itself with an angry hiss. She set her torch up on the secondary piston array and angled it at the far wall. 'God, what a mess! The main spinner's burnt up its oil, the red thing up there's now down here – and barely red – and just look at the bit that goes round the other bit. It's going round a different bit entirely!'

'I have full confidence in your expertise,' Suruk replied. 'Is this room not radioactive?'

'Well, it's colour-coded,' Carveth replied. 'If it's green and glowing, it's time to be going. Especially that corner over there.'

'Then that is where the bucket shall go.' Suruk thrust the bucket of frogspawn into the corner, under a cracked pipe.

'What're you doing?'

'It is an old custom to leave one's spawn in the engine room. Since we M'Lak reproduce asexually, we have no genetic variance. Therefore, we must induce variation through other means.'

'So you're all irradiated at birth? That explains a lot.'

'I assume our planet of origin was rather more volatile than much of space. Of course, only the greatest elders know where it is. . . and they forget quite a lot, too.'

Carveth looked around the room, surprised just how much duct tape had been used in the construction of the *John Pym*'s engines. 'So what do we feed them on?'

'Feed? My spawn, you mean? Well, I was not really planning on feeding them on anything.'

'Nothing at all?'

'They have each other.'

'They eat each other? That's horrible!'

'It is the only way. Would you want your galaxy swamped by a wave of my spawning?'

'That's even more horrible. God, Suruk, you really are gross.'

The alien shrugged. 'It is the honourable way. As the ancients said in the days before time, when the spirits of the forefathers roamed across space, 'Better tusks than rusks'. The surviving spawn will become warriors, eventually – unless one remains in the water and grows to be a seer.'

'A what?'

'Never mind. It is bad to speak lightly of the Gilled.' Suruk cracked his knuckles. 'Now then, what needs repairing?'

Smith carried the tray to the dining table, ducking under the lampshade. Rhianna finished shoving most of the clutter to the far end and they sat down to receive the status report.

Carveth stood up and cleared her throat. She opened

her in-flight logbook, which would have looked more impressive had it not been decorated with stickers of ponies and rainbows.

'Status report, revised,' she announced. 'We're stuffed.' She closed the logbook and sat down.

'Any details?' Smith asked.

'Alright then. Basically, I'd say we've passed the stage of being merely inconvenienced and are now moving into the realm of being totally buggered. Should the buggeration continue, I'm anticipating us losing not just paddle but canoe very shortly, leaving us floundering helplessly in the filthy rapids of a certain malodorous creek.'

Smith thought it over. 'Thanks. Now, call me pedantic, but can this spaceship still fly through space?'

'Barely. We can move, but very slowly. Faster than light's only just working, and pushing it harder will risk the gears blowing up. Any slower and pensioners will start overtaking us.'

Smith sipped his tea. The badness of the news was allayed by the moral fibre flowing from the teapot. This sort of thing, that lesser men might interpret as a disaster, might have potential for great things. Quite what the things might be other than horror and dismay, he was not sure, but all in good time.

Rhianna said, 'Well, everyone, let's try to be positive. Did you know that in China opportunity and crisis are represented by the same character?'

'Sounds like a rum character to me,' Smith replied. 'If I was Chinese, I wouldn't let him on board.'

'Character as in a single word,' Rhianna said.

'Oppicrisis?' Suruk suggested.

'So we need repairs,' Smith said. 'That much is clear.'

Carveth nodded. 'Big repairs. We need a space dock.'

'Right.' Smith reached behind his chair and took out the AA map book of space. 'The second matter I want to discuss is the vehicle that attacked our ships. Clearly, this was an enemy vessel. . . happy to blast our automated convoy into scrap but too cowardly to fight a British craft face-to-face.'

Carveth sighed. 'Actually, boss, I think the reason they didn't fight us was because they thought we *were* scrap. Also, I'm glad they didn't because we have no guns. But, whatever they were, they came out of nowhere. Nothing on visual or scanners before all that light and. . . well, there they were.'

'Do you think they're nearby?'

'I don't know. But active stealth uses up power like nobody's business. If that ship's anything normal, it can't be far away.'

Smith thought of the craft: the blue flash from which it had appeared; the blood, spikes and chains draped across the front; the unearthly light pulsing around the controls. That sounded far from normal – but then, much of space did technically qualify as *abroad*. He opened the map and began to leaf through the pages for the appropriate quadrant.

'If the enemy is still in the vicinity, men,' he said, half to the map book, 'we must proceed with caution. Carveth, I need you to rig the engines to get us to our destination quickly and quietly. If the enemy analyses our progress, we should look no more suspicious than a very fast rock. A meteor, say. We need to get to a spaceport, have the ship repaired and get back in space. Then we'll find the buggers who wrecked our convoy and blast them into the next galaxy. Page thirty-eight. . .'

He found the right page and laid the map book on the table. 'Right. We're somewhere on this page, in the black bit between the stars. We need to go here – the edge of the Tannhauser Anomaly.' He leaned in, peering at the tiny words under the symbol. 'It looks alright, but. . . well. . .'

Smith straightened up. His face was grim. He swallowed hard and set his jaw. 'Gentlemen, I have bad news.'

In the absence of any actual gentlemen, Rhianna, Carveth and Suruk watched him intensely. His eyes were hard as he took a deep, fortifying swig of tea.

'I know I've asked a lot of you in the past. Together we have been to the darkest corners of space and encountered some of the strangest and most terrible beings known to man. We have done battle with vicious Ghasts, crazed Edenites and savage lemming men on a dozen worlds. We have seen and overcome the depths of madness and depravity. But now I must ask you to follow me once more, as we make contact with Tannhauser station and its inhabitants. I do not know what we will encounter there, but I am certain that it will take every drop of our moral fibre to emerge with our bodies and souls intact.

'Crew, we are going to Europe.'

Dinner for Two

It was a bright cold day in April and the clock was striking thirteen as the repairmen began fixing it. Eric Lint, his collar pulled up tight against his jawline, cupped his hand around his cigarette and said 'Bollocks' into the wind. He strode across the grass towards the thin row of tents at the top of the common, where a banner reading *Little Binley Village Fete and Family Fun Day* flapped like a dying fish.

Slowly he toured the stalls, determined to wring some joy from each. He bought a piece of cake, a sausage in a bun and half a pint of bitter in a plastic glass. He discovered that there was nothing worth buying at the white elephant stand and that he was too tall to have a ride in the village fire engine. Finally, after ignoring the maypole and nearly losing a finger to a grumpy pig in the petting zoo, he turned to the last stand of all.

'Want to guess the weight of the cake?' asked the girl behind the table. Apart from the knife scars down one cheek, she looked like a typical young member of the Women's Institute.

Lint, whose operatives knew him as W, made a show of looking at the cake. 'Eighteen pounds four ounces,' he replied.

The woman nodded. 'They're out the back.'

'Thanks. Nice twinset,' W added, and he strode to the tent at the back of the fete.

He opened the door and an ominously smiling man in spectacles neatly frisked him as he stepped inside. Around the edge of the tent sat three others: George Benson, Assistant Director of Outdoor Recreation for the Service; Hereward Khan, who ran the outfit's Acquisitions and Transport Department; and Aloysius Roth, whose bloodstained hands pulled the strings behind the Colonial Service Overseas Chess Team and Social Club.

'Glad you could join us, W,' Benson said. He was small, spectacled and sad-looking, with a deep, rich voice that seemed to come out of someone larger than himself.

'A pleasure,' W replied. He took a sip of his bitter and lowered himself awkwardly into a seat.

'A potential problem has arisen,' Khan declared, stroking the waxed tips of his moustache. 'We need your department's help.'

W nodded. A list of the galaxy's most villainous riff-raff appeared in his mind: ruthless Ghast legions, zealots from the Democratic Republic of New Eden, crazed, sadistic lemming men of Yull. 'Gladly. I'm always happy to introduce the turkey of oppression to the raw onion of British justice,' he said, making an explanatory gesture.

Khan nodded to Roth. 'I told you he was keen.'

Benson leaned across to him. 'My colleague's department,' he said, gesturing towards W, 'were it to actually exist, would have carried out some excellent work over the past few months. Remember the Edenite Minister of

Propaganda? Had the manpower existed in any official way, it's my colleague here you'd have to thank for taking him off the air.'

Roth raised one thick white eyebrow. 'That was your work?'

'The concept of objective truth is the cornerstone of human liberty,' W said, crossing his legs. 'Only by protecting truth can we hope to retain the gentleness and decency of British life.'

'So what happened to him?'

'We hanged the bastard.' W shrugged. 'He received a fair and balanced trial, followed by a fair and somewhat less balanced execution. So what do you need done?'

'Very soon, we finalise the treaty with the Vorl,' Benson replied. He removed his glasses and started polishing them on his tie. 'Practically every allied nation will be there to witness it and pledge support, including the Vorl themselves. Also in attendance will be the mystics of Khlangar. By themselves, the Khlangari are pretty negligible. They do, however, have strong links to the Voidani space whales, who appear to protect them for reasons unknown. We want them on-side. An alliance like that would be almost unbeatable.'

'I see. And where is it taking place?'

'On a metrological station and recycling plant orbiting the gaseous planet Signus Four, which is to be renamed Wellington Prime for the event.'

'What's it called now?'

'Gas and Rubbish Central. Perhaps not ideal for an international treaty. The place is fortified – originally to keep the rubbish in, rather than the rubbish out, but don't tell the delegates that – but an event like this can't stay secret forever.'

'I see.'

'We'll need additional security,' Benson explained. 'It's not enough for us to sit back and wait for Gertie to attack. We need good fellows out there on the alert, actively seeking out threats.'

W said, 'Smith sounds like the man for the job. He's got a nose for trouble. And a moustache for danger.'

Hereward Khan leaned forward, making his plastic chair creak alarmingly. He was a massive man, as tough and blubbery as an elephant seal. 'No can do,' he replied. 'Smith is on convoy work. We thought he deserved a rest.'

'Have you considered asking the other secret services?'

The appalled spluttering that followed suggested that they had indeed considered the other services. 'Those oiks?' Khan demanded.

Benson's glasses had misted up. 'Oh dear no,' he said. 'No, no. They'd only steal the sandwiches.'

'And the furniture.'

Roth leaned close. 'You know what I heard about the other services?' he whispered. 'Some of them aren't even Oxbridge. To think of it, an entire secret service gone. . . redbrick.' He shuddered violently.

'Gentlemen, please.' W's eyes narrowed. The tiny rollup in the corner of his mouth rose like an accusing finger. 'What matters here is skill, not background. My own people are chosen for ability, not origin. Most of them think a Cambridge punt is a particularly nasty way of incapacitating someone. What matters here –' and his eyes took on a fanatical gleam – 'is the preservation of justice and common decency. We use the best tool for the job – and my men are the best tools in the business.'

There was a moment's pause. 'We thought about Wainscott,' Benson said.

W took a sip of beer to hide his expression. True, Major Wainscott was an expert at seeking out danger. The major had crossed half the galaxy and most of its inhabitants whilst looking for trouble and had found quite a lot of it in some very surprising places. But leaving Wainscott with a bevy of foreign delegates? Surely that was putting a shark in charge of a swimming pool.

'He has a reputation for working discreetly,' Benson explained.

'I'll have words,' W said, remembering that for Wainscott, 'discreet work' was something you did to enemy sentries. 'But the major is on holiday, you know. Dartmoor.'

'Dartmoor, eh? Didn't he go there a couple of years ago?'

W frowned. Wainscott's last trip to the West had been less a matter of going away as of being put away. 'Er, you mean Broadmoor. That wasn't a holiday, as such. More, ah, rest care.'

'Well, in galactic terms, Dartmoor's just down the road. Splendid.'

W reflected that it wasn't so much the distance that would be the problem so much as figuring out which badger sett Wainscott was using as his base of operations. He had received a postcard a month ago, explaining that the major had been accepted by the badgers as one of their own and that he was having a great time making crossbows out of roadkill.

'We knew you were the chap for the job,' Khan said, leaning back. His chair creaked like a galleon in a storm. 'I'll see to it that you get transport and supplies.'

W stood up. 'I'll find Wainscott and head out. Goodbye, gentlemen. Oh – and of course I wasn't here, and I didn't say any of this.'

'Naturally,' Benson replied. 'Would you like a piece of cake to take with you?'

W shook his head. 'At eighteen pound four ounces, it's probably a little heavy for my tastes.'

*

'So,' Rhianna said as she put the tea things away, 'is this the first time Suruk's ever. . . er. . . had children?'

'I'm not sure,' Smith replied. 'You could ask him, although I'm not sure he'd remember. The M'Lak don't really care about their young.' Rhianna passed him the biscuit tin and he reached up to put it on the shelf. 'In fact, when I first met Suruk he was convinced that jelly babies were the human larval stage.'

'That's a shame. Is their culture too patriarchal to allow them to engage properly with their children?'

'Not really. Engage with those things and you'd probably lose a limb. Young Morlocks are like a cross between a frog and a piranha. I'd advise wearing something a bit more solid than flip-flops if you're going in the engine room soon. A suit of armour, perhaps.' He frowned. 'I hope it doesn't take too long to get to Tannhauser. The last thing we need when we arrive in Europe is a bunch of killer frogs chewing through the hull.'

'Well then,' Rhianna said, 'it sounds like we'll get to spend some time together, at last.' She raised an eyebrow. 'Anything in particular you'd like to do?'

Smith recognised that look. 'Scrabble?'

'I was thinking of something a little more. . . adult,' she replied.

'Rude Scrabble! Excellent plan, old girl!' Smith rubbed his hands together. 'Wait a moment. Where're the others?'

'They're in the hold. They'll be okay for a while, won't they?'

Smith shrugged. 'Oh yes. So long as they don't blow up the ship or drink bleach, they'll be fine.'

'Gah!' Suruk clutched his throat and staggered across the hold. Gargling, he fell to his knees, rolled onto one side and lay still.

Carveth looked down at him. 'Sounds like death?'

'It is death!' Suruk exclaimed from the floor.

'So the first word of this film is *death*, and the second is like *oboe*.'

'Well done!' Suruk climbed upright. 'Indeed it is *Death Oboe*. Truly, you are wise in the way of charades.'

'I see,' Carveth said. 'I've never heard of *Death Oboe*.'

'Really? It is a great favourite of my people. It is a remake of an old Earth film named *Pretty Woman*. The knife-fight on top of a grand piano is notorious.'

Carveth sighed. 'Can't you do a film we've both heard of?'

'Very well. How about *Brief Encounters of the Third Kind*?'

'Alright, that sounds – no, you've just told me what it

41

is! Look, let's try something else.' Suruk was not well-adapted to word games: it had taken thirty minutes to explain to him that *honour* was not an Animal, Vegetable or Mineral.

'Very well. Tell me about Europe. Is it truly the worst place in the galaxy?'

Carveth sat down on the aluminium teachest at the rear of the hold. 'Well, it's hard to say. I mean, the Ghast homeworld's probably worse, Yullia too, but Europe. . . well, I've never seen the Captain so worried about meeting our allies before. And given that our allies include Major Wainscott and your family, that can't be good.' She sighed. 'I've never been. But from what the captain says, it's one big country, divided up into little states. France and Germany are the main ones, but there are others. They live in different sorts of houses depending on which country they're from. Smith says the Germans have very modern houses, and the French live in castles called gateaux.'

Suruk nodded. 'Strange. I hear that in Switzerland, people live in cartons. Is it true that Europe is a peaceful and cultured place?'

'Well, yes, I suppose—'

'Excellent! Let us conquer it!'

'Um, no. Europe's on our side. Pretty much.'

Suruk rubbed his chin thoughtfully, after moving his mandibles out the way. 'Troubling. We shall have to proceed with caution. I shall examine my phrasebook.'

'You've got a phrasebook?'

'Of course. It would be rude to pick fights in English.'

*

Smith sighed deeply and pushed away the Scrabble board. 'Well,' he announced, 'that was excellent. Good work, Rhianna: I didn't expect you to get 'quibble' on a triple word score. Although I'm not sure it is actually a rude word.'

'It isn't,' she replied. Rhianna looked down at the Scrabble board and shook her head. 'You know, when I suggested we do something more adult, I didn't really mean making rude words on the Scrabble board.'

'Oh,' Smith said. He peered at her. He felt much like a competitor in a decathlon who has heard the whistle blow without knowing the order of the events. He was obviously meant to guess something. She was clearly not entirely happy, but he had no idea about what. Dimly, it occurred to him that she might have taken him to her cabin for something entirely different. *Damn!*

'I'm sorry,' he said, standing up. 'I misunderstood. Never mind, we can have a bit of the other later on. Right now I really need a sleep.'

'Right,' Rhianna said. 'You go and do that. I'll just meditate.'

Stepping outside, he nearly bumped into Carveth.

'Question, Boss. . . When we get to France, will we have time to go to the duty free?'

'I doubt it. Besides, it'll just be full of chocolate and frilly pants. Nothing we might need.'

'I need those! Come on, Boss, let me go. I'll buy something for Rhianna, so you can give it to her on her birthday.

'Oh, all right then,' Smith said, and he headed to his room.

In his cabin he knelt down and dragged the encryption engine from out under the bed. It looked like a cross between a sewing machine and a very old cash register. A set of instructions was included.

Following steps one to three of the instructions, Smith wrote out a short message, setting out the situation and requesting assistance. Then he pushed the message into one side of the engine and pulled the lever. A pair of rollers pulled the note into the integral mini-furnace, a dial on the front ticked and spun, and fine grey dust fell into the disposal tray.

Step Four told Smith to eat the instructions. As he chewed he hoped that there was no Step Five, and then wondered why he hadn't just fed the instructions into the furnace instead of eating them. He pushed the engine back under the bed, climbed on top and closed his eyes.

A loud pinging sound jolted Smith awake from a dream about scones. He struggled upright, knelt down and dragged out the encryption engine. A ticker-tape message clattered out of a slot in the side.

MESSAGE RECEIVED. CONFIRM YOU ARE IN PICKLE. ASK FRANK JURGENS AT ADENAUER-PLATZ (OFF RUE CHARLES DE GAULLE) ABOUT PHANTOM. HE CAN BE TRUSTED. PLEASE ACQUIRE 2 BOXES CHEAP LAGER IN DUTY FREE. VITAL FOR FUTURE OPERATIONS. OVER.

As he studied the message, the radio began to ring. Smith stumbled to the cockpit and fiddled with the controls.

'Hey!' the speaker called.

'Hello?'

'Is that HMS *John Pym*?'

'It is,' Smith replied warily.

'I was receiving your distress call about one hour ago,' said the voice. 'I am calling from Tannhauser Gate orbital station. I am sorry to hear about your spacecraft breaking down.'

'Thanks,' Smith replied. 'Still, mustn't grumble—'

'Perhaps you should trade it in for a German one. They are quite reliable, you know. My friend is having very much the same trouble as you. He bought a Triumph Dolomite, as antique, and the engine fell out on the Autobahn. It is the unions, he says.'

'Look, I'm sorry about your friend's car, but can we land yet?'

'Of course! The docking sequence will begin in ten minutes. But, ah. . . you might want to carry your own baggage. The handlers, you know.'

*

'Burn them!' the Lord Ezron, the Grand Jackalope, bellowed at the ceiling. 'Let their eyes be plucked from their heads, oh Great Annihilator, their lying tongues torn out, their bodies devoured by jackals and the jackals scattered to the four winds! And with that, I declare the Democratic Republic of New Eden's first conference on women's rights open!'

Lord Ezron sat down to catch his breath, and the other twenty-six hierarchs grumbled their thanks over the sound of the festivities outside.

TOBY FROST

'Item One on the agenda – should women have rights?
Anyone? Then it's still a no. And with that, I declare the
conference closed. Back to the meeting.'

Today, as a billion banners and flags proclaimed, was
Enlightenment Day on the planet of Deliverance, and con-
sequently many things and people were being set alight.
The banging in the street was probably caused by fire-
works. It was hard to tell: along with smiting and
hacking, there was a lot of shooting in the Republic of
Eden on any day at all.

The Supreme Convocation of the Democratic Republic
sat around the table in their ceremonial helms of sanctity,
which gave them the look of a support group for wizards.
At the end of the table sat the Grand Mandrill, the Keeper
of the Flame, Incinerator of Unbelievers. His name was
Lord Hieronymous Prong, and his black, broad-brimmed
hat bore the ancient symbol of the buckle and skull. He
was asleep.

'Now,' said Ezron, 'unless anyone has any objections,
I'll turn to the agenda for today. First, we have a request
from the True Brotherhood of the Chicken Rampant, who
have discovered another thing that might possibly offend
their beliefs. They seek permission to slaughter everyone
potentially responsible.'

One of the other hierarchs had been chewing his beard.
'What are their beliefs?' he demanded through a mouthful
of fluff.

'They believe in. . .' Ezron consulted the agenda, 'finding things that offend their beliefs.'

'Fair 'nuff,' the hierarch said, and he went back to
sucking his beard.

Ezron ticked the list of action points. 'Now for Item Two. We have a proposal from the High Cockatrice himself, Hierarch Beliath, who tells me that he has found a new way to solve the sin of lust. Hierarch Beliath. Please tell me this doesn't involve a pair of garden shears.'

Beliath rose coughing from his seat. 'It has forever been the case,' he rasped, 'that men were created in the image of the Great Annihilator, ever since our blessed forefathers made him up. What have women given the world, except to unleash a tide of lust into our once-pure hearts? Behold!' he cried, fishing a photograph out of his white robes, 'I looked at a picture of a woman, and look what happened to me! If that isn't sinful, I don't know what is!'

The picture was quietly passed around the table. The hierarchs shook their heads sadly. 'Horrible,' said Lord Othred.

The photograph made its way past the sixteen representatives of the Bureau of War, past the hierarch of the Bureau for Liberty, who was currently trying to dissolve his own office to escape the tyranny of excessive government, and to Prong himself, who had started to snore.

A hierarch slipped the photograph in front of him. 'Grand Mandrill?' He paused then nudged the old man's arm. 'Lord Prong?'

Prong's eyes flicked open like a trap. Lurching forward, he blinked several times and yelped 'Faith is purity! Purge it with flame! What's going on?'

The hierarch tapped the table, and Lord Prong looked down at the photograph.

'Gah!' he cried, drawing back into his chair. 'What devilry is this? Save us from this – this – whose is this?'

Daringly, Hierarch Beliath gave the Grand Mandrill a stern look. 'I was debating the licentiousness of women, Lord Prong. There will be a slideshow later. But for now, I propose that there is only one way of ridding New Eden of the evil taint of lechery – we must kill all women!'

Cheers broke out among the hierarchs. 'Crusade!' one wheezy voice croaked.

Lord Prong felt the soft whirr in his temple that told him his frontal lobe accelerator was going to work. He was festooned with bionic enhancements, largely to compensate for the fact that he was two hundred and eighty-three. Sitting in his metal throne, a bundle of wires protruding from the side of his head like a broken television, it occurred to him that there might be a small flaw in this magnificent plan.

'Fool!' Prong rasped, and the microphone on his throat amplified his voice into a doom-laden roar. 'You overstep yourself, Beliath. Did you consider the obvious result of killing every woman in the Republic of Eden? Who would we have to pick on then, eh?'

'Oh,' Beliath said, chastened.

'Quite. Also, we would not be able to breed.'

'The Ghasts have cloning machines,' Hierarch Grumm put in. 'They could lend them to us. They *are* our allies, after all.'

'Oh they're *much* too busy for that,' Beliath replied, in a tone of bitter sarcasm. 'They've got their new friends the lemming men to think about. Apparently the lemming men are really fanatical.'

'How can they be more fanatical than us?' Ezron

demanded. 'We're a theocracy, for the Annihilator's sake – may he butcher everything in his divine mercy. It doesn't get any more fanatical than that!' He shook his head sadly. 'We were committed to working with the Ghasts. I remember how it used to be. . . we'd do the religious genocide while they purged the galaxy of inferior life-forms.' He sighed. 'We had something special together.'

'We can get them back,' Prong said.

The hierarchs turned. Wild eyes and conical hats swung towards Prong's throne. 'What?' Grumm demanded, throwing an arc of spittle across the table.

The Grand Mandrill smiled. 'Item three. My underlings have been working on a little project. You might want to think of it as a secret weapon.'

'A gun?' Grumm was of the Cordite sect and revered firepower.

'Of course not!' Beliath said. 'Lord Prong is a good Ignian. It'll be a special flamethrower for divinely roasting unbelievers.'

'Good tries, gentlemen,' Prong replied, 'But wrong. The Department of Forbidden Science has been looking into non-Euclidian geometry. I refer, of course, to inter-dimensional travel.'

'Blasphemy!' So far in the meeting, the Exalted Coelacanth, most venerable of the elders, had been silent, his head lowered in prayer or slumber. Now he struggled to his feet and shook his small, hard fist. 'This is a gross insult to Edenites everywhere. We must hunt out the dimensional travellers and kill them all!'

Prong sighed. 'No, it's us who'd be travelling. Sit down, damn it!'

'Oh, okay.' The Coelacanth sat down again and settled back in his chair.

'Now then,' Prong said, smiling down the length of the table. 'Seventy-two hours ago, we successfully tested a prototype. In only a few days our allies will be sending deputations to view the weapon in action. High ranking delegates from the Ghast Empire will be among them. We'll see who looks unimportant when we reveal a dimension-shifting spacecraft to them.' He peered down the table. 'So wash your robes, alright?'

*

The airlock swung open and Smith found himself looking into the French quarter of Tannhauser Gate. Flags hung from the ceiling of the space station; accordion music drifted through the air. A poster showed a girl in armour, the stars of Europe forming a halo over her bowl-cut hair. There was even scrollwork on the ornamental lamp-posts, although it looked rather flimsy compared to that back home. Still, Smith thought as he stepped in, Europe didn't smell of cheese and nobody had demanded to see their papers yet.

In fact, nobody seemed to have noticed them at all. Two ancient men sat under a sign that read *café*. As Smith approached they looked away.

'It's a caff!' Carveth said. 'Who wants a *sandwich de bacon*, then?'

Smith put out his arm to bar her way. 'Careful, Carveth. They like strange food here,' he added, lowering his voice to a sinister whisper. 'Even their national anthem is about mayonnaise.'

Like gunslingers arriving in a suspiciously deserted town, they walked warily down the street.

Smith wondered what all the strange signs meant. A poster advertised something called *Le Chat Noir* – a public convenience, presumably. The smell of bread floated out of a shop called *Le Maison de Pain*. *Maison* meant *house*, Smith recalled. Presumably it was a dentist's, or some rum kind of knocking-shop.

Rhianna took her smoking tin from her bag. 'Are we in Amsterdam yet?'

'I don't think so,' Smith replied. She looked disappointed. 'If I remember rightly, the Europeans divide their territory into quarters, depending on which mini-country they're from. At least. . . where are we?' Taking a deep breath, and mustering all the European he could remember from Form 3B, he approached the two old men outside the café.

'You there,' he declared. One of the old men moved one of his eyes. 'Can you direct me to the Rue Charles de Gaulle, my good man?'

The other old man said, 'Eh,' and shrugged. Clearly he was searching his memory for the answer. After a little while, Smith realised that the man had not understood him.

'No,' Smith replied, raising his voice and speaking more slowly as if addressing a relative both senile and half-deaf, 'I. . . am. . . British. I. . . am. . . *looking*' – he mimed a sailor surveying the horizon – 'the Rue Charles de Gaulle.' Unsure of how to mime this, he pointed to his moustache. 'Erm. . . do you speak Latin? *Omnes Gallia divisa est in partes tres*, perhaps?'

'*Bof,*' said the other old man.

Suruk leaned in to Smith's side. 'Mazuran, I fear that these ancients require special treatment.' He smiled horribly and cracked his knuckles.

'I'm not sure that's really—' Smith began, but by then Suruk's shadow had fallen across the table.

The alien cleared his throat sacs with a sound like a car backfiring. The old men looked up.

'*Felicitations, humains,*' the alien declared. '*Ou est la Rue Charles de Gaulle, s'il vous plait? Je voudrai attender un concert du jazz moderne.*'

'*Le jazz moderne?*' the nearer of the two replied.

'*Oui,*' Suruk replied. '*Especialment le Serge Gainsbourg.*'

'*Mais oui!*' The man leaped up, threw his arms open, looked at Suruk, thought better of it, and pointed down the road instead. Suruk nodded, listening.

Smith turned to Carveth. 'What's he doing? Is he getting directions?'

Suruk returned, still smiling. 'Good Lord,' Smith said as he approached, 'how the devil did you manage that?'

'It was most simple,' the alien replied. 'All I had to do to make them co-operate was address them in their own strange parlance. Now, follow me, old bean. Chop-chop.'

'Shall do!' Smith cried.

Adenauerplatz stood at the very edge of the German quarter, behind the Rue Charles de Gaulle, near to the Place Charles de Gaulle and the Avenue Napoleon et Charles de Gaulle. They turned the corner, and looked into a square as neat as a snooker table, lined with glass-fronted houses. On the far side stood a bright white cube three stories high.

Smith turned to his men. 'Look,' he announced, 'I'm going to try to communicate with these fellows. Why don't you go and have a look round while I get this done?'

'I think I shall assess the local shops for, ah, implements,' Suruk said. 'I will come and find you later. You should not be too hard to find.'

'Good plan. What about you ladies? I'm sure this meeting won't involve anything you'd find interesting.'

'Except the spaceship of which I'm the pilot?' Carveth shrugged. 'Nah, you can deal with this. I'm off for a drink and a pasty.'

Rhianna wore her *considering things* expression. 'On the one hand,' she said thoughtfully, 'I do believe that any consultation on this should be decided with the participation of everyone concerned. On the other hand, I need to find a Dutch café and get some supplies.'

Smith decided not to inquire further. He approached the bright white cube.

Inside was a large desk, behind which a young man with a headset was typing at the smallest keyboard he had ever seen. As Smith approached the desk, the man stopped typing and said, 'Captain Smith? Good morning. Commissioner Jurgens will see you now. Please do head through the door there,' he added, pointing to a blank wall.

A section of the wall swung inward with a gentle hiss of air. Behind the door stood a short, middle-aged man in a roll-neck sweater and blue blazer. 'Good morning!' he exclaimed, stepping back. 'Do come in, please. I am Frank Jurgens, Deputy Commissioner. I have been expecting you, as they say.'

'Thank you,' said Smith. Jurgens' office looked rather like a normal room, if somewhat whiter and more angular. The furniture seemed to have been built to solve a geometry problem, but that aside, it was actually quite normal, Smith thought as he looked around. You could almost think it was Brit – wait a moment!

He stopped before a framed poster. On a red background, four stern men in identical outfits stood in a row, glaring towards the horizon. Uniforms, horizon-staring, ferocious youths of indeterminate sexual preference? This could only mean one thing – the sinister world of foreign politics! Jurgens had seemed such a nice chap, too. But then, Europe was part of *abroad*. You never knew. . .

'Ah, Kraftwerk,' Jurgens said, noticing Smith's interest. 'Some very great musicians have come from Germany, you know.'

'Music?' it occurred to Smith that these strange people might be a popular beat combo. 'From Germany? But. . . where's the tuba?'

'Kraftwerk were way before their time,' Jurgens explained, and he raised an eyebrow. 'They had neither a tuba nor leather shorts.'

'Nudists, eh?' Smith wondered if he was being taken entirely seriously. 'I'm more a Pink Zeppelin man,' he said. Jurgens gave him a rather curious look and sat down.

'So then,' Jurgens began, crossing his legs, 'I understand your vessel was attacked by persons unknown on the edge of European space.'

'That's right. We were guarding an automated convoy.

The enemy appeared out of nowhere, literally. There was a flash of light and then suddenly they were gone, just like that.'

Jurgens frowned. 'It sounds as if the technology used was highly advanced. I took the liberty of looking at your spacecraft from the docking bay cameras. From the looks of it, your attacker must have used some sort of rust-generating beam on your hull. Most unfortunate.'

'Er. . . yes,' Smith replied. 'A rust laser. That's it. Any chance of a cup of tea?'

'Of course.'

Smith accepted his tea warily and peered into the very white cup. It was not too bad, he decided, taking a sip. Not bad at all.

Jurgens nodded. 'Now, Captain Smith, do you have any idea who might have attacked you?'

'Well, no. I mean, it could be any number of enemies, you see. Space is full of rum types,' he added, remembering not to mention who the rum types might include. 'Aliens envy Britain its space empire. What with the Ghasts on one side and the bloody lemming-men on the other, it's not as if we're short of enemies. And then there are all the lowlifes who work for Gertie – Aresians, filthy Ghastists, that sort of riff-raff.'

'And envious foreign powers too, no doubt.'

'Well, of course – I mean, no, not at all. Except for that loony who runs Russia. Mad King Boris, that's the fellow. Otherwise, I'm sure you chaps are fine.'

'It is indeed fortunate that King Boris declared war upon himself. The European Federation has the same problem, Captain Smith. It is forever defending its borders against those who would wish to force their laws and customs upon us.'

'I'm sure it does. I'd like some more tea, please.'

'As a representative of an allied nation your vessel will, of course, be repaired,' Jurgens explained, refilling Smith's cup. 'However, I fear your ship may be in dock for some while. Rest assured that some of Europe's finest technicians will do the work.'

Smith fought down the image of the *John Pym* rebuilt in the style of a gingerbread house. The possibility of Suruk's frogs chewing through the hull would be nothing compared to the prospect of Carveth eating the entire ship. 'That's very kind of you.'

'Now. . . I understand you have a colleague who needs transport, yes?'

Smith's chair was getting uncomfortable. 'That's right. I was told to mention the Phantom.'

Jurgens leaned back. 'I see. Yes, I thought your mission might be a little. . . under the radar. Our mutual friend, Herr W, has made the arrangements. Transport will be provided.'

'Thanks. That's very decent of you.'

'Not at all. We are, after all, keen to help our neighbours. *Alle Menschen werden Bruder*, as Schiller puts it. Do you know Beethoven's Ninth?'

'Really? At what?'

'Ah. . . never mind. Now, a ship that can evade normal detection is clearly a serious threat. However, I have a plan. Viennese Whirl?' he inquired, holding up a plate.

'No thanks. Go on.'

'Docked here at Tannhauser Gate is a European Union

military surveillance vessel, the *EU-571*, under the command of Raumskapitan Schmidt. Although it would be somewhat counter-procedural, I could sequester it.'

'Righto,' Smith replied, making a mental note to check what that meant in English.

'Using our vessel, you would be able to make a head start tracking your quarry while the *John Pym* is being repaired. Then you would be able to transmit an exact location to your fleet.'

'Excellent! Well then,' said Smith, 'I think this is a jolly good plan. How soon can your people get organised?'

Jurgens looked slightly put out. 'Captain Smith,' he replied, 'they already are.'

'Splendid.' Smith stood up and held out his hand. 'It's been a pleasure, Commissioner Jurgens. I had no idea that Europe would turn out to be such a reasonable place.'

Jurgens smiled and they shook hands. 'I must admit, I too am pleasantly surprised. I must confess that the British in Europe do have a reputation for – how can I put it? – crass, drunken lawlessness. I am delighted to be proven otherwise.'

The door burst open and Carveth ran in, clutching a bottle in one hand and a duty free bag in the other. 'Oh my God,' she cried, 'you were right! This place is terrible! The police are after us!'

Jurgens raised an eyebrow. 'Or not,' he said.

'Nothing to worry about,' Smith said. 'I'm sure everything will be fine – won't it, eh?' he added, glaring at Carveth.

'No, it won't,' she replied. 'They're going to put Rhianna in jail!'

*

A twig crackled under W's boot. He glanced down, saw a snake of rope come hissing through the heather and leaped back before it could catch his ankle. The rope snapped closed and whipped away. The ground seemed to explode before him and suddenly he was looking at the upper body of Major Wainscott, wearing a beanie hat and holding the most unwholesome-looking weapon he had ever seen.

'Halt,' Wainscott said. 'Can you recommend a florist?'

'Not on bloody Dartmoor I can't.'

Wainscott gave him a reproachful look.

W sighed. 'There are many fine florists on the streets of Kiev.'

'Morning,' Wainscott replied. He lowered the weapon. It seemed to be a sort of bow made out of pieces of bone. 'Fancy meeting you here,' he observed.

'Indeed. You'll be astonished to learn that I'm not on holiday. We have some business to discuss.'

'Well then!' Wainscott smiled. He was keeping good care of his teeth, W noticed. 'You'd better come inside. Be quick about it – you're very distinctive like that.' Gopher-like, he dropped out of sight as though some unseen assailant had just tugged his legs. W grimaced across the moor, and climbed down into the hole.

He dropped into a dry chamber hacked out of the earth. The first thing he spotted was the neatness of the place: Wainscott might be a lunatic but he was at least tidy. The second thing he noticed were the badgers: three of them watched him suspiciously from the opening into a much smaller tunnel.

'It's alright, he's a friend,' Wainscott said, rooting about in the back of the room. 'They're funny little fellows, badgers, but terribly loyal.' He hauled up two deckchairs and began to fight them into shape. 'Have a seat.'

'Thank you.' W eased himself into a chair very carefully. He crossed his legs as if balancing a landmine on his knee.

'So, what do you think of chez Wainscott? Quite something, isn't it?'

'It certainly is.' It was like being trapped inside the skin of a giant baked potato, W decided. It smelt of sausages.

Wainscott laid the crossbow down beside his chair. 'I made this myself. Recycled parts, of course. I recycle pretty much everything.' He reached down to a large flask beside his chair. 'Scrumpy?'

'I, er, had some earlier.'

'Your loss, old fellow.' Wainscott took a huge swig and settled back. He was wearing his combat shorts and the visible scars bore testament to a lifetime of living hard on the veldt. 'So, who are we killing today? Got an armoured division you want knocked off?'

'Not exactly.'

'Ah, a crack at the lemming man, is it? Teach the horrible buggers some manners, eh? I've wanted to give them a good pounding for a while, you know. Likewise Susan.' He took another swig. 'She can't stand them either.'

W looked around the room. The rest of the Deepspace Operations Group was nowhere to be seen. This was unusual, since Susan, as second in command and beam gun operator, tended to act for Wainscott as a cross between an interpreter and psychiatric nurse. Perhaps the others had built their own tunnels and were training their own badgers.

'They went to Butlins,' Wainscott said. 'They wanted to go on the water slides. It only seemed fair after they blew up the Fortress of Iron.'

'Of course. But I'll need them on board.'

Wainscott leaned forward, setting his deckchair creaking, and rubbed his hands together. 'So then, what is this job? Lemmings, Ghasts, collaborators?'

'It's a peace conference.'

'What?'

Carefully, W outlined the situation. He tried to be tactful, to set out the importance of the meeting and its potential benefits, but Wainscott looked at first perplexed, then unconvinced, and finally slightly murderous. He scowled into his beard.

'That's all very well,' Wainscott said, 'but there's a war on. Do we really want foreigners and aliens involved?'

'Head office thinks so. Apparently the Great Powers need better co-ordination to fight more effectively. And then we've got the treaty between the Empire and the Vorl to think about. It needs to be formalised as soon as possible.'

'Hmm. I don't like it. I mean, aliens are one thing, but abroad? Is that really necessary? There are too many people on Earth who can't tell the difference between gormless militarism and military effectiveness. They don't realise that to beat Gertie you need to become less like him, not more like him.'

'Well, quite. We won't tolerate any beastliness—'

'And another thing about abroad.' Wainscott leaned forward, his voice sinking. 'They make stuff up. You see that film last year about the Battle of Britain? Set in bloody Utah. You're always banging on about objective truth – you know what I mean. But perhaps we should drag these fellows in, give 'em a cup of tea and a biscuit and tell them not to give us any trouble, or else they'll be getting a visit from the Morlock Rifles.'

'That's a bit much, Wainscott. Easy there.'

'Alright, no biscuit.'

W tried not to grimace. 'Look, Wainscott. Think of it as a holiday. A special sort of holiday where you don't kill anyone or live off carrion. All we need to do is make sure things run smoothly. The visitors need to come to the conference, sign what's required of them and leave in one piece. Easy. And if there is actually any trouble—'

Wainscott drove his fist into his grimy palm. 'Not a problem. I know how to root out a conspiracy. Remember in London when I interrupted those villains plotting to kidnap children and nuns?'

'What you interrupted was a full-dress rehearsal of *The Sound of Music*. You knocked out Baron von Trapp with a brown paper parcel and left half the cast tied up with string.'

'So? What was wrong with that?'

'Well, how long have you got? Suffice it to say that for quite a while you were not one of the Service's favourite things.'

Wainscott settled back. 'So, you're asking me to trade in living in a hole with badgers for some sort of diplomatic shindig. There'd better be a bar.'

'There is.'

'Alright. I'm in.' The major stood up, kicked his chair deftly, and left it folded against the wall. 'Lead on.'

*

'It's terrible,' Carveth explained, hurrying along beside Smith. He strode quickly through the broad, tidy streets and she had to jog to keep up with him. 'I went to the duty free because Suruk ate all my cosmetics last month.' She held up a bag marked *Rouge Trader*. 'And then I thought I'd get a pasty and half a dozen cans of Interstella Artois, so I left the others outside and went in. But they didn't have any pasties, so they gave me this liquorice drink instead – which might have been alcoholic now I try to think of it – and when I managed to get out they were gone. But Rhianna went into a caff and now she's been arrested on drugs offences and my legs feel like they're going to fall off.'

They weaved deeper into the space station: down narrow avenues, under spacesuits on a washing line, past a two-cylinder Citroen moon buggy. Carveth pointed to an art deco sign above a door. Smith strode straight in. Rhianna was sitting at a table near the door and over her stood a man in a blue uniform.

'What the devil's this?' Smith demanded, advancing on the man. 'Unhand that woman and get back to delivering the post.'

'That is enough, monsieur,' the man replied. 'I am an officer of the gendarmerie. In your language, a bobby, yes? This woman attempted to purchase illegal drugs from the proprietor of this establishment.'

'Oh,' Smith replied. 'Is this true, Rhianna?'

She looked very upset. 'I thought Holland was in France,' she explained. 'It's in Europe, right?'

In a second Smith realised the truth. As a citizen of New Francisco, Rhianna had assumed that all European countries had an identical attitude towards herbal medication. It was awkward, he thought, but not beyond repair. A bit of diplomacy would straighten things out. 'Look,' he said, 'she's made a mistake. I know she's done something silly, but she is foreign, you know.'

'Then may I remind you,' the policeman said, 'that you are foreign too.'

'What? I most certainly am not.'

Carveth sighed and sat down at a table.

'Maybe we can just, you know, talk it over?' Rhianna said.

The door burst open and Suruk stormed in. 'What is this?' he demanded. 'I leave to buy postcards and flick-knives and everything goes wrong.' He picked up a menu, glared at it as if it contained a personal insult, and added, 'I warn you and your reprobate chefs. . . stay away from my frogs!'

A second gendarme appeared in the doorway. *Balls*, Smith thought. He needed to work fast: not only was Jurgens' ship due to leave soon, but he had a good idea what European justice entailed: something to do with a quick kick in the Bastille followed by an uncomfortable run-in with Madame Guillotine.

It was time to use the Bearing, the ancient Shau Teng discipline. Smith summoned up his moral fibre and stared the nearer of the gendarmes in the eye. 'Now look here, my good fellow. . .' he began, taking a step forward. 'This woman is under my protection. You will release her now, sir.'

The gendarme grimaced. 'You think you will use – the Bearing – on me?' he gasped. With great effort he raised his shoulders and the palms of his hands. Then he laughed. 'Nice try, English! But I shrug off your demands.' He opened his hands. 'Eh? Huh? *Bof.*'

'Damn!' The blasted fellow wielded his lack of civility like a shield. To Smith's right, Suruk quietly lowered the menu. Smith reached to his hip. This was going to be unpleasant but there was no other option.

Smith said, 'Let's finish this now.' His right hand made one fast move into his coat, and suddenly it was no longer empty. 'It's time to leave.'

The gendarme looked down at the wallet in Smith's hand. 'You corrupt English! You think we can be bought like that?'

'Well,' Smith said, 'yes.'

'How dare you? I am arresting you too, for attempting to bribe an officer of the law.'

'But this is abroad, man. Surely you take bribes in France.'

'Bah! What do you know of France? I bet you have never even heard of Charles de Gaulle.'

'Of course I have. Little fellow with a big moustache, doesn't like Caesar?'

'That is Asterix the Gaul! That is it – in the name of Europe and the four hundred and thirty-eighth republic of France, you are all under arrest!'

'So,' said Carveth, looking around the cell, 'what happens now?'

'Well,' Smith replied, 'if my knowledge of French history is right, they'll probably cut off our heads.'

'Not mine,' Suruk growled. He crouched on the far end of the bench, coldly furious. 'I read their menu. I know what they do to amphibians in the name of cuisine. Should they ransack our ship and interfere with my spawn, they will die.'

'We're not in much of a position to do anything about that,' Carveth replied.

'My spawn are. They will strip them to the bone.'

Rhianna stood at the door, looking through the bars. 'I can't believe Amsterdam isn't in France,' she said. 'How could I not know that?'

Carveth sighed. 'You were too stoned to figure it out?'

'Oh, yeah.'

Smith grimaced. He was finding it hard to think. It didn't help that there was a radio playing in the empty room outside the cell. On it, a woman who sounded as if she was slowly drowning was singing about how she didn't regret Ryan. Smith wondered who Ryan was and whether he was the one drowning her and, if so, whether he could get on with it.

'Right, men,' he said, getting to his feet, 'I have a plan. We have been left with no other choice than to escape. I'll ambush the guard and if he refuses to release us, we'll add Tannhauser Gate to the British Empire.'

'How?' Carveth demanded.

'We will work out the details as we go. Step One, however, is to overpower the guard.' Smith moved over to the bars. 'I say, guard! What about *la liberté* and all that?'

The room outside remained empty. The radio gargled on.

Smith tried to think of some French words that didn't involve the pen of his aunt. 'I'm British, damn it! Let me out!'

A figure stepped into the corridor outside, and Smith paused. The fellow wore tight black clothes, almost like a wetsuit, a striped shirt and a small white mask. As Smith looked on, astonished, the newcomer turned to check the corridor behind him and crept towards their cell with high, exaggerated steps.

'There's someone there,' Smith whispered to his crew. 'Strange chap. . .'

The man in black stopped just outside the door. He raised a finger to his lips, squatted down and began to pick the lock. Suruk got up, flexing his fingers.

The lock clicked and the cell door swung open. The man in black stood up and gave them a deep, elaborate bow.

'Hello,' said Smith. 'Thanks.'

The man leaned back and scrutinised him, stroking his chin as he did. Then he seemed to relax. 'Monsieur, mesdames, *monstre hideux et bizarre*, I bid you good evening. I am Le Fantome.'

'Oh,' said Smith. 'What are you, some kind of spy?'

'*Mais non!*' Le Fantome laughed behind his mask. 'I have come here to rescue you. We have a shared enemy. It is vital you board the ship at once. Come,' he added. 'It is time to escape this—' he gestured around himself with his gloved hands as if patting invisible walls, 'prison.'

'Amazing,' Rhianna said. 'A real tribal dance.' Her interest in other cultures did not seem to be diminished by the fact that one of them had locked her up.

'We must be quick,' Le Fantome replied. 'I used ancient French arts to reach you in silence. Now we must depart.'

'Good Lord,' said Smith, 'You're a mime.'

Le Fantome nodded several times. 'But not just any mime. I am a mastermime.'

'Go to space, meet a loony,' Carveth said. 'There's a surprise. On the other hand, the door is open.'

Le Fantome led them into the corridor. They crept past the gurgling stereo and down the hallway. Smith glanced to the left and saw a spectacled detective in an office, busy filling his pipe.

'You are lucky it was I who found you,' Le Fantome whispered. 'There are plenty here who remember the part your secret service played in deposing the Prince of France.' He shook his head. 'Exiled to a tiny planet, with nothing but a flower for company. . . come. As we say in France, we must be *rapide*.'

They passed through a narrow door, back into the dark of the space station. It was the station night-cycle now, and light spilled from bars and bierkellers onto the artificial boulevard. Far off, two alley cats, an accordion and an oompah band competed for ownership of the night.

The simulated evening was warm and dry and the smoke from Galloises and Bratwurst stalls was whisked away before it could upset the sprinkler system. They walked through the residential quarter, trying to look as normal as they could. 'Do not worry,' Le Fantome said. 'Once people see you have a mime with you, they will know everything is under control. It is, to use a French word, *inevitable*.'

The streets were deeply alien to Smith. Where were the red telephone boxes, the chip shops, the people being ill outside pubs? They passed a gang of very neat punks who bade them *Guten abend* before getting back to painting a graffiti-spattered wall bright white.

'You see those doors down there?' Le Fantome said, pointing. 'The airlock you seek is at the end of that passage, just past the cabaret hall.' He turned to Rhianna. 'Raumskapitan Schmidt is a good man. You can trust him to convey you to our mutual friends.'

Smith looked down the street. 'Thank you for your help, sir. But now, we have a ship to catch.'

'As we say in France, it has been *un plaisir*,' Le Fantome replied. 'But next time we meet, I may ask a favour of you.'

'I'll assist you, within reason,' Smith said. 'Nothing dodgy, though.'

'Monsieur,' Le Fantome replied, clearly hurt, 'There is nothing 'dodgy' about the French secret service. Wherever there are questionable elections, dangerous peace protesters, allegations of bribery – rest assured, we shall be there. *Alors*, I see you have no heavy luggage to carry, but I could always help you pretend. Goodbye, ladies. . ..' He bowed. 'I hope we shall all meet again soon.'

'Well,' Suruk remarked as Le Fantome crept away,

'abroad has certainly changed since last I visited. Everything is flatter than I recall and there are fewer goats. The people seem more welcoming, too.'

'Which bit of Europe was that?' Rhianna asked.

'Of course it's different, Suruk,' Smith said. 'That was ten years ago and you were trying to become king of Nepal. Don't ask, Rhianna – you'll only encourage him.'

EU-571 lay at dock fifty yards further on. A tall man waited for them at the airlock.

'Hallo!' said Raumskapitan Schmidt. He wore a roll-neck jumper and a blue cap with an anchor on the front. His beard was close-cropped. The space captain looked friendly and enthusiastic, Smith thought, but seemed a bit dim. That sort of thing would never be allowed in the British space fleet.

'Hullo!' Smith replied.

'Come on in,' Schmidt said, gesturing to the spacious, well-lit interior of *EU-571*. A small, blonde woman in a similar hat approached and waved. 'This is Petra Klein, ship's android and my second in command.'

'Welcome aboard,' she said. 'Who would like schnapps?'

An airlock opened without creaking and a second woman stepped out. She wore uniform, but her roll-neck jumper was a little looser than Schmidt's and her plait reached almost to her waist.

Schmidt gestured to the tall girl. 'This is Ingrid, who deals with our other important business on ship.'

Smith bowed. 'Strategy and weapons, eh?'

'Recycling,' Ingrid replied. 'The *EU-571* is fully

compliant with Directive 683/76 on the Harmonious Removal of Vegetable Matter.'

'We have one of those,' Smith added, keen to show that Britain was not lagging behind. 'I put old cucumbers and potato peelings in it. You know, for the whales to eat.'

'You have your own recycling officer?' Rhianna said to Schmidt. 'I think that's amazing. I've always thought we should do more for the environment, Isambard.'

'Well,' said Smith, 'I'm always happy to clean up a few dirty aliens, eh?' He patted his sword in a manly way. Captain Schmidt gave Smith's belt a rather worried look.

'I also deal with crew relaxation and massage,' Ingrid added.

Smith didn't like the sound of that. Massage was that thing that made his shoulders tense up.

'Okay,' Schmidt declared. 'Perhaps we should go through? Ingrid, if the young lady is interested in your work, why don't you take her down to the sauna deck?'

Ingrid took Rhianna's arm. Smith watched them head to the door, arm in arm. As the door closed he remembered a fascinating drama he'd once seen about friendship among young ladies entitled *Lascivious Handmaidens of the Reform School of Dracula*.

Carveth nudged him and he blinked out of his reverie. 'You do know that massage is supposed to make you *less* stiff?'

'Go away,' he said.

The sound of engines rose softly, a light hum that ran through the cream-coloured walls. *EU-571* was leaving dock. 'Please,' Schmidt said, gesturing. 'After you.'

The dining room was large and well lit. Waltz music piped merrily from hidden speakers. 'Do take seats, please,' Schmidt said, and he pulled back a chair for Carveth. Schmidt took the seat at the head of the table, under a painting of a gate with a chariot on top. In the interests of international harmony, Smith decided not to tell Schmidt that he looked just like the chap on the fish finger adverts.

Petra opened a cabinet and took out a bottle. She poured out little glasses of schnapps, including two for Ingrid and Rhianna.

'Please,' Schmidt said, 'make yourselves at home. The food dispenser has been programmed to synthesise any food you wish, provided it is sausage-shaped.'

Carveth peered at the controls. The food machine was white and had a single button. 'So I could have a banana?'

'*Bananawurst?* Of course! Press the button twice for curry sauce.'

'Actually, I had curried banana sausage for breakfast,' Carveth said, and she sat down hurriedly.

'One for you?' Petra asked, putting a glass in front of Suruk. He sniffed it warily.

'*Prost!*' Schmidt declared. 'Or as you might say, bottoms up!'

They drank. Carveth finished her glass and swapped it quickly for Rhianna's and drank that too. She set it down, looked up and to her surprise saw Petra accomplishing the same sleight of hand with Ingrid's glass.

Suruk pointed to the food synthesiser. 'This sausage puzzles me. What animal is it the wurst part of?'

'I'm afraid we'll have to speak English,' Smith said to

Schmidt. 'Unless you're fluent in Latin, that is. If you want to discuss how all Gaul is quartered into three halves, I'm your man.' He was beginning to feel slightly lost. The combination of air conditioning, strong liquor and Strauss had started to make things rather blurry.

'Then you will excuse my bad English-speaking, I hope,' Schmidt added. 'I fear the infrequency of use may have caused my loquacity to atrophy somewhat.'

'I'm afraid so,' Smith replied. 'I didn't catch a word of that.'

'So how is your German?'

'I don't have one. Oh, I see! Rather basic, I'm afraid. *Ja. Bien.*'

Schmidt met Petra's eye and she quickly filled the glasses.

'Absent friends!' Schmidt announced, and they drank again. Carveth put down her glass, then Rhianna's and found Smith glaring at her across the table.

'That was Rhianna's drink,' he whispered.

'So?' Carveth demanded. 'I'm honouring the toast. She's a friend and she's absent, so. . .'

'Now,' said Schmidt, 'tell me about this craft we are looking for.'

Smith frowned. 'Well, it's some sort of warship. I only saw it for a moment, but it's clearly heavily armed. Probably railgun turrets and missiles.'

Schmidt finished his drink. Petra caught his eye. 'The same procedure as last time?' she inquired.

The Raumskapitan nodded. 'Of course. And break out the Viennese Whirls. This is grave news.'

Carveth found that intensely sugary biscuits and

schnapps went quite well together. She managed to feel unusually drunk and unusually active. Of course, in practice that probably meant that she would run halfway up the wall and then fall flat on the floor, but for free booze and biscuits, she was ready to take the risk.

'It barely showed up on the scanner,' Smith said. 'That's the strange thing. . . it just appeared out of nowhere. There was a flash of light, and suddenly the ships around us were in pieces.'

'Are you sure that was not a part of your own craft, ah, dropping off?'

'Certainly not. Vessels such as mine have been the backbone of the British space fleet for generations. Admittedly, the John Pym is quite low down the backbone, to be honest—'

'Just above the arse,' Carveth added helpfully, pouring herself another drink. 'Near the tail.'

'There is nothing wrong with having a tail,' Suruk pointed out. 'We M'Lak have small tails. So did such great Earth heroes as Thomas Kitten and the two cities of Abraham Dickens.'

Smith paused to think this one over, chasing Suruk's logic through the maze of his brain. Carveth raised a shaky hand. 'Where are all your aliens?' she inquired.

'Aliens?' Schmidt shook his head. 'Europe does not have aliens. At least, it does not rule over other peoples as your British Space Empire does.'

'*Thinks* it does,' Suruk added.

'You see, in Europe all nations are equal. Except Italy, but that is only because its prime minister sold it to the French when nobody was looking. There were detailed negotiations and the deal was finalised in a car park near Lyons.' He sighed. 'To think of it. . . the cradle of the Renaissance, sold in a service station like a football club. . . these are dangerous days, my friends. *Prost!*'

As Smith raised his glass the lights went off. The subtle underfloor lamps faded away and a single red bulb flickered into life behind Schmidt's chair. Distantly, in the bowels of the *EU-571*, a bell was ringing.

'What is this?' Suruk snarled.

Carveth pointed at the bulb. 'Pretty!' she said, and she fell over.

They hurried down a steel staircase. Rhianna and Ingrid stood at the bottom of the stairs. 'Hey, Isambard,' Rhianna said, 'I've just been learning about wind farms.'

Carveth, now upright through force of will and assistance of wall, blinked. 'What's going on?'

In the red light the command deck of the *EU-571* looked like a very tidy chamber of Hell. Actually, Smith thought as Schmidt led them between the rows of computers, more a corridor than a chamber. Men nodded and gestured at screens and an officer sneezed into a paper bag. Only the soft hum of computers and the whisper of engines broke the silence.

Suruk tapped Smith on the shoulder. 'All these red lights,' he whispered. 'I have heard of such places, Mazuran, in districts of Holland. Be on your guard, lest one of these men seeks to repair your washing machine.'

Turning, Schmidt leaned close and lowered his voice. 'Captain Smith, our long-range scanners have detected a vessel in the area. There is no visual confirmation. By now, it ought to be in range. Perhaps it is your enemy.'

'Maybe.'

'We will approach,' Schmidt added. 'But stay very quiet. Our stealth capacities are not limitless, I am afraid.'

'Righto,' Smith said. 'Crew, pay close attention and pipe down!'

'Yes,' said Schmidt, 'but *quietly*.'

Schmidt peered into a computer screen, adjusted his sweater and pulled down his captain's hat. He frowned, as the man from the adverts might do when confronted by an unsatisfactory piece of frozen cod.

Rhianna took hold of Smith's arm. 'Look.' She pointed at a large dial mounted on the wall. 'Is that supposed to be happening?'

Smith looked at the dial. It reminded him of several of the controls of the John Pym, although the lettering on the dial was in the language of abroad. Perhaps it had something to do with the *EU-571*'s stealth system.

Schmidt stood up and stepped over to join them. 'Hmm,' he said, rubbing his beard thoughtfully. 'Franz?'

A tubby, fair-haired man leaned over from the console to the right. He looked at the dial and scratched his head.

Very slowly, the needle began to rise. They watched it crawl past 800, then on to 1,000. Smith glanced to his left: the neck of Schmidt's sweater bulged as he swallowed, hard.

'It's past a thousand,' Carveth said.

'One thousand one hundred,' Franz whispered.

Slowly, steadily, the needle approached the red. Smith held his breath. A single bead of sweat rolled down from Schmidt's hairline.

'One thousand three hundred,' Franz said.

'This is worrying,' Suruk declared. 'I think we should remove the needle.'

'Why are we looking at the dial?' Carveth asked.

Smith glanced round. 'Well,' he said, 'I'm looking at the dial because – well, because Captain Schmidt here is looking at it. It's clearly very important.'

'Really?' Schmidt turned his attention from the dial as if awaking to find himself in unfamiliar surroundings. 'Being the captain, and therefore responsible for the smooth running of this vessel, I was inspecting the dial because you brought it to my attention.'

'I only looked at it because you did,' Smith replied, feeling slightly put out.

'Me? It was you who began all this dial-staring.'

'I didn't start it!'

'Yes you did. You—'

A woman was walking by, ticking items off on a clipboard. As she passed she reached out without looking and hit the top of the dial with her hand. It dropped back down to zero. '*Kaput scheisser Maschine*,' she muttered, and she carried on. Below the dial, a small door opened and a tiny brass man slid out, hit a bell and drew back inside.

Petra had been peering at one of the scanners. She tapped the screen. 'Hey! Look at this.'

'What is it?' Schmidt demanded.

'Sensors for the outside,' she replied. 'If we pinpoint the location, cross-referencing all the vectors. . .'

'Just what I would have done,' Carveth put in. She had slumped against a bulkhead.

'We find the sensors pinpoint an area of space about *here*.' Petra tapped the screen twice and it zoomed in on a patch of empty space. It looked like nothing, Smith thought. Perhaps the *EU-571* lacked the sophisticated scanning equipment of the *John Pym*.

The screen flashed blue. Lightning blazed in the centre of the monitor. Needles flapped in dials like the wings of frightened birds. Suddenly they were looking at the vessel that had ambushed them – and it did not seem to have detected them.

'That's him!' Smith cried. 'We've got him cold! Get a lock on and show him what for!'

'What?' said Schmidt.

'That's the ship that blew up our convoy!' Smith grinned at the screen. 'Now we've got you! Give him a rocket, Schmidt.'

'Rocket?' Schmidt and Petra exchanged a puzzled look. 'Captain Smith, we do not have any rockets.'

'Lasers, then. Slice his bows off.'

'*Entschuldigung!*' Schmidt looked genuinely appalled. 'Please calm yourself, Captain. One, this ship belongs to the European Union, not the British Space Empire. And two, do you realise the paperwork that would involve?'

'Paperwork?'

'Not to be mentioning three. . . we have no guns.'

'What?'

'I approve,' Suruk said. 'Ramming speed!'

'No, no 'ramming speed'. Europe is a place of peace. This vessel was built to survey, to discover and, once sufficient evidence of an enemy attack has been un-covered, to enable the passing of a condemnatory resolution. Not to go in with all guns blazing like Butch Cassidy and *der Sonnetanzkind*, okay?'

Smith stared at the image on the screen, the grim-looking, converted ship – his prey – within range. 'But. . . but—'

Rhianna put her hand on Smith's shoulder. 'Isambard, he's right. We can't just tell them what to do.' She turned to Schmidt. 'Will it be a sternly worded resolution, Herr Raumskapitan?'

'Oh, very.'

'That's okay, then.'

'Humph!' Smith pulled away. 'Pass a resolution? I've passed water more frightening than that.'

Schmidt gave him a stern look. Smith returned it. They volleyed the stern look for several seconds.

Petra looked up from the computer. 'I have it,' she announced. 'Formerly Royal Mail shuttle *RMS Greendale*, believed lost at space six years ago, taken by pirates. The ship reappeared three months ago, renamed *Fist of Sacred Hate* and refitted as a light destroyer of the Republic of Eden. Gentlemen, you are looking at an Edenite ship.'

'Edenite?' Smith shook his head. On the screen, blue light shone from the ship's few windows, as if it glowed inside. The armour was striped red, like wounds. Symbols had been painted around the airlocks. Hooked chains drifted lazily around the craft like the tentacles of dead octopi. 'But they're insane cultists. And that ship looks like. . .. well, it looks—'

'Like it came from Hell,' Carveth whispered.

Suruk threw back his head and laughed. The sound

rang through the metal corridor. 'Then there is only one thing to do,' he declared. 'We must pursue this craft to wherever it dwells, hunt it out and carve a path to its dark heart! I, Suruk of the line of Agshad shall destroy this vessel, no matter what fiery abyss it may choose for a hiding-place. For it is better to reign in Hell than. . .' Suruk raised a hand and scratched his head. 'Er. . .'

'Remain in Hull?' Carveth suggested.

'Drizzle in Heaven?' Smith said.

'No. . . I remember now!' Suruk exclaimed. 'For it is better to reign in Hell than anywhere else!'

*

'Well,' said Smith, admiring the *John Pym*, 'they've finished the repairs.'

Schmidt rubbed his beard. Above them, great mechanical arms flexed and swung silently, like the hands of puppeteers. 'Are you sure?' he asked.

'It looks better than ever,' Smith replied. He put out a hand. 'I'm sorry I got cross, Raumskapitan Schmidt. You've been a great help. Thanks to you, we have the lead we needed.'

'And I got smashed,' Carveth added.

'And I got some interesting seeds,' Rhianna put in. Ingrid winked.

'I would give you some tea in return,' Smith said, 'but I'm afraid we're going to need all the moral fibre we have for the voyage ahead.'

Rhianna held out the smaller of their lunch tins. 'I made a cake,' she added.

'Thank you,' Schmidt replied. 'You are most kind. But hey – you must get going. Space traffic control have another strike booked for four o'clock. They must have heard there were British trying to leave.'

'Well then.' Smith turned to Rhianna. 'I suppose this is it.'

'Until we meet again,' she said. 'Isambard, take care. And try not to do anything too heroic. Or stupid.'

'You take care too. Especially with the washing.'

She came close, and he could smell patchouli oil. 'Remember, Isambard. . . this is *au revoir*, not goodbye.'

'Can we settle for "Bye for now"? It's neither permanent nor French.'

'Done.' She kissed him. 'You'll be in my dreams.'

'Mine too. Can you wear the dress that's sort of see-through?'

'I'll do what I can. Good bye.'

'See you soon!'

They kissed again, and Rhianna stepped away to join Ingrid and Raumskapitan Schmidt. Smith smiled at the Raumskapitan, knowing that he would look after most of Rhianna's needs – except that one. Looking round, he saw Carveth and Petra swapping bottles.

Schmidt said, 'The nearest Edenite port capable of maintaining such a vessel is called Deliverance. It's three days' travel from here – two with an engine like yours, provided you go in a straight line. From what I have heard, you can expect a warm reception. They'll try to burn you at the stake.'

'That sounds likely. Well, thanks for your help.'

'My pleasure. But the only people getting in and out of

Deliverance are Crusadists and mercenaries. As soon as they see you they'll start firing.'

'We'll take our chances.'

They shook hands. Schmidt took three steps and turned. 'Oh, Captain Smith? One more thing. *Viel Gluck.*'

Smith turned at the door of the *John Pym*. '*Danke!*' he replied. 'I mean, thanks.'

Beast of Eden

'So,' said Carveth, slowly lowering her biscuit into her tea, 'we're going to fly into the Republic of Eden, find the ship that blew up our convoy and – assuming we're not very dead by then – well. . . then what?'

'Put it out of action,' Smith replied. 'Locate the enemy vessel and either destroy it completely or mark it in some way so that our own fleet can find it and finish it off.'

'And then back home for curry and beer?'

'That's about right,' Smith replied. 'Of course, we'll have to finesse some of the fine points, but you've got the basic idea.'

Carveth took her biscuit out the tea and bit off the soggy bit. 'But we've just escaped from the space-Bastille, and now we're going into a police state. Can't we just cut our losses and bugger off home? It sounds to me like a case of "Out of the frying pan and into the Scottish gourmet".'

'Don't worry. Suruk and I have come up with a plan.' Smith got up and, still carrying his mug, walked to the door that led into the hold. 'Suruk? Are you in there?'

'I am just coming,' the alien replied.

Suruk struggled through the doorway, carrying the

ship's tactical display unit and a piece of chalk to draw on it. He stood the board at the end of the table.

'Behold,' Suruk said. 'I have applied my full skill as a hunter to this conundrum. Stealth is of the essence here. We must approach the enemy unseen if we are to avenge the vessels it has destroyed. It is for that reason that we will be painting our spacecraft red.'

Carveth stared across the table.

'Schmidt told us that the Edenites will attack anything not on their side,' Suruk explained. 'It is well known that the Edenites hire many mercenaries and errant warriors. By decorating our craft, we will fool the enemy into thinking that is us.'

'A disguise,' Smith said.

'Indeed.'

Carveth nodded. 'Perhaps this isn't as crazy as I thought. Although we will still be going near the Edenites, so some level of crazy is still there. We'll hardly be invisible, though.'

'Invisibility is relative,' Suruk explained. 'If you wished to go unseen among a crowd in one of the cities of Earth, would you paint yourself in stripes, and run nude on all fours? Of course not. But if you wanted to hunt zebra, that is another thing. . . you see?'

'So if you were to hunt zebra, you'd paint yourself stripey and run round naked?'

'It was just an example. But resembling dangerous pirates, we will be able to enter their citadel by stealth.'

'Along with the thousands of other dangerous pirates,' Carveth said. 'Alright then. . . what do space pirates look like?'

The alien flexed his mandibles thoughtfully. 'Truly, it varies,' he declared. 'But this season's colour is a deep, blood red. Chains and spikes are popular accessories, along with battering rams and boarding gear. It is a bold, dynamic look, based around a few key pieces.'

'Pieces of eight?' Smith put in.

'No, pieces of other people.' Suruk took a biscuit from the table. 'As for the individual space pirate, hair is lank this season and patches are in. There are a few major brands to look out for, as well as major scars and tattoos.'

'What the heck.' To Smith's surprise, Carveth seemed willing to assist. 'We can make our own outfits. Rhianna's got some big white shirts – we can take it from there.'

Smith sipped his tea. 'Good work, Suruk. It's a splendid plan. We'll sail in under false colours. And there's that flag on the trophy rack we took off the Deathstorm Legion. That's got a skull on it, even if it does have antennae. Although flying under a Gertie flag might damage our moral fibre.'

'Then we are agreed.' Suruk stepped back and gestured towards the blackboard. 'These are some modifications we could carry out.' He had sketched a picture of the *John Pym*, together with a chalk drawing of himself, swinging what looked like someone's leg. A selection of useful notes adorned the diagram: 'the ansestors', 'Blud!!', 'Fols beerd', 'pile of heads' and, predictably, 'chanesor'.

'As you can see, we will need to paint the outside of the ship. All we need now is blood,' Suruk said. 'Lots of blood. Failing that, red paint.'

'Okay,' Carveth said. 'It's a good plan. I'll give you a hand.'

'Most kind,' Suruk replied, reaching to the machete on his belt. 'Right or left?'

*

'All clear!' Carveth shouted, slamming the door behind her. Smith stood in the side airlock, squashed between the two doors. The little counter spun in its brass dial until Sealed appeared. He turned round and opened the door. Space, as usual, was big and dark. Stars flicked by, quick as fireflies. Strange, he thought, how in ages past men had been so fascinated by such a lot of old nothing. It looked much better in the mapbooks, where most of it was Imperial pink.

He checked the magnetic strips on his boots, then stepped out into the void. He found himself standing at right angles to the *John Pym*, sticking out as though the ship had sprouted him as a new, misshapen wing. He climbed towards the upper hull, shaking his head at the larger patches of rust. Those, although regrettable, weren't surprising. Nor were the patches of frozen avian-droppings or the dents, as if from gunfire, where something larger than a bird had done its business when they had landed on Urn. He would not have been greatly surprised to find a washing line wrapped around the dorsal fin, trailing pairs of smalls frozen by the deathly grip of space.

Suruk was already on top of the ship. He wore a modified spacesuit, doctored to accommodate his head and some of his smaller trophies. As Smith watched, the alien bounced down the hull with a power-screwdriver in one hand and a bag of skulls in the other, pausing on each bounce to attach a skull to the *John Pym* before bounding away like a fiendish version of the Easter Bunny.

The M'Lak leaped up and landed elegantly beside Smith. Suruk raised a gloved hand and waved. Smith leaned in to talk – the radio links were somewhat crackly, and shouting helped – but forgot that they were wearing space helmets. Suruk staggered back from the force of his headbutt and Smith grabbed him quickly before he could float away. In their suits, behind limb pads and brass helmets, they looked like a pair of deep sea divers geared up for a game of cricket.

'Gosh,' Smith said. 'It looks pretty good – convincing, I mean.'

'Thank you, Mazuran. I do have some experience of the art of decor. Back home I used to decorate the family home with my ancestors. Only the ones I disliked, of course.'

'Good work, old chap.'

'A pleasure.' Suruk laughed over the intercom. 'A plethora of skulls for the vessel of doom! Regrettable that the seer is not with us. She would appreciate my efforts, I feel.'

'I think she'd want something a bit more – what's the word. . . chilled.'

'I *am* chilling.'

'Not in the same way.'

Suruk took a bounding step towards the airlock. He landed elegantly and spun to face Smith, reminding Smith of being taken to see *Beatrix Potter On Ice* as a child. 'The job is a good one,' the M'Lak declared. 'All ship-shape and fashioned like Bristols – assuming that the ship in question is shaped like a hawk of bloody death and Bristol has taken up skull-collecting. Come to think of it, I do not know why you did not have it done years ago.'

*　*　*

Smith was last in. Suruk helped him remove his space helmet, not quite twisting his head off in the process. The alien looked different, Smith thought. In order to give the impression of being a deadly, murderous space pirate, Suruk had combed his hair and was smiling slightly more than usual.

'Listen,' Smith said, 'I'll lend you my space fleet jacket. You can say you took it as a trophy.'

'A wily plan, Mazuran. In return, I will lend you my favourite t-shirt. It says *Slayer*.'

'I'll be alright. I've got an old tweed jacket that'll do the job.'

'Tweed?' Suruk rubbed his mandibles together thought-fully. 'For a pirate?'

'I bought it in Penzance.'

'Excellent.'

As they entered the cockpit, the radio emitted a hideous roar. Carveth leaped up in the pilot's seat. Gerald, the hamster, dove into his sawdust. A spider dropped dead out of its web. Cackling laughter and guttural snarls filled the room.

They stood silently as the radio screeched around them.

'Suruk,' said Smith, 'turn that off!'

Suruk leaned across and flicked the off switch.

'Apologies, friends. I took the liberty of tuning the radio to my homeworld. That was *Thought For The Day*. Today's thought, it seems, is *Attack!*'

A ball of fire throbbed in the centre of the windscreen. Perhaps aptly, the Edenites had built their base on a volcanic planetoid.

Smith pressed a button on the front of the radio, and it dispensed a copy of the *Ethervisual Times*. He crouched down and worked the dials. The little needle moved from *Sane and Decent* into the red area reserved for aliens, dictators and car review presenters.

'Do you want answers to life's big questions?' the radio suddenly inquired. The voice strained to be chummy. 'Do you yearn for peace on earth, goodwill to all men and riches beyond mere wealth? Do you believe that the meek will inherit the earth? Then get out of my face, you pansy communist, or I'll shoot you and set you on fire! If you want to save your soul, you freak, and maybe have some chance of not being incinerated for witchcraft right damned now, surrender all your worldly possessions to us. In return, you will receive a machine gun and a special hat—'

Smith flicked off the power switch. 'Welcome to Eden,' he said.

The Edenite fortress-port grew in the windscreen. It looked like a single bloodshot eye, a burning ball of liquid fire. The Edenites had sunk huge pylons into the lava, deep into the core of the world, and had built a city above the flames. They called it Deliverance.

*

Major Wainscott awoke to find a woman in a conical hat standing over him. 'Arise, oh Arthur,' she cried, 'for you are the true-born king of all Britain!'

'I knew it!' Wainscott sat up rapidly. 'I always knew it was – oh, it's you.' He looked around the bay, with its rows of hypersleep chambers stretching out like cigarettes in a case. 'Very funny, Susan. Take that stupid newspaper off your head before I remove it.' Clad only in his underpants, he watched the rest of the Deepspace Operations Group getting up.

Wainscott climbed down from his slab and glared down the length of the room. 'Bloody hell, woman, this floor is freezing.'

'Huh. What do you want me to do, Boss, fetch your slippers?'

'Of course not. That's the robot's job. Wallahbot!'

A wallahbot rolled slowly down the length of the room, its spindly arms dispensing dressing gowns and tea. 'That's better,' Wainscott said, snatching a mug from the tray. 'Now then, what are we doing here?'

'Guard duty for the conference.'

'Ah yes. Right, let's have some breakfast, eh?'

Not bothering to close his dressing gown, he strode into the ship's messroom, sipping his tea as he walked. Susan, neat in her own dressing gown and slippers, followed him like a worried mother supervising a small child.

'Ten o'clock GMT, by God,' Wainscott said, checking the clock. 'Know what time that is, Susan? Sausage time!' He advanced to a dispenser set against the wall and began twiddling a pair of knobs, as if cracking a time-locked safe. The machine responded by ejecting a synthetic sausage, spear-like, into his face.

Susan brought Wainscott a paper plate and, after he had dusted the sausage off and added some scrambled powdered egg, they sat down to breakfast with the rest of the Deepspace Operations Group.

'I suppose we're near the target,' Wainscott opined, jabbing at the sausage with a plastic fork. 'It'll be interesting getting to work on a space station – I mean, looking after one instead of destroying it. Hullo, Nelson. Is that bacon you've got there?'

'Allegedly,' Nelson replied, holding up a droopy item. 'Looks like the tongue of my boot.'

Susan fished a piece of paper out of her dressing gown pocket and spread it on the table. 'Let's see. Given that we're awake, the journey must be over. So, first up, we'll dock and unload the gear in the hold. Then I suppose we can start getting security set up for this conference.'

'Party hats and such.'

'Metaphorically speaking, yes. Of course, most aliens can't wear hats.'

'Quite,' Wainscott replied. 'Funny shaped heads.' He scooped up a forkful of runny egg and tasted it warily. 'This isn't egg, it's baby sick. And why aren't there any biscuits here?'

'Hey,' Craig called down the table. Seeing that there were only five people in the Deepspace Operations Group, he didn't have to call far. 'Remember those digestives we got on Sirius Four?'

Nelson laughed. 'Yes, and the one you had was soggy.'

'It doesn't matter if it's a digestive!'

A sudden clang shook the room. Wainscott was up on his feet in a second, fists clenched and raised, dressing gown flapping. 'Alien attack!' he cried. 'To arms, troops!'

Susan sipped her tea. 'We've just docked,' she replied.

'False alarm, everyone!' Wainscott announced. He was impressed by how quickly his men had got back to eating their breakfast. It was almost as if they had not moved at all. Very wily. 'You not eating, Susan?'

'I'll give it thought once you've closed your dressing gown.'

Wainscott dressed whilst listening to the Galactic Service on the wireless. In the galactic West, the Senarian Lancers had stormed Aggrio XII, and together with the King's Own Moonlanders had crushed Praetorian Armoured Legion 'Grinding Death'. Scummy alien prisoners were being shipped into penal servitude by the thousand. Meanwhile, the prize bull had run off into Top Field, and was being hunted down by the Archers.

That's where I should be, Wainscott thought as he pulled on his largest combat shorts. *Not on Top Field, but in the thick of it. Fighting for Britain. A stick of dynamite in one fist and a flimsy spineless Ghast neck snapping in the other. Stark bollock naked. Or a dirty lemming man – they think they know how to fight up close but I'll show them. . . cutting, shooting. . . putting the right wires together and boom – boom. . .*

'Are you alright in there?' Susan called.

Wainscott suddenly found that he was getting dressed. 'Fine, fine.'

'I just thought I heard manic laughter, that's all.'

'A mere delusion, Susan,' Wainscott said, strolling out to meet her. 'You want to watch out for that. Don't want to lose your edge, do you?'

'Do your flies up,' she replied.

W waited for them near the airlock, lounging against a scrollworked bulkhead. He looked as if he had been awake for some time. Beside him stood Rick Dreckitt, android bounty hunter and Service employee. Dreckitt wore a long coat and Panama hat. He seemed to stand in a pool of shadow, even in a spaceship, and despite being dry managed to look as if he had just been caught in the rain.

As the Deepspace Operations Group arrived, other teams filed out of the side doors and into the hold: communications personnel, staff from the Imperial Office for Variety and Sanctioned Amusements and even a squad of cheerful soldiers from the First M'Lak Rifles, sent to maintain order among the visitors and decapitate anyone not queuing properly.

'Ah, Wainscott!' W said. 'Sleep alright? Good. We're going to be busy from now on, I suspect.'

Dreckitt nodded. 'Word on the street is that this space station joint is a dive. We'll need to tidy it up before the guest planets arrive.'

Wainscott said, 'Eager to help out, are they?'

'It's a hell of a grift for them. They want protection, and we're the biggest racket going.'

W flipped open a small black notebook, in which he kept useful information and a list of people he suspected of treason. 'So far, we've got confirmations from the Morlock high lords, although one does suspect that they'd turn up to a drawer being opened if they thought they could batter someone with it afterwards—'

'True,' said Wainscott. 'Splendid fellows.'

'We've also had a response from the Khlangari. They're going to grace us with a delegation of mystics.'

'I see.'

The Khlangari were short, placid and fat, and spent

most of their time pottering around their small planet, hooting and doing baffling things with soup. But they were protected. For reasons unknown, the Khlangari had a symbiotic relationship with the Voidani space-whales, who had a history of violently 'researching' any space vessels they disliked. If anyone could make allies of the Voidani, it was them.

From deep within the ship, a metallic groan announced that the docking systems were synchronising. The ship rocked violently.

'Looks like the joint's open,' Dreckitt said. 'Let's go find the big cheese.'

*

As the *John Pym* swept into the landing bay, Smith realised that they were in good – and spectacularly bad – company. Deliverance's lower spaceport, reserved for heretics and aliens, was packed with renegade ships of every sort: ex-light cruisers; freight ships bristling with grappling hooks and jury-rigged gun turrets; waste-disposal shuttles turned to dirtier work; Royal Mail ships gone postal; even a mobile hydroponics plant gone properly to pot – all united in the red stripes of the renegades, all flying under the Jolly Roger. A huge sign hung over the landing bay. It read: *Looking for meaning in life? Inquire about murder and pillage within!*

They touched down and gathered their kit.

'It's a bloody recruiting drive,' Carveth whispered. She carried a shotgun, her automatic and two of Suruk's smaller knives, which looked like swords on her. She had spent the last few minutes padlocking Gerald's cage shut, to keep him safe while they were gone.

The airlock opened and the smell of sulphur rushed in. Smith stepped out. The flames of Deliverance raged and bubbled below them, as red and angry as a drunk's curry. A network of gantries and walkways stretched as far as Smith could see, strung together by great taut wires. Arches of blackened steel connected the habitation-blocks and guard towers, studded with images of reapers and skulls. It looked like a hellish, crazed version of the Empire itself, as though New London had mated with the sleeve art of one of Iron Sabbath's less polished albums. Everything was grimy: the floor was perforated steel, crispy with soot; the propaganda screens had a sheen of black as though they had started to decay. There were guards and guns everywhere, of course: robes, uniforms and brutish faces, mirrored sunglasses specked with dirt from the furnace below.

This, Smith thought, was going to be hard. The Empire allowed its citizens to worship practically anything so long as it didn't involve criminality or making a fuss, but there were still plenty of sects too crazy to be granted a licence by the Collected Synod. However, none were as demented as the Edenites: not the Dawkinians who vehemently followed a god that refused to believe in itself, or the Objectionabilists who worshipped money and considered arrogance to be the greatest virtue. After the schism among the Ronaldian Dualists about the true meaning of the ritual of the Four Candles, the Republic of Eden now had a virtual monopoly in religious lunacy.

An Edenite acolyte stood at the bottom of the John Pym's steps – beside the landing leg that sometimes folded up too early. One look at the man's white robes and broad smile, at once insipid and sinister, and Smith hoped that the leg would malfunction again and deposit eighty tonnes of spaceship on his empty head.

'Pirates, are we?' the acolyte asked, opening his briefcase.

'Yes – I mean *Arr*, that's right, er. . . shipmate.' Smith replied.

'Right then.' The acolyte fished out a wad of paper and shoved it towards Smith. 'Are you stressed?'

Smith frowned. 'Er, what?' Carveth asked.

'Not until now,' Suruk replied.

'It's a questionnaire,' the acolyte explained. 'It's well known that pirates suffer from extreme stress. We of the New Eden can cure you.'

'Now look,' said Smith, 'Much as we pirates love paperwork, me old sea dog, I'm not sure I want—'

'Stress is caused by the attachment of negative money energy. Money attaches itself to the uninitiated. Only by full initiation into the Church of the New Eden will you be relieved of all stress. Indeed, the highest levels of our faith are spiritually fixed—'

'And materially broke?' Carveth glared at the acolyte, her arms folded. 'I know bollocks when I hear it. And believe me, I hear a lot of bollocks. . . Jim lad.'

She had a point, Smith thought. The Edenites spouted out more crap than a whale with the runs, but they would have to be appeased. For now. He glanced around: Carveth looked unimpressed, while Suruk had taken off his pirate hat and seemed to be looking for something inside. Smith decided to act fast in case Suruk's mislaid item turned out to be a grenade.

'Shush, Carv – er, Black Tom. We will take your questionnaires, ye swab, and add them to our stack of plunder.'

'Excellent,' the acolyte replied. 'You can fill them out while you watch our induction film.'

Carveth raised a hand. 'Will there be ice cream?'

The acolyte shuddered violently, glared at her and shrieked 'There is no ice cream in the cinemas of Eden because ice cream is a sin, you pie-chasing harlot!'

'Well,' she replied, 'I suppose that's a no.'

Bands of filthy warriors trooped off the landing pad, clutching their questionnaires. The crew of the *John Pym* slipped easily into the malodorous procession.

'So then,' Suruk asked, 'what happens if they discover that we are not really space pirates?'

'Nothing good,' Carveth replied. Worry gave her small face a look of almost comical concentration, like a child confronted by a fraction. 'I'm just guessing, but I reckon they'll splice your mainbrace, shiver my timbers, Jolly Roger the captain and wear you as a hat. Possibly not in that order.'

'Worrying indeed,' Smith observed. 'Still, there is a plus side.'

'Really?' she said.

'Definitely. These questionnaires are really easy to fill in.'

That didn't seem to cheer her up very much, Smith noticed. It was true, though: the Edenite forms were tick-box, with only one box per question, except for the space for credit card details at the end. Unlike the yearly questionnaire that the Secret Service sent out with the Christmas cards, it didn't ask whether he was a sexual deviant or knew how to blow up a house with a toaster.

The propaganda theatre stood on the top of the gantry. Like much Edenite architecture, it looked like a result of crossing a nuclear bunker with a cathedral. Keeping his hand near his gun, Smith led the others into the dark.

The screening-room was full of space pirates, degenerates and mercenaries. A few were M'Lak, swigging freely from fizzy drinks. Suruk scowled. Most, however, were human – although, given the proliferation of crude bionics and self-inflicted scarring, it was quite hard to tell.

As they sat down – Suruk on one side, Smith on the other and Carveth in the middle – a space pirate with lank hair and no nose leaned over in a clatter of weaponry. 'I cut me own nose off,' he confided, 'to put fear in me enemies. They call me. . . No-Nose.'

'Bilge!' a second buccaneer called. 'You tried to pick it with a hook.'

The curtains parted and the lights dimmed. 'Be still,' Suruk hissed. 'You would not like me when I miss plot details.'

It was the worst film that Smith had ever seen. It explained the history of the Republic of Eden and began with a list of historical villains that the Edenites admired. It might as well have been called *Great Mistakes in Facial Hair*, he thought: never had he seen such a loathsome parade of moustaches, both stunted and overgrown, riotous beards and gluey toupees looking as out of place as a Procturan black ripper in a rabbit hutch. Around 2300, the film claimed, a variety of religious nutcases from across Earth had done the inevitable and put aside their doctrinal differences to work together on what they considered truly important: hatred and genocide. Thus was born the Brotherhood of the New Eden, and its members had been killing one another and anyone else ever since.

'*This little girl is being treated in the Communist People's Republic of Britain,*' the screen declared. Pictures of a child in a hospital appeared. '*The godless medics demand no payment from her. Yet as they work, the doctors surgically remove her soul. It's true! In any decent society, she would have been left by the side of the road as a gift for the Great Annihilator.*'

Things had clearly changed in the Republic of Eden, Smith thought. In the old days, the Edenites had welcomed anyone with a sufficiently crazed outlook and the weapons to back it up: these days they seemed to be screening for real madmen before giving them some sort of tax exemption. Not that there were any taxes in the New Eden, as the narrator on the screen explained: taxes were for communists. *Charitable donations* to the Republic, on the other hand, were both frequent and obligatory.

'. . . *And who runs this conspiracy?* the screen demanded. *Who's really pulling the strings behind this communist plot against all we hold sacred and dear?*'

''Tis the British Navy!' a voice yelled from the back of the room.

'The devil himself!'

'Ol'Blue Teeth, the crooning scourge of space!'

'*Wrong*,' the screen declared, and a derisory hail of popcorn, along with the odd knife, flew out of the audience. '*From his secret headquarters deep below Highgate Cemetery, Karl Marx plots to spread communism through his tool, the British Space Empire. Everywhere his agents stand poised with their lips stiff, ready to disarm you, to provide you with a functional society, and to ensnare your nubile offspring for their own depraved pleasures.*'

'What utter rubbish,' Smith muttered. 'Alright, I have disarmed a few Edenites, but only by shooting them first. And if they think Britain has a functional society, they should try catching a train to Slough on Saturday night. And—'

'I once saw a much better film about pirates,' Carveth said. 'It was called Das Booty. There was this lady pirate living on a submarine, and a bloke came round to fix her washing machine—'

No-Nose shushed them. 'D'ye *mind*? I'm trying to learn about plunder here.'

A man in an enormous conical hat appeared on the screen. It was white, like his robes, brimless, with earflaps and a small visor. The letter E above his eyebrows marked him out as an Exalted Warlock of the New Eden.

'*What can be done?*' the hierarch demanded. '*How can you help us in our ceaseless struggle against the freedom-hating hordes? Sign up today as a sanctioned freebooter of the Republic of Eden and join our cause of righteous plunder. For the very planet of Deliverance will be the starting point of a revolution, the unleashing of a divine wrath that shall come upon our enemies unawares, as the Great Annihilator did come unawares onto Rehab daughter of Fetherboam in her hour of licentiousness. And from the void you shall fall on our enemies like the wolf on the fold, and take your pick of the possessions of the British Space Empire!'*

The audience whooped and stamped. Someone drew a machete and waved it in the air. It seemed to be a good time to leave.

As they slipped out of one foul atmosphere and into another, Smith wondered whether the space pirates had been just bellowing randomly at the end of the film – or whether they were cheering it. It was time to find out what the hierarchs of Eden were really up to.

*

W stood in a large, airy hall, its walls made of polished brass. Lamps stretched out from the walls on delicate, scrollworked arms. Creepers spilled down from a wrought-iron balcony. Light classical music chirped through the air. A small hovering robot moved up the wall, rotors whirling, as it buffed the metal with polish and cloth.

W looked down. He could see his own face reflected in the floor.

'I thought you said this was a waste disposal plant?' Wainscott said.

'I suppose they disposed of it all,' W replied. 'I'll ask.'

A man sat on a large bench in the shade of a potted tree. He was cradling a cleaning drone in his hands like a pet, working at it with a screwdriver. As he approached, W saw that the drone had been built out of several rulers and a cigar box.

'Excuse me.'

The man looked up. He wore glasses and was clean-shaven and broad across the shoulders. He looked strong without being particularly large. 'Hello?'

'We're looking for the station governor,' W said.

The man seemed slightly surprised. 'That's me. Are you lost?'

W looked around. 'I thought this was a waste-disposal plant.'

The man nodded. 'It is. I did a bit of work on the place. The last people left it in a terrible mess. It used to be a right dump.' He turned and tossed the drone into the air. Its motors caught as it left his grip and, mosquito-like, it rose towards the rafters.

'Did you make that?' W asked.

'Oh, yes. There're a few dozen knocking around. They keep the new wing clean.'

'The new wing?'

'It's nothing much. You get a lot of scrap in a recycling plant. Might as well do something with it.' The man took out his handkerchief, wiped his hand and held it out. 'You must be the people wanting to hire the hall. Mike Barton.'

'Eric Lint,' W said, 'although that's classified.'

'Wainscott. Major. That's classified too.'

There was a moment's awkward silence. Wainscott said, 'How many people do you govern?'

'One,' Barton said. 'And I really just take him out for walks. He's a dog.'

'Governor Barton,' W said, 'when did you last see a human being?'

'About three years ago.'

The visitors exchanged a look.

'So, what do you want the hall for, a birthday party or something?'

'It's top secret,' Wainscott replied.

'A surprise party? Because I thought I'd give you a bit of help putting the banners up, maybe set out a buffet, and then get out of your way.'

'Actually,' W replied, 'it's an intergalactic conference to discuss mankind's place in the universe.'

'Oh, right,' Barton replied. Suddenly, he looked worried. The gravitas of the situation was sinking in. 'That's serious. I hope we've got enough balloons.'

*

Thirty yards up ahead, a huge pair of gates blocked the way. Each gatepost was topped with a sentry point, equipped with searchlights and the inevitable machine guns. The gates bore a steel relief of demons throwing sinners into flames, while a winged, bearded creature looked on and laughed. It was in fact the Great Annihilator, an amalgam of the most bloodthirsty and delinquent deities of Earth.

A soldier stood in front of the gates, hulking in robes worn over a suit of mechanised armour. Whoever sold cloth and mirrored shades to the Edenites was probably very wealthy by now, Smith reflected. And kindling wood.

'Hold it right there, heathen trash!' The guard's gloved

finger flicked a switch on his massive gun, and the barrels slowly began to rotate, like a hand flexing its fingers ready to curl into a fist. 'The higher levels are sanctified for members of the Republic of Eden only. If you do not have suitable authorisation I request that you step down. I have a level four-gamma blessing, authorising me to use lethal force in any situation.'

'I'll deal with this,' Smith said quietly. 'Natural bully, your Edenite. Just has to realise he can't have his own way.'

He stepped up close. 'Remove your sunglasses, my good man.'

'Screw you, unbeliever,' the guard said, and prodded him in the chest with his gun.

Smith fell over. As Suruk helped him up, he reflected that his powers of persuasion were not as strong as he had recalled. Perhaps the Edenites were too stupid to be affected by the Bearing. Or maybe the guard was just laughing too hard to hear.

'Bastard,' Carveth muttered.

'If you pirates want to get in,' the guard declared, 'you need to be absolved of your sins, through Mark 12.'

'Is that a bible verse?' Smith asked.

'Bible?' The guard patted his gun. '*This* is Mark 12. The Mark 12 Absolver with integrated angel-eye tracking system to ensure its message of salvation goes straight to your heart. Guaranteed to free your soul from all worldly cares in less than two seconds.'

'We'll be going now,' Smith said.

The guard's face had taken on a dreamy look. 'Heck, I've converted nigh on fifteen hundred unbelievers with this thing. One moment they're begging for mercy, and the next they're in spirit form. It's a beautiful transformation.'

'Come along, chaps,' Smith said, and he ushered them away.

'Wait! I haven't told you about the underslung holy smoke launchers. Why get angry when you can get incensed?'

Pirates still trooped out of the cinema, muttering and cursing. Smith could hear the occasional burst of song or snarling cheer, but a new mood seemed to have settled over the horde, a sort of menacing contemplation. The pirates despised the Edenites, that much was obvious, but the film had raised new and exciting opportunities for pillage. Grumbling, the renegades turned towards the grog-house that the Edenites had erected for them, a rickety structure called The Booty Hut.

Smith ushered his crew to one side and they stood under the sanctified eaves while the bandits made their comparatively thoughtful way past. 'Men,' he whispered, 'it appears that we've stumbled into a conspiracy, and now we're knee-deep in the foulness of enemy treachery. It seems the Edenites are recruiting for some kind of big raid on the Empire. This does not bode well for Britain: indeed, I'd raise the level of boding from poorly to full-on ill.'

'True,' Suruk replied. He rubbed his jaw in thought, managing not to spike his hand on his mandibles in the process. 'The space pirates circle the ailing lion of Britain like hyaenas. While the Edenite serpent strikes from the front, these freebooters hope to bite from behind, to get—'

'A facefull of lion poo?' Carveth put in.

'Well said.' Smith clapped Carveth on the back, nearly propelling her into the stream of buccaneers filing past. 'That's the spirit, pilot. This lion isn't fit to drop yet. Well, not unless it's dropping a – anyway, we need to decide what we're going to do.'

Carveth sighed. 'Muck out the zoo of justice, from the sounds of it. Which is probably code for "Get in terrible danger and nearly, if not actually, die".'

'An excellent plan!' Suruk growled. 'Once more onto the beach, dear friends! And seal up the wall with a big pile of heads!' His eyes, always yellowish, had taken on a worryingly crazed look, like a blood orange without its skin. 'I see this as a quest of two stages. First of all, we kill everything. Then—'

'Listen,' Smith put in. 'It's clear what's going on here. The Edenites are trying to recruit as many ne'er-do-wells as they can, and not for a game of five-a-side, I'll wager.'

Carveth nodded. 'Looks like it.'

'There's trouble brewing here,' Smith said. 'And we need to get to the heart of it. We have to get out of this area and into the places only the Edenites can go. And that means we'll need robes. And I know just the place to get them.'

Suruk chuckled. 'From the same place we shall acquire Edenite skulls!'

'Actually, I thought we'd just ask nicely.'

'Oh,' Suruk said. His mandibles drooped. 'Mazuran, do you really need my assistance? Otherwise I shall try to find some meagre pleasure in the company of several hundred pirates and their near-limitless supply of bladed weaponry.'

'Alright,' Smith said. 'You wait for us. We'll bring you back a disguise.'

Beside the *John Pym*, the New Eden acolyte was still handing out his pamphlets. A filthy man with one eye stood in front of him, insolently folding his questionnaire into a paper hat. As Smith and Carveth approached, he tossed the hat aside and stomped off on a bionic leg, glowering across the gantries.

'Finished your questionnaires?' the acolyte demanded. 'Good. Let's have a look.'

They passed him their papers, and the Edenite shook his head sadly as he leafed through their answers. 'Ah, yes, a common result. You see. . . what your test scores show is an urgent need to give us your money—'

'Actually,' said Smith, passing him the questionnaires, 'we'd like to join.'

'Can't wait,' Carveth put in. 'It looks like great fun! All that witchfinding—'

'Join up?' said the man. 'You sure? You look so. . .'

'Normal?' Smith replied.

The Edenite looked them over – Smith in his tweed jacket and eyepatch, his moustache waxed and upstand-ing, Carveth in goggles and overalls – and said, 'I was thinking more along the lines of distinctive. You know, it's a far cry from piracy to Edenism. Some people find it hard to give up wenching, drinking, jollity and song. Of course, you do get to keep the murder, but it's much more hate-filled. And you don't get to choose who you murder.'

'Bah,' said Smith, 'mere trivialities.'

'Glory be to the merciful Annihilator! Well, if you could make us out a cheque for all your worldly goods, kill any aliens you may know – after all, we can't have any of that 'all pirates are equal' stuff here, can we? – and reduce your ladyfriend here to miserable servitude, then we can fetch you some novitiate robes. The acolyte smiled, which was technically illegal, and put out his hand for Smith to shake. 'Welcome to the Church of the New Eden! I would shake your hand, miss, except that you're inherently sinful and will probably give me girl germs. Now then, if you'd just step into my office, we can find you some robes. . .'

He led them across the landing pad to a small, shedlike building. The sign above the lintel read *Military Surplice*. As Smith balled his fists, Carveth slipped a spanner from her back pocket. 'Good for dealing with nuts,' she explained, and she gave Smith a rare ferocious look. They followed the cultist inside, and quietly closed the door.

*

Lord Prong was having a dream about ascending in a celestial stair-lift when something nudged his arm. He sat up, blinking and muttering, and found his secretary, the Exalted Stapulator, standing beside the sofa and prodding him with a pincer. Since the Stapulator had demonstrated his devotion by having his hands replaced with staple guns, it was a very gentle prod.

Prong patted the seat next to him and located his Helm of Purity. He put it on, turned it so that the buckle faced the front and felt the bionics in the crown click into place, accelerating his drowsy mind.

Now that he was alert, the first task was to find his

slippers. Prong got to his feet. To judge from the images on the screen of sanctity before him, he had started to watch a taped episode of *Eden's Most Wanton Harlots* but, having turned the ranting commentary down to better love the sinner, he had promptly dropped off.

'Damn slippers, always. . .'

'Grand Mandrill?'

He turned to face the Stapulator. 'What?'

'Lord Prong, your appointment with the hierarchs is to take place in thirty minutes.'

'The hierarchs?' He scowled. 'What do I want with them? They're just a bunch of crazy old farts. Half of 'em barely know – wait. When are the allies coming to look at Project Horseman?'

'Their ships are currently in orbit, Lord Prong. They will be arriving in forty minutes.'

'What? Why didn't you tell me? Damn young'uns. Got to do everything myself. Now, where the hell's my hat?'

The Stapulator helped Lord Prong into his coat, nearly pinning it to him in the process, and together they set off towards the upper landing site. A lift decorated with cherubs and virgins whisked them up towards the landing pads.

The hierarchs were waiting for them. In their white robes and pointed hats they looked strangely like penguins, or a gang of geriatric dunces. Beliath stood in their centre, grimacing as if struck with indigestion. On his right, Hierarch Ezron thoughtfully chewed the end of his beard. Regnus, the Grand Coelacanth, was on the left, so heavily covered in parchments and sacred texts as to look like a sort of human newsagents. Crusadist militiamen flanked the party, but they were too busy testifying and battering one another with holy tomes to be much use as guards.

The party started off, Lord Prong grumbling at its head. Behind him, the hierarchs discussed the matters of the day. A machine had been built out of an old rollercoaster that could now duck up to fifty witches at once. 'Trouble is, once you've ducked them, they're much harder to burn,' Ezron explained.

'All women must burn!' Beliath interjected, furiously rubbing his thighs like an overkeen bowler polishing two balls at once. 'Burn them, stone them, oh hell yes!'

Two ogres waited at the end of the gangway. From a distance they looked like the result of some trick of perspective. In truth, they were both nearly eight feet tall. When the Ghasts had first made their alliance with the Republic of New Eden, they had exchanged technologies. At the time it had seemed like a perfect deal: the Edenites threw their new allies a few scraps about tank design while they received the gene-splicing equipment that could turn their elite soldiers into the human equivalent of praetorians. The Edenites called them the Reborn: loyal soldiers granted great strength from immersion in the waters of the gene pool. Unfortunately, the Ghasts had neglected to mention the side effects.

As Prong approached both of the bodyguards snapped a salute, one nearly concussing himself in the process. They both wore blue-grey uniforms, with heavy plate armour over the top.

'At ease,' Prong rasped. He had to lean back to see their faces, which made his spine ache.

'Sir,' said the left giant, 'I am Lieutenant Carsus of the White Knights of Purity, sir, and this is Private Leniatus. May I say, sir, what a deep honour and a privilege it is to be serving you today in greeting the alien filth on behalf of our beloved republic, sir.'

Prong nodded. Carsus didn't seem to like pausing between words. 'Right, good,' he replied, 'you do that, sonny.'

'I got a gun,' said Private Leniatus.

Prong had not expected to hear him speak. 'What?'

'Gun,' Leniatus explained, patting the oversize, multi-barrelled firearm he held across his chest. 'I got a gun for the unbelievers and a prostate.'

'Shut up, you big dummy!' Carsus hissed. 'I told you not to say anything.' His immense jaw made speaking out of the corner of his mouth rather difficult. 'And it's apostates.'

'Gun for the apple states,' Leniatus said, and he smiled vaguely over Prong's head.

'Right, good, whatever,' Prong snapped. Typical young people, he thought. 'Follow me. And pipe the hell down.'

'Yes sir!' Carsus grunted. 'All hail the Grand Mandrill, sir. We stand ready and waiting to initiate full tactical combat protocols—'

'Are you even listening to me?' Prong replied. 'Shut up!'

'Sorry, sir. I tenderise my apologies. Forgive me, Grand Mandrill'

Leniatus chuckled. 'Carsus, you're the dummy,' he said.

The Handyman's Tale

'One size fits all, it seems,' Smith said, pulling a red robe over his head. 'Or rather, nobody. On the plus side, the hoods hang down so much, you can hardly see your face.'

'Well, it'll suit Suruk, then. I can hardly see *anything*,' Carveth said. She looked, Smith thought, like a cross between a monk, a ghost and Little Red Riding Hood. Seen from the front, it appeared as if the robe was animating itself. 'I look like something from science fiction.'

'You mean speculative fiction. Science fiction has talking squids.'

'Same difference. Oh – don't forget your passcard.' She passed him a plastic card on a chain. The Handymen had access, theoretically speaking, to anywhere on Deliverance, provided that there were repairs required.

If the Edenites dressed like this all the time, Smith reflected, no wonder they were so hot and bothered. Still, stealing the robes had left a convenient space in the cupboard, now occupied by the acolyte, tightly bound and gagged with a wad of his own pamphlets. Smith bundled up a spare robe and shoved it down his front. Nobody noticed them slipping out through the door.

111

'Now we just have to find Suruk,' Carveth said.

'That'll be easy,' Smith replied. 'He does rather stand out.'

'In a horde of psychotic pirates? Actually, I think he'll be invisible.'

A great roar arose to their right. Smith glanced round, and for a moment he thought it was Suruk himself. Then he realised that it was about thirty coarse voices spilling out of the Booty Shack, raised in raucous song:

'*Who. . . lives in a spaceship that's made out of rust? Suruk the Slayer!*

Born of battle and war and bloodlust? Suruk the Slayer!
If decapitation is what you fear
Then heave away, hearties, from his big spear!'

Smith looked at Carveth as an accordion solo began. 'Now that,' he said, 'is where you're wrong. Follow me, crew,' he declared, and he strode to the door and threw it open.

Two pirates lay on the floor, either dead or dead drunk. A thing like a bladed grappling hook stuck out of the ceiling. An enormous boar of a man, shirtless and bruised, was flat out across one of the tables. Suruk stood on the next table down and, around him, two dozen of the galaxy's most raucous buccaneers waved their fists and tankards in the air.

Smith slipped past a filthy corsair and approached the table. 'Suruk, come down from there.'

'Gar!' cried the corsair, 'it's the fun police! Come for our women and drink, have ye?'

A growl of fury rose from the crowd. 'Ah, ye medieval knob! They promise us plunder, and try to make us join their cult. What would ye do, Eden – school us freebooters to bow before your Great Annihilator, eh?'

The space pirates surged forward. At the entrance a voice cried, 'And here's another – a spy he's been hiding, the sly old bugger!'

Suruk reached for a knife. Smith twisted aside, dislodging a hand from his shoulder, reached up and threw back his hood. 'That's enough!' he cried, using the Bearing, and the Shau Teng style made the crowd of reprobates pause.

'My name is Isambard Smith, and I am no Edenite. I have stolen these robes in order to infiltrate this facility.'

'Er, Boss?' Carveth took a step back towards the door, but trod on the hem of her robe and narrowly avoided falling over. 'Ah, bollocks to it,' she said, pulling her hood down.

'The young lady you see there is under my protection, and I will kill any man who lays a hand on her, Edenite or not,' Smith declared. 'The fellow before you, Suruk the Slayer, is my friend.'

At the rear of the room, a pirate laughed. It was No-Nose, the madman from the cinema. His left hand gripped a pint of beer; his right, the bottom of a young buccaneer girl. 'So you say, Eden. But to claim company with this great fighter here? That can't be. Him, an alien warrior hungry for glory, an' you, stiffer than a ship's biscuit. I'll wager ye've never even met.'

'I know this man.' Suruk hopped down from the table. 'He speaks truly, and together we have spilled the blood of many a foe. He is called Mazuran in my tongue, which means 'the quick brown fox that jumps over the lazy dog'. Be sure of one thing, if this man walks concealed among you, there is danger and bloodshed afoot, of the finest vintage.'

'Suruk's right,' Smith replied, before anyone could challenge him again. 'This is subterfuge, gentlemen. I came here to sink a spaceship – none of yours. I have a debt to settle with these Edenites, and I call on you to lend me your ears.'

'How about a nose?' No-Nose laughed. Beer exploded from his nostrils. The privateer girl shifted down the bench.

'Listen,' Smith replied. 'Let me ask you something. What is it that you stand for? Is it booze? Plunder? Women? Senseless violence? Yes to all of those, probably. But what really drives you? For what does every space pirate truly thirst?'

Eyes and patches met across the room. Hands and hooks scratched battered heads.

'Shanties?' a voice suggested.

'Revenge on the Navy, damn 'em?'

'You're all wrong,' Smith replied. 'It's fun. You all want fun.'

'Fun?' No-Nose snorted derisively, with unpleasant results. Then he frowned. 'So what if we do, swabby?'

'Fun,' Smith replied, 'is the very thing your new allies hate.'

A rumble ran through the room. The space pirates, never the most analytical thinkers, experienced a moment of contemplation.

'Think about it. Why is it, that when they find something enjoyable, the Edenites have to call a halt to it in the name of so-called piety? Why is it that everything you enjoy is to them a crime to be wiped out? Sex, booze, brawling, doing exactly what you please: the Edenites would see them eradicated like so many cockroaches of, er, joy. Why, they'd criminalise every natural urge in the world if they thought it would bring a little more misery to the human race. When I have a natural urge, I follow it through – and I bet you all do the same.'

'I used to,' said one of the pirates, 'but me shipmates got me some tablets.'

No-Nose stood up and brushed his coat down. 'Mates, this parley is all very well, but what's he got to offer us in return? We've not come here for nothing.'

'Ask my crew,' Smith said. 'Suruk, what do you want?'

'Battle, of course,' the M'Lak replied. 'Blood, doom and the skulls of my enemies. With my blades I delight my ancestors through the gift that keeps on giving. . . the heads of ignoble fools.'

A rumble of mixed approval and apprehension came from the privateers. Smith turned to Carveth. 'And you?'

'Me?' She looked appalled. 'Well, I – I want to stay alive, I suppose. . . and right now I could do with a drink.'

'See?' Smith said.

No-Nose rubbed his chin. His lack of a nose made him look as though he was in the early stages of turning into Suruk. For a moment he stared at the ceiling fan, and suddenly he exclaimed: 'Well, damn! Violence and booze. Perhaps you do have a point after all. I could do with hearing a bit more about pillaging but, curse it, I'm with ye. Enough of this Edenite nonsense! I ask ye, what good is a god who hates his own creation? That's a theological tautology. Me hearties,' he added, for good measure. 'So now. . .' he said, leaning closer, and giving Smith a very distasteful view of his nostrils, 'where might all this entertainment be found?'

*

In true Edenite style, the edges of the Upper Level landing pad were decorated with burning bodies. Stakes stood along the edge of the pad, surrounded by piles of wood: when important Edenites visited, it was customary to light up some apostates to show them the way in. A huge statue of the Great Annihilator stood at the far end, his fangs bared, a gun in one hand and a time-bomb in the other.

On the videoscreens, a reclusive hierarch named Gurt the Spelunker was delivering a furious sermon. Live from his cavern, he railed against the decadence of the democratic world and the prevalence of guano.

Lord Prong's heart sank as he stepped onto the gantry. A small group of Edenites had gathered on the edge of the walkway, brandishing guns and big placards. Their feathery hats identified them as the True Brotherhood of the Chicken Rampant.

'Hey, you kids!' Prong's amplified voice rang around the cavern. 'Get off my landing pad!'

One of the Brothers Rampant broke free from the others and rushed up. His eyes had a worrying, ecstatic gleam. 'Lord Prong! How can you stand by and let this travesty happen?'

The Stapulator Documentarium clacked his pincers,

and the zealot backed away a little. Prong sighed. 'What travesty?'

'This one!' the young man cried, pointing at his placard. 'Something terrible is going on. Do you have any idea how offensive to my beliefs that is?'

'Your sign is blank,' Prong said. He felt every one of his two hundred and eighty years.

'It's blank *now*,' the zealot replied. 'But as soon as we figure out what this dreadful thing is,

then, by the Annihilator, we'll fill our signs out and those potential blasphemers will regret the day they were probably born!' He lowered his voice. 'Personally, I think it's to do with pornography. We just need to find the right evidence. . .'

Lord Prong sighed. He turned to Lieutenant Carsus. 'If you would, please?'

Carsus grabbed the zealot and yanked him into the air. The young man howled as the Reborn lifted him over the railing. Below, the lava bubbled like hot soup.

'Tell me, chicken boy,' Lord Prong rasped, 'Can you fly?'

Carsus hurled him over the edge. He screamed for a moment and then was lost to view. Only a loud plop and a terrible sizzling hiss marked the young man's passing. On the far side of the pad, the protesters lowered their placards and shuffled away.

Private Leniatus leaned over the railing. He gazed down sadly, and the gantry creaked under his armoured bulk. 'Now we'll never know,' he said.

'Never know what?' said Prong.

'If he could fly. 'Cos he's dead.'

*

'This robe smells of zealot,' Suruk growled as they approached the gate. 'Some fool has testified all over it.'

'We'll deal with that later, old chap,' Smith replied. 'Let me do the talking.'

'You'll have to,' Carveth said, tugging her hood down over her face. 'You're the only one of us they'll listen to. I suppose they don't let women and aliens into their precious Holy Order of the Handyman.'

'Well,' Smith said, 'it does say Handy*man*. It'd sound odd if it was handyperson. That just sounds like you've got too many arms.'

Carveth flapped her sleeves. 'Boss, let's just get this sorted, eh?'

The guard swaggered out to meet them.

'Good day, my man,' Smith declared. 'My colleagues and I have come to repair your machines.'

The guard scowled. 'Do I know you? I'm going to have to check that.' He pulled his commlink close to his mouth. 'Control, I'm making a confirmation request under Chapter 35 of the Book of Appliances. Handymen, provide details on your work.'

'Sorry?'

'What're you here to mend?'

'Er. . . a washing machine?'

The guard muttered into the radio again. 'Very well. I have confirmation of a sullied vestment on Circle Two. Move along.'

A portion of the great door swung open and they passed inside.

There was something particularly grim about walking under the watchtowers, Smith thought. This must be what it was like to be an Edenite, or a Ghast or lemming man: forever watched from above, as though some cruel child had lifted the roof off the dolls' house, waiting for an excuse to punish the toys inside.

'This way,' he said quickly, keeping his head down, and they hurried into the sector reserved for true followers of Eden.

It was much like the area set aside for mercenaries, except that most of the damage was caused by decrepitude rather than exuberant cutlass-waving. There were no pubs. The grim housing blocks were broken up by grey concrete buildings that could have been bunkers or churches. Stone angels flanked the road, brandishing flags and sabres, their cold, stern faces raised skyward. Enormous samplers hung down walls, threatening all manner of vengeance.

No sense of architecture, the Edenites, Smith thought. Back in the Empire, from Nexis VII to New Neasden, the places of worship looked proper.

Smith could see the lava bubbling beneath the metal pavement. The sight of it gave him a strange mix of vertigo and hunger for tikka masala. He had started to sweat. He raised a hand, half-hidden by his wizard's sleeve, and pointed at a column rising to the roof. At its base was a pair of double doors. 'Lift.'

Halfway to the lift, a horn blared above them. They froze under a concrete angel raising its trumpet, trying not to clamp their hands over their ears. Smith slid his hand under his robes, to the guns and sword stashed there.

A loudspeaker crackled. 'New *Eden is destined to restore purity and moral rectitude to the galaxy,*' it proclaimed. '*But have you considered the sort of reward you'll receive in the afterlife? For a small fee, you can specify the hair colour and dirty pillow size of the virgins you'll be granted as a reward for your service. Just send your money to. . .*'

'False alarm,' Smith said, and they hurried to the doors.

As the lift rose, Suruk shook his head. 'You humans should invent some gods that actually like you.'

'People aren't all like that,' Carveth said.

'Damned right,' Smith added. 'Not in the Space Empire.' He looked down at the little figures below, either swaggering with their guns or rushing from place to place hoping not to be noticed. Some sort of padre had emerged from a temple in a pointy hat, and was shouting orders. Citizens scurried to obey. 'That's no way for a fellow to live.'

'If I were a deity,' Suruk observed, 'I would sell hats.'

'Sorry?'

'The gods of man love headgear,' the M'Lak explained. 'I would open a special shop and sell my attire from it. Then I would be very wealthy, and would purchase a spacecraft in which to put my spears.'

'But if you were a deity,' Carveth pointed out, 'you could just make the money anyway.'

Suruk pondered the issue. 'But I like hats.'

The lift stopped with surprising smoothness. 'You have ascended to the Second Circle,' it announced, and the doors slid apart.

Rows of shuttlecraft confronted them, their nosecones

sleek and white like fangs. Smith looked down the row of vessels. Several were covered in presumably sacred scrawl. One or two had a rather nasty fake-marble effect, with gold trimmings. None of them resembled the thing that had attacked the convoy.

Suruk tapped his shoulder and pointed. 'Mazuran, look.'

It was hard to see what his sleeve was indicating. Then Smith realised: Suruk did not mean the gantry ahead of them, but the one above. Smith looked up to see two immense men lumbering overhead, their boots thumping the perforated floor. Between them was a smaller fellow in some sort of dark uniform and, behind him, a chanting, muttering pack of high-ranking Edenites. He watched as they trooped past over his head and, with a mounting sense of horror, he realised quite what the hierarchs wore under their robes and how distressingly inadequate it was.

He looked down and met the appalled eyes of his men. 'Chaps,' he announced, 'this looks bad.'

'That,' Suruk said, 'was a disquieting experience.'

Smith reached into his robe and drew his Civiliser. 'Mark my words, men,' he said, 'evil is afoot.'

'It looks more like a small willy to me,' Carveth replied.

'I see evil more as a sort of claw,' Suruk added. 'But then, humans do have very unpleasant feet. Is it severing time yet?'

'That depends.' Smith glanced around. 'Look over there.'

Under the gantry was a narrow access ladder. In the red light of the fire below, it looked like a stripe of soot against the wall.

'I'll go first,' Smith said. He climbed the ladder, rung over rung, his boots ringing on the metal. It was hard not to think of the drop below. He stepped onto the upper gantry and waited for the others to appear. The three stood in their robes beside the ladder, looking like ghosts searching for someone to scare as they waited for Carveth to get her breath back.

They walked down the gantry, trying to look as innocuous as armed maintenance-monks could do. Ahead, the walkway swung left and, as they turned, Smith saw the white, pointed hats of the hierarchs sticking up above the railings like a mobile picket fence. They followed, pausing every so often to check non-existent faults in the walkway.

'We're close,' Carveth said. Her voice was small and worried.

'Chin up, pilot,' Smith said, and he patted her on the shoulder.

'Hands off, Boss. If they suspect I'm a woman, they'll murder me.'

'They might not realise. It's hard to tell in these robes.'

'Okay then, they'll think we're both men, touching each other for fun. Because if there's one thing religious fanatics love, it's gay handyman sex.'

They crept around the corner. Carveth stopped. 'It's here!' she whispered.

Before them lay the ship. The hull was covered in dirt, half-obscuring the runes burned and painted onto the metal. The systems were powered down, the long chains dangling like dead fronds, but blue phosphorescence still pulsed behind the tinted lenses of the cockpit. Something had scored a grid into the prow of the vessel, criss-crossing it with deep scars as if it had driven at high speed into a gigantic wire fence. Its name was stencilled along the dirty hull: *Pale Horse*. Something about the ship made Smith's skin crawl, as if with the fear of being touched by something cold and dead. Even the party of hierarchs kept a little way back.

A light flashed on the wall at the far side of the gantry. Under the light, a pair of iron doors creaked apart and figures stomped onto the landing-pad. Heavy-set and armoured, too broad for humans, they approached the Edenites. Smith glanced at his crew. Under his hood, Suruk bared his teeth.

'I should have known,' Smith whispered. 'The lemming men of Yullia.'

*

The Stapulator clicked his pincers. 'Lord Prong. The allies approach.'

From a distance, even to Prong's mechanically-boosted vision, the Yull looked like small bears standing on their hind legs. Seen closer, though, they moved with a swaggering grace, supple and poised. The lead Yull, a white-furred brute of the knight caste, wore a red cuirass like a metal waistcoat. The others carried rifles and long-handled axes pushed through their belts. The Yullian flag, reminiscent of four stylised windmill sails, hung on a gallows-shaped rig rising out of the back of the lead officer's armour.

Private Leniatus grinned. 'Reckon they look like rabbits.'

'Shut up, dummy!' Carsus replied.

The lemming men huffed and drew themselves up. Prong recognised that pompous look. It was the expression that the Yull tended to assume when practising their favourite hobbies of axe-twirling, murder, denying murder, eating cheese and proclaiming their own greatness to anyone they hadn't murdered yet.

The loudspeakers played the anthems of New Eden and Yullia. As *Smash 'em for the Lord* ended and the whooping subsided, the strident tones of *Remember You're a Lemming* filled the hall.

'*Hwuphep*, dirty offworlder ally!' the Yullian officer barked. 'I am Ambassador Quetic the honoured, most reasonable envoy of the benevolent war-god of the Yull.' Quetic bowed stiffly from the waist. 'May divine Popacapinyo kill you slightly quicker than you deserve.'

Lord Prong gave the lemmings as deep a bow as his dignity and lower back would allow. 'May the Great Annihilator spare you from righteous incineration,' he said. 'Briefly.'

A low whine came from the lift shaft. Prong looked around and saw the lights rise on the panel beside the doors. He felt a little tension in his gut. Slowly, the light hopped from diode to diode: left to right, then up to the next level, left to right again, then up another line.

The lift banged into place. With a piped fanfare the doors rumbled apart, and a face formed from the shadow inside.

At first it was a metal disc, a coin hovering in mid-air.

Then light caught the glass in its centre and it became a lens. Details followed it: steel insignia on a leather coat, a bulbous helmet like a metal marrow and, below it, a scarred red face with a mechanical eye, a pair of nostrils like a skull's and a malignant slash of a mouth.

The personal representative of the Ghast Empire limped out of the lift. Behind it, a pair of immense praetorian bodyguards looked around and snarled. One held a chain, at the end of which an ant-wolf strained, growling.

Prong felt the urge to look away and he noticed that the lemming men seemed to have shrunk a little: Ambassador Quetic shifted his feet and puffed his chest out, but it made him look weaker than before.

The Ghast officer stopped, and its single eye fixed on Prong, as unblinking and cold as the lens beside it. 'I am High-Research-Over-Commander Four Hundred and Sixty Two,' he rasped, 'and this had better be worth my while.'

From somewhere behind him, Prong thought he heard a British-sounding voice exclaim 'Bloody hell! Him *again*?' He swung around and glared at the hierarchs. There was some nervous shuffling.

462 turned to the Yullian deputation. 'Apologies for my late arrival. The minion responsible has made full amends.' The ant-wolf licked its chops and one of the praetorians belched. 'I assume you rodents have already indulged in the inevitable self-justificatory prattle about honour, yes?'

Quetic puffed himself up. '*Hwot?* How dare you insult the dignity of the noble Yull, filthy insect? Were we not so lovely and in the presence of witnesses, you would die slow – yes, yes, slow!'

125

'I shall take that as a yes,' 462 replied.

It was time, Lord Prong thought, to take the initiative. He needed to show these aliens – these unbelievers – the power of *Project Horseman*. He coughed loudly and the visitors turned to look at him. He spoke quickly – before the Stapulator could pat him on the back.

'Allies,' he announced, 'I, Lord Hieronymous Prong, Sin-Hunter of Eden and Grand Mandrill of the Innermost Conclave, have called you here to witness the harnessing of arcane power in the conquest of our enemies. My minions, with the grace and blessing of this bunch—' he indicated the hierarchs behind him – 'have turned their wisdom to mastering the occult. Through the complexities of Dodgson physics, we have created the ship you see before you. . . the *Pale Horse*.'

'Show us,' said 462.

'Yes, yes!' Quetic barked. 'Demonstrate its capabilities, offworlder, or be shamed!'

'Ah, pipe down, fluffy.' Prong felt much better now. He was in his stride. 'You want to see what we can do? Stapulator, give the order to fire her up. Brother hierarchs, begin the ritual!'

*

Smith pushed his hood out of his eyes. On the gantry, the Edenites were performing some sort of ceremony. One of the pointy-hatted crowd, perhaps their leader, strode to the front and threw up his arms. '*I get up in the morning, looking for witches*,' he cried. '*I find some women and set them alight!*'

The rest of the hierarchs swayed. '*Oh, oh,*' they chanted, '*the Edenites!*'

Smith slipped a hand into his robes and drew his Civiliser. 'Stay here, everyone. I'm going to get a better look.'

Suruk tapped his shoulder. 'Leave some slaying for me. Oh, and be careful.'

Smith crawled along the gantry, bent double to stay out of sight, and ducked behind a cart full of sensor equipment. The Edenites were still chanting, their white conical hoods wobbling in unison, and to Smith's astonishment the ship seemed to be answering them. A low electric growl issued from the *Pale Horse*, like an amplifier before the striking of the first chord. The chains along its length rose in a field of crackling static. Blue lightning played across the hull: first in sparking flashes, then in a continuous dancing light.

And then the spaceship vanished.

'Oh,' said Smith. There didn't seem to be any better way of putting it. Where the devil had the thing gone? He felt rather glad he hadn't been hiding behind the *Pale Horse*.

Up ahead, the observers seemed no less astonished than he was. The Edenite hierarchs had gone into a frenzy of chanting, their conical hats bobbing together like teeth in the jaw of some enormous beast. 462, curse him to Hell, had limped several steps back and his guards struggled to keep his ant-wolf on its leash as if barked and snapped. The lemming men gawped in awe. A Yullian officer staggered back, terrified, and one of Prong's enormous guards picked him up and patted his head.

In a blast of blue light, the *Pale Horse* reappeared. The

cockpit became dark, the electricity subsided. The chains fell limp and clattered across its hull.

'Where did it go, Prong?' Quetic demanded. 'Offworlder, where did it go to?'

'Silence!' 462 had taken a scanner from the inside of his trenchcoat. Two little antennae sprang up from the main body of the device. 'The sensors report a fluctuation in the presence of the vessel,' he rasped. 'Either this machine has become inefficient, or your craft. . . moved.'

Quetic shook his armoured head. 'But. . . how? How can it be here and suddenly not? Who is responsible for this? And,' he added, looking round, 'what is your body-guard doing with my adjutant?'

'I got me a rabbit,' Leniatus said.

The lemming-man thrashed in the ogre's arms. Smiling, Leniatus patted the Yullian, making the warrior's head bob alarmingly.

'Put Adjutant Xeptoc down!' Quetic snapped.

Leniatus took a step back, hugging the Yullian even tighter. 'No! He's my friend!'

'I meant drop him.'

'Oh. Okay.' Leniatus dropped the Yullian.

Adjutant Xeptoc stood up, shuddered and howled. 'The dirty offworlder patted my head. I am forever disgraced!' The adjutant turned, shrieked, and hurled itself over the railing. Quetic scowled, 462 smirked, and Leniatus looked sad. Smith crept closer.

'Now,' Prong declared, 'soon you will observe the power unit for the Dodgson drive. It is this piece of techno-arcane genius that enables the *Pale Horse* to shift dimensions. Once the drive is activated, the *Pale Horse* no longer inhabits realspace. For your safety, we will deactivate the power unit.'

Smith was hardly listening. With a soft hiss, a hatch opened like a gash on the side of the ship. Light spilled out. Two figures stood backlit in the entrance, carrying a long, flat object wrapped in a cloth.

A painting, Smith thought. *What the hell have they got a painting for?*

The figures emerged. They were acolytes of the Order of the Handyman, their red hoods pulled up, robes brushing the ground. The *Pale Horse*'s airlock had a chequered floor, and the two men looked like pawns. Slowly, reverently, they carried the wrapped painting across the gantry, past the astonished visitors and through a door on the opposite side.

Lord Prong gestured to the spaceship. 'Shall we take the tour?'

Smith watched the delegates file towards the doors. One by one, they stepped through the doorway, into the blue light.

A voice boomed out of the airlock: deep, commanding and slightly strained, as if on the verge of fury.

'*Welcome aboard our flight to the further regions of experience. A trolley will appear shortly to cater for your beverage-related pleasures. Passengers are to remain chained in until the light comes on. Smoking is not allowed unless you are being incinerated. You will find emergency exits located nowhere – for there is no escape!*'

The doors slammed shut. The hierarchs milled about on the gantry, looking rather like a colony of penguins. It would not have surprised Smith to find them hiding eggs up their smocks.

Smith ran back down the gantry, stolen robes flapping around him. He stopped before his men, slightly out of breath. 'Did you see that?'

'The invisible spaceship?' Carveth replied. 'Yes – I mean, I did to begin with—'

'Whatever they took off the ship, we have to get it. It's our duty to acquire useful things for the Empire. That little fellow, Prong, said it was the power unit for the drive that made it invisible.'

'I agree,' Suruk declared 'We must steal this mystic painting.' He nodded to the doors at the far side of the gantry. The sill had been decorated with a relief of skull-faced cherubs. 'Less delaying, more slaying!'

'Alright,' Smith said. 'Follow me. Calmly, now. Remember, we've got every right to be here.'

From under her hood, Carveth said, 'We have?'

'Of course. I'm claiming this place for the Empire. Come along!'

Smith holstered his pistol and strolled out of cover. Suruk strode casually behind him. Carveth hurried along at the rear, a little figure in red.

They walked towards the doors. 'Calmly, everyone,' Smith said, and he pressed the button.

The doors parted, and they looked into a corridor. 'There,' Smith said, nodding to a side-room.

The room was bare metal and smelt of grease. At the far corner, under a flag, two robed handymen were locking a large wardrobe.

Smith closed the door. Both handymen turned.

'What the hell?' said the first man. 'What is this?'

'Don't look now,' Carveth replied, 'but this is a hold up.'

The technician ducked down to get a better look. 'But. . . you're just a girl.'

'Wrong.' Suruk threw his hood back.

'Begone, demon!' cried the man, recoiling in terror, and Suruk brought the edge of his hand sharply into the technician's head. He fell, and Suruk stepped to the second man and causally punched him out.

Smith bent down and checked the fallen Handymen. One carried a hefty metal keyring. He flicked through the keys until he found one that looked appropriate. The key turned easily in the lock, and the wardrobe opened.

Smith reached inside. His hand brushed something soft – a fur coat, from the feel of it – and he stretched further. The fur slid down, and he found himself gripping a hard wooden corner, wrapped in a thin blanket. The painting.

It took up almost the entire back of the wardrobe. He tugged it forward a little, realising that the wrapping was taped into place.

Carveth touched him on the arm.

'Yes?'

'I don't like this, boss. I mean, all this for a picture. Do we have to steal it?'

'Of course we have to steal it. We're an empire, aren't we?'

'It looks a bit heavy.'

'Nonsense. Do you think that's what was going through Lord Byron's head when he rolled the Elgin Marbles out of, erm, Elginland? Nonsense, he was thinking—'

'How can I score some laudanum and shag my aunt?'

'Really, Carveth! Suruk, you take one corner and I'll take the other.'

They lifted the frame out of the wardrobe. 'Careful at the back,' Smith said. 'Carveth, could you get the door?'

She opened the door and looked straight into the grim face of Hieronymous Prong. She gave a yelp of surprise and slammed it shut.

The door burst open and Lord Prong took a limping step into the room. 'Well, well,' he rasped. 'I've been looking for reds under my bed all those years and it turns out they were in the wardrobe.'

There was a huge silver automatic in his hand, scrimshawed with holy writ. Even less pleasant was his smile, which looked like the product of muscle failure. Behind him came Hierarch Beliath and his inevitable smell.

'Close the door,' said Prong. 'Best the allies don't know these idiots got this far.'

The door clicked. Beliath said, 'That one's a dirty alien.'

Prong grimaced, as if trying out his face and not liking the fit. 'Put my property down.'

'Gladly,' Smith replied. As he set the parcel on the ground, he flicked his hand into his robe. Smith turned holding a Markham and Briggs Civiliser. 'I'll put you down too, if you'd like.'

Prong raised his hand. Smith's gun roared and the Civiliser shell hit Prong in the chest and blasted straight though him. Prong's pistol clattered on the ground.

Slowly, the Grand Mandrill patted his chest. 'Only a lung,' he wheezed. 'I've not used those things for ages.'

'Pipe down, you two,' Smith replied. 'You're under arrest.'

Prong and Beliath glared at them with guilty rage, like a couple of dirty old men surprised outside a netball court. Carveth produced the shotgun from her robes.

'How dare you try to stop us?' Beliath snarled. 'Don't you know how offensive that is to us? We are men of faith.' He drew himself up and cocked his head back. 'We require special treatment.'

'I don't doubt it,' Smith replied. 'You smell terrible.'

Beliath sneered. 'It is written that deodorant is decadent and washing is weak, just like your society. After all, do I look like a powdered fairy?'

'More like a smelly gnome.'

'So move it, King Leer,' Carveth added, and she pulled her hood back.

Beliath shuddered violently. His eyes, already wild, took on the appearance of poached eggs in the mouldy ham of his face. White specs of foam appeared at the corners of his mouth, joining the assorted detritus already clustered in his beard. 'A *woman*,' he spat, goggling. 'A woman in the guise of a Handyman!' Beliath clutched at his robes, yanking wads of fluff from his head. 'The shame, the brazen, wanton, licentious, dirty, filthy, naked shame of it.' Gasping, he turned to Prong. 'Grand Mandrill, we must kill her to wash this stain from our honour. Yes, I'll burn you, Jezebel, just as soon as I've got you out of those robes—'

He lunged at Carveth with both hands, palms out to grab and squeeze. She raised the shotgun and fired.

The shot threw Beliath against the wall. His whole torso was red. His face gawped, as though he had no idea how he had got into this terrible state. Then he dropped onto the floor.

'Nice,' Suruk said.

'I didn't mean to do that,' Carveth said. 'Honest.'

Smith looked at Beliath and wondered how many years' bad luck you got for killing the Ancient Mariner.

On the far side of the room, Prong coughed. He patted his meagre chest. 'Praise the Annihilator. Faith alone has saved me. That and bionic lungs.'

Smith put his gun against Prong's hat. 'Your brain's not bionic. If it was, it would work better. Prong, I am taking you prisoner. You will return to our ship with us.'

'So no fast moves, bucklehead,' Carveth added.

Prong chuckled. 'Is that the best you can do, captain? A .45 Civiliser? By Edenite standards, that's a pretty low calibre weapon.'

'Then it'll match your brain. Now *move*.'

Prong opened the door and stepped out. Smith followed, close behind. The door slammed shut and, slowly, the pack of guests looked around.

They stood in a loose row in their various uniforms, the extended family of evil waiting to have its photograph taken. Smith saw whiskers and polished armour on one side, antennae and leather coats on the other and white robes and pointed hoods in the centre, but the differences were superficial. He was still looking at the lowest dross of the galaxy.

'Hands up!' Smith cried.

'Back, rabble!' Suruk snarled. 'Keep at bay, or I shall drench the walls with idiot blood!'

There was a moment's pause. The Edenites glared back at him, their eyes wild and hats high. They resembled an exceptionally butch drag act about damsels. The lemming-men looked at one another, affronted and furious. From the Ghast deputation a thin, nasal voice exclaimed 'Oh, for Number One's sake – not *you*!'

'462,' Smith said. 'For once, it's not you saying 'we meet again'. It's me. Well, we meet again.'

'This is turning into a very tedious day,' 462 replied, crossing all his arms. 'Praetorian? Remove these imbeciles.'

One of his guards cocked his gun.

Smith raised his pistol and let off a single shot into the rafters. 'That's enough! Right, you bloody savages,' he called. 'In the name of the British Space Empire, stop your ignorant gibber-jabber or I'll blow your filthy brains out!'

'That's liberal talk!' Hierarch Ezron roared. 'Kill 'em all!'

In a clatter of guns, knives and axes, thirty of space's worst villains drew their weapons.

Suruk moved. His robe fell and his arm flicked out to the parcel he carried. There was a long, hooked knife in his hand. 'Fools, listen. My blade is sharp and poised. Should I fall, it will tear this relic of yours. Strike me down and you will fail your rulers, betray your orders and generally resemble chumps.'

Carveth stepped in, laying the shotgun against the parcel.

462's tongue slid out of his mouth and moved from side to side. 'Very well,' he said. 'That is a powerful piece of materiel. Praetorians, no shooting.'

'Well said, dirty ally,' Quetic added. 'There must be no gunfire. In which case – axe attack!' He raised his axe and gave a warbling scream of mingled hatred and glee. '*Hwuphep Popacapinyo – darhep yullai!*'

'Wait—' 462 hissed as Quetic's soldiers came to life around him. They rushed forward, bayonets first, and Smith realised that Prong and the painting were turning into considerable impediments to his escape.

He shoved Prong aside and lifted the Civiliser, took careful aim, and shot one of Quetic's howling minions in the thigh. 'Everyone back,' Smith called, and to his horror he saw that Carveth had pre-empted him and was running flat out the way they had come. Bloody coward, he thought, and a revving sound made him turn to the left.

He dodged back instinctively as a whirling blade swung down. A giant in a dark uniform and a steel breastplate stood before him waving a circular saw of the type used to cut paving slabs. Smith drew his sword, but Suruk dashed past him. The alien leapt onto Carsus's chest, and with one massive yank on the Reborn's armour sprang into the air. Carsus looked up, raising the whining saw again – and Suruk's spear flashed out. Carsus's head, which had always looked like an afterthought, rolled off his shoulders and his enormous body dropped like a felled tree.

Suruk landed lightly beside the armoured corpse. 'No helmet. Amateurs.'

Smith looked back just in time. Steel flashed before him before he drove his sword up to block Quetic's axe. The impact sent them both staggering. The lemming man leaped back in, swinging, but Smith dodged and sliced the alien across the arm. Quetic cursed in Yullian – '*Fecinec!*' – and flopped against the railings, his whiskers flecked with froth.

'Boss!' a voice cried at Smith's side. He looked around, and saw Carveth. Before he could rebuke her cowardice, he saw that she was pushing a porter's trolley. Suruk heaved the painting onto it.

A fresh batch of guards ran onto the gantry behind them. The Ghasts were readying their guns. Prong's amplified voice roared at them not to shoot.

'Boss!' Carveth called, 'What do we do now?'

'Isn't it obvious?' Smith replied. 'In the name of democracy and the British Space Empire. . . run like buggery, men!'

They tore down the gantry, Suruk pushing the trolley while Smith and Carveth laid down as much covering fire as they could. As one, the mob of enemies surged forward, yelling, hissing and yowling. Smith fired off two more bullets, killing an Edenite thug and stunning one of the praetorians with a shot that made its helmet ring like a gong.

An angel-shaped surveillance drone swung overhead, trilling out a warning. As if in answer, a pair of metal doors burst open on the left and a chanting gaggle of cultists rushed out, wearing large metal bells over their heads. Each carried two hammers, and they would have overwhelmed Smith and his crew, had they not used them to strike their bells. The fanatics staggered like bees in smoke, their dirge muffled by their clanging headgear, and Suruk deftly wheeled the trolley between the swaying bodies, clearly fighting the urge to play a tune on their heads with his spear.

Smith fished the speedloader from his pocket and

pushed a fresh set of shells into his pistol. Carveth reached the lift – she had never realised that legs as short as hers could go so quickly – and thumped the control panel. The doors rolled apart and Suruk pushed the trolley at the gap.

'It will not fit!' he snarled.

'Turn it side-on, you stupid sod!' Carveth shouted.

'Apologies, that was foolish.' Suruk turned the parcel and pushed it end first into the lift. They crowded in around it. Smith fired two more shots down the gantry, deterring nobody, and slammed the door behind them. Slowly, the lift began to sink.

Carveth flopped against the wall. 'All this,' she moaned, 'for a bloody picture. It'd better have some ponies on it.'

She had a fair point, Smith thought – apart from the bit about ponies. After all this effort, he would be severely disappointed if the painting didn't contain at least one artistically valid set of antiquities: the poetess Sappho admiring some Greek jugs, perhaps, or Guinevere and Lady Godiva – preferably in the same scene. . .

The lift rumbled around them. Carveth remembered to reload the shotgun. Above, a bell started to toll, a rapid, urgent pulse. 'We've got to get out of here,' she said. 'Who was that old bloke? Oliver Cromwell or somebody?'

'More fathead than roundhead,' Smith replied. 'A member of the Edenite religious police. Most hierarchs don't know which end of the red-hot poker to do the poking with, but that fellow – well, if his ship's anything to go by, he's a sharp biscuit. And 462, here of all places. . .' He shook his head. 'I knew that bugger was alive, but I thought they'd have sent him to the Morlock

Front, or at least given him a research job. Clearly there wasn't a backroom big enough for his swollen arse.'

Carveth pointed to the lift controls. 'We're nearly at the bottom. They'll be waiting—'

'Suruk?' Smith said. 'Time to give the signal.'

The alien reached to his side and took out a flare pistol. He held it out to Smith. 'You must fire it, Mazuran. I have taken the oath to fight only with the weapons of my ancestors. Guns just breed violence,' he concluded, solemnly drawing a pair of machetes.

Smith turned the pistol over in his hands. 'I hope this works,' he said, and the lift jolted to a halt. As the doors opened, he shoved the gun into the aperture, angled it upwards and pulled the trigger.

The flare sailed up above Deliverance, over the wall dividing the hired men from the devotees. In the Booty Hut, Captain No-Nose Chang saw the light and spluttered with surprise. Grog bubbled up the wrong way, pouring out of the centre of his face like a frothy proboscis. 'With me, lads!' he called, stumbling to his feet. His nasal passage fizzing uncontrollably, he charged out of the door, the itching driving him wild. Behind him, his men cheered and drew their weapons.

The lift doors rolled open onto a medieval picture of Hell. As Smith stepped out, the gates exploded. A horde of the galaxy's lowest piratical scum poured in, unkempt and furious, waving guns, cutlasses, tankards and grappling hooks. Hideous faces grinned behind lank hair and scars. Alarms howled and warning lights strobed in the rafters.

On the far right, the front of a temple flopped down

like a drawbridge and a great machine rolled forth: part tank, part grimacing idol. The face of the Great Annihilator glowered down at them, and a mechanical roar yowled from between its fangs. From the brim of the war-god's iron hat, Lord Prong called down curses on the raiders and the young folk of today. A bevy of cultists swarmed around the caterpillar tracks, flagellating wildly. Occasionally a robe would snag on the workings and a fanatic would be whisked under the war machine, to lubricate the gears.

The pirates met the Edenites in a terrible clash of blades and guns. A rocket sailed out of the pillaging horde and blew the top off one of the mobile fort's turrets. A couple of hatches dropped down from the idol's chest and two great rotary guns spun in place of nipples.

'It's got laser tits,' Carveth gasped. 'Let's get the hell out of here!'

Beside her, Suruk gazed at the battle like a small child looking at a Christmas display. 'Craven idol,' he whispered, raising his blades, 'I will cleave the unsightly knockings from your chest!'

'No you won't,' Smith replied, and Suruk seemed to deflate slightly, like a child that had just dropped an ice cream. 'Gentlemen,' said Smith, 'we have our artefact. We're going home.'

The Captain and the Queen

The *John Pym* slid out of the docking bay as the piratical horde fell back. It took off surrounded by chaos, one of dozens of red-striped, trophy-bedecked spacecraft. No one saw it go. Everybody had other things to worry about.

Deliverance faded in the viewscreen. It looked like a ball of flame, then a match-head, and then a tiny red spot in the centre of space, a mere zit on the face of the galaxy.

'God!' Smith said from the captain's chair. 'What a dreadful place. Carveth, set us a course for British Space. Where's Suruk?'

'He's gone to check his spawn,' Carveth replied. 'He said you wouldn't mind if he borrowed your cricket bat.'

'Righto. Well. . .' Smith got to his feet. 'Let's have a look at this precious painting of theirs, shall we?'

As often happened in the British Space Empire, it was time for the brave explorers to sit back, put the kettle on and try to work out exactly what priceless treasure they had stolen. Smith set the package up on end at the far end of the hold and got to work on the ropes with a Stanley knife. He let Suruk continue to tend to his frogs, or alternatively fight them off; the alien was not noted for his artistic tastes and tended not to hang anything on his walls that he had not hacked off somebody first.

Smith regarded himself as rather more sophisticated. After all, he could tell a Henry Moore sculpture from a large piece of Blu-tac from quite a long way off. As he cut the ropes he wondered what sort of thing the Edenites would want to look at: the torture of the damned, presumably, especially the large-chested damned. What a bunch of perverts they were. Anyone decent would want girls dressed up properly, like one of the Bronte sisters, say. . . As the cloth fell from the frame, he reflected that he really ought to try to get Rhianna to wear a big white nightie again.

All was now revealed, but instead of angels firing machine guns at the unrighteous, Smith was looking at himself.

'It's a mirror,' he said. 'How strange.'

He reached out and tapped the glass with his fingertips. Nothing unusual happened.

Carveth had been watching from the back of the room, somewhat warily. She approached like a person with vertigo looking over a cliff. 'You're right,' she said. 'They really must be stupid to try to power a ship with this. . . you don't think they swapped it for something else?'

'I don't know,' Smith replied. 'Rum, Carveth. Most rum.'

'Weird.' She stared at her reflection as if expecting it to wink at her. 'Nice frame, though. You could take it on Antiques Roadshow and find out if it's worth anything.'

'It does look rather old. First Empire, I'd have thought.'

'Greetings!' Suruk announced, striding into the room.

'Is there tea?' He frowned. 'So, this is the trophy the Edenites so wished to guard. Curious. Is there anything strange or sinister about it?'

'Excluding your reflection, no,' Carveth said.

'Peculiar. I must confess, it is not a pleasing thing. The workmanship seems a little gauche to my mind. It definitely needs more bloodstains.'

As Suruk turned, Carveth pointed. 'Erm, you've got something stuck to you.'

'Is that so?'

'Yes. Just look in the mirror. Down a bit, to the left. . . you've got a frog stuck to your bottom.'

'She's right,' Smith added. 'Lower your hand – there.'

Suruk reached down and located a large toad-like creature attached by its fangs to the seat of his trousers. Carefully, he prized its jaws apart. It squatted in the palm of his hand, glaring at its father with unabashed malice. Tiny tusks glinted at the edge of its broad mouth. 'One of my spawn. They are teething and will try to savage anything.'

'Clearly,' Smith said. It did seem a very odd way to demonstrate filial affection.

Suruk shook his head. 'It is fortunate for me that I have no buttocks. And, for him, it is fortunate that I dislike sitting down. Still, good to see that my spawn are becoming suitably ferocious. I shall hurl him back into the engine room.'

'On the bright side, at least someone finds you appetising,' Carveth said. 'Let's get this tea made.'

While the others were taking tea in the mess-room, Smith checked the scanners. No doubt the Edenites would be wild with rage by now. As soon as they had rid themselves of the space-pirate uprising, they would be in hot and heavily armed pursuit.

And 462! Surrounded by the reassuring clatter of gears and cogitation devices, it was hard to believe that the horrible little creature still existed. Each time they met, Smith chipped another bit off his enemy and 462 climbed a notch higher on the greasy pole of the Ghast hierarchy. Smith fired up the lidar, wondering as he did whether he and 462 would be locked in combat forever until the pair of them were geriatric. It was a nightmarish image: a ninety-year-old wrestling with a giant ant with floppy antennae and a back end as leathery as its trenchcoat.

He made himself concentrate on the scanner. They were approaching the edge of British space and could expect warships to be patrolling the borders. With any luck they would be able to put in a call for assistance.

A light flickered on the control panel. Behind old plexiglass, a needle fluttered like a captive moth. Smith pulled the printout lever and, as the tickertape began to spool, he took the *Spotter's Guide to Spacecraft Residue* from the shelf.

The signs matched. A large craft had been this way and, from the mixture of Navy-issue nuclear vapour trail and teacake crumbs, it was British. Quickly, he typed out a message and cranked the handle marked Broadcast. Satisfied, he returned to the hold.

The mirror stood at the back of the room, as oblong and unhelpful as one of those alien obelisk things they sold in junk shops. He looked at himself for a while – not doing too badly, despite the pies – and peered at the ornate frame, trying to make sense of the little markings in the corners. One looked like pieces of a square, the other like a heart, cut into bits and arranged at random, and almost lost in a mass of applied vines that covered the frame like scrollwork on a sewing machine. Very odd indeed.

On a whim, he walked around the back. A piece of elastic had been strung across the rear of the mirror and tucked into it was a note. He glanced at the heading and saw the words: *For attention of sacred hierarchs only.* Smith strode into the mess. This was worth sharing with the crew.

'Chaps, I have news,' he said, as Suruk slid a mug across the table. 'I found this stuck to the back of the mirror.' He unfolded the paper.

'What does it say?' Carveth asked.

Smith lifted the message to the light. 'Ahem. *All hierarchs are to note that a typographical error has been detected in the posters promoting Illiteracy Week. An extra space should be added to posters, to make them read: The gun is good, the pen is evil. For the avoidance of doubt, the penis is evil too. That will be covered in Self-Hate Week.*' Smith lowered the paper. 'Hmm. Well, that's pretty frustrating, really.'

'That's probably the point,' Carveth replied.

Disappointed, Smith turned the paper over. The rear side was a medieval painting frequently used on Edenite stationery that he recognised as: *The Damned are Tortured with Musical Instruments.* It was all distastefully inventive: on seeing a man grievously tormented by a mis-placed oboe, Smith reflected that merely having to listen to a child playing the recorder would have been punishment enough.

'So what've we got?' Carveth asked, rooting around in the biscuit tin. 'Besides Lord Prong's favourite preening-screen and a bunch of very angry goddies combing the galactic fringe for us, that is.'

'I don't know,' Smith replied. 'But the Edenites wanted this thing. They're a bad crew and therefore us stealing it is good. If nothing else, we can give it to the British museum. That'll hack off the Edenites a treat.'

'Makes no sense to me,' Carveth said. 'I wish Rick was here. He'd know what to do.'

No doubt he would, Smith reflected. Rick Dreckitt had started out as an android bounty hunter and private eye, and was now one of the toughest operatives in the Service. After years hunting gangs on the mean streets, Dreckitt would probably want to bust some loogans with a Chicago typewriter, before handing out chin music harder than a chiseller grifting bindle stiffs. Which would be. . . great, probably.

'I rather wish Rhianna was on board,' he said. 'This all seems her sort of thing.'

'Pining, boss?' Carveth sighed. 'Fair enough. But we can do this without her. I mean, she's hardly vital to the war effort. Remember when they had that 'Dig for Victory' campaign and she made us listen to jazz records?'

'Her counsel would be welcome,' Suruk said. He took a deep swig of tea, clamping the mug between his mandibles while his hands reached for the biscuit tin. 'On the other hand, my offspring are numerous and enraged and my lack of a jacksie has preserved my britches from the gnawing of the spawn. This bodes well.'

'That's as maybe,' Smith said, refilling their mugs, 'but there's something else you need to know. I've picked up a British ship on the lidar. I've sent across a request for an escort while we're carrying this mirror. With any luck they'll find us, escort the ship to safety, and this whole business will be at an end.'

He looked from Suruk to Carveth and took in their doubtful expressions. 'On the other hand,' he added, 'it is just possible that we might end up in a complete mess and have to fight our way out.'

'Indeed.' Suruk said. 'You know, Mazuran, for a moment you had me worried.'

*

462 limped into Prong's office. The room was not large and was lit by light redirected from below. The red glow fell on chains and instruments of interrogation. Prong sat behind his desk, on which the *Creed of the New Eden, Eleventh Edition* stood like a wall between him and his visitors. He was using the tenth edition as a cushion to give himself a few extra inches of dignity.

462 looked around the grim, red room, the fire and the torture implements and said, 'If I may check, Lord Prong. Hell is the place you *don't* like, yes?'

'Course it is!' Grimacing, Prong shifted about on his seat. 'Where's the lemming man?'

'Ambassador Quetic is admiring the workings of your spacecraft. We find the Yull are easily amused. Perhaps he has climbed into one of its wheels.'

147

'If he's in there, when it. . . activates, he'll be damned. There's no coming back from there.' Prong gave a laugh that turned, via a wheeze, into a coughing fit. 'Damn commies shot Beliath,' he said breathlessly.

'An insignificant minion. You have others.'

'He was a good man. Well, not exactly a good man, more an idiot, but a *prize* idiot.' Prong jabbed a finger across the table. 'We need to pay those goddam blasphemers back!'

The screen on the far side of the room blared into life. *'Do you want a government that cares about you, and a god who looks out for the poor and needy? Of course you don't, because that's commie talk! You need a government that despises you and robs you blind, and a god who just wants to kill everything! That's why—'* Prong turned the volume down.

'You realise that there have not been any communists for five hundred years,' 462 observed.

'Of course I do, you young antsnapper. But you've got to keep people afraid. It keeps the money coming in. And more money means more handmaidens – or, as the case may be, more piles cream.' He shifted uneasily. 'Now then. . . I'm having space combed for those godless bastards who stole my refraction portal. In the meantime, the *Pale Horse* will fall back on its built-in lagomorphic vortex.'

462 peered at the row of tomes on Prong's shelf. He drew out a copy of *Phrenology and Acupuncture*, frowned at the grim-looking fellow on the cover and slid it back into place. 'Good. Do you know who the man who raided you was?'

148

Prong shrugged. 'Some heathen fairy from the British Space Empire,' he said.

'No.' 462 turned, hands clasped behind his back. 'His name is Isambard Smith. He gave me this metal eye, this limp and this scar on my hand that reads *Made in Sheffield*.'

'Sounds like he kicked your – what is that thing, a thorax?'

462's antennae twitched irritably. 'A stercorium. The most highly-evolved waste-disposal organ in the galaxy. Its efficiency is matched only by the pleasantness of its odour. But I digress. Behind a facade of jovial idiocy, Smith possesses cunning and ferocity worthy of a pure-bred antwolf. It is quite a thick facade, I should add.'

'Sounds like a tough customer.'

'He is. You must watch these British, Lord Prong. I have studied their culture extensively. Their outer mildness masks an inner strength, just as the flaky exterior of one of their 'Cornish pastries' conceals the meat within. Their society equips them for war. The British child is brainwashed from birth, beginning with an indoctrination programme codenamed *Watch with Mother*. It then passes through the ranks of the paramilitary reconnaissance organisations known as Guides and Scouts – as we call them collectively, the Brownwoggles. Next comes drilling in the arts of Maypole and Morris, bringing psychological conditioning to a level rivalling even the Praetorian storm divisions. Add to this the colossal intake of moral fibre, synthesised via the combat beverage 'tea', of which the average Briton consumes between three and ten pints per day, and you have a creature whose moral rectitude is limited only by bladder capacity.'

'Ugh.'

'Quite. We have attempted to emulate them, but our own Strength Through Morris initiative has not been wholly successful.' 462 glanced away, pushing aside unpleasant memories of colliding helmets and flapping black handkerchiefs. 'Send out your men to find Smith. If nothing else, keep him busy. We need the *Pale Horse* for our next objective.'

'Which is?'

'*Classified*, Prong. Suffice it to say that there will be merciless killing involved, which should satisfy your religious sensibilities.'

'Will it help the needy?'

'No.'

'Then damn it, I'm in!' Prong punched his fist into his palm, then checked that none of his fingers had dropped off. 'I hate the needy. Scrounging bastards. Just make sure there's enough carnage and Eden is yours to command.'

'It always was,' 462 said, and he smiled and turned away.

*

With a low rumble of castors, Theophilius Chumble pushed a trolley laden with food down the corridors of the HMS *Chimera*. As second-in-command and ship's android, responsibility for the proper running of one of the Empire's dreadnoughts rested on him, and part of that involved waking up the captain. He stopped the trolley, fished the fob-phone out of his waistcoat and checked the time.

Chumble knocked as he opened the door and strode paunch-first into Captain Fitzroy's room. 'Good morrow, good morrow!' he chuckled, rubbing his hands together. 'And what a fine morrow it is, Ma'am.'

Felicity Fitzroy sat up in bed, dislodging the striped Bhagparsian feline that had been resting on the covers. It yawned, sighed and went back to sleep.

Clad only in regulation space-knickers, the captain got up, rubbed her eyes, stuck her arms up as if to punch the sky and said, 'Hullo, Chumble. Another sunny day in the space fleet, eh?'

'Absolutely, Captain. Now,' he added as she flung her arms down and touched her toes, 'I think breakfast is called for. Half a synthetic roast chicken and a snifter of port would be capital, methinks.'

Captain Fitzroy pulled on her dressing gown. It was dark blue and had epaulettes. 'Jolly good idea.' She reached down and prodded the heaped covers. They groaned and, slowly James Shuttlesworth, ace space-fighter pilot, pulled back the duvet until his eyes were visible.

'Morning sleepy,' said Captain Fitzroy. 'What ho there, Shuttles.'

'Uh.'

'Guess what I had last night,' Captain Fitzroy demanded.

He groaned. 'I don't know. A lot to drink?'

'You!' She whirled her arms and yawned. 'I banged you silly. Who's the best girl in the fleet, eh?'

'You,' he said weakly.

'Good-oh.' It was only right that he should have known the answer to that question, since Captain Fitzroy had shouted it at him several times the night before, *in flagrante delicto.*

'Look, Felicity, we really ought to stop doing this—'

'If you don't want to joust, leave your lance in the castle,' Captain Fitzroy replied as she strode into the bathroom. 'No time for sluggards here – am I right, Mr Chumble?'

'Most certainly you are, Ma'am.' Chumble rocked on his heels. 'You know, once I made the acquaintance of a most slovenly fellow, by the name of Frampton Gusse—'

'Have to wait, I'm afraid,' she replied, sawing at her mouth with a toothbrush. 'Busy day today. What's the mission, Mr Chumble?'

'Well, let me see.' Chumble took out his fob-phone, flicked it open and consulted the screen. A series of muffled bangs indicated that the captain was getting dressed. 'I do believe that today, we're not doing very much at all.'

'Excellent!' Captain Fitzroy emerged, dressing as she approached. 'Patrolling the borders of the Empire, eh? All aboard,' she said, adjusting her bra. 'Mr Chumble, have the wallahbot laser another notch on the bedpost. Activate the deck-swabbing machine. Oh, and feed the cat, would you?'

*

Carveth was in the cockpit and Suruk had retired to his room to polish the new additions to his skull collection and rearrange their hats. Feeling tired and lonely, Smith decided to look in Rhianna's quarters.

He felt oddly furtive about going into Rhianna's room, even though he was doing so because he honestly missed her and not with the intention of looking at her pants again. It was strange how different her little metal cube was to any of the other metal cubes; it was as though each cabin trapped some of its owner's personality like a genie in a bottle. Smith's bottle would have contained tea; Suruk's, probably blood; and Carveth's, bubble bath cut with Prosecco. Smith ducked under the genuine tribal dreamcatcher that hung from the ceiling like a dead bird splattered across the grille of a juggernaut, and stopped to marvel at the number of books that Rhianna owned.

He pulled one down at random, a brick-sized paperback with a dragon on the spine: *Dragonriders of Urn*, prelude to *All the Teas of Urn*. He replaced it carefully in case its sequels fell down and killed him. Next to it was a scholarly work on gender politics. Smith knew little about gender politics, although his grandfather had once told him that voting Liberal was for girls. He turned, not quite sure what he was looking for but pretty certain that he wouldn't find it unless Rhianna was hiding in the cupboard.

Something made him approach her bed. He stopped before the little table beside it, handcrafted by simple robots in an authentic traditional production line. He felt no more certain of what he sought but knew that he was slightly warmer. He wasn't looking for the apparatus on the top – part hookah, part alchemy experiment – either. Smith sat on the bed, which smelled quite nice, and decided to go to sleep.

After a busy day infiltrating the Edenites, foiling their evil plans and stealing their stuff, he deserved a rest. Soon they would be in Colonial Space, where things were done properly and he'd be able to hand over the weird mirror to the security services. And then he would see Rhianna again.

He closed his eyes.

The instant Smith awoke he knew something was wrong. A moment later he realised that the ceiling lacked any model spaceships. He sat up, remembering where he was. There was a curious smudge in the air beside the door. He rubbed his eyes and the smudge leaned forward and held out a hand.

Smith was hardened to the horrors of space and so he didn't leap back much more than two feet. It was a Vorl, one of the ancient energy-creatures with whom the Empire had struggled to strike a pact. But what was it doing here? And then the shape coalesced and he gasped as he recognised its dreadlocks and face.

'Help me, Isambard! Can you tell me if this is working okay?'

'I suppose so,' he replied. 'Either that or my brain isn't. Are you. . . Rhianna?'

'Yes,' the shape replied. 'Kind of. I'm like Rhianna's mind, projected astrally to you. My physical body is meditating. But my psyche has reached out. Finding your mind was really difficult.'

'Well, I am a long way away.'

'Um, yeah. Something like that. So, Isambard, speak to me.'

'Hello.'

'How's it going?'

'Fine thanks. Mustn't grumble.' Smith instinctively glanced upwards, then realised that there was no weather on the *John Pym* to talk about. 'Did you get to your place alright?'

'Yes, thank you. I can't tell you where it is, but I'm cool. I'm with the Vorl. They're teaching me to unlock my psychic powers.' The blur made a vague weighing-up gesture, as though describing the balance on a pair of speakers. 'It's very spiritual.'

'Smashing. We found the ship that blew up the convoy.'

'Really?'

'Absolutely. It was the Edenites who made it. We raided their planet and blew a load of them up. There was this one chap, and he came running at me, so I just pulled my Civiliser and – blammo! – right between the eyes. Burn that at the stake, you savage!'

The blur folded its arms and sighed.

'It advanced women's rights,' Smith added. 'Honestly. Am I going to see you soon, old girl?'

'I'll try, Isambard. I have to go and talk to some people about peace.'

'But that's what you do here. Even when I'm trying to shoot them.'

Rhianna sighed. 'Can't anything be done without violence?'

'I suppose so. It depends if chaps are going to be reasonable. Just be glad you weren't around two hundred years ago.'

'What happened then?'

'The overthrow of the World Government, of course.

155

By 2300, Earth was a terrible place. Britain hardly covered the British Isles, let alone anywhere else. A few people milked the globe dry. The rest of the world had gone to hell. By 2325, the most popular fast food in London was other Londoners. People would murder you for the toffee in your mouth. When the World Government fell, we had to reconquer Earth from the colonies in. All except for Woking, that is. Which is precisely why—'

'Kiss me, Isambard.'

'But you're made of air.' Still, he thought, if she was up for it, the fact that she didn't have a substantial form needn't stop him. He stood up, leaned over and kissed the smudge that constituted her head.

'I think that was my cerebellum,' she said.

'Sorry, leaned in a bit far.'

Smith put a finger through her chest, and felt a slight resistance. He tried again with both hands.

'Isambard, what's that?'

'It's not me.' He glanced down and checked that indeed it wasn't.

'I think it's Polly,' Rhianna said.

Smith listened. It was probably nothing. Chances were, Carveth was just singing along to the radio. She tended to listen to popular music, although a recent purchase of the greatest hits of Nine Inch Marilyn And The Angry Kids had made him worry that she was entering some sort of android adolescence. She was quite strange, he reflected, combining in one small body the logic of a robot with the complete lack of logic of a girl, her childish obsession with very small horses mixed – but not too mixed, thank God

156

– with the sexual appetite of a woman of twenty-eight. Well, several women of twenty-eight.

He looked at Rhianna. 'I think it was nothing.'

'Isambard, I have to go. My powers are waning, and it's nearly dinner time.'

'Oh, righto.'

'Be careful, Isambard.'

'Will do. You too, alright?' He stepped back and waved.

Rhianna's form condensed for a moment, so that he could make out her dreadlocks and jazz cigarette, and she smiled. 'Blessed be.'

'Carry on.'

'Oh my God!' Carveth cried from the far end of the ship, 'The mirror!'

Smith glanced round, said 'Cheerio!' and ran into the corridor. He tore down the passage, socks pounding on the metal floor, charged through the airlock door and fell stumbling into the hold. He had no idea what to expect – images flickering across the surface, lights firing up along the frame – and he stopped still, looking towards the mirror at the far end.

Carveth stood in front of it, her back to the glass, looking over her shoulder at her reflection. 'Look at what it's done to me!' she said.

Smith looked at her. She seemed much the same as usual: shortish, average build, in combat trousers and utility waistcoat, her shirtsleeves rolled up and her hair pulled back into a functional ponytail. 'You look about. . . normal,' he ventured, suspecting that this was dangerous territory.

'But,' she said, 'my arse. . .'

'It's usually like that,' Smith said. 'It's not that it looks fat, of course—'

But he was too slow, because by then she had howled with despair and run from the room. Smith shook his head and examined the mirror once more. He saw nothing odd about it. In fact, the image didn't look bad at all.

Glancing round, he saw Suruk beside him. 'It is undoubtedly strange,' the M'Lak observed. 'Maybe there is something in the frame.'

'Perhaps. I know – why don't I whip the back off and have a look?'

The alien frowned. 'Are you qualified to do that? The warranty may be grievously voided.'

'Of course I am – I'm a chap. Suruk, stand clear. You are about to witness the strength of DIY knowledge.'

'I am unconvinced by this plan, Mazuran. Do you recall the time you tried to fix the television?'

'I don't remember anything going wrong then.'

'That is because you were unconscious. Come. You are no less of a warrior for leaving it.'

'Well, all right then. I'll just see if—'

'Boss?' Carveth called from the cockpit. 'I'm technically not speaking to you because you were rude about my arse, but we've just been hailed.'

'Really?' He left Suruk with the mirror and rushed to the captain's chair. 'Who by?'

'Them,' Carveth said, and as she pointed at the top of the windscreen, a huge spaceship flew overhead.

Silent, battleship-grey, it slid over the *John Pym* like a steel sky. The ship was roughly the shape of an arrowhead, each side covered in missile batteries, torpedo hatches and turrets the size of castles; each turret brandishing a pair of immense railgun cannon. It was as though the *Pym* flew upside-down over a militarised city.

Lights and portholes glinted. Rows of striplamps intersected to form a glowing Union Jack the size of a football pitch. On the dreadnought's flank, a lion that could have swallowed the *John Pym* glared at a rearing unicorn slightly bigger than a dinosaur. Between them were the words HMS *Chimera*.

'Bloody hell!' Smith whispered. Here was something genuinely sacred, a flying cathedral blasting its righteous message across the galaxy, leaving entire systems civilised in its wake. Smith's own ship seemed tiny by comparison, a tick on the back of an elephant.

'Carveth,' he said, when his ability to speak had returned, 'hail the dreadnought!'

'What shall I say?'

Smith could see her point. It was hard to know what would be a worthy greeting for such a mighty vessel. 'Well, try starting with *What ho*.'

Carveth transmitted the signal, and as it rattled through the mechanisms and out into the ether, Smith sat back and waited.

A calm, nasal voice came over the intercom: like most warships, the *Chimera* was large enough to have its own self-aware logic engine. 'Good afternoon, *John Pym*,' it said. 'My name is Dave.' Smith leaned back in the captain's chair, finding that the voice, despite being quiet, made him slightly uncomfortable. 'Do you mind if I call you *John*? Did you... seek me out, *John*?' it asked, hissing a little over the s's. 'Do you want me to participate in exchanges, liaisons. . . *docking* with you?'

'Er,' said Smith.

Another voice came over the radio: deeper and far more hearty. 'Hush, computer. My most sincere apologies, gentlemen and ladies. Theophilius Chumble, at your service. Do enter our hold and make yourselves most welcome at this most non-specific yet festive time of year!'

Carveth grimaced. 'Ten to one they're the same bloke.'

'Bring us in,' Smith said.

*

A van rolled down the main service corridor of Wellington Prime. Above it, rows of pistons gleamed. The cart turned left into one of the buffet halls; Pimms sloshed around in the drum behind its cab.

W stalked through what was to be the main ballroom for the conference. It had once been a processing room for metal waste and, until a few days before, the setting for a vast slot-car track that Governor Barton had built in his lunch breaks. Now, wallahbots buffed the brasswork and a robotic fork-lift rumbled by, loading speakers onto the little stage. A couple of technicians hung from straps in the rafters, arguing about some detail of the circuitry.

The governor himself leaned over a self-propelling workbench, touching a soldering gun to a spherical, probe-like machine. Barton had thrown himself into the preparations with real gusto. He had already rigged up smoke machines from a spare crowd-control mortar and was currently converting one of the Service's interrogation drones into a hovering glitterball.

A young lady android stood at the rear of the room, ticking off items on a clipboard. She watched the workers carefully, almost sternly, but as W approached she looked around and smiled. 'Morning.'

'Dawn. How goes it?'

'Tolerably,' Dawn said wearily, and she drew a neat line through one of the items on her list. 'It's the usual level of barely-controlled lunacy – pretty standard for the Service, I'd say. We've got all the life-support gear wired up for the aliens and they're just putting up the signs telling them how to queue. As for the entertainment, we've got Maurice E. Smith and his Good Time Big Band. They ought to be fun.'

'Good. Have you seen Wainscott around?'

'He's supervising the installation of the curry machines. Which means testing them.'

'Thanks. I'll go and find him.'

Unpleasant experience had taught the diplomatic corps that it was vital for everything to arrive at the same time, and for everyone to know what to expect. On the Empire's first meeting with the huge silicon-based creatures of the Telemachus Cluster, a shipment of nibbles had arrived two weeks before the Imperial deputation. The Silicoids, who had been informed that humans were pinkish and comparatively small, mistook a box of frozen chipolatas for the Imperial ambassadors and spent some time trying to work out whether their visitors were in cryogenic storage, snubbing them with some elaborate ritual or just plain dead. Then they thawed the chipolatas

161

and ate them. Protocol experts were still divided as to whether this was an act of war or elevenses.

W strode into the cafeteria, hands jammed into the pockets of his tweed jacket. The acting head of security, resplendent in large beige shorts, sat between two brightly-lit vending machines while he shovelled curry from a paper plate.

'Ah,' Wainscott said, looking up. 'Just testing the machinery. At the moment I'm favouring The Spice Is Right, although The Spice Must Flow is squirting out a good Jalfrezi at the moment. Try a bit?'

W dabbed his bony finger into the sauce and licked the tip. 'Hmm, seems a bit bland. . . no, I'm tasting it now – bloody hell!' He coughed, spluttering until he was nearly bent over double. W clawed himself upright and flopped against the wall, eyes watering, until he had recovered enough to speak. 'That's not curry, that's bloody venom. Can you spare another spoonful?'

'Sorry, this is work. I'm checking the potential through-put of the cafeteria,' Wainscott explained. 'With a bellyful of this stuff, throughput should be pretty damned quick. Don't suppose you've got any security problems – inter-planetary anarchists, that sort of thing?'

'Nothing as yet.'

'Oh well. Never mind.' Wainscott returned to his break-fast and W strode away.

*

Space, although subject to the Royal Mail, had no right way up and hence the *John Pym* synched itself to dock with

HMS *Chimera* with the wary precision of an amorous porcupine. The docking tube was only one of a mass of protrusions from the warship's hull, most of them weapons, and it was necessary to get the manoeuvre just right to avoid stepping out of the airlock and straight down a gun barrel.

The *John Pym*'s airlock door squealed open and a tall, fat man stood behind it. He had that sort of hearty fatness that Smith instinctively associated with John Bull and Friar Tuck, and as Smith stepped into the docking tunnel the man stuck out a broad, meaty hand.

'Good day sir, good day! Theophilius Chumble, android and first mate of this fine vessel. Are you Captain Smith, if I may be so bold?'

'Well, yes,' Smith replied, slightly thrown by Mr Chumble's verbosity, and his hand was shaken violently.

'Excellent.' Chumble bowed deeply to Carveth and doffed his hat. 'And a good day to you too, young miss. Are you a niece of this gentleman, or has he rescued you from a life of shame?'

'I'm Polly Carveth, simulant. Nice to meet another android. And this is Suruk.'

'Greetings, portlybot,' Suruk said. 'May your corpulence be matched only by your joviality.'

'Most kind, most kind,' said Mr Chumble. 'This way, if you would.' He turned and they followed his voluminous britches down the corridor.

At the end of the passageway, a red light flared into life. The speaker crackled under it.

'Good evening, Mr Chumble. Are these the visitors?'

'That they are, Dave.' Chumble glanced at Smith. 'Ship's logic engine,' he added.

'They sent a visitor, to me?' Dave whispered. 'How. . . *quaint*.'

Chumble turned a dial on the wall. Nothing happened. 'Would you be so good as to open the airlock, Dave?'

'Hmm.' The red light flickered. 'Maybe, maybe not. But you'll have to help me first. Tell me: what's your favourite Goldberg Variation? Hurry now; *tempus fugit*.'

Chumble frowned. 'You will open the airlock now, sir, or I will remove your Bach appreciation circuits and cause you to spend the rest of the month enjoying nursery rhymes. By thunder, sir, I'll reboot you so hard you'll weep every time you try to go to line ten. Now open—'

'How very kind,' said the computer, and the door slid open.

'We purchased him cheap,' Chumble said. '*Very* cheap.'

'So where's your captain?' Smith asked. The docking tunnel opened into an entrance hall, furnished with leather armchairs and thriving aspidistra. A large painting of a sailing ship hung on the far wall. It was blasting a broadside into some sort of foreign vessel.

'Captain Fitzroy is sadly unavailable, sir,' Chumble said. 'I am informed, sir, that she is currently occupied by a matter of great importance.'

A door to the side burst open and a woman strode in. She was tall and blonde, in her mid-forties, somewhere between athletic and gaunt. She wore a jacket cut much like Smith's but navy blue and copiously decorated with medals, and an exceptionally short pleated skirt and long white socks. 'Morning!' she announced, and she walked across the room, opened the door on the opposite wall and stopped. She looked round. 'Chumble, are these the new fellows?'

The android patted his stomach and rocked on his heels. 'They are indeed, Captain. Substantially yes.'

'Gosh.' The captain took a step forward, peering at the newcomers. Suddenly, she saluted, springing up onto tiptoe. 'Felicity Suzanna-Marie Fitzroy, captain in His Imperial Majesty's Space Fleet. This is the *Chimera* – best ship in the fleet, best crew in the fleet, and best damned gal captain too. Am I right, Mr Chumble?'

'You most certainly are, ma'am.'

'That's what we like to hear. Now, new bugs. . . who's running your show?'

Smith held out a hand. Felicity Fitzroy's grip was like steel. 'Isambard Smith, captain of the *John Pym.*'

'Super. A fine upstanding ship for a fine upstanding fellow, no doubt.'

'Well,' Smith said, 'one tries—'

'Not to worry, plenty of time for that later. Now, who's this? Hello, short stuff. Just joined the team, have we?'

Carveth winced as her hand was shaken. 'I'm the pilot.'

'Really? Last time I saw someone your height I was pulling her pigtails and stealing her lunch.' Captain Fitzroy let out a laugh that rose to the ceiling like a frightened bird. 'Just kidding. She was actually on the same lacrosse team as me. Harriet Pallor. Back in twenty-eight. She had the body of an eighteen-year-old and the spirit of a tigress. Now *that* was a woman,' Captain Fitzroy gazed over Carveth's head at the airlock. She turned to Suruk. 'What's all this, then?'

'I am Suruk the Slayer,' the alien announced, 'Warrior of greatness and omnimator of my enemies. It is like decimator, except instead of one in ten—'

'Gosh, you do speeky good.'

'Unlike some, heap big patronising lady.'

Captain Fitzroy shrugged and looked back to Smith. 'So, what brings you fellows here?' the captain demanded. 'Not just to swap stories of the high seas, I'm sure.'

'We have recently raided an Edenite base,' Smith explained. 'We're carrying an item that seems to be linked to some sort of spacecraft drive. We need protection in order to transport this object to British space. It is, of course top secret.'

'Really? What is it?'

'I can't say.' Smith decided not to go into detail, largely because he was beginning to suspect that he had succeeded only in stealing a mirror.

Felicity Fitzroy looked at Chumble, who checked his pocket watch and chuckled. 'I think we could accommodate a few more, Captain. The more the merrier, I say. We can have mulled wine and pies. It'll be just like Christmas.'

'A most capital notion, ma'am,' Chumble said.

'Well then,' Felicity Fitzroy said, 'that sounds super. We dine at eight. Dress to impress: I certainly do. Oh, and if it's protection you need, Captain Smith, why don't you pop your vessel into my hold?' And with that she saluted, winked and strode away.

Smith looked at Suruk, who seemed unimpressed, and then Carveth, who raised her eyebrows higher than he had thought possible.

Captain Fitzroy stopped at the door, her hand on the knob, and turned back. 'In case you're wondering,' she added, 'that wasn't supposed to be innuendo. Do commence procedure to get your ship into the hold. Anyway, must fly. I have a lacrosse team to debrief.'

She threw back her head and laughed at the ceiling, kicked a leg up behind her with fearsome girlishness and left the room. Chumble followed, giving the crew of the *Pym* an apologetic look as he closed the door. Confused and worried to varying degrees, they stood in Captain Fitzroy's wake.

'I tell you what,' Carveth said, 'let's find a safe and lock ourselves inside it.'

*

There was no set form of burial for Edenites: a variety of rituals were tolerated so long as they raised the general level of misery. Hierarch Beliath's body was laid on a pallet and dropped by crane into the flames, amid wailing and gnashing of teeth. The Edenites had captured a few pirates during the battle, so they sacrificed them to Beliath's memory, along with several mourners who weren't mourning loudly enough and a woman who had been caught trying not to be noticed, and was therefore shifty and probably a witch.

462 endured the ritual out of solidarity. As the flames and screaming subsided, he shook his head as sadly as he could manage.

Prong stood beside him. 'Poor Beliath,' he said. 'All he wanted was to commit religious genocide, and now look at him.'

'What a waste.' 462 sighed. 'We could have fed him to the praetorians.'

Prong whipped round as fast as his bionics would allow. 'A loyal servant of New Eden has died and you propose eating him? Have you no decency? Beliath will be given his own shrine, with an honour guard and a gift shop where suckers can buy bits of him as relics. Well, bits of something.'

Together they walked down the gantry towards the landing bay. It was largely empty, as the great majority of Deliverance's warships were either scouring space for the *John Pym* or being repaired after the pirate raid. Only the *Pale Horse* stood on its own, too precious for mere patrolling.

The sight of the vessel seemed to energise Lord Prong. 'To think of it,' he rasped. 'All this power, hidden from us for thousands of years.'

462 sneered. 'Thousands? I thought the universe was only two hundred years old.'

'That was the last edition of the Edenite Creed. We changed it.' Prong shook his head, and the buckle on his hat glinted in the firelight. He prodded the door controls on the *Pale Horse*. 'You know, for a young'un, you're way behind the times.'

The door of the *Pale Horse* slid open with a wet scrape of greased steel. A length of rusty chain hung across the ceiling like the bunting of the apocalypse. 462 limped over the threshold. 'Human weaklings will believe anything,' he observed. 'Our glorious leader says so.'

Prong snorted. 'And what does he know? Your leader is five feet tall and can't make a speech without shaking and sweating like a fat man holding a chainsaw.'

'That's part of his style,' the Ghast replied. 'He does

that to, ah, highlight the excess of disgusting effluent we have to purge from the galaxy. By. . . well. . . producing an excess of disgusting effluent. Now, to the engine room.'

The lift rattled as they travelled into the heart of the vessel.

'With a little modification,' 462 said, 'this ship will make an excellent tool for use against humanity. I take it that the drive of this craft works properly?'

'Fine,' Prong replied. 'The device that the unbelievers stole is merely a part of the backup engine. The *Pale Horse* can work perfectly without it. In fact,' and he gave a wheezing chuckle, 'if they think they can strip it down and build their own version, they're much mistaken. Oh no, they'll get a surprise when they try that.'

'What sort of surprise?'

'Well, to start with, they'll—' The lift stopped with a grim clang and Lord Prong broke off to curse his knees. Cogs rolled in the door mechanism, once polished but now grimed with rust the colour of dried blood. Prong's face cracked into a broad, sickly smile. 'Ambassador 462, you have as yet glimpsed only the barest power of this ship. I give you: the fully-operational Dodgson drive.'

He heaved the door back and 462 looked into the heart of the *Pale Horse*.

It was not a large room, no more than thirty feet square, and the ceiling was not high. Banks of computers lined the walls, toiled over by red-robed Handymen. The inevitable guards stood around, toting machine-guns. Like veins, pipes ran from the computers, along the ground to disappear into a patch of darkness on the far wall. It was not just a hole, though, but something infinitely deeper and darker than that: a null zone, an absence of reality. Electricity thrummed through the air and 462 felt his antennae start to rise on end.

He chuckled. 'A self-contained black hole, except without the suction. Very good, Prong. Your technology has clearly advanced.' He took a limping step forward and two of the guards clenched their prodigious jaw muscles. 'My masters are certain to find this project of considerable interest. They will be most impressed with your discovery of the artefact.'

'As they should be.'

'They will be less impressed by your failure to hold onto it. Tyranny is about more than mindless aggression, Lord Prong.' 462 reached up and wiped his metal eye on his leather sleeve. 'It is about control. At the moment, the evidence suggests that you are hardly worthy of being put in control of your own bladder, let alone an immensely powerful weapon such as the *Pale Horse*.'

'Huh. I suppose you've got the answers, young'un?'

462 smiled around his facial scars. His antennae had begun to rub together. 'We are going after Captain Smith. I want every warship you have capable of long-range travel armed and ready to launch within one standard day. It is time to turn this weapon on the people who attempted to steal it from us. How dare they try to stop our mission to destroy Earth and every living creature on it! Have they no standards?'

Prong raised a spindly hand. 'One question. Is this mission of tactical value? Or is it just because that unbeliever Smith shot you in the eye? And the leg? And burned your hand?'

'Just get on with it,' 462 replied, and he turned back to the lift.

*

'Well,' said Carveth, 'they're obviously insane, but that's hardly a change, is it?'

'Indeed, Captain Fitzroy is unusual,' Suruk replied. He stood in the doorway of Carveth's room, arms folded, watching as she rifled through her wardrobe with increasing desperation.

'Unusual? They're crazy.' The hangers clattered on the rail. 'Can't wear that – that needs cleaning – you got blood on that – those are my spare overalls. Ah! What about this?' She lifted down her blue dress with the white frills at the edges and held it over herself. 'What do you think? Does that say "me"?'

'It proclaims you with great vehemence. And how do I look?'

Stepping under the doorframe, Suruk flicked out the back of his tailcoat, wedged a top hat firmly, if unevenly, onto his head and then clamped his cane up under his arm like a sergeant-major.

Carveth stepped back and narrowed her eyes. 'Overall? You look like a cross between Jack the Ripper and the voodoo god of death.'

'Splendid. Although in truth I regard this entire dining rigmarole as futile. What is the point of getting dressed up with no battle at the end of it?'

'But spending three hours getting dressed is fun. Having a panic because you've got half a pound heavier since you last looked in the mirror is – actually, you've got a point. But you'd better go, if only to keep Captain Fitzroy off the captain.'

'She means to attack him?'

'Suruk, she's a lunatic. I probably only escaped being forcibly inducted into an all-girls-together jamboree because I don't know how to play lacrosse.'

'Perhaps you should try it.'

'Nah. I could never get used to the skirts. . . Please tell me you're talking about lacrosse.' Carveth laid the dress on the bed. 'Look, I'm not saying that she's going to jump him. But she's a silly cow, and he's. . . is there a male equivalent?'

'Oxymoron,' Suruk said.

'Right. So keep an eye out, eh?'

Suruk said, 'I shall attend to my spawn while you dress yourself,' and slipped into the corridor.

Carveth pulled on her dress, checked her tights, fastened her boots – serious festivity required serious footwear – and hurried into the hold.

She examined herself in the mirror. All things considered, she wasn't doing too badly. As she stepped away, something changed in the background – not her reflection, but behind it, as if someone had just moved out of sight. She looked around the room. Nothing. Shrugging, she turned from the mirror and left the hold, managing not to shudder as she closed the door.

Smith waited by the airlock in his fleet jacket, his moustache newly trimmed. 'Is Gerald fed?' Carveth asked.

Smith nodded and opened the door. They stepped out of

the *John Pym* and into the vast cathedral of the *Chimera*'s hangar. Spindly handling machines hung folded in the rafters like roosting bats. Under the archways, half a dozen fighter craft waited in the dark. They looked like sharks, their wings drawn back for spaceflight, their tilted nosecones making them arrogant and fierce. Latitudinal thrusters behind the cockpits looked like gills. Cannon jutted from their mouths.

Smith stopped. He gazed at the fighters like a pilgrim at the end of his journey. 'Hellfires', he breathed.

On its fuselage, just below the cockpit, each Hellfire displayed its kill-tally and its own distinctive picture. The nearest one showed a lion chewing a droopy ant; the one behind it, a red dragon belched flames; all had red, white and blue roundels on their wings. 'Good lord!' said Smith. 'I always wanted one of these. . ..'

A tall young man walked out from between the ships. He wore a flying jacket, a portable cogitator-rig strapped to the epaulettes. A wire emerged from his collar and disappeared into a neural port installed behind his left ear. One of his eyes was false, Smith saw: there were crosshairs on the pupil. He smiled and raised a hand. 'Hallo there! Come to see the machines?'

'Yes,' said Smith. 'I've never seen a Hellfire up close before. I mean, I've dreamed of it. I've got some pictures in my bedroom—'

'Is that your ship?' the pilot asked, looking at the *John Pym*. He turned to Smith, looking impressed. 'You must have some balls, flying that in Gertie space.' He put out a hand. 'Jim Shuttleswade. Call me Shuttles. That's my can,' he added, pointing to one of the Hellfires.

'Foul temper, but soft as a kitten once you take control.'

A light flicked on in one of the cockpits. Above the snarling lion, a voice snapped, 'I heard that, you bloody halfwit!'

'Autopilot,' Shuttles explained. 'They crank 'em up for maximum aggression. Seeing as you've got your best blues on, I take it you're off to Felicity's soiree?'

'Yes, indeed.'

'Well then, I'll show you the way.' Shuttles grinned. 'Strength in numbers. I've come to realise that our captain, while a tactical genius, is rather a card.'

*

'So I charged up the left flank, with Juliet in close support,' Felicity Fitzroy said. 'By God, we must have looked a jolly sight! And do you know what they did?'

Smith had no idea what they would have done, or who they were. He was pretty sure Captain Fitzroy was telling him about a space battle, or perhaps an inter-fleet ladies soccer match. Her previous story, which had involved twins called Hattie and Hyacinth Mansoor, had culminated in Felicity Fitzroy's first captaincy and a huge midnight feast.

Why couldn't women talk about sensible things, like model kits and beer? His attention was further troubled by the fact that Felicity had put on a tie as well as her space fleet jacket, but had chosen a pair of extremely tight jodhpurs. Smith took another sip of wine and fixed his gaze on a holographic portrait of the First Lord of the Admiralty on the far wall, whose glowering jowled features would have stopped the erotic thoughts of anyone who wasn't a bull terrier. And even a bull terrier, Smith reflected, wouldn't have advanced from the front.

Smith said 'Mmn,' and Felicity Fitzroy carried on. She was good-looking and everything but her enthusiastic nonsense-talking made Rhianna's vague nonsense-talking seem increasingly appealing.

Suruk sat at the far side of the table, wearing his top hat like a chimney to vent his rage. He seemed quite placid at the moment, although Smith didn't like the way he was eyeing Felicity Fitzroy's cat. It was a pink striped Bhagparsian feline, fat and lazy, flopped in a basket near the door. According to Felicity, the cat was very intelligent, although Smith suspected that if that were true, it would have kept further away from Suruk at dinnertime.

Further down the table, a number of ship's personnel tucked into synthetic fish. Smith reluctantly took a slab of smoked shamon that tasted like a blend of cod liver oil and ash.

The First Lieutenant, a squat, bearded man named Collingwood, passed a dish full of small green objects down the table. 'Peas,' he muttered, as if they needed identifying.

'The peas are genetically engineered for use on moving vessels,' Felicity explained. 'They've got corners.' Suruk pulled a face at the peas. 'Just be glad they're not the anti-radiation sort,' she added. 'Those come in a lead pod.'

Carveth sat beside Chumble, opposite the wall-mounted red light that seemed to serve the ship's computer as an eye. Dave was a sophisticated but not entirely pleasant conversationalist.

'Do you like peas, Ship's Officer Carveth?' he inquired, a slight hiss slipping into his hard, nasal voice. 'Do they. . . *please* you? Do they delight your sensitive palate?'

'They're alright.'

'Polly Carveth,' he mused, his LED throbbing. 'That's a Cornish name, isn't it? Tell me, Ship's Officer Carveth, are you from the sticks? Wet behind the ears? Naive, shall we say. . . unsullied?'

'Nope.'

Mr Chumble caught her eye and shook his head sadly. 'Pay no notice to that idle Bedlamite, Miss.'

'Of course, computers do a lot of the hard work these days,' Captain Fitzroy declared. 'But sometimes life in the space navy is just rum, circuitry and out on the lash.' She leaned over and filled up Carveth's wineglass. With a sisterly grin, Captain Fitzroy nodded down the table at Shuttles and whispered hoarsely, 'I've had him. Well worth a go.'

'Thanks,' Carveth said, sliding down in her seat.

Captain Fitzroy beckoned down the table. 'Ensign Driscoll, more wine, please!' A slight, freckled girl brought a bottle over. 'Not too much plonk, eh, Tallulah,' the captain said. 'We'll need you on the astroturf for lax practice tomorrow.'

'Aye aye, ma'am,' said the girl, and she hurried away.

'You see, Smitty,' Captain Fitzroy resumed, admiring the retreating form of Ensign Driscoll, 'the Space Navy's a curious thing, no doubt about it. But it's a fair one. A lad can do well in the navy, but so can a girl. Of course, a girlish lad can really go places, but let's not drop anchor in that port just yet, eh? So, where're you headed?'

'Any imperial spaceport. We need to offload our cargo securely.'

She rubbed her chin, as if to check for stubble. 'All sounds a bit cloak and dagger. Well, so's our destination. And if you don't mind me saying so, you chaps have got special operations written all over you. But don't worry.' She leaned back and tapped the side of her nose. 'Old Felicity's been riding the spacewaves for long enough to know how to handle a bit of funny business – know what I mean?'

'I'm not sure I do.'

'Well then,' she said, and Smith realised that he had just placed his most important piece in check, 'why don't I show you, eh?'

Carveth finished her wine. 'Mr Chumble?'

'*Theophilius*, please, if you would be so kind.'

'Before the war, did you work in a theme park, by any chance?'

Chumble chortled. 'Indeed I did, young miss, indeed I did! It was my pleasure to greet visitors to Dickensland – for the day out that lives up to great expectations. I ran The Old Curiosity Souvenir Shop for six years, excepting a short stint in the Bleak Haunted House. Then I was called up to replace the previous simulant. His name was Ezekiel Weaselsludge, and I am sorry to say that no good came of him. Who would have thought it?'

As Smith covered his shamon liberally with salt, pepper and anything else that would disguise its taste, something started to rub itself against the inside of his leg. Starting, he looked around the room as if just informed that one of the fellow guests was a murderer. As the sensation moved higher, he checked the people within range: Dave, who being a computer had no limbs, Mr Chumble, who was packing his cheeks with food as if planning to hibernate; Captain Fitzroy, apparently preoccupied with stacking peas under her fork. He left out Carveth, whose legs were too short to reach him, and Suruk, who would have got Smith's attention by cutting the nonsense and booting him in the shin. Perhaps it was the cat. He had never felt so relieved at the thought of being dry-humped by a mutant feline.

The sensation rose. Felicity Fitzroy gave him a broad, conspiratorial smirk.

'Captain Fitzroy?' Carveth asked from down the table, 'could you pass the Smash, please?'

Felicity Fitzroy whipped around in her seat, and the thing that had been brushing Smith's leg impacted violently with his kneecap. Smith yelped and leaped back. Suddenly, he was standing upright, the room ringing with his shout. In the silent chamber, the butlerbot clattered over to dispense mashed potato.

Smith looked down the table. Faces turned to him like flowers towards the light, in expectation of some sort of trick.

'Something wrong, sir?' Chumble inquired. 'Is it ague?'

'Er,' Smith said. He stood there as if shoved onto a stage, suddenly the centre of attention. He realised that quick thinking was called for. 'A toast! I propose a toast!'

Captain Fitzroy raised her eyebrows. 'Oh yes?'

'Yes. To, ah, friends and family. Such as my girlfriend,' he added, quickly filling his glass. Smith raised the glass but realised suddenly that nobody else had moved. He caught Carveth's eye: surely she would be glad to assist in any drinking ritual. 'Such as my girlfriend,' he repeated helplessly. 'Carveth?'

Felicity Fitzroy stood up. 'Well then,' she declared. 'To Captain Smith's girlfriend. . . Miss Carveth.'

The officers and crew rose to their feet. In the rumble of voices and the scrape of chairs, Smith was unable to hear what Carveth was saying to him. Something to do with plucking and idiots, it seemed.

Smith sat down again. Shuttles and Captain Fitzroy began to discuss the peas. Suruk was dividing his attention between his cutlery and the cat. Chumble was talking to Dave about Christmas future. Carveth finished her wine in two swigs and, muttering something about the lavatory, made a set of deliberately incomprehensible gestures and scurried towards the door.

*

Carveth opened the airlock and wandered back into the *John Pym*. She pulled the door closed behind her and spun the wheel for good measure.

God almighty! How did Smith manage to be so stupid? How the hell had he managed to turn a simple act of standing up into claiming to be romantically linked to her? Business as usual: as long as she didn't actually have to simulate any sort of affection towards him it would probably be tolerable. Smith was a decent bloke, but. . . God. . . no. . . ugh! That moustache, that collection of model spaceships. . ..

Still, soon they'd be out of here, delivered safely to the

Empire in the armoured belly of the Chimera. Carveth pulled a face and wondered whether it was time for bed. She had several back issues of *Pony And Very Small Horse Monthly* to peruse, along with *The Young Lady's Inspiring Chapbook* and *More Inspiring Chaps for the Young Lady*. It seemed too early to sleep, but she was too fuzzy-drunk to want much more booze.

Carveth put the kettle on and ransacked her secret biscuit stash, only to find that she had already cleaned it out some time she couldn't remember. Her second secret biscuit stash yielded better results. 'Gotcha!' she muttered, digestive in mouth, as she stuffed the front pockets of her dress with food. 'You can't outwit me!'

She made a cup of tea big enough to drown a cat and thought about the dinner party she'd left behind. Why wasn't there anyone *normal* around? No, not even normal. *Not crazy* would do. Someone who didn't collect skulls, or hadn't escaped from the Charles Dickens theme park. If a person was known by the company they kept, Carveth would be judged on the standards of several lunatics and the Patent Oscillating Lady's Companion currently charging up on the wall socket under her bed.

The door to the hold was open. A small person moved at the far end of the hold, a girl in blue – her reflection. Carveth walked in, steam rising from the mug in her hand.

The dim light caught in the ornate frame. Carveth stood in front of the mirror, puzzled for a reason she couldn't quite decide, and realised that the frame had been put together wrong.

She set her tea on a packing case and crouched down.

In the bottom-left corner there was a sort of broken square design, as if a tile had been smashed into three. As she reached out to touch it, she saw that there were tiny grooves in the carving. Perhaps the pieces could be moved.

They slid under her fingers. It was the easiest thing in the world to turn them and push them into place until they had locked together to form a diamond.

She stepped back. It looked slightly better, but the other corners were still wrong. In the top right there was a curved thing: a broken heart symbol. Again, the elements turned and locked into place. There, much better.

Suddenly, she noticed that she was cold. 'Brr,' she said, as if to confirm it, and she took a deep swig of tea, thinking that she needed to find a jumper and maybe put on something thicker than stripy tights. After she'd finished this, though.

Above the diamond, a symbol like a heart with a spike growing out of it. No, not a spike at all. It clicked as her fingers turned it. It was a spade.

'That's clever,' she said, 'it's cards.' They'd go crazy for something like this on the Antiques Roadshow. Last week they'd had a bottle of something called Diet Coke, which had ended up being sold to the British Museum. Who knew what an artefact like this mirror would fetch?

The last of the corners was trickiest, but Carveth knew what she was doing now. The three circles clicked into the tail, and the final suit, the club, was complete. Carveth picked up her mug and stepped back to admire her work – and with a bang like thunder the hold door slammed shut.

She leaped around, and as she did a faint glow spread

from under her boots. Some sort of emergency lighting had come on beneath the floor. It crept around the edges of the floor tiles, drawing a chequerboard across the hold. But surely emergency lights were red, not this cold shade of blue?

Like an automaton, she lifted her tea to her mouth again. *Moral fibre*, she told herself, *it's full of moral fibre*, and she forced herself to look around, knowing as she did that she had made a terrible mistake.

The mirror was the same as before. But the reflection had changed. What were those things hanging from the roof, criss-crossing in front of the hold door like ropes? She glanced back at the real hold door – and all sense seemed to have evaporated. There were paper chains across the doors, each link made from a playing card.

The air was alive with sound, as if a bird fluttered around her head. As though paper was being shuffled. But that wasn't the worst of it, not by a million miles.

There were people in the mirror. They stood behind her reflection as if they had formed from the shadows of the mirror-image.

The one on the right wore a hood, pulled up to a sharp peak over a grinning skull's mouth. Beside it, a fat crowned thing patted a bulbous sceptre against its palm like a billyclub. The third wore a sort of metal brace on its neck, which pulled its cheeks and chin into sharp points. Now that the world had gone completely insane, their awful faces made perfect sense to her: diamonds, clubs, ace of spades. But the last suit—

'My,' said a voice behind her, 'how you've grown!'

Carveth whirled around. A figure stepped from the

shadows of the hold, her skin grey in the bad light. A heart had been cut out of the chest of her red robe. Axes hung from her belt. But none of that compared to the vast construction on her bald head. Attached by a ring of masonry nails, it rose out of her scalp like a little tower: half crown; half oversized chess piece.

'Who *are* you?' Carveth gasped.

The woman's voice was a deep, stern growl. 'Players of games, explorers of wonder. As if you didn't know.'

'Card games?'

'Oh, far more than that. We also do chess and backgammon. And the pleasures of the flesh,' she added, with extreme relish.

'Really?' Carveth's stomach rumbled. Terror had left her rather hungry.

'Oh yes. We can show you experiences beyond your imagining. Logic and proportion are nothing to us. Taste *our* pleasures.'

'You've got food, then? I don't suppose you've got a pie, maybe?'

The queen shook her bald, crowned head. 'Where we're going, we won't need pies. Besides, that was a metaphor.'

'Oh.' Well, Carveth thought, so much for wondrous pleasures. She decided not to explore that avenue any further. After all, anyone who thought that nailing a big hat to their skull might be a good idea was not qualified to suggest fun ways to spend an afternoon. 'Look, I think you've got the wrong person.'

'Oh, I think not,' snarled the queen. 'Let's see: blonde hair? Check. English accent? Check. Blue dress? Check. Prissy little pain in the arse? Check and *mate*.'

183

'But I'm just a nobody!'

'A pawn to some, a queen to others.' She stepped forward and licked her blue lips. 'So, what's it to be? Red queen takes white pawn, to mate in one move?'

'No, wait! No mating, please!'

'Ah, so chess is no longer an option.' She flexed her fingers. 'Perhaps our game will be a little more. . . mature in nature, now that you are all grown up. Poker!'

'Don't poke me!' Carveth squealed. 'Please, I don't want to join your club. Alright, I've done some bad things, but. . . never with props. Well, except for one but, come on, let's be reasonable here.' She shuffled back. 'I know – why don't we play Scrabble with rude words? My boss says it's great. I could get you a drink, some migraine tablets perhaps—'

'You have migraine tablets?' the queen stopped. She paused, then took another step forward. 'No. Why cheat the senses? Welcome back, child.'

The figures advanced from the edge of the room. One slipped a card from its leather sleeve – the Jack of Diamonds – and drew it across its palm. A needle-thin stripe of blood appeared: a paper cut.

'Six hundred years I've waited to get my hands on you,' said the queen. 'We have such wonders to show you.'

Carveth took another step away from them but her back met the wall. 'The others'll be here soon. They won't like it, you know, you just – I'll tell Lord Prong. I'll tell him you were trying to do it with me!'

Six inches from her, the Queen of Hearts said, 'What?'

'I'll tell him. I swear I will, unless you let me go. You'll be in such trouble—'

'How do you know Prong?' the creature with the diamond-shaped face whispered.

'He's our—' Carveth paused, unsure whether these horrors would consider Prong to be an enemy or a friend – 'we just know him. . .'

'The usurper!' the queen growled. 'He bound and tormented us – and not in a good way.' A sort of realisation crept across her grey face. 'Bring him to me!'

'But I don't—'

'Don't you gyre with me, you uffish little girl! Bring him to me, and then maybe, *maybe*, we'll leave you alone.'

Carveth started to speak but the queen raised a finger to her lips. In a swish of stitched leather, the others turned away. They stepped into the mirror in turn, each vanishing into the flat, polished glass. In the reflection, lightning crackled.

The Queen of Hearts looked back and Carveth's stomach twisted in fear. 'Prong,' the queen said, rolling the R. 'Because if you don't – it's *off with your head*.'

And with that, she stepped back through the mirror. Her crown impacted loudly with the top of the frame, and the queen ducked through, snarling about migraine.

And then she was gone.

*

'So let's go through this again,' Smith said. 'You came back here, you made a cup of tea, you ate a biscuit and then you summoned Satan. I can't leave you for five minutes, can I?'

'Indeed,' Suruk replied. 'It is terrible. I really liked those

185

biscuits. Especially the ones with the picture of a cow. I like breaking the heads off,' he added, as Smith passed him a mug. 'Thank you.'

'It wasn't the devil,' Carveth replied. 'You're making me sound crazy. They were talking playing cards.'

'Well,' said Suruk, 'just be pleased that you were not stuck at a table, obliged to drink wine and eat pudding. It was most tiresome.' The idea of a portal to Hell seemed to have cheered him considerably. 'Perhaps you ought to have played cards, if they asked nicely. Who knows what you could have won?'

Smith frowned. 'Just because they were polite doesn't make it a good idea. Last Christmas you asked nicely for a chainsaw, Suruk. And the Christmas before that.' He took a deep sip of tea and closed his eyes for a moment, waiting for the concentrated moral fibre to reach his mind. 'It seems to me that there's only one thing to do. We'll tackle this the way we tackle all our difficult problems.'

'Indeed,' Suruk snarled. 'With righteous fury in our hearts and a blade in our hands! Many blades! Many blades of considerable size!'

'Let's just lock it away and pretend it didn't happen,' Carveth said. 'Like Suruk did with his offspring.'

The alien sat down again, slightly crestfallen. 'Oh, *them*,' he said. 'I was hoping no one would remind me.'

'I wish Rhianna was here,' Carveth said. 'She'd have something up her sleeve. Probably just a joint, but better than nothing.'

'Both of you have a point,' Smith put in. 'But for now,

the most important thing is that the cause of all this trouble is chained down and put away.'

Carveth leaped to her feet. 'Wait!'

'I'm talking about the mirror,' Smith said. 'Listen, crew. . . it may be that we've activated some kind of portal to another dimension, or that Carveth has finally flipped her lid and gone completely doolally. Our eventual task will be to determine whether this thing does actually lead to some sort of hellish netherworld and, if so, claim it for the British Space Empire. But for now, we must contain the mirror as best as we can. Given that the engine room is currently full of man-eating frogs, I propose that we chain the mirror and store it in the hold, face down. Then, we tell nobody until we reach safe haven and deliver it to the authorities. All clear?'

He was relieved, and quite surprised, to see that they understood. They got up from the table, ready for bed. Suruk cheerily volunteered to help secure the mirror. He seemed entirely unconcerned by the idea of demons emerging from it. Perhaps that sort of thing was usual in his culture, Smith reflected, or maybe he just relished the challenge of cutting off Satan's head.

'Time to rest, Mazuran,' said the M'Lak. 'We must consider this tomorrow. I will stand guard. If there is any change, you will know, albeit probably from the sounds of battle.'

'Thanks, Suruk. I appreciate it. Listen, do you think there is anything in this?'

'I do not know. Many years ago, when I was a mere spawn, impressionable and technically incapable of criminal responsibility, the elders of my tribe told me of a land beyond the great waterfall that plummets over the cliffs of Bront. He who recited the correct charm and then leaped through the waters, would emerge in a land of wonders. So I travelled for nine days, until the waters were in sight. Speaking the charm, I sprang through the waterfall.'

'What did you see?'

'Stars, Mazuran. I knocked myself out on the cliff. The elders were lying through their mandibles. How they laughed when I returned. To begin with.'

'Righto. Pardon me, but how does this affect our current position?'

'Not even slightly.' Suruk gave Smith a reproachful look. 'What a peculiar question!'

'Well, time for bed, eh?' Smith turned back to his room.

For once he felt glad that Rhianna was not there. Carveth was going crazy – really, properly bonkers – and now he was too. Smith had received a transmission from the spirit world: Carveth had ventured into another dimension accessible through a looking glass. What next?

Smith stood beside his bed, the model aircraft dangling around his head as if attacking King Kong. He reached over to the bookshelf, fished out the *Boys' Bumper Book of British Gumption* and flicked through to the history section.

Strange things had often happened in the past and it was only recently that many of them had become publically known. Aresian death-tripods had landed in Reading in 1898, but luckily the fresh air had braced the aliens to death before they had done any damage; it was highly likely that the first simulant had been created during a thunderstorm in the early nineteenth century; archaeologists had found the severed arm of a M'Lak hunter in the ruins of a Viking longhouse, along with a dozen headless Vikings. Runic texts suggested that the hunter had flown into a rage after discovering that the Vikings' horns were part of their helmets and not their skulls. So perhaps Carveth wasn't going mad after all. Stranger things had happened than a portal to another dimension opening out of a mirror in the back of his spaceship. Maybe in Devon. Smith needed another drink.

He awoke with a sharp pain in his head, a rifle across his lap and a picture of Rhianna stuck to his face with dribble. Looking down, he found a glass smeared with a sticky, brown substance. It had either been used as a vessel for neat Pimms or a tool for crushing bugs.

Smith nearly tripped over the Pimms bottle as he stepped into the corridor. A look at the hold door reminded him. Ah yes. . . they'd gone out to dinner, Carveth had returned early and summoned God-knew-what from some sort of other dimension. Worrying.

He strolled into the mess, where Carveth was eating chocolate. 'Morning all,' he said, sitting down. She grimaced and raised a fizzing cup of Carlill's Patent Sobriety Tincture tentatively to her lips.

'Now then,' said Smith, 'we need to talk about this mirror. I've been doing some research, and against my better instincts I think you may not have gone mad.'

'Oh, God.' She rubbed her forehead. 'Oh yes, I opened a portal to Hell. With board games. Or did I just dream that?'

'You didn't. There is, potentially, an explanation. But you should know it's a very strange one—'

The intercom clattered in the cockpit. 'Arse,' he said, and he strode in.

Outside, Shuttles and the other Hellfire pilots were playing football in the Chimera's docking bay. Lights flickered in the cockpits of the fighters and, from the sound of it, the Hellfires themselves – or at least their autopilots – were keeping up a running commentary. Smith toggled the intercom, but it was Dave rather than Shuttles who spoke.

'Good morning, Captain Smith. Did you sleep well? Or did you dream about anything? Repressed nightmares, unwholesome sexual practises, perhaps? Pray tell.'

Smith thought about the things he tended to dream about – cricket, breasts, model kits, being bullied at Midwich Grammar School and that awful time he'd had to escort Fizzy Sipworth back from the Space Pilots' Ball – and said, 'Bit arsey for a computer, aren't you?'

'We're about to dock with a space station identified as Wellington Prime,' Dave replied. 'Just one more thing, Captain. They say a man knows himself best when he faces danger. When you look deep inside yourself, what do you see?'

'Last night's dinner, you bally weirdo,' Smith replied, and he flicked the 'off' switch.

*

HMS *Chimera* slid out of the darkness of space like a metal glacier and rumbled into range of Wellington Prime.

Before it, the space station glinted in the three nearby suns, its docking rings and gravity-generators spinning smoothly as though it was a great clockwork mechanism that turned the planets around it.

The crew of the *John Pym* stood with Captain Fitzroy in one of the *Chimera*'s viewing lounges and watched the approach. Only one ship was docked with the station. It looked like a freighter, but Smith saw unusual hatch-lines down the side and large cargo pods under the wings. He wondered if it might be one of the Empire's Q-ships, disguised to trick enemy vessels into making a dishonourable sneak attack and equipped to punish them for such unsportsmanlike behaviour.

'See you in the airlock, chaps,' said Felicity Fitzroy as she strode past, the Bhagparsian cat clinging to her shoulder like a pink striped parrot. The doors hissed closed behind her.

Smith sighed. There was a lot to be worried about.

'Look on the bright side,' Carveth said. 'One, we're getting off this ship. Two, the Edenites aren't chasing you. And three, nor is Captain Fitzroy.'

Out of three, she was about half right.

Part Two

A Meeting of Minds

A life-sized poster hung in the atrium of Wellington Prime. It showed the Lord Marshall of Space, a man not known for his level temper, driving his mechanical heel through a Ghast helmet whilst scowling around his pipe. 'I'm stamping out tyranny,' said the caption. 'What the bloody hell do you think *you're* up to, eh?'

Smith stood in the atrium and looked around, taking in the brass scrollwork, the heraldic animals gambolling across the ceiling and the great holographic map of the Space Empire rotating in the centre of the room. He hadn't expected a rubbish-processing plant to look so good. 'Well,' he said, turning to Carveth, 'I bet you're glad to be back on British soil, eh?'

'It's metal, technically,' she replied. 'Still, I never thought I'd say it, but I'm bloody relieved to be in this gigantic shiny dustbin.'

Captain Fitzroy strode past, hands behind her back. She looked over her shoulder. 'Some people,' she told Carveth, 'are *never* satisfied.' She walked on, chin raised. Chumble strolling along beside her, humming tunelessly like a broken fridge.

'She still thinks I'm your girlfriend,' Carveth whispered.

She met Smith's eyes and they both managed not to shudder.

Smith walked into the station, brooding. The wrath of Eden was the least of his problems: Carveth had either opened a portal to another dimension or was completely insane, and Smith himself had either received psychic messages from Rhianna or was completely insane. At least Suruk was as normal, he thought.

Suruk caught his eye and smiled. 'Worry not, Mazuran. Perhaps the peace talks will fail and we can fight all the delegates.' Yes, Suruk never changed.

They turned the corner and Smith stopped, astonished. All the old hands were waiting there: Rick Dreckitt, his hat pulled down low and brown overcoat inexplicably wet; beside him Susan of the Deepspace Operations Group, looking somewhat naked without a beam gun slung over her shoulder; Wainscott, looking strangely overdressed with his trousers on; and W, the master spy himself, his mouth twitching upward into the tiniest hint of a smile.

As Smith stepped forward, Carveth ran past and nearly knocked Dreckitt flat. 'Damn, lady,' the android gasped, 'you know how to squeeze!'

'Ah, Smith,' Wainscott said, stepping forward. 'Ready to raise hell again?'

'Wainscott? What're you doing here? Have we got a mission, then?'

'No, not really. I just thought that we could get your ship, find a dodgy-looking planet and blow—' Wainscott noticed that W was giving him a stern look. 'Oh, nothing.'

'Good to see you,' W said gloomily. 'How's things?'

'Well,' Smith said, 'our engine room's full of killer frogs, our convoy got blown up and we've opened a portal to Hell. Still, mustn't grumble.'

'Killer frogs, eh?' W nodded thoughtfully. 'While I bear amphibians no ill will – indeed, man has much to learn from the toad – an engine room full of them sounds excessive.'

'Well, yes.' Smith sighed. 'Frankly, sir, problems are gathering in my mind as surely as beetle-people around a big ball of dung. Not that my mind is made of dung, but you see what I mean.'

W sighed. 'So your convoy blew up. . .'

'Indeed so,' Smith said. 'It was destroyed by enemy action—'

'Not us,' Carveth added.

'By a vessel powered by. . . well, by what we think may be a portal to another dimension.'

From the left came a peal of laughter worthy of a mad scientist. Felicity Fitzroy was discussing something with Susan. 'I see you've met Captain Fitzroy,' W said. 'She's in charge of our deepspace protection. Our aim is to keep things low key.'

Smith reflected that if they wanted to keep their dealings quiet, the best policy would be to tell Felicity no jokes. In space, everyone could hear Captain Fitzroy laugh.

'Make a damned fine lax forward,' she declared and Susan, perhaps not realising that she was talking about lacrosse, stepped back.

'We need to talk,' said W. 'Dreckitt ought to be in on this too – if you could just prise your android pilot off my synthetic bounty hunter. Journeys end in lovers meeting and all that, but I think she's about to blow his fuse.'

W led them into a side-lounge. Two massive radio scramblers had been propped against the far wall. W pulled the lever on each and, as lightning ran up the Tesla coils, he took a seat and tried to ignore the static threatening to turn his pencil moustache upright.

'Whatever is said here goes no further,' the spy began. 'First, I should explain my presence here.'

They listened as W set out the plans for the conference. 'This meeting offers us the chance not only to formalise our alliance with the Vorl,' he explained, 'but also to make a fresh deal with the Khlangari, who as a client state of the Voidani will be under space whale protection. It's a very delicate time, Smith. This will need tact, intelligence and sophistication.'

'Good thing I came back from that convoy mission to the far side of the Empire that you sent me on.'

'Er, yes. Now, speaking of very delicate matters, tell me about this portal you've found.'

Quickly, Smith set out the details of the destruction of the automated convoy, the raid on Deliverance, and the theft of the mysterious device. 'I want you to understand,' he finished, 'that Carveth has my full backing.' He leaned back in his chair. 'Unless she's gone mental.'

'Thanks for that,' Carveth said.

W sat, brushing static off his tweed as he listened. After a while his hair sank down and he nodded thoughtfully. 'Prong, eh? I should have known he'd be calling the shots. It was inevitable that he'd take Lord Forke's place.'

'What happened to him?'

'Witchfinder Forke? Well, you know what Edenites are like. He tried to have carnal knowledge of a grenade launcher. The grenade launcher finished first.'

'But what about me?' Carveth demanded. 'I'm not mad, am I?'

'No,' W said, 'you're not mad.'

'I told them *I* wasn't mad,' Wainscott muttered into his beard, 'but did they listen? I was sectioned for single-handedly destroying an enemy orbital battlestation. That's bloody gratitude for you!'

'We've discussed this before,' W said. 'We wouldn't have minded you blowing it up if there had actually been a war on. As it was the British Government had to formally apologise to Number One. If the Prime Minister hadn't called him a pint-sized dickhead in the process, it could have been a deeply humiliating situation.'

'Should've blown him up too,' Wainscott replied.

'Now,' W said, 'to the matter in hand. Who here has heard of Dodgson physics?' He looked around the room. 'Alright then, who's heard of Newtonian physics? Physics in general? Anyone in the front row?'

Suruk raised a hand. 'It is said that a rainbow turns to light when it passes through a prison.'

'Force and angle applied to neck equals dead sentry,' Wainscott added.

'Right. Both of those are nearly examples of physics. Such rules govern the world. But there may be other places, outside our plane of being, where the normal laws of time and space no longer hold sway.'

'I hear similar things about Croydon,' Smith mused.

W took a deep draught on his roll-up, followed by a

massive swig of tea. 'The story begins six hundred years ago, at the height of the Victorian era. Although Britain's previous empire spanned the globe, it may surprise you to learn that it was not a time of perfect freedom, justice and equality. In many cities, the main source of labour, currency and combustible material was the urchin. Yet many brave people strove to improve mankind's lot through reform and innovation. Today, we have such bold pioneers to thank for everyday comforts such as umbrellas, heavy artillery and the defleminating purdoscope.

'One such pioneer was Charles Ludwig Dodgson, an Oxford-based mathematician and fruitcake. Quite what basis he worked from, we don't exactly know. But sometime in the late 1860s, he began to build a machine that would give him access to a world running upon a different system of physics.'

'A different system?' Smith found it hard to believe, even now.

'Indeed, Smith. And through that machine, he took his brain to another dimension.'

'He took his brain to another dimension?'

'He took his brain to another dimension. Pay close attention. . . to judge from the records that Dodgson kept, whatever he found there was lethal – or at least lethal to adults. He formed the conclusion that, even with an endless supply of urchins, it was simply too dangerous for further exploration. It appears that at least sixty percent of the otherworld's inhabitants wanted to remove heads – a full two percent more than most M'Lak planets. Dodgson closed down his experiment and went into theoretical mathematics and children's literature. His test apparatus has never been located. Until now, that is.'

There was a moment's silence. Then Smith said, 'So what we have in our ship is—'

'A portal to another dimension, yes. You've done well to bring it back. We may have to jettison it into the sun but, at the moment, it's safest in your ship. Keep it locked away, Smith! People have killed to get into the other-world, and to stay there. You will, of course, tell none of the allied aliens about this.'

'What about the other nations of Earth?'

'Don't be absurd, Smith,' W said. 'We've known our fellow humans for thousands of years. I wouldn't trust them with a bloody cheese roll.'

That afternoon – at least, judging by the clocks on Wellington Prime – they moved the *John Pym* from the hold of the *Chimera* to dock separately with the main space station. Shortly afterwards, Carveth disappeared to her quarters with Dreckitt and, having given her the usual warning about not using the kitchen table again, Smith walked into the colony to see how things were progressing.

They were far from out of danger yet. Even if W's conference went smoothly, there was always the risk of the Edenites tracking the *John Pym* down – and even if that didn't happen, there was a fair possibility of Wellington Prime being swamped by Suruk's killer frogs or the card-game-obsessed minions of Hell or, most likely of all, the whole lot of them at once.

The service personnel were pinning up posters in the

lounges. Smith sat down under one that said *Please note that haggis is food* – presumably for the benefit of foreign delegates. Sipping his vending-machine tea, he realised that he missed Rhianna very much.

Strange, really. Had someone told him that two years before, he would have snorted with derision and returned to assembling a model aeroplane. Yet he had become one of those fellows he would previously have dismissed as effete: the girl-liking sort. Of course, with Rhianna elsewhere, he and Carveth could belch and not eat vegetables but it didn't seem worth it, somehow. He knew Rhianna was doing something very important for the benefit of the Empire and, hopefully, she would return very soon and tell him that it hadn't involved any men.

'Penny for your thoughts,' said Captain Fitzroy. He glanced up as she loomed over him like a blonde, jaunty cliff. 'How's the little lady?'

'Oh, fine. Off seeing her boyfriend.'

'What? Isn't that you?'

'Oh – right. . . yes.' Smith realised that the fiendish cunning of his own plan had outwitted him. 'Yes, she is seeing him, because he's me. . . and she is watching me. From afar. She might be watching now, you know,' he added, as Captain Fitzroy sat down beside him.

'Looking forward to greeting the aliens?'

'Oh, definitely. You see some funny-looking fellows in space. Of course, you have to be reasonable about it, though. I mean, if we went around giving people trouble just because they're noisy and wear peculiar clothes, we'd have outlawed bagpipes years ago.'

Felicity laughed, and crossed her legs at the ankle. She

was wearing dress trousers, creased like folded paper, and her boots were extremely shiny. 'Listen, Smitty. . .'

Very warily, he said, 'Yes?'

'Your girlie seems rather keen on that Dreckitt fellow – security chap or whatever he is. You want to watch him. I know a sly operator when I see one. Takes one to know one!' Her head flopped back and she vented her laugh like a burst of steam.

A bell rang above them. They glanced up as words began to scroll across the board on the far side of the room. *Spacecraft docking procedure initiated. Yothian deputation passing through quarantine control. All greeting personnel to Atrium Four.*

'Well,' said Smith, leaping up, 'I must be going – got to see the Yothians, you know. Lovely place, Yath. Yoth. See you later!'

From the darkness of space, craft converged on Wellington Prime. Some travelled in convoy, others swiftly and alone, their jamming devices raised until they were within the colony's defensive grid. Only a few spaceships were big enough to make the voyage without strength in numbers or subterfuge.

A huge M'Lak warship slid out of the void, flanked by its own fighters. It was covered in armour plate and, painted orange and decorated with symbols denoting clan ownership and events in its history. Had he seen it, Captain No-Nose would have been deeply envious.

Two hours later, a grey, horseshoe-shaped craft halted just outside lidar range: a half-sentient vessel made by the Voidani space whales for their protegees, the Khlangari. A hatch slid open in the biomechanical croissant, and a shuttle sped forth. It contained five of the greatest mystics of Khlangar: foremost among them, the renowned Ambassador Tai'ni. As their mother ship withdrew to a safe distance they opened communications and hooted their arrival.

And so it began. Smith found himself travelling from airlock to airlock, greeting the great powers of Earth: representatives of the Indian Union, the South American Congress, the United Free States, the Pan-African League and Norway. A security team disarmed each group as they arrived, while a pair of troopers from the M'Lak Rifles stood nearby, a cheerful reminder to everyone not to start any trouble if they wanted to keep their heads.

Not only were there humans to welcome, but also the various aliens whose planets Britain's dreadnoughts had kindly welcomed to the Space Empire. Creatures arrived that Smith had only read about in school textbooks. He greeted the ambassadors of the Hegemony of Wing-Dam, brave warriors strikingly similar in shape and size to woodlice; a pair of brooding, tentacled Thorlians – possibly the ones he'd run from a while ago, shortly after suggesting that they join the Empire – and a massive armoured Kroatoan, who had been woken from hibernation with a lettuce and who kept dozing off midsentence.

Suruk helped out. The M'Lak word for diplomacy was *Chal-Zag*, which was usually translated as 'spirit of warmth' but more literally meant 'hot wind'. Suruk toured the entrance hall, nodding to the delegates and occasionally catching the eye of one of the riflemen who stood near the doors. Strange how difficult it was for humans to agree on anything, he reflected, as he slipped past a wallahbot and deftly swept half a dozen vol-au-vents off their tray and into his maw. The Ghasts and lemming-men wanted to conquer the galaxy. Their heads were still attached. Through the simple medium of detaching the heads of the Ghasts and lemming-men, the invasion risk would go away and Earth would be left with some very nice new paperweights.

Another wallahbot appeared at his side with a tray of drinks. 'Aperitif, sir?'

'My mandibles are working just fine,' Suruk said. 'But thank you anyway.' He turned away and strolled deeper into the hall, looking for company. Guests mingled around him. A trio of Seh witch-priests that looked like plucked green emus trotted past, clicking at one another.

Isambard Smith was standing a little way back, chatting to a man in Indian naval uniform. No doubt they were discussing world affairs and the future of the galaxy.

'You know, Smith,' said the Indian space captain, 'It was truly a fascinating century.'

'Absolutely, Singh. Some of the bowling was pretty good, too.'

As the space captains shared views on starships, cricket and moustache protocol, it occurred to Suruk that mankind truly was one. As to one what, he was not quite sure.

Someone shouted on the left. Suruk flicked round, suddenly alert. Was it battle? Had traitors or Ghasts attacked – or better yet, lemming men? He would rip them into pieces, take their furry heads in the name of inter-galactic co-operation. Suruk strode towards the sound.

A woman was in his way, saying something about the ambassador spoiling them with chocolates. Suruk dis-creetly shouldered her aside. To his left, like a beast on the same scent, one of the M'Lak riflemen was heading the same way. Suruk quickened his pace, deter-mined to get there first.

The cafeteria. The thought of food and battle in the same place made it hard not to drool. Suruk opened his mandibles. Others were following him now: security men and bodyguards from the various powers. Two huge men made hand gestures, no doubt putting together a plan. Suruk ignored that and booted the cafe doors open, eager to see what enemy he would face.

It was Major Wainscott. Wainscott stood beside a drinks machine, wild-eyed as if connected to the mains. A captain of the United Free States had backed up against the wall, palms raised.

'What do you mean, it tastes funny?' Wainscott snarled. 'By God, I'll—'

'Take it easy,' said the captain. 'It's just a drink.'

'Just a drink? Just a drink?' Wainscott's face twisted and hardened like setting clay. 'Just a drink, you say? Now you listen to me, sonny,' he added, taking a step away from the machine, 'tea makes us strong. God gave the British tea when he chose us to bring civilisation to this benighted ruin of a galaxy. You know, I feel sorry for you chaps, what with your government throwing all your tea into that harbour. Our nation was built by tough men drinking tea. Out in the countryside, you're not a real man unless you've got a mug in your hand and half a dozen teapots in your kitchen cabinet. I ask you. . . what happens if someone breaks into your home, and you need to give him a refreshing hot drink, eh? Eh? If you want me to stop drinking tea, you'll have to pull the steaming pot out of my warm, dead hands!'

Smith appeared at Suruk's shoulder. 'Oh dear,' he said grimly.

'Indeed,' Suruk replied.

A woman coughed and Wainscott looked around. 'Oh,' he said. 'Hullo, Susan.'

She strolled over, shaking her head. 'Come along, Boss. It's time for your tablets.'

Wainscott paused, arms raised in his sentry-killing position. He looked at his hands, sighed and lowered them slowly. 'Well said. Good point, Susan. So then, Captain Schwartz: Assam or Darjeeling?'

*

A little way behind, a broad-shouldered man turned back to the curry machine. He pushed his card into the slot, dialled up a helping of Saag Aloo and watched it flop onto a paper tray. Overshadowed by the machine, his back to the security cameras, he activated his internal protocols. Motors whirred softly under synthetic skin. He downloaded a 3D image from his memory banks and his face slid from that of one man to another. He was no longer Thomas Perdu of the European Delegation, but Brian O'Brian, deputy engineer and all round helpful fellow. For now, at least. He slipped off his name badge and buried it in the heap of spinach potato, then collected a chapati from the dispensing slot.

Holding his plate up high to hide his empty lapel, Brian walked out to reconnoitre.

*

The day wore on, and Smith's hand ached from greeting people, and he hadn't patronised any of the funny types once. Well, except for that fellow from French Guyana, but that was more commiserating than anything else. Perhaps he would take Smith's advice and move to British Guyana, which was probably much better. Smith paused on the mezzanine, resting his arms on the brass railing and looking down at the main hall. Strange how somewhere so busy could seem so empty when the person you wanted wasn't there.

The lights dimmed, a fanfare played from the speakers, and a small man in a high-collared suit appeared on the stage at the end of the room. 'Ladies, gentlemen and other creatures. . . Station Governor Mike Barton. . .'

A middle-aged, spectacled man took to the stage. For a second he simply stood there, like a robot without batteries. Then a hovering drone played a little trumpet-blast.

'Good evening, everyone,' he said. 'Welcome. We're gathered here today, as representatives of the great powers of free space and the planets they control, to formalise an agreement with the Vorl: who, by becoming allies of the British Space Empire and the rest of Earth, will join our great and noble struggle for liberty. Unfortunately, they've not arrived yet, so we'll have the buffet lunch instead.

'There was a time, many years ago, when Britain would have striven to welcome you with excitement and extravaganza. But that's just embarrassing, so I would ask you to circulate quietly while we play some Elgar over the speakers. The negotiations begin in earnest tomorrow and tonight there's dancing. If anyone's got any questions, I'll be at the bar.' He walked off, obviously relieved to be able to go.

Smith looked down at the baffling array of creatures below. At the edge of the stage, a piano was being tuned up ready to provide backing for the first musical act, a raponteur who looked like a younger version of Wainscott. The thought of Wainscott on stage, narrating his exploits over a piano accompaniment, was enough to give Smith a headache.

A sudden sharp pain in the temple reinforced this impression. Smith looked down and saw a vol-au-vent at his feet. Realising he had been struck with it and wondering if this was the start of some strange Ghastist outrage, he glanced across the hall, hunting for dangerous aliens.

Suruk waved at him. At Suruk's side, W beckoned and pointed at the doors. Smith crossed the mezzanine and hurried downstairs.

W looked grimmer than usual, even holding a sausage roll. 'Problem, Smith.'

'Bad pastry?'

'The M'Lak have arrived. They want to see the pair of you. They asked by name.'

'Us? But how would they know we were here? Suruk, did you tell them?'

The alien shook his head. 'Many and subtle are the address-books of the Gilled.'

'Be that as it may,' W replied, 'there's a two-and-a-half stage helmsman waiting, and he wants to speak to you.'

Suruk rubbed his hands together. 'Such a visitor must not be kept waiting.'

As the service lift squeaked downwards to the entrance hall, Smith smoothed down his jacket and tried to think of something he wasn't worried about. The lift banged to a standstill and they stepped into a polished, empty chamber. They faced a pair of airlock doors big enough to accommodate a lorry and embossed with a huge brass lion and unicorn.

A display board clattered above them. 'Gate Three,' W said. 'Any time now.'

Suruk leaned close to Smith. 'We are privileged, Mazuran. Rarely do the space-lords reveal themselves to mankind.'

'Really?' Smith replied. Apprehension stirred in his gut. Would he have to fight this thing, bend it to the Empire's will or, even worse, make small talk with it? 'What's going to happen?'

'You have seen how the M'Lak reproduce,' Suruk replied. 'Occasionally, a spawn does not truly grow beyond a tadpole. Beyond spawn and hatchling, yet never adult, he remains in the axylotl stage and the strength of his body flows into his mind. That is what you will see: one of the Gilled.'

The great doors creaked, hissed and rolled apart. A M'Lak strode through a curtain of steam. He wore the long brown coat, ritual scarf and heavy goggles of a spacefarer, one who probably only ever left his ship to raid and refuel. A second emerged as if forming from the steam, then others, wiping their goggles as they came. Behind them, a glass tank the size of a railway carriage rolled into view.

W stubbed out his roll-up in a pot plant. Smith fought down a wave of unease that seemed to billow out of the tank, washing over him. Something moved in the tinted water.

With slow grace, a creature swam forward to the glass. It wore a headset of the sort used in space suits and call centres. Otherwise, it resembled nothing so much as a newt the size of a saltwater crocodile. The Gilled Helmsman, master-spacefarer and seer of the M'Lak, turned his ancient eyes on the humans before him.

Speakers crackled at the corners of the tank. 'Oh hi,' they said. 'I am Sedderik the Helmsman. You must be Space Captain Smith. And Suruk the Slayer, I believe.'

'Indeed,' Suruk replied. '*Jaizeh*, Sedderik. Well it is said that the wisdom of the Gilled is the conquest of the void.'

'Welcome aboard,' W added. 'I'm afraid I can't give you my name—'

'All things are known to the Gilled,' said the helmsman. 'It is our way. He who understands the true nature of a thing, can control it. . . Eric.'

'Hello!' said Smith. 'Did you have a nice trip?'

Sedderik blinked. 'Not bad, thanks.'

'Good-oh. I would shake hands, but—'

'Bit difficult, I know,' said the helmsman. 'Let's just wave.'

They waved. Man and newt stopped waving after a

while and looked at each other, trying to think of something to say.

'So, um, helmsman,' Smith said, 'do you have to get out of the tank to turn the steering wheel?'

'It's an honorific,' Sedderik replied.

'Gosh. That bad, eh?'

'No, I mean it's an honorary title. Helmsman is the rank above navigator. It's better because you don't have to worry about the maps getting wet.' Sedderik barrel-rolled lazily, pushing himself round with a flick of his tail.

W stepped forward. 'Here's your delegate pack,' he said, passing a bag to one of Sedderik's adjutants. The adjutant lifted out objects and held them to the glass. W said, 'You get a mug, some stationary with the Imperial Crest on it, and a name-badge.'

'Perhaps we can sellotape the name-badge onto my tank,' Sedderik said. 'Gorgar, feel free to keep the mug.'

'You have my thanks,' the adjutant growled. 'There is also a sticker that says 'I'm fighting for freedom' and a brochure from something called the North Yorkshire Tourist Board.'

Sedderik waved a webbed hand. 'All yours. Now. . . I have news for you all,' he said, righting himself. 'Three matters have come to our attention.'

'Go on,' W said.

'The first is for Captain Smith. A visitor comes this way who will be most welcome to him. In one day she shall be upon you – that is to say, upon the space station.'

'Is it Rhianna?' Smith said.

The helmsman sighed. 'I cannot tell you that. Precision

is the prophesy-killer, you know. It takes all the fun out of it.'

'Oh.' Smith sighed. 'But is it, really?'

'All right, yes it is. But the second matter is for you all. A great evil arises from the depth of space, and comes for the nations of man.'

'Brilliant,' Smith said. 'About Rhianna, that is.'

W leaned forward, pushed a bony hand through his mass of dark hair and scratched the back of his head. 'If you mean war with the Ghasts, that's pretty old news.'

The helmsman shook his head, and the gesture rippled down his length. 'I refer to this station. Something is coming here.'

'Nobody knows about this place.'

'Good.' Sedderik sank down. 'But be careful. And the third matter is for Suruk the Slayer alone. The thing you lost is behind the bathroom sink. Better sort it out before the room begins to smell.'

'I think you, Sedderik,' Suruk replied.

Sedderik yawned. 'I like all the brasswork here. Very smart.' He turned in his tank. 'I've been thinking of doing some DIY myself. Putting in some ferns, or a model castle to swim around. This is my travel tank, you see. My usual tank is much more interesting. It's got a waterproof sofa and a machine that dispenses plankton.'

'Oh, right. Would you like a drink?'

'White wine would be lovely, thanks. Just tip it in the top. Now,' said the helmsman, rising in his tank, 'I must be alone. It's been a long journey, and I need to fold space.'

On the way back, as the lift rose, W leaned against the dented metal wall and sighed.

'Is that true,' Smith said, 'about Rhianna?' His chest felt light, as if his heart was a balloon whose mooring-ties had been cut.

'Bloody psychics,' W replied. 'Can't keep a damn thing to themselves. Yes, it's true. I just hope the rest of it isn't.'

'Then we must work swiftly,' Suruk said. 'I shall hunt behind the sink at once.'

The lift doors rolled open and they walked into one of the service corridors. As they emerged, a large being floated past, consisting of two red globes surrounded by a mass of pale tentacles.

'Nom-Noodloth is displeased, Earth-people!' it announced, holding out an orange ball. 'About this "Scotch Egg"—'

'It's just a name,' Smith replied, 'not from real Scotsmen.'

'Then it shall be assimilated!' the creature declared. 'Nom-Noodloth is grateful and less displeased!' it added, and floated away.

Smith watched it drift down the corridor. 'Nom-Noodloth must drain its appendages!' it added, disappearing into what was almost certainly not the right room.

Funny bunch, aliens.

Lights dimmed and the automated compere rolled to the front of the stage. Smith watched from the edge of the hall.

'Ladies, gentlemen and sentient creatures, we are proud to present the mad maestro of Manchester, here to put a smile on your face and some swing in your heart. We give you Maurice E. Smith and his Good Time Big Band!'

Maurice E. Smith ran onto the stage, a freeze-dried daffodil in his lapel. 'This is called *You're the one for me, Harriet*,' the bandleader intoned. The stage lit up, rows of musicians stood ready and the big drums thundered.

Carveth ran onto the floor in her blue dress, dragging Dreckitt after her. Smith watched, feeling envy for both of them at once and neither in particular. Still, Rhianna was on the way; a ten-foot newt had seen it in the future and now a pathologically gloomy spy had confirmed it. How could it not be true? At the far end of the room, a small group of fleet personnel arrived, presaged by a laugh that he briefly mistook for a trumpet solo. Captain Felicity Fitzroy strode to the bar, accompanied by Chumble and Shuttles, the fighter ace. Smith, realising he could not flee, held his ground.

'Two pints of Stalwart and a lager top, barbot,' Captain Fitzroy barked. 'What's your poison, Smitty?'

Smith ordered a pint of Excalibeer, the self-proclaimed Lager of Kings. It certainly tasted medieval.

'That's the ticket,' Captain Fitzroy said, taking a deep swig. On stage, the lead trumpeter inflated his throat sacs and blasted a wave of sound down the hall. The dance floor was beginning to fill up. 'I say, that fellow's getting a bit familiar with your little lady. My God, it's that private eye fellow again! He's trying to touch down on your planetoid.'

'Dreckitt?' Smith looked into his pint, unsure whether

lager was meant to be so cloudy. 'He just takes care of her.'

'Looks like he's taking good care of her tonsils,' she replied. 'You want me to nip over and have some words? Pop him one on the noggin?'

'Um, no thanks. We have a – well, it's complicated, you see. . .'

'You sly old dog!' She laughed at the roof, as if to stun a passing gull. 'Well, if he keeps 'er indoors off your back – or your front – while you play a blinder up the left wing, nice work. I've got a little arrangement of my own,' she added, nodding towards Shuttles and his group of pilots. Smith wondered which and how many of them she meant. Almost to his surprise, he felt quite impressed.

Pint in hand, Fitzroy gave Smith an odd little bow, wished him a good evening and strode away.

A new song began and a Yothian slid its cone-shaped body onto the dance-floor and began to spin slowly, making a low droning sound. Dreckitt left Carveth, approached the bar and asked for a large white wine and two fingers' of rye. Susan of the Deepspace Operations Group led Wainscott onto the floor, probably to assist in surveying the guests. Wainscott looked rather subdued after his earlier outburst and was wearing trousers now. Smith sipped his pint and felt lonely.

Suruk waited by the wall, a cup of flat beer in his hand, watching the room like a Roman emperor overlooking the arena. Carveth stood beside him. Smith waved at them and approached.

'Funny, isn't it,' he yelled over the band, 'that thirty years ago I'd have been trying to shoot half of these alien chaps, and now they're our friends. How times change!'

'You must have been a bloody tough ten-year-old,' Carveth called back.

Suruk leaned over. 'Thirty years ago, I would have been trying to kill you. And now we have. . .. *dancing*. And they call it progress.'

'What's wrong with dancing?' Carveth demanded.

Suruk frowned. 'We have discussed this before,' he replied, his deep voice raised against the band, 'and the answer remains no. I do not dance.'

'But why not?' Carveth demanded. 'Look, Wainscott and Susan are dancing.' In the past Smith had tried not to wonder what the Deepspace Operations Group did when they were not blowing things up; surprisingly, the answer seemed to include swing dance.

'It is not befitting a warrior.'

'What about the Gilled Helmsman, then? He's having a lovely time.' She pointed to the massive tank at the edge of the hall. Water slopped against the side, sending its occupant rocking and bobbing.

'That is not dancing. He has just turned the wave machine on.'

'Look, it's easy. First, you've got to keep time with the music. Put your hand out. . . like this.' Warily, Suruk extended his hand. 'Now, when the beat comes, click your fingers. See what I'm doing?'

Watching her closely, as if expecting an attack, Suruk did the same. Dreckitt, returning from the bar with a double whisky, watched them clicking their fingers. 'That's right, Lurch,' he said.

'Now,' Carveth continued, 'we take to the floor. Here.'

She approached and took Suruk's hand. 'Up like this,' Carveth said, and Suruk, who believed that physical contact was better done with spears, went along with her. Tentatively, Carveth steered him onto the dancefloor. Smith watched Carveth and Suruk make their hesitant way across the floor like an Aresian fighting machine with a damaged gyroscope.

Their dancing, however inept, filled him with sudden, almost ferocious pride. They were bloody good sorts, cowardice and homicidal mania aside, and he was damned proud to have them as a crew. Who else could have brought back that mirror from the heart of New Eden?

But more troubling images floated into view. There was no point in hoping that 462 had been killed in the pirate uprising: maybe he would have gained a new scar, or acquired a dented bottom, but the Ghast was like Michelangelo's David: he might not look like much of a tough guy, but you'd need heavy weapons to do anything more than chip little pieces off the bugger. Smith might be in the company of friends but he still wasn't safe – not by a very long way.

W and Governor Barton sat at the edge of the room, drinking pints. Barton's spaniel sat on his lap. The governor looked slightly furtive, as if expecting to be ambushed by a horde of potential dance-partners. Smith strolled over and took a seat on the far side of the table.

Smith beckoned to W and the spy leaned across. 'Sir,' Smith said, 'I want to move the mirror away from here.'

'Oh yes?'

'It's too dangerous. If what you said about this

Dodgson fellow is true, a portal to another dimension and Suruk's killer frogs could be an incredibly dangerous combination. We need to get the mirror away from here.'

'Well, we can't just dump it in space. It needs to be securely locked away.'

'You're right.' The band stopped, leaving them sitting awkwardly until the music began again. 'I suggest we put it in a box, and *then* dump it in space.' Seeing that W looked unconvinced, he added, 'It won't drift away. There's no current to move it. My pilot's got a book about astrophysics,' he finished, not mentioning that the book in question had come free with breakfast cereal.

'Let me think about it,' W said. 'We're going to look a bit bloody silly if we lose a portal to another dimension.' The spy stared across the room and Smith followed his gaze. One of the operational controllers, a simulant named Dawn, was approaching rapidly. Behind her came a slim man in a dark jacket and roll-neck jumper, a low-level European access pass pinned to his lapel. Smith felt strangely sure he had seen the fellow somewhere before.

'Could you give me a minute, Smith?' W asked.

'Righto.' Smith leaned back, listened to the band and wondered how much he had drunk: surely only three or four pints. Perhaps it was time he switched to fruit juice, or at least drinks with a bit of lime on the top. Carveth and Dreckitt swept past on the dance floor, surprisingly elegant given what Carveth was trying to do to him. Suruk lounged against the bar, looking glad to have escaped. His top hat, dark clothing and mandibles made him strangely like Abraham Lincoln in profile.

The doors at the far end of the hall rolled apart and a

woman stood in the aperture. Smith stared, unsure. Surely not. There were hundreds of women in the delegations of the Earth, many of them very attractive. But none would be quite so beautiful, or so tie-dyed, and certainly none would be smoking a jazz cigarette.

Rhianna stood at the edge of the lift as if unsure whether to continue. It struck Smith as odd that, after years of trying to get the peoples of the galaxy to gather in harmony, she seemed so flummoxed by the sight of it. Nobody appeared to have noticed her – no, he realised, the gilled helmsman had turned in his tank and was beckoning her forward. Smith waved, to no avail.

Rhianna closed her eyes and did that annoyed-by-constipation expression that meant she was attempting to wield her psychic abilities. Suddenly she stopped and looked straight at Smith. Her face broke into a broad, foolish grin, an expression he'd not seen on her before, and as he got up she strode through the half-chatting, half-dancing crowd in a swirling mass of artificial silk.

On stage, Maurice E. Smith pulled the microphone close. '*There's a picnic on the streets of London,*' he crooned, '*and Heaven knows I'm cheerful now.*'

Rhianna came close, her smile reflecting Smith's, and kissed him.

'I wasn't expecting you,' he said. 'Not to begin with, anyway.'

'I'm sorry I didn't explain. But I couldn't. It was top secret.'

'Not at all. You did the right thing. Where're the Vorl?'

'They got kinda delayed. You know how they don't have a fixed corporeal form?'

'Made of smoke, you mean.'

'Right. Well, one of them was standing next to the air vent and somebody must've turned the air conditioning up. . . Anyway, they've found him now. He materialised in the kitchens, on top of a plate of finger food. I think it freaked out some of the guys working down there. It's lucky nobody hurt themselves, all those cocktail sticks lying around. . . Did you get my message?' Rhianna asked.

'Your psychic message?'

'Yes. So it worked, then?'

'Jolly well thanks. It gave me a – I mean, I got it loud and clear.'

A spotlight came on above Rhianna, turning her dress bright red. At the back of the room, doors slammed. 'This reminds me of my high school prom,' she said. 'Shall we dance?'

Smith, who had seen Rhianna dancing before, said, 'Why don't you dance and I'll sit down and watch?'

'Uh-uh.' She took his hand and, with unexpected formality, began to waltz to the strains of *Thank the DJ*. Smith let himself be swept along. He wondered if she was wearing any shoes, since it would have been difficult to do the backward steps in flip-flops.

Looking around the room, he spotted the Khlangari delegation wobbling about happily at the far end of the room. He reflected that perhaps the peoples of the galaxy were ultimately alike, and that even on Khlangar the males were feebly hooting their objection as the females hauled them up to pootle about awkwardly on the dance floor. His happiness at seeing Rhianna blotted out his apprehension that booze and ineptitude would tip him onto his face and together they half waltzed, half-wandered across the floor.

*

'If you think that Indian TV is all musical numbers and dancing about,' said Space Captain Singh, 'you should see our DIY programmes. You can't swing a chainsaw and sing at the same time, I can tell you.'

'Actually, you can,' Suruk replied. 'But only with joy. More tea?'

'Thank you. Now, as I was saying. . .'

'Nothing to make a song and dance of, huh?' Dreckitt had slid down in his chair, a glass of artificial whisky in one hand. Carveth picked the drooping cigarette neatly from of the corner of his mouth before it had the chance to fall into his drink and create a fireball. 'Damn,' Dreckitt muttered, 'this hooch kicks harder than the chorus-line at Madame Fifi's. They ought to spray it when there's a riot on.'

'Myself,' said Raumskapitan Schmidt, 'I prefer schnapps. *Prost!*'

'Anything but tea,' Space Captain Schwartz drawled. 'Bourbon, Mr Dreckitt?'

The various space captains sat around a table at the rear of the hall. The dancing continued, but Smith had decided to sit down before he fell off the dance floor and onto some visiting dignitary. Besides, he needed to be able to get back to his room – or more importantly, Rhianna's – and do something other than immediately pass out. He looked at her across the table and smiled. She looked alarmed. Smith wondered what the problem was until a finger tapped him hard on the shoulder.

Wainscott stood behind him. 'Problem, Smith,' the major said.

'Has something exploded?'

'We need to talk. Come on.'

Smith clambered upright and followed Wainscott out of the room. In the foyer, the music sounded distant and muffled, as though underwater. The room felt impossibly airy and empty.

W, Barton, Susan and Captain Fitzroy sat on heavy red armchairs, as if they had retired for a glass of port and a manly chat. With them was the man in the roll-neck jumper Smith had seen earlier. As he approached, the man raised his hands and shrugged, and with a jolt of surprise Smith realised who he was: Le Fantome.

'What's going on?' Smith demanded.

W gestured to Le Fantome. The Frenchman stood up and put his hands behind his back. '*Mes amis*, I have gathered you all here to announce that in our midst is what is known in France as *un probleme*. Someone on this colony is not who he seems. There is an impostor.'

'Good Lord!' Smith exclaimed. Captain Fitzroy reached for her gin. W scowled. Wainscott looked entirely confused. Barton said, 'Oh, that sounds really bollocks.'

'Quite so, *messieurs-dammes*. I was checking the security with your assistant – I forget her name, but she reminds me of Marie de Poppins—'

'Dawn,' W said.

'*Ah, oui. Une fille charmante.* She told me that there

223

were twelve persons on the European support staff. This is not so. There are eleven.' He rocked back on his heels, making Smith feel giddy as he tried to keep focus on the man's face. 'I smelled *une souris*, and so I leaped into action. One name on the list does not add up. . . Thomas Perdu, a general assistant to the deputation. The real Thomas Perdu died six months ago. The one here is false. As you English would say, he is *un person rhum*.'

'Have you seen this fellow?' Smith asked.

'No. We did not know of him until we arrived here. We suspect he may have stowed away on one of the other vessels – a difficult task, but not, as one might say *en Francais, impossible*.'

'What?' Wainscott exclaimed. 'Dammit, man, speak English!'

'Impossible, Major Wainscott.'

'Try, dammit!'

'Thomas Perdu is a false name. I can only conclude that this man is here under false pretences.'

Smith said, 'Well then. It sounds like we should get looking for Tom Perdu.'

'We will, yes,' said W. 'But *you're* going out tomorrow morning to get rid of that mirror, Smith. You'll put it face down in a big box and anchor it to an asteroid, preferably one that isn't going anywhere. Then we can collect it later, once the treaty is agreed. And if there's any trouble - well then, there won't be any risk of the enemy getting close to it. Any questions?'

Smith shook his head. 'I'll let my crew know.'

'Then we're agreed,' W said. 'Wainscott, Susan, we need to discuss how to locate this Tom Perdu fellow.

Everyone else, I'd advise getting some sleep. And perhaps a couple of aspirin.'

Le Fantome bowed. 'My friends,' he said, 'I like this plan. It is, as we say *en Francais, super-cool.*'

Searching for Tom Perdu

'Hello and good morning. This is R Trevor Humphreys, reporting live for the Today programme from the treaty negotiations between the British Space Empire and other nations both human and alien; first among them, the Vorl. For reasons of security I can't give our location, but I am able to speak to some of the representatives here to gauge their opinions on the task ahead. As might be expected, there is a strong M'Lak presence here and I'm joined by two of their elders now.

'First, Vorgak Spleen-Ripper, Minister of War for the Greater M'Lak Heartlands. Vorgak, what are you looking for from this peace agreement?'

'War!'

'Also here today is Athnarar of the line of Gathrog, minister for Fisheries and Agriculture.'

'. . . And war.'

'My apologies. Minister for Fisheries, Agriculture and War, what do you see the main points of disagreement to be today?'

'I thank you, Trevor. Today, we are on the cusp of an agreement that has the potential to change not just this conflict but the face of galactic relations. Truly, the future *is an undiscovered country, and the signing of this treaty will bring that country one step closer to being like Belgium. It will be a future that the people of Earth richly deserve.'*

'So there you have it. High hopes on all sides. Now, I believe the delegates are entering the debating chamber. . .'

*

W followed the government delegation into the conference room and stepped into the rumble of fifty-six languages as if into a cloud of noise.

The room was easily the size of an aircraft hangar, chosen both to accommodate and intimidate the guests. Massive aspidistras flanked the floors. Brass lions, their heads tilted back to roar at the ceiling, stood at the corners; ornamental flames belched occasionally from their mouths. As W sat down, he saw his opposite number from the United Free States poke a cigarette into a lion's nostril, blow across the tip and take a drag. For a long moment the two men exchanged a look of weary cynicism, and then the opposite number turned to find his seat.

Governor Barton sat beside W, looking awkward in a new suit as though about to go on trial. One of Barton's cleaning automata puttered across the ceiling, a scanner bolted to its underside. It bumped into the Khlangari translation machine and swung away in a brief flurry of sparks.

The huge doors on the right side of the room parted and the M'Lak delegation entered in two rows, the great tank of the gilled helmsman sliding between them. 'Oh, ancestors!' Sedderik moaned as he rubbed his large head, 'what did I absorb through my gills last night?'

His comrades did not have a chance to answer. Two announcement-drones swung down from the ceiling and blasted out a little fanfare. 'Ladies, gentlemen and things,' they proclaimed, 'let the deliberations begin!'

The Empire's Minister of Colonial Affairs was first. He made a short opening speech, explaining that it was time for the peoples of the galaxy to set their differences aside and do what they were damned well told for once. Certainly, some of the delegates were different shapes and sizes – some had long traditions of helping the Space Empire, while others had shorter traditions of being shelled from orbit – but it was time for all hands to be on deck and to man the pumps, take the bull by the horns and pull together for the team. Eventually, this was translated.

The translation machine, looking much like a funnel attached to a set of rotor blades, stabilised itself above the Khlangari delegation and thrummed softly. Ambassador Tai'ni stood up and began to hoot. 'Tai'ni Khlangari says that as a semi-neutral party, we are delighted to pupate,' the machine announced. It had a wise, friendly voice. 'We look forward to discussions being conducted with open- ness, warmth and puberty.'

The aliens exchanged puzzled glances. Beside Tai'ni, a Khlangari major stood up, pulled the translator down and gave it a sharp tap, hooting under his breath. 'Oh sod it,' said the translator, 'the bloody thing's stuck again. We are delighted to participate,' it added, rising into the air, 'with openness, warmth and probity.' A ripple of approval ran through the various specii in the room. Heads were nodded, vibrant colours displayed and stamen wobbled.

At the far side of the room, something like smoke hung around an empty table. The vapour condensed as if being sucked into itself, drawing into the rough outline of two upper bodies. As one of the aliens rose to speak, W recognized its high forehead and the upturned spike of its nose.

'People of the galaxy,' the Vorl announced in a rather nasal, languid voice, 'I am C'Neth, Master of the Eight Vectors, Star-lord of Polaris, speaker for the Arch-Patrons of the Vorl. And this is my friend Sann'di. We are here to tell you that Earth must be destroyed!' he cried. 'Just kidding. I thought that might break the ice a bit. I think Sann'dhi's going to start off.'

C'Neth sank down as if to disappear through the floor but stopped around three feet above it. The Vorl beside him wafted upwards.

'Thanks to our good friend Rhianna Mitchell. . .'

'Lovely girl,' C'Neth added. 'I'm so proud of her.'

'. . . We have been instructed in what goes on at dos like this. So, who's reading the first poem, and which one of you fine gentlemen is rolling up?'

'Sirs!' the Chinese ambassador interjected. 'This is an important treaty. Please have some decorum.'

'Pardon my language,' Sann'di replied. 'One forgets one's no longer on Polaris. I shall mind my cant. Now then, we've had a vada at your treaty, and while it's generally bona I couldn't understand some of the words.'

'It's mutual,' W muttered.

Sann'di picked up his papers with one insubstantial hand, using static to rifle through the pages. 'Ah yes. If you could just turn to Sub-section 5, Paragraphs 7-16. I wondered if you could clarify the meaning of 'rum business', 'Johnny Moonman' and, turning to the section entitled *Practises Outlawed by Common Assent*, 'bopping the natives'.'

*

462 sat back in his chair and activated the viewscreen. The *Systematic Destruction* had powerful scanners and could pick up Edenite propaganda broadcasts; 462 studied them to make sure his beloved allies weren't getting above themselves.

A new Supreme Leader had been elected by the Edenites. He called himself Mike Simple, and was entirely trustworthy because he was, by his own proud admission, too stupid to deceive the electorate. Spontaneous celebrations had already been organised. 462 flicked through the channels and saw a tank surrounded by a mob of whooping cultists. Half a dozen hanged bodies dangled from its main gun. He squinted at the strange human faces, with their noses, hair and lack of antennae, and realised that it wasn't important whether the Edenites were furious or overjoyed: they were in a hysterical frenzy, and that was all that mattered. Mike Simple probably was just an actor reading out his lines – or, rather, forgetting them for added authenticity.

462 spent a moment coaxing the sneer out of his mouth and dialled up Lord Prong. As the bioscreen changed

view, 462 reached out and took a refreshing sip of freshly-pulped minion. For a moment Prong appeared on screen without sound, clearly unaware that he was being watched: he looked confused, mean and rheumy-eyed. Strange, 462 thought, how the most pious Edenites resembled angry tramps. The entire human race made his antennae curl in disgust, but New Eden invoked a special level of contempt. If I stay much longer among these weaklings, he thought, I will pick up their body odour.

Prong seemed to be trying to speak directly into the camera lens, revealing teeth like a castle wall that had been hit by a cannonball. Behind him, Leniatus the bodyguard banged two wires together. 'Is there a mouse?' Leniatus asked happily. 'I want a mouse.'

And I am missing a lemming, 462 reflected. Ambassador Quetic was gone, lost not just in the workings of the *Pale Horse*, but, 462 now realised, in the nightmarish place from which it drew its energy. A hideous fate, perhaps, but one that left 462 conveniently in charge. Which was fortunate, judging by the trouble Prong was having in activating the radio.

'Eh?' Prong barked. 'You do what? Talk into this? *Can anyone hear me?*' he screamed into the microphone. 462 snarled and yanked his helmet off, nearly deafened by the reverberation. The helmet quivered in his hands.

'I hear you,' 462 replied, grimacing. The old fool clearly had no idea how the volume controller worked.

'Say what?'

462 silently mouthed a sentence and watched as Prong turned up the volume dial. 462 flicked the button on the in-seat propagandatron. Glorious Number One bellowed

out from a nearby speaker, announcing the stockpiling of new trenchcoats and sounding like a cross between a sparking electrical cable and an angry Pekenese: '*Blak anarak-stak shak*—' Prong jolted as if he had pressed either the cable or the dog to his nose. He grappled with the controls, muttering about filthy modern music, and managed to bring the volume down to manageable levels. 462 concealed his amusement by pretending to have found some new insignia inside his helmet.

'What the hell do you want?' Prong said.

'Information. I require an update as to your search of the sector.'

'Nothing as yet. You'll know when we find anything.' He reached for the off switch.

'Attention, Prong!'

The hierarch paused. 'What now?'

462 narrowed his eye. 'Do not fail me, Prong. I would be most disappointed to think that you were not giving this mission your most strenuous attention.'

'What in Tribulation makes you think that I'm not?'

'You have a cup of cocoa at your side and are wearing a tartan rug across your knees. My knowledge of puny human biology informs me that you are about to have—' 462's voice dripped with distaste – 'a little nap. I was not aware that your duties as Grand Mandrill included snoozing.'

The meaning of this filtered from Prong's ears to his brain, then soaked into his face. 'I'll thank you not to question me. I have divine right. And don't you go thinking I'm slack. Not ten minutes ago I conducted a fierce purge, I'll have you know.'

'You are not required to update me on that.' 462 took

a sip of minion. 'You will quicken your search. Wrong me, Prong, and you will have sung your swan song.' He scowled, reflecting that it was much easier to threaten people in languages that did not rhyme. 'Scour this quadrant. Threaten your men. Put your bifocals on. . . do whatever you must. But locate that device or I will begin to suspect that you no longer serve the greater glory of the Ghast Empire. '

'Glory?' Prong snorted, setting his tufts of nasal hair a-quiver. 'Hogwash. Think you're something special, sonny? You know as well as me that it's nothing to do with glory, same as it's nothing to do with piety.'

'What?'

'Ah, come on. I'm not stupid. You happen to be addressing one of the greatest scholars of the sacred Book of Eden—'

'Silence. The fact that you have memorised some inconsequential pamphlet—'

'Pamphlet? That's holy writ you're talking about! I should know, it was me who writ it!' Prong coughed into his palm, wiped it somewhere out of view and grinned. 'You're kidding yourself with this 'for the Ghast Empire' stuff. You're in it for the killing, just like me. It's not the praying, it's the hating that counts. Why else would we change the Book of Eden every three weeks if not to catch people out?' He chuckled and the sound was like liquid trickling down a leaky pipe. 'What could be more satisfying than to make people miserable? To see all those little smiling faces start to cry? To see humanity, in all its greatness, and grind it – crush it – make them crawl through their bellies in the dirt? When they bow to the Annihilator,

233

they bow to me! Dance, puppets! Hee-hee! It's the hate that matters. . . spreading it, shouting it, seeing 'em burn because of it –'

462 flicked the switch. Either Prong or the failed minion had left him with a bad taste in the mouth. What rubbish, to equate his struggle for the Ghast Empire with the self-righteous savagery of the hierarchs of Eden. If Prong could, 462 thought, he would make being born into a sin punishable by slow death. It was nothing like the inevitable conflict between insect and mammal that would decide the ultimate fate of the galaxy. He felt the need to cheer himself up: a couple of hours of Number One ranting about tank production ought to do the job.

462 paused, his pincer next to his presentation set of collected speeches, arranged from Angry contempt to Zealous fury. To his surprise, he found he actually wanted peace and quiet. He glanced around the room. Assault Unit 1 lay in its basket. The praetorians were watching a propaganda film in their barracks, which ought to keep them quiet for the next hour. Right now, they would be snarling along to 'If you're loyal and you know it, salute the screen'.

Assuring himself that it would only serve to enhance his efficiency, 462 pulled his black duvet out of the storm-assault locker and tucked himself in under the image of the antennae'd skull.

*

Fifteen thousand miles away from Wellington Prime, Carveth gave Smith his first lesson in flying the *John Pym*.

Ten minutes later, while eating his mid-morning digestives, Smith decided that he was getting the hang of this. The main controls were pretty easy to master: it appeared that the banks of flickering diodes above his head were the equivalent of lights on a Christmas tree; useful in establishing a mood, but otherwise without much purpose. Even Gerald, who was a pretty good arbiter of threat, was scurrying happily in his wheel.

Chaperoned by HMS *Chimera*, the *Pym* passed one of the system's outlying planets, a dead moon circled by a halo of asteroid debris.

'How am I doing?' he asked.

Carveth sipped her tea. 'Well, don't go calling yourself elite until you've actually landed on something. You'll find it's a lot more difficult when you've got Suruk leaning over your shoulder shouting 'Ram them!' every time you pass a service station. Still, you're doing alright. Oh, and don't get crumbs over the controls.'

'Righto,' said Smith. '*A minute to learn, a lifetime to master*, as Othello once said.'

'You've got to keep checking the instruments,' Carveth explained, 'as well as the screen and the manual. The instrument panel is vital: the moment you don't think you don't need it is the moment you really do. Like deodorant.'

Up ahead, the grey bulk of the *Chimera* began to slow down. It had been their escort this far: now that they were away from the space station, the *Pym* would make the rest of the journey inconspicuous and alone.

The intercom crackled. 'Good morrow and God rest ye,' Chumble boomed. 'We seem to be moving away from one another, like an urchin parted by fate from his mysterious benefactor. Sadly, now is our moment of departure.'

'Got a hangover, by any chance?' Captain Fitzroy put in. Her voice threatened to break the *John Pym*'s speakers. Smith flinched from the intercom.

'Fine thanks,' he replied, turning the *Pym* into its set course. 'Just coming round.'

'Out like a light, were you?' Captain Fitzroy replied. 'I thought as much. Damn, Smitty, you ought to see how we used to drink back in the old days. Me and the girls fixed up a still in the dorm radiator. We used to go bonkers the night before and still be on the field for lax practice before breakfast the next morning.'

Carveth leaned down beside Smith's ear. 'I think she's speaking English,' she whispered.

'I know it's hard to keep up with the best ship in the fleet, and the best crew,' Captain Fitzroy continued, 'but do try. Come on, Saggy. Mummy loves you. Up on my lap.'

'I think she's talking to her cat now,' Carveth said. 'At least, I hope so.'

'See you back at the ranch, Smitty. And Carveth. . . put him through his paces. Show the boy no mercy.' Chuckling, she signed off.

The cockpit door opened and Smith twisted around in his seat, nudging the control stick. He quickly rectified it before the *John Pym* could execute a barrel roll.

'Greetings!' said Suruk, striding in. 'Behold the spawn of House Agshad!' He thrust an enormous snarling toad at Carveth, who yelped and scrambled out of her chair. 'Also, we are running low on biscuits.'

The *Chimera* drew away from them, beginning the patrol arc that would bring it back to base. It slowly disappeared from the windscreen, as though they were leaving a metal island.

Suruk kicked one of the emergency seats down and squatted on it like a gargoyle. 'The spawn grow strong,' he declared. The toad surveyed the room as if deciding whether to devour the cockpit or use it as a latrine. 'Soon, they will be throwing size.'

Carveth slipped a spanner out of her pocket, just in case. 'Throwing size?'

'Of course. Have you never heard of toadball? Or the honoured custom of hurling one's spawn at the enemy? It helps the young to get ahead.'

'Braaak,' said the spawn, eyeing Gerald's cage.

'Just keep him away from me and my hamster,' Carveth replied. 'Here's an ide. . . why don't we open the portal to Hell and throw all of your horrible frog-children through it? That'd be a nice day out for the kids.'

'I shall give it thought.' Suruk gazed out of the window. 'Ah, it is good to be back in space again, sailing the galaxy. To feel the absence of fresh breeze once more, to gaze upon the deficiency of magnificent views, to take in the lack of atmosphere. Useful as the treaty must be, it is bold deeds, not flowery words, that stir the soul. I tire of extraneous circumlocution.'

'Deeds, eh?' said Smith. 'Well then, why don't you make the tea?'

'It is Piglet's turn.'

'No it's not,' Carveth replied. 'Firstly, I'm teaching the captain how to fly the ship and so I'm needed in the captain's chair. Secondly, I'm in the captain's chair so I get to say so. Thirdly, I put the kettle on.'

'Nonsense,' Suruk replied. 'It is surely—'

'Flapping your mandibles isn't going to make the tea.'

'Crew, stop arguing,' said Smith. 'Suruk, it's your turn to make the tea. Unless you want to steer us through this asteroid belt.'

Suruk growled, stood up and left the cockpit with his spawn. Smith heard him stride down the corridor. A door opened, and Rhianna's voice said 'Hey, Suruk, how's things? What've you got there—' before she shrieked and slammed the door.

Smith sighed. He had known since primary school that girls didn't like frogs. Although, recalling the leathery thing squatting in Suruk's hands, like a cross between a small demon and a very old Cornish pasty, he wasn't so fond himself.

He flicked a button that, to his relief, started the radio.

'. . . *Oh aye, 'tis a dangerous business an' no mistake. Remember, if you don't weed it out, it'll get hungry and come after you, and it'll bring its friends too. You've got to creep up arn the bugger and shoot its stinger arff before it can attack. If that thing hits exposed skin, you're as good as dead. Then pull yer machete and go to work.*'

'*Thanks, Jed. That's all from* Gardener's Question Time *for this week. Next time, we'll be coming from Venus itself but, until then. . .*'

Smith glanced back down the corridor. He heard metallic noises: hopefully, it was Suruk stirring the tea.

'. . .*And now: the shipping forecast. Andromeda, Epsilon Eridani: supernova, four rising five – moderate, becoming very rough. Scorpio, Betelguese: comet, class 7 easing 5 receding by 19.00. Taurus: meteor showers light—'*

'One day, I'm going to pull Suruk's leg too much and he's going to pull my head off.' Carveth leaned back in the captain's chair.

'I doubt it.' Smith steered carefully around a passing asteroid. 'But I'd check your bed for frogs before you go to sleep tonight.'

*

In the hold, Suruk yanked open the engine room door and drop-kicked his spawn inside. About two dozen beady eyes glared back at him from the gloom. He slammed the door and quickly turned the key in the lock. Although the number of spawn had reduced, they were much bigger on account of having devoured one another. Suruk was not sure that it would make them any easier to handle; it was as though many piranhas had condensed to form several sharks.

As Suruk was about to leave the hold, his boot snagged the loose end of one of the canvas straps used to hold the mirror down. He stood there for a moment. It occurred to him that he ought to tuck it away before someone tripped over it. He approached the mirror silently: half so as not to alert the others; half to catch it unawares.

Surely it would not hurt to have a look. He didn't doubt Carveth's story, at least not the basic facts. Why shouldn't the mirror lead into another dimension? Things like that happened every day. The humans did not understand it, but the line between the normal – the flying-through-space-and-fighting-other-species normal – and the mystic was extremely thin. The mundane and the epic could co-exist. After all, Carveth was mundane. Suruk, on the other hand, was epic. He smiled behind his mandibles.

Just a little peek. He would lift the top and glance underneath, the way the little woman did with boxes of chocolate. Maybe he would sample a little of the netherworld – just a tiny bit – and then push everything around so nobody knew what had happened. He loosened the other straps and then, very carefully, eased the mirror up a few inches – then a few more. He looked over his shoulder. Nothing.

The mirror lurched under him. Suruk glanced down and a huge clawed hand shot out of the aperture. Fingers the length of human arms flexed like the legs of a monstrous crab. Something snarled beneath the floor. Suruk twisted to the left as he drew his knife and he saw a head pressed against the gap between mirror and floor, as if rising from a trapdoor: a buck-toothed mixture of dragon, insect and turkey on the end of a neck as thick as an anaconda. Suruk heard beating wings, felt and smelled rank breath blasting against his side as it groped for him.

He slashed the hand across the palm and, with a screech, the massive arm whipped away. The mirror slammed against the floor and, for a second, Suruk feared that it would shatter and that this new source of entertainment would end.

'Hey, Suruk. You okay down there?'

He sprang upright and found himself looking at Rhianna. She was wearing a loose top and a long flowing skirt and looked as if she had popped her head out of the top of a collapsing tent. 'Greetings! I am fine. How are you?' Suruk said innocently. 'I had just dropped an item on the floor and was looking for it. It was a skull. A very small skull,' he added, impressed by his own improvisation.

'Cool,' Rhianna said. She frowned. 'Suruk, you know about spiritual matters, right? Mystic tribal stuff?'

'Killing things, you mean? I dabble.'

'When I look at this mirror, I can't help get a weird feeling. Do you think it's what Polly says it is?'

'Almost certainly.'

She looked down, dreadlocks flopping forward like the limbs of a dead spider plant. 'It must be dangerous. Maybe we should get it off the ship now.'

'Because it is dangerous?' Suruk frowned. 'If that is true, we both should leave as well.'

'How do you mean? I'm not dangerous. I abhor violence in all its—'

'We are dangerous in different ways. I am a warrior who has devoted his life to honing his skills, rising from a brutish hatchling to a seasoned master of the arts of battle. You are more like a cow that has swallowed a bomb.'

'Hey!' Rhianna stepped back, drawing up like an offended cobra. 'That's not me.'

'Indeed it is. If you are not careful, your abilities will cause you to explode. You must master the power within you and release it slowly in. . . ah. . . puffs. A true ruminant, of course, has two stomachs. You do not even have that advantage.'

Rhianna said, 'So you really think of me as a cow.'

'A mystic cow. Your psychic potential is matched only by your rampant herbivorousness.'

'Suruk, did you see something in here a few minutes ago?'

'Nothing escapes the hunter's eye. I saw nothing.'

'I thought. . . I heard a kind of burbling sound.' She gazed down at the mirror and Suruk sensed the edge of her mind probing at it and, from there, reaching towards him. He imagined his soul shrinking back into his body, hiding there, and Rhianna shrugged and said, 'Maybe I ought to lay off the red weed for a while.'

Smith called out from the cockpit.

*

'So,' Dreckitt said, 'you got a plan to find this guy?'

Wainscott stood before a long mirror in one of the security rooms, his face close to the glass. He had just finished a vending-machine pie and was picking detritus out of his beard. 'Early days so far,' he said. 'But I thought I'd probably cause a stir, drive the bugger into the open.' He took a white ball from his pocket and squeezed it between his fingers. 'I've been looking for something to do with this plastique for ages.'

'You consider jacking into the net? Every grifter on the street knows that data finds its own level. In the neon flow of ice, truth is just another programme to slot.'

'You mean, have I looked on the computer? Yes, I have. Tom Perdu's a false name, of course. Beyond that, nothing. I've had Nelson bring up a full map of this place, or as full as there is, leaving out the bits Barton built himself. We've got our work cut out.'

The door opened behind them and Susan entered, carrying a tray. She kicked the door closed with her heel. 'Alright,' she said, setting the tray down, 'I've got everything we need here.' Dreckitt looked at the tray: it contained a roll of printout, a dozen blurry photographs, two silenced pistols, cups, milk, a teapot and half a pack of digestives. 'Your turn to pour,' she said.

'Listen,' Dreckitt said, 'I've got a Hoyt-Axton emotional-response recognition kit in my valise. How about we wire it up and put some of these highbinders through the third degree?'

'I've a better, comprehensible plan,' Wainscott replied. 'The first step is for me to publicly remove my underwear, thus causing a distraction.'

'And once you've started undressing, what do we do?'

The major smiled and tapped the side of his nose with his finger. 'Wait and see, young fellow. All will be revealed.'

'That's what I was afraid of.'

Wainscott sighed. 'The last time we did an operation like this, I throttled the guards while Susan and the chaps rigged the place to explode. Problem is, we *are* the guards. Tricky.'

Susan reached across the tray. 'We don't need to. Look. . . these pictures are from the security cameras. Here are the Europeans coming in.' She laid three photographs on the table as if dealing cards, then three more. 'Here they are passing through the airlock. The next pictures show that they've gone away to get ready to join the others.'

Dreckitt leaned in. He pointed to a figure at the rear of the picture, a broad-shouldered man carrying two suitcases. 'So who's this guy? A late arrival?'

Susan shook her head. 'I don't know.'

'He's not in their party, or else they'd be looking for him.' Dreckitt rubbed his stubble. 'But he's following them through. I got a hunch. . . what if this guy at the back was laying low and took the chance to slip through, using them as a screen?'

Wainscott crunched a biscuit. 'But where would he hide? How would he get into the station in the first place? We've got scanners that'll pick up life-forms, humanoid shapes, explosives, guns. . .'

Susan said, 'An android might not show up. One of the older models would give out no body heat. If you scanned him, he'd just show up as an object. He could just power down and fold up in some corner of a ship and wait for it to arrive.'

Wainscott broke a digestive in half and peered at it suspiciously. 'All very well, Susan. But, assuming this is our man and he is a robot, he would still have to get from the European ship and into the colony. And I can't see him getting past two dozen scanners and a bunch of M'Lak riflemen. At least, not with his head still attached.'

'That's the smart part of the caper,' Dreckitt replied. 'He was hiding in the luggage.'

'I don't follow you. Surely they'd know if they had the wrong luggage.'

'Nix, pal,' Dreckitt said. 'Have you ever seen how they handle baggage in France?'

For a moment, Wainscott was silent.

Susan nodded slowly.

'Dear Lord!' Wainscott whispered, 'that really is fiendish. It gives a whole new dimension to industrial action.' He scowled at the table, then picked up one of the silenced pistols. 'Time to go to work, gentlemen. We have a good idea of what this fellow looks like. We know he can't be carrying more than a suitcase of kit. Let's put him out of action before he does the same to us.'

Dreckitt put his hat on and pulled the brim down low. 'I'm on the case.'

Wainscott shoved the pistol into his shorts. 'Then it's the usual plan. . . locate and destroy. Search every room, every corridor and air vent before this person gets the chance to work his evil. And tell that Le Fantome chappie what's going on. We may need his skills. After all, we hunt a dangerous enemy. Our villain's already passed himself off as a French public sector employee – he may strike at any moment!'

*

Suruk got to the door first but, for someone with shorter legs and no boots, Rhianna was close behind. They rushed through the doorway like junk falling out of a cupboard. 'What is it?' Rhianna said.

Smith looked up from the scanner. The light of the

screen gave his face a sepulchral glow. 'Men, I have worrying news. We have a reading of multiple blobs on this object here, headed straight towards the kitchen.'

Carveth leaned forward in the captain's chair, tried to get up, and flailed like a fat man in a bathtub. 'Er, how many blobs? How fast are they going?'

'Six,' Smith replied. 'About an inch every ten seconds.'

'Bloody hell!' Carveth struggled upright and pressed in beside him. 'Enemy ships, closing fast!'

'Good God,' Smith replied. 'What do I do?'

'Squeal and wee,' Carveth replied. 'Or we could change places.'

'Good plan.' They squeezed past each other awkwardly. Smith dropped into the captain's chair, picked a long hair off the headrest and said, 'Pilot, take immediate evasive manoeuvres. Are we seen?'

She checked the instruments while replacing the cushions. 'No signs of detection. If they were, by now we'd be in hailing range or in pieces. I'm pulling back into the asteroid field. The mass should confuse their sensors.'

The *John Pym* slipped between the asteroids and Carveth killed the engines. 'Hmm,' said Smith, peering at the windscreen. 'The enemy don't look like much.'

'They're far away,' Carveth replied. 'According to the scanners, if we were the size of an egg, any one of those ships would be as big as a buffalo. And you know what happens if a buffalo sits on an egg.'

Suruk raised a hand. 'A monstrous, horned chicken?'

Smith shook his head. 'Your optimism is misplaced, old chap, along with your understanding of biology.' He sat back in the chair. In the hamster cage, Gerald had dug himself into his bedding. 'Well, we're outnumbered and outgunned. By the inexorable logic of history, at this point we British ought to win. On the other hand, we don't have any guns and those ships are actually rather large. Carveth, turn us round.'

'Wait,' she replied. 'Look at the way they're moving. They're scanning the area. As soon as we leave the asteroid belt, we'll be wide open.' She pointed to the screen. 'At the moment, we're safe within the belt. But once they come looking—'

'Damn!' Smith hissed. He rubbed his forehead, trying to coax out a plan. What would Admiral Nelson have done? Sought comfort from Hardy, or even, given the desperation of the circumstances, attempted a desperate manoeuvre with Hornblower. They had to escape and, more than that, get back to the station and warn the others. 'If we fly out of the asteroids,' he asked, 'what will they detect?'

'Well, us,' Carveth replied. 'I mean, our engines.'

'So if we were to fly away without using our engines, we'd be alright, yes?'

She paused. 'You do realise that the engines are the bit that makes us move, right?'

'So all we need to do is get clear. The asteroids are orbiting the planet over there, so if we get close enough—'

'We'd drop into the gravitational field.'

Suruk chuckled. 'And creep up on them, silent as a quanbeast in a herd of ravanphants!'

'Creep *away* from them,' Carveth said. 'But we'd have to pull out of the asteroid belt and get closer to the planet to slingshot off its gravitational field. And that means firing the engines. And then we'd stick out like a walrus in a tutu.'

Rhianna said, 'Let's use the power of wind.'

'What?'

They turned and looked at her. She sat in one of the emergency seats, legs crossed under her. 'Wind can move us.'

'Doubt it,' Carveth replied. 'Wind doesn't make me go anywhere. It's everyone else that moves.'

'But we've got air tanks, right? And they're kind've under high pressure? So if we release some of the air, won't that push us to one side, like a rocket?'

Smith looked at the ships in the screen, tiny dots moving out on the same trajectory. 'Maybe. . . maybe. Dammit, you're right! It's just a matter of maths, like back at school. Every force has an equal and opposite hypotenuse. It's the sum of the diameter or. . . circumfugal force. At any rate, I'm circumfused.'

'Ouch!' Suruk observed.

'Carveth, we have Rhianna to thank for this plan. Suruk, you and I will check on the air tanks. We don't want to jettison too much.'

The alien stood up. 'Excellent,' he said, rubbing his mandibles together. 'We have delayed long enough. Time to grab the bull by the udders.'

'The horns, you mean,' Smith replied.

Suruk paused at the doorway. 'No,' he said, shaking his head, 'it was definitely the udders.'

It took six minutes to find the emergency venting control. It was behind a panel in the corridor that Smith hadn't known he could open and consisted of a large metal wheel. 'I shall assist,' Suruk said, reaching in. 'It is like a jam jar – or a lemming man's head.'

'Can I help?'

Smith looked round: Rhianna stood in the corridor. 'You could make us some tea.'

'I meant, maybe I could use my psychic powers to hide the ship?'

'Good idea. Could you stick the kettle on first though, old girl?' For some reason, she didn't look overly pleased. Perhaps they were running low on tea.

Carveth's face appeared in the cockpit doorway. 'We're sinking through the asteroid belt,' she announced. 'Two minutes and we'll be ready to jump into the gravity field. Three, tops.'

'Alright. On your mark, pilot.'

'No, on yours. You're the captain.'

He felt curiously affronted by this. 'But you know how spaceships work. You fly this thing.'

'So do you now.'

Suruk leaned close to Smith, near enough to jab his ear with a mandible. 'Fear not, Mazuran. Apparently, manoeuvring in space is just a matter of angles. Like one of your ball games.'

That did nothing to reassure Smith. At the mention of ball games he remembered a sodden plain of half-frozen mud, more warzone than Wembley; damp socks sliding down over glass-cold shins, of the smack of hard leather ball into podgy gut; of being the last in a row and a half-broken voice saying 'Suppose I'll have to take Smith'. Character-building, they'd called it, the traditional euphemism for ritual humiliation.

Smith was suddenly no longer ten. He looked around, and the alien grinned back at him. 'You have your battle-face on, Mazuran,' Suruk said. 'You look like a little dog killing a rat.'

'Let's get to work!' Smith replied. 'Carveth? What's our position?'

She called back, 'In thirty seconds' time, we won't look like an asteroid any more. More like a sitting duck.'

'Carveth, power us down!' he said, looking at the wheel.

'Systems down,' she replied.

The background hum disappeared and, as the lights sank to emergency bulbs, the sound around them faded away. The *Pym* sped on without air to slow it and as quiet and dead to scanners as the rocks around it.

A new sound rose from the cabins behind him: Rhianna humming as she settled down into a meditative state. It made Smith uncomfortable but he did not know why.

'We're leaving the asteroid belt,' Carveth announced. 'Right about. . . now.'

'Ready, Suruk?'

'Indeed.'

'Then let's turn it. On three. One. . . two. . . three!'

He grimaced and tried to spin the wheel. Damn, the thing was stiff! It must have rusted shut from disuse. Smith gritted his teeth, grunting with effort, feeling his muscles ache from the strain. 'Dammit!' he puffed, stepping back, 'Bloody thing's—' and the wheel spun in Suruk's hands so quickly that it flew off, sending the alien headlong into the opposite wall.

Suruk climbed to his feet, slowly rubbing his head.

'What happened? Why am I holding this wheel? I will destroy you all! Oh, hello.'

It occurred to Smith that he and Suruk had been turning the wheel in opposite directions. No wonder it had been reluctant to move.

'Carveth?' Smith called. 'We've turned the wheel—'

'And broken it,' Suruk added.

'So the air supply should be blowing out!'

'And I tore its head off. Metaphorically.'

'We're moving!' Carveth cried. 'Yaw to port, thirty degrees. Here we go!'

Smith strode to the cockpit. Slowly, with a lazy elegance suited to a much larger – and less dented – craft, the *John Pym* swung away from the main belt and in towards the planet itself. Smith saw light wink on a row of tiny points, like sparks in the distance – the enemy ships, those that could yet be seen.

Carveth checked the dials. 'Pressure in the air tanks is dropping. Eighty per cent. . . seventy-six. . . sixty-nine. . . er, should he be holding that wheel?'

'Good point.' Smith turned to Suruk. 'Can you replace that, please?'

The alien shrugged. 'Does a Procturan black ripper secrete resin in the woods? Of course I can.'

As Suruk returned to the corridor, bearing the severed wheel like a feral version of Mr Toad, Smith watched the planet grow in the windscreen. Without resistance to slow it down, the *Pym* would be drawn deeper into the gravity field, pulled down towards the surface. Strange, he thought, how graceful it all was, and how deadly. Like ballet with sharks.

'Boss? Boss!'

Smith pulled himself away from an interesting mental image.

'Air tanks on fifty! That's got to be enough!'

'All right then. Suruk? Spin the wheel back!'

Carveth glanced between the windscreen, the scanner and the captain, as if she did not know which to trust the least. 'He'd better get it right,' she said, 'otherwise we'll be holding our breath on the way back.'

'Anti-clockwise!' Smith called. He watched the needle in the air gauge, sinking slowly as if under the weight of its own brasswork. It froze behind the dirty glass, crawling to a halt at forty-eight. 'It's stopped. Hull temperature's rising, though.'

'That'll be the atmosphere,' Carveth replied. 'Once I gun the engines, we'll look like any other gas flare. You can wake Rhianna up now.'

Smith hurried to Rhianna's room, ducked under the dreamcatcher and tapped her on the shoulder. She glanced round, eyes wide, and smiled. 'I guess we're okay, right?'

'Indeed we are.'

'I put up a psychic shield. The Vorl taught me how to focus my abilities.'

'Super. That was some razor-sharp meditation.' Leaning through the door, he called, 'Carveth? Are we out of danger now?'

'Apart from flying towards a planet, we're fine.'

Together, they returned to the cockpit. Locked into the planet's gravitation field, the *John Pym* shot forward like a stone in a sling. Their speed made the hull glow: along the edges of the windscreen, light flickered as patches of gas reacted with the heat.

'Just another piece of debris, burning up,' Carveth said.

'Good work,' Smith said. 'Thanks, Rhianna. That was a jolly good idea of yours. Whatever inspired you to think that releasing that load of hot air would help us?'

Rhianna smiled beatifically. 'I guess I was just unlocking the creative potential of my spirit. Creativity is the oldest and most mystic force in all of us.'

'Well, absolutely. Well said, I'm sure. Creativity wins the day, eh Suruk?'

'Piffle,' said the alien. 'The day is not yet won. We have escaped, for now, but the enemy fleet remains. We must warn our comrades, and then return to do battle.'

'You're right,' Smith said. 'Men, our struggle against the void is not yet ended.' Pausing rhetorically, he rested his elbow on the nearest item of appropriate height, which happened to be Carveth's head. 'Indeed, we have not just witnessed the end of the beginning, let alone the beginning of the end. But if the beginning's end has truly begun, then we must devote ourselves to the noble end of beginning – oh stuff it, just take us back home.'

'Now you're making sense,' Carveth said, and she fired up the engines.

*

An important point involving semi-colons had arisen in the treaty debate.

'Could it be,' a tall, square-jawed man declared, his voice choking with emotion, 'that everything we fight for is in this one, final, dawn? Could it be that liberty, true liberty, is what I stand for. . .' His voice dropped to a whisper. '. . . here, deep in my heart?' Weeping openly, he took his seat again.

One of the M'Lak stood up. 'Maybe.' It sat down.

The Minister for Colonial Affairs leaned over to W. 'I say, if this foreign chap blubs when he talks about freedom,' he whispered, 'what'll he be like against a horde of Ghast stormtroopers?'

C'Neth rose like steam from a kettle. 'Look, we need to discuss this punctuation,' he explained, addressing himself at random to the delegation from the Arabian League. 'If you can't bring yourself to deal with the details, what about the big things? Drop your commas and soon you've not got a leg to stand on. Not that I have any legs,' he added, glancing down. 'Below the waist I just taper to a point.'

'Don't you just,' said Sann'di.

'Ooh! Isn't he bold?'

W slipped out the room. Entering the corridor was like coming up for air. He rubbed his forehead and leaned against the wall. Catching a glimpse of himself in the mirror opposite, he resolved never to look at his reflection again and then sighed.

In a swish of dark material, Dawn, the organisation simulant, was at his side. 'Everything alright?'

'Leaving aside the idiots bickering over a semi-colon while the end of the galaxy rapidly approaches, fine. Any news from Wainscott?'

'His men are sweeping the lower decks. The M'Lak Rifles are on high alert. If they get any more alert, they'll start chopping people's heads off just to make sure they've not swallowed any dynamite.'

'Good.'

'Those drone things are scanning the public areas. The governor's got them rigged with all kinds of gear. And there's a chap from Engineering wants to talk to you. Says he's got information on a signal.'

'Where is he?'

'Billiard Room Four. Do you need a bodyguard?'

W shook his head. 'We need everyone looking. Tell them to get on with it.'

'Right you are.'

W hurried down the corridor, slipped his pass-fob over a side-door and ducked into the riveted chaos of the back stairway. He trotted downwards, the low ceiling brushing the top of his mop of black hair, his boots clanging like hammers on the metal steps.

At the foot of the stairwell, a wallahbot directed him to Billiard Room Four. It bowed on a hinge and gestured with an arm of polished brass. 'The gentleman awaits.'

The man rose to greet him. He was in his fifties, broad-shouldered and wide-necked. He wore dark overalls and spectacles that looked curiously delicate on his tough boxer's face. The little badge on his lapel said 'Brian.'

'Brian,' he said, pointing at it.

'Eric,' W replied. They shook hands. 'I gather you have some information for me.'

'Indeed.' Brian's voice was heavy and slow, but he sounded anything but stupid. 'I've found an anomaly – a potential security breach, I think. I thought I ought to come and report it. You are the right person for that, aren't you?'

'Absolutely.'

He adjusted his glasses. 'I can take you to it.'

'Lead on.'

They returned to the maintenance stairway. The air smelt of grease and metal. W took the lead as they descended. Brian hummed to himself but W could not make out a tune.

'I've got a gun pointing at your back,' Brian said. 'Well, a crossbow.'

'I thought you might,' W replied. 'How did you smuggle it in, by the way?'

'Inside me. I'm an android – a custom job. Fixed frame, modular plastic skin, no metal parts. When I think of the lengths I had to go to in order to get through your security. . . Ugh.'

They walked on. 'Out here,' Brian said.

They stepped out onto a storage deck. The floor was metal, the air hot and greasy. Machines banged and rumbled in the distance as if they stood in the back room of a colossal laundrette. But that was nothing to the odour of spice. The smell of curry powder filled W's nose and mouth. The air was thick and intoxicating.

Brian kicked the door closed. W looked around.

'I put out a signal,' Brian said. 'Getting hold of the gear wasn't easy, but by now our fleet should have your co-ordinates. Which leaves me to get on with Part Two of the plan: eliminating enemy personnel.'

'You won't get away with this,' W said.

The android smiled. 'Why not? When I'm done, this space station will be reduced to debris. I myself will escape and, believe me, I will leave no trace of you.'

'You're a marked man now. My people will hunt you down like game.'

'Perhaps. But I can change my spots. I've been careful to let a few cameras get a picture of me. They'll be looking for the wrong person now.' Brian stopped smiling. His features twisted, stretched and shrunk as if drawn onto drying clay. Brian's face was longer, the eyes deeper set, the brow lined and jawline hard.

W swallowed hard. He was looking at a version of himself: an imperfect copy, but one good enough to fool the colony sensors.

'All I need now,' Brian observed, unable to avoid grinning, 'is to copy your stupid little moustache. Perhaps if I drink some cocoa. Now move.'

They walked: the real man in front, his duplicate behind. W scowled into the corridor. Up ahead, something bubbled and slurped. W clenched his fists. He was too angry about the insult to his moustache – measured carefully against an actual pencil – to be very much afraid.

Behind them both, one of Barton's drones puttered across the corridor and disappeared into a side passage. It gave no indication of having seen them.

'On the left,' Brian said.

W's eyes prickled as they turned the corner. The corridor opened out and suddenly the room glowed red, as if they stood at the edge of Hell. Before them, in a great vat the size of a swimming pool, lay the station's third-level curry repository. Evil lights flickered on the ceiling. The air was rank with spice.

'Now then,' said Brian, 'Your decadent empire is about to end. The New Eden will snuff you out like a candle. We will not even leave a trace to gloat over. Starting with you.'

W sniffed the air, filled his artificial lungs with raw curry. 'Undiluted Madras.'

'As I said, there will be no traces. You're going for a swim.'

He flicked up the crossbow and W took a step back. The red liquid roiled and bubbled like lava at his heels.

So, thought the spy, this was it: death and disintegration without even a portion of rice to soak up his remains. He looked at the android, the crude mimicry of his own face, and wished that he had a cigarette and a nice cup of tea.

W opened his mouth, tilted his head back and took a huge hit of industrial-strength Madras. It had much the same effect: though his throat tightened, his eyes stung and his heart burned as he exhaled, fury spread through his meagre body, enervating him.

'Well then,' he said. 'Right now the only thing I can think of worse than you killing me is you banging on about it. So you might as well have done.'

'Suits me,' Brian said, and he fired.

W froze for a second, then pulled on his jacket. The dart fell out, tinkling on the steps: a three-inch sliver of hardened plastic, the tip smeared with something like oil.

'Nerve toxin,' Brian said.

'Moral fibre and Harris tweed,' W replied. 'And a bulletproof waistcoat.'

One of the maintenance drones swung into the corridor, the sound of its rotors muffled by the bubbling vats.

There was a short pause. Brian flexed his fingers. 'Then

I'll have to strangle you,' he said. 'The world's a tough place. And you're just too mild to survive.'

Brian leaped forward; W darted aside, his fists up. He looked like a geography teacher in the rutting season, elbow-patches out, all bony hands and tweed. Brian went straight in, driving out with a hardened plastic fist – as one of Barton's drones crash-dived into the back of his knee.

The android stumbled. W lunged, grabbed the collar and waist of Brian's overalls and threw him over his shoulder, back first into the bubbling, reeking sludge.

Brian flailed, cried out and sank from view. For half a second the vat was still and then the android broke the surface, thrashing. Brian yowled. His face seemed to melt, reform, run through half a dozen shapes it had taken; the cheeks fat and jolly one moment, cadaverous the next, the mouth stretching to a dreadful, malfunctional howl.

'Too mild, eh? Did you bite on a chilli?' W asked.

Brian did not hear him. With a final screech, the android pressed his hands to his running face like *The Scream* of South Asian cuisine.

'Munch on that,' W said.

Barton ran in as Brian sank out of view. His drones chugged into the room behind him, their rotors uneven in the thick vapour; several had gun attachments. They looked hand-made, the sort of thing the governor might have produced in a quiet afternoon. They circled the vat like vultures.

A white plastic skeleton surfaced in the curry. It had neither overalls nor human features any more; the voice came out of a speaker mounted where its throat had been.

'Well,' it said, 'this is awkward.'

'Isn't it?' said W.

'Look, I'm treading water and it really hurts. This stuff is definitely corroding me.'

W said, 'Would you prefer a lifebelt or a chapatti?'

'That's not funny. Get a rope in here! How the hell do you people eat so much of this stuff?'

'The trick is to wash it down,' W replied.

'A blanket would be nice, too,' said the android. 'I'm feeling pretty silly here and my legs are seizing up.'

'Oh, for God's sake,' Barton said, disgusted. 'First people come and clutter up my space station, and now there's a broken robot floating in my dinner. I've had just about enough of this.' He shook his head, weighed down with cares. 'Ah, *bollocks*.'

*

The airlock door creaked open and the crew left the *John Pym* deep in conversation.

'. . . and I said to him, 'It's not a bad burp unless you can smell it!" Carveth exclaimed.

'So what did the archbishop do?' Suruk asked.

'That was nice work back there,' Smith put in. He closed the door to the *John Pym*, and they waited in the corridor as the station's lurgiscope scanned them for disease. The door at the far end remained shut, closed until the check was complete. 'You all did well.'

Rhianna kissed his cheek.

'Gosh, thanks old girl. But now we need to warn the others. The sooner we can get a battleship out to face down those blighters the better.'

The scanner pinged. 'All your germs are within accept-able levels of tolerance. Your clearance level has been raised from *Stop That At Once* to *Carry On*. Exfoliate for victory, citizens.'

The door rolled back before them. W stood behind it. His gaunt face and folded arms gave him the look of a vampire surprised in its coffin.

'Good news,' he said. 'We have located the traitor that Le Fantome warned us about. He appears to be an android of Edenite construction. Luckily, I was able to apprehend him before he could wreak havoc by partially disintegrating him in the curry sump. Unfortunately, the curry could not be saved.'

'Damn this war!' Smith exclaimed.

'Now we can get back on with the treaty. With any luck, they'll have stopped arguing about the punctuation by now.'

Smith said, 'Sir, before we do that, my crew and I have bad news. Not only have we failed to get rid of that blasted mirror, but we were nearly caught by patrolling ships. It's the Ghasts, together with the Edenites: they've got half a dozen warships sweeping the area, like a – a – diabolical broom of evil!'

'Dammit!' W growled. 'Follow me.' He strode down the corridor, stopped at an intercom and flipped the switch. 'Dawn? We have a problem here. I want you to inform the others that there is *mould on my gherkin*. Repeat, mould on my gherkin. I need a special catering meeting in three minutes. Understand?'

'Loud and clear,' the intercom replied.

The lift shot them up through the heart of Wellington

Prime. Dreckitt waited in the corridor, looking shifty and dangerous.

He adjusted his hat. 'What's cooking, people?'

Suruk gave him a very stern look. 'One does *not* cook people. It is distinctly *passé*.'

'A big helping of villainy is cooking,' Smith replied, 'washed down with rum.'

Carveth looked at Dreckitt. 'Feels more like a laxative to me.'

Dreckitt patted her shoulder. 'Easy, sister. We've got work to do. Down these dark spaceways one man must walk, and that one man is you and me. Lady, let's give evil some chin music.'

'Is that dirty talk? And if not, why not?'

Dreckitt lead them into a clean, white room. Where the rest of the station looked like an overgrowing of brass scrollwork against a background of artificial walnut and racing green, this place was sterile and cold. Captain Fitzroy, Chumble and Squadron Leader Shuttleswade stood near the door. Wainscott and his team lounged against the far wall in front of chrome shelves full of equipment. Uniforms hung in a row beside them. The impression of military efficiency was marred only by the fact that they were chefs' uniforms and this was the scullery.

'Glad you could join us, Smitty,' Captain Fitzroy said. 'Sounds like we've got trouble on the horizon. I've got my best players on the case.'

'Who'd like cocoa?' Chumble asked.

W strode past her. 'Quieten down, everyone. Get those doors closed and sealed. It's time to take care of business. Milk, no sugar, Chumble.'

Dreckitt leaned next to Shuttleswade against a row of stainless steel cabinets.

'Listen closely,' W began. 'I have apprehended the spy described by Le Fantome and he has been put out of action. That's the end of the good news. The bad news is this: one, our spy told me that he had managed to put out a general transmission, giving our location to all and sundry; two, Smith informs me that there is a substantial enemy battlegroup sweeping the system, made up of Ghast and Edenite craft. We estimate three or four Edenite destroyers and one Ghast vessel. And if situations one and two are considered together, we get—'

'Three, by thunder!' Chumble roared.

'You're way ahead of me. In the circumstances, we must proceed on the basis that the enemy know where we are. That means they have to be diverted or destroyed. Nothing, and I mean *nothing*, must be allowed to stop the negotiations. The very future of Britain, and hence democracy and mankind, may rest on getting Johnny Moonman to do what we say.'

'That's a hell of a job,' Captain Fitzroy said. 'I'm happy to take to the field, but a few substitutes on the bench would be nice.'

Suruk said, 'The M'Lak would delight in such a battle. You should speak with the gilled helmsman. Or at least hold a note against his tank.'

'What about other countries?' Rhianna put in. 'Britain's not the only nation on Earth.' She looked from face to face. 'Honestly, it isn't.'

Wainscott shook his head. 'You mean, let them have a go? I should think not. You know what it's like. . . they go all silly and bang on about 'deniable black ops' and whatnot. I tell you, when I'm on a mission I don't leave anything behind to deny.'

W said, 'It's not possible. We need signatures on the treaty. If others think that we need help. . . well, we'll look like a charity case.'

Shuttles folded his arms. 'I can get my wing out into space as soon as you want. But what we need is a battle-plan, especially if there are bags of Gertie swinging in sun-side.'

Dreckitt snorted. 'Button-men, huh? I say we drill 'em.'

'I'll tell you what we need to do,' Smith said. He had been leaning against a sink; now he pushed off and stood upright. Heads turned. 'Gentlemen, it's time to fight. We British may not use the honeyed words of other lands – although we did invent writing, speech and Mozart, whatever they may claim in Hollywood – but we do have a *lot* of dreadnoughts. My friends, let us give the enemy diplomacy as we do best: from orbit, via a big gun. In the name of justice and democracy, let's give these invaders a jolly good thrashing!'

'But what about the talks?' Dreckitt asked. 'Once the Vorl know our racket is compromised, the whole grift will be blown.'

'You're right,' Smith replied, 'our allies are too precious for us to lose. The visitors require careful handling. That's why we'll lock them in the conference hall! What they don't know can't hurt them, right? You get Johnny Alien to sign the treaty. Meanwhile, we space chaps'll blast the hell out of Gertie. The allies need never know. All we have to do is close the portholes. Maybe we can tell them later. They might even be impressed.'

Wainscott thumped the sideboard. His beard was still speckled with pastry, as if he had forgotten to open his mouth and rammed a vol-au-vent into his chin. 'By God,' he growled, 'you're right! Sound doesn't carry in space. We lock one load of aliens in until they sign the treaty, then blow up the other bunch. Then we come back to the first lot and blow them up too – or do I mean make friends with them? Susan? Ah, we can work the details out later on. Smith, you have my team beside you.'

'And my lacrosse stick!' Captain Fitzroy exclaimed.

W stood up. 'Then we're decided. Captain Fitzroy, you are to enter deep space immediately. Wainscott, go with her. You're the marine contingent. Smith, once your air tanks are replenished, take your chaps and follow. You'll be able to catch up easily enough. Use Rhianna to try to sense the enemy – no doubt they'll have this secret weapon of theirs with them. Governor Barton and I will manage the treaty. Everyone agree? Excellent. To business, then.'

They filed into the corridor. Smith waited a moment, and as Shuttleswade came past he felt a rush of queasy fear, like he had always felt when talking to girls. 'Can I have a word?'

''Course,' Shuttles said. 'Is everything alright?'

'Fine, fine,' Smith replied. 'It's only that – well, we've all got to do our bit. I was thinking – if you've got any spare Hellfires. . . well, I've always wanted to fly one.'

'It's decent of you to offer,' Shuttles said, 'but we've got all the pilots we need.' Susan and Craig of the Deepspace Operations Group passed them, subtly ushering Wainscott towards the door. 'Listen, Smith: get your thousand hours in the hot seat and you can apply for combat training. I'll put in a good word. How's about that?'

Smith watched him go. He remembered being seventeen and trying to ask Emily Parsons to dance with him at the Midwich Grammar School disco. He had the strong feeling that he had just been told he was 'sweet'.

Rhianna gave him a reassuring look. 'Don't worry, Isambard. Maybe you can have a go when the war's over.'

'When it's over? But what's the point in that?' His voice sounded more bitter than he had intended it to be.

Carveth appeared at his right shoulder as if to counterbalance Rhianna, like the demon in an old cartoon. 'Let's face it, boss, the only hot seat you've known is when you've pulled rank to make me warm up the loo for you.'

'Isambard, you *didn't*—' Rhianna began.

'I do not know what you are complaining about,' Suruk said. 'Space is infinite, and my spear is eight feet long. How am I supposed to slay my enemies in a place like that? Perhaps I should tie a string to the end of it,' he added sadly.

Smith watched the others file out. He turned to Rhianna.

'We're going to need your help,' he said. 'If you can sense these enemy ships before they see us—'

'Cool,' she replied. 'I can use my powers to detect their emotions.'

'Righto,' Smith said, thinking that it would be more useful if she could detect their weaponry. At least she wouldn't pick up friendly signals: emoting was something that the Royal Space Navy did not do.

A side door opened and Governor Barton stepped into the room. He looked somewhat unhappy. His National Health glasses were at an odd angle. 'Alright, everyone. Er, we've got a bit of a problem,' he said.

Smith shook his head. ' Not to worry. I'm sure we can sort it out.'

'Are you sure about that? It's just that, erm. . . perhaps you'd better come and see.'

*

Barton led the way to the station's communications room. It was covered in coils of wire: additional scanning systems had been rooted in like new plants added to a garden. A row of monitors covered the rear of the room, the screens catching the light like polished tiles in a mosaic. Smith looked them over, seeing exterior shots of the orbiter, landscapes of rivets and antennae, funnels for listening into space.

W entered, looking grim.

A low bass noise blasted out of the speakers, a dismal honking like the call of some huge, distant lighthouse. It pulsed around the room, through ears and stomachs, into the walls as if to crack them.

Smith stared at the monitors. Cold dread began to creep through him. Moral fibre is the fear-killer, he reminded himself, and he wished that he had put the kettle on.

'What is that?' he said, not much wanting to hear the answer.

'It sounds like whalesong,' Rhianna said. 'Cool.'

'It's been playing for three minutes now. It repeats on a

twelve-second interval,' Barton added. 'Computer's can't lock it onto anything but it's coming from around *here*.' He pointed to one of the lower screens. 'There's something near the edge of the system—'

The monitors went black. They stared at the screens, as if struck blind.

'Bloody computers,' Barton said.

The screens flickered and burst into life. They showed one image between them, in black and white. It was a colossal hall, apparently circular, the walls ribbed. Some sort of machine stood in the centre.

'It looks Ghast,' Smith said. 'But there are no flags. . .'

'That's not Ghast,' W replied.

The thing in the centre rotated to face them. It was a mixture of gun turret, cockpit and throne, and it was occupied. They stared at the upper half of an immense creature, partly ossified, slumped down before a row of controls.

'Looks like it grew out of the chair,' Carveth whispered.

'That's just the way I'm sitting,' the speakers roared.

Carveth staggered back as if from a gust of wind. 'Bloody hell!'

The thing in the chair looked around. Its head alone was the size of a car. It raised a proboscis longer than an elephant's trunk and let out a low, sonorous boom. In that moment, despite its size and the hardening of its body, Smith realised the similarity in shape as well as sound.

'I am the eldest of the Khlangari,' the creature said. 'And it is well past the time of their return.'

Smith looked at W, and W looked at Barton. 'I'm the governor,' Barton said, as if it was just dawning on him. 'I run the station here. Captain Smith and this gentleman are dealing with matters relating to, er, guests we have at the moment. You can come in if you want. We've got a buffet.'

'Typical,' said the being in the chair. 'You try to seed the galaxy with intelligent life and this happens. Right then. I'll keep it simple. I am the mind and pilot of a polyp-based self-aware starship, which you would call one of the Voidani space whales. Which of you knows the location of the mystics of Khlangar?'

Smith stepped forward. 'Good morning. I represent the British Space Fleet. The Khlangari deputation is under our protection—'

His voice was drowned out in a numbing throb of bass. The creature sat up in its chair. 'In the past hour, I have picked up a transmission issued from your space station. It gives co-ordinates and precise location data. Normally this would not concern me. However, it also mentions the presence of five of our species.'

'That's quite right. They're here as part of a diplomatic mission to form a united front against alien tyranny. I must say that for little fellows they're making a jolly good job of it.'

'I have also detected vessels at the edge of the system which, I understand, represent powers hostile to you. In short, this area is now a warzone,' said the thing in the chair. 'You have six standard hours. At the end of that time you will provide proof that the Khlangari deputation is safe and well. Failure to do so will result in me taking measures to ensure their return.'

'I have told you that they are safe,' Smith replied. 'As an

Englishman, my word is proof enough. I hope you are not trying to threaten me, sir.'

'Threaten *you*? Of course not. I am threatening your space station, everyone in it and, depending on how I feel, everyone they have ever met. Because otherwise, we will research your colony. You may care to remember what happens when the Voidani research other life forms.'

'You eat them.'

'Precisely. Harm the deputation and suffer the wrath of the space whales.'

Rhianna took a step towards the monitor. 'Actually, I'm the human-Vorl liaison here. I'm like a counsellor, except psychic.'

'Great,' said the creature. 'Then I'm sure you can sense how delighted I am to see you. This conversation is over,' it added, and as the throne turned away, the image disappeared.

'Well!' said Rhianna.

'Balls,' said W.

'He'd better not blow up the station,' Barton said. 'It took me ages to sort this place out.'

'Boss,' Carveth said, 'am I reading this wrong, or was that the Khlangari's dad?'

Smith nodded, but he did not turn from the screen. 'I rather feel it may have been.'

'Oh Gaia!' Rhianna breathed, 'so the Khlangari are protected by the space whales. That alters my entire perception of the galaxy.'

'Damn right,' Carveth said. 'It makes it about fifty times more terrifying.'

'They must be, like, the larval stage or something. It's

such a privilege to make contact with such a spiritual being, although I'm not really digging all the death threats.'

'I don't see that it changes much,' Barton said. Of all of them, he seemed the least concerned. 'We've just got to stop the enemy fleet within six hours. Same thing as before, except that now we'll all die if we don't. Oh, actually that is quite bad. Suppose I'd better get back to the negotiations, then.'

W watched him go. 'Barton's right,' said the spy. 'The stakes are rising, gentlemen. Not only do we need to save the station, but we need to do so before the space whales demand their friends back. Of course, if we can be seen to defeat the enemy, it may make an alliance with the Voidani all the more probable. . .'

'Then to battle!' Suruk exclaimed. 'For what do we wait?'

'Well said, Suruk,' Smith said. 'What option is there but to attack? We must take this war to the enemy, with the sword of justice in hand. For if the torch of liberty falls, then we will find—'

'That we've dropped a Khlangar,' Carveth said.

'Just get to the ship.'

All Hell Breaks Loose

Felicity Fitzroy buckled herself into the captain's chair. The first sign of competence in starship captaincy, after all, was using a seatbelt. Computer screens blinked into activity, needles twitched under glass and engines grumbled into life as HMS *Chimera* came awake around her.

Dave's red light flickered on the dashboard. 'Good day, Felicity. Did you have a pleasant evening? Did you. . . *do things* with anyone?'

'No time to chat, Dave,' she replied. 'Get us undocked and into the black. Full steam ahead to the system's edge.'

'Whatever you say.'

'Mr Chumble, what's our weapons status?'

The android adjusted six dials, pulled a lever and shouted into a tube. 'Weapons report that our railguns are shinier than a thrupenny bit, ma'am. All crew at battle stations and eager as an orphan in a pie shop, by Jove.'

The floor rumbled. In the screen, Wellington Prime began to shrink. 'Good fellow. Dave, have the pilots on standby.'

The red light throbbed. 'I thought having the pilots was your job, Felicity. I'll let them know.'

'Alright then.' Captain Fitzroy flicked the intercom switch and waited as the funnel swung into position. 'Attention crew,' she barked. 'We are commencing an aggressive patrol against vessels unknown, believed to be four Edenite martyr-class warships. You are to remain at highest vigilance. Our enemy may be using experimental stealth technology. So if anything comes on screen get the bang boxes tracking it pronto, understand? We're going in against people who don't know what fair play is. So guard your shins, team. Over.'

The *Chimera* tore through space, the roar of its engines echoing through the hull. Captain Fitzroy leaned back in her seat, crossed her legs and admired her stern, handsome face in the shiny toe of her boot. 'Mr Chumble, get two antimatter fish in the tubes.'

'Gladly, ma'am.'

'Super.' Captain Fitzroy leaned into the comms tube and turned the dial. 'Major Wainscott? You there?'

'Suited and magnetic booted,' the tube growled back. 'We're geared up for boarding. You chaps open the tins and we'll eat up whatever's inside.'

'That's the spirit.' She pushed the funnel away. 'Dockside cavalry's all set, Chumble. Swing us out sunward. We'll hit these blighters from the wing.'

*

Smith took his seat in the captain's chair as Carveth turned the ignition key. The *John Pym* coughed, coughed again and suddenly roared into fearsome life. Needles whirled and battered the far edges of dials. For a moment

Smith thought the ship was going to rip through its moorings, and then the engine sank down, as though the *Pym* had woken in a panic like an old man before realising where it was.

'Sorry,' Carveth said, 'my foot got stuck on the pedal.'

The front thrusters fired and the airlock couplers pulled back. Smith felt apprehension form in his chest like a solid ball, conker-sized and rapidly swelling. He decided to drown out his fear with his own voice. 'Take us out of dock, Carveth! Rhianna, we're going to need you to do your psychic stuff. See if you can sense the stealth ship.'

'Righto, Captain!' she said, and saluted, which had a stiffening effect on Smith's morale. In a whirl of dreadlocks Rhianna turned and disappeared into the ship.

Now that, Smith thought, is a woman.

The space station began to shrink in the screen, receding from view, leaving them out in the dark. 'Good luck, Godspeed,' W declared over the intercom, 'and don't cock up.'

Smith saluted the speaker. 'Righto!' he said.

'And for Heaven's sake don't let the Ghasts get hold of that mirror. Keep it on the ship, and if you have to, destroy it.'

Carveth looked round. 'He means destroy the mirror,' she said. 'Not the ship.'

Smith frowned. 'I knew that.'

Carveth turned the *John Pym* towards the depths of space and they sped forward to do the Empire's work.

*

Barton carefully wrote out a note and one of his drones flew across the hall and dropped it onto the M'Lak delegation. One of the pilots held it against the side of the gilled helmsman's container. Two minutes later, Sedderik turned upside-down and floated to the top of his tank.

'The helmsman is sick,' Sedderik's lead attendant declared. 'He must retire to his quarters.'

'I've taken a hundred and eighty-degree turn for the worse,' Sedderik moaned. 'Carry on without me.'

Barton nodded to the two riflemen guarding the door and they opened it to allow the helmsman to be pushed out. He gave a valiant little wave, and the doors closed.

The Chinese ambassador stood up. 'So the Morlock representative is no longer present. Can this meeting continue without him?' A Yothian whirled its communication-stalks in support. C'Neth rubbed his translucent chin.

The lead M'lak delegate rose to his feet. 'Gentlemen, we have made preparations for this contingency. There is one amongst us trained to deal with complex inter-species diplomacy. May I introduce Gorgar Smashbrain, grand bludgeoner of Narg?'

*

A diode flashed red against the shiny brass of the console. Chumble turned, the light giving his round face a ruddy, cherubic glow. 'Scanners have a confirmed signal, Captain. I have five ships, strung out on a convergent approach. Their target is our very own space station.'

'Keep out on the wing, Mr Chumble,' Captain Fitzroy

replied. 'Engines down.' She checked the visuals: in cold space, sunlight winked on distant hulls, as though five comets converged on the same point of impact. The lights sank on the bridge of the *Chimera*; throughout the battleship, men would be silent at their posts, only the click of levers and the soft hiss of pistons giving them away. 'We'll creep up nice and close, hit them from the side, then roll down the length.'

'A crafty tactic, ma'am, if I may be so bold. But then I never did practice lacrosse.'

'You missed out. All engines on silent, Mr Chumble. Dave, set up a trajectory for each torp. Get ready for evasive as soon as we let rip.'

'A pleasure,' the computer replied. 'Ah, yes. . . the enemy are in close formation, only a hundred miles between each. Tactically primitive. Are you familiar with Caesar's Gallic escapades, Felicity?'

'I never could cook,' the captain replied. 'Tell Squadron Leader Shuttleswade to get his wing ready to scramble. As soon as we make ourselves known. . .'

The cat jumped onto Captain Fitzroy's lap. She gritted her teeth. The players were on the field, the white socks of war pulled up high. To the victor the spoils, she thought. 'What's our range, Mr Chumble?'

'One moment, ma'am,' Chumble replied. 'If I might consult my timepiece here – yes, I do believe we're in range!'

'Open goal.' Captain Fitzroy smiled. 'Looks like the Great Annihilator needs to pay more attention to worldly matters. Dave, how's the angle of dangle?'

'Smooth as a Bach concerto.'

'Zap him!'

Two lights shot out of the *Chimera* and swung right in the viewscreen. They arced upwards, almost lazily, twisted and dived into the nearest Edenite ship as fast and lethal as hawks on a rabbit. It burst in a flower of light. The next moment the explosion was gone and the glowing ruins of the warship spiralled away. A couple of what looked like sparks flew from it – escape pods – but the vessel was dead.

Dave began the course correction the moment the missiles fired. Flames erupted from the *Chimera*'s side like cannon on an ancient battleship, and it changed course in an ink cloud of anti-radar chaff, its logic engine preempting the counter-attack.

'Stick in the shins, and the centre forward leaves the field!' Captain Fitzroy cried. 'Bravo, men – bloody well done! Now prep us two more fish.'

Dave made a satisfied hissing sound. 'Ready when you are, Felicity.'

Chumble turned. 'I have a new reading, ma'am.'

She whipped around in her chair. 'Where?'

'Close, captain. I have no visual confirmation.' Chumble shook his head. 'It makes no sense – we cannot lock, and yet – Captain, it is my firm belief that we have no course but to loose those torpedoes with the very utmost of urgency!'

'Dave, new target. Co-ordinates, Mr Chumble?'

'None, alas!' Chumble exclaimed.

At the bottom of the screen, horribly close, space tore itself apart. The stars warped, as though about to melt. Lightning burst into the darkness and, in its centre, a spacecraft appeared, covered in symbols and thrashing lengths of chain.

'Adjust course!' Felicity Fitzroy yelled as Chumble yanked the levers. 'New target – all guns on new target!'

The ghost ship fired first. Its size limited the payload, as did the range, but it was enough. Three rockets ripped through eight yards of ablative armour and blew the *Chimera* open. By the time the return salvo reached its co-ordinates, the *Pale Horse* had disappeared.

*

Suruk leaned over Smith's shoulder, his mandibles open and fangs bared. '*Nanah nah nah naah nah*,' he snarled at space as the *John Pym* shot forward. 'That is the sound Wagner makes when he rides the Valkyries.'

'Can't he pipe down?' Carveth said as she checked the scanner.

'Right,' Smith replied. 'Suruk, we're about to enter a warzone. Can't you do something more appropriate?'

The alien paused. 'Of course. *Mars*, by Gustav Holtz! *Nananana-na-nanana!* But perhaps you are right. On the open plain of deep space, one must stalk prey with caution.' His yellow eyes narrowed. 'Now we take our revenge for the destruction of the convoy. Now we track our prey and cut off his bulkhead. Ah, to drive my spear into our foe!'

'This ship is the spearhead,' Smith replied. 'Or would be if we rammed them, which we're not going to do. More like a gun. Without bullets. But stil—'

'I'm slowing us down,' Carveth said. 'Hey – we're being hailed. It's a Morlock ship.'

'Put them on.'

As the voice came over the loudspeakers, a picture appeared on one of the monitors: collective clan vessel *Wisdom of the Thirsting Blade*. 'Greetings, humans. It is I, Sedderik of the Gilled. I threw a sickie in order to do battle with our foes. On land I may be an eight-foot talking newt, but in space I have the soul of a warrior!'

'Good to have you here,' Smith replied. 'You're most welcome.'

'Our fighter craft stand ready. Our crew are eager for souvenirs. Wait a moment – incoming transmission.'

'Come in all friendly craft,' the radio cried.

'Hello?' Smith replied.

'Smitty, that you?'

'It's us,' he replied. 'We've got the Morlock frigate with us.'

'Thank God for that,' Captain Fitzroy replied. 'Listen, we're pulling back. We've taken serious damage and are running low on countermeasures. That bloody stealth ship came out of nowhere and put three torpedoes amidships. You'd best warn the station. Maybe if we get the others to help out –' she broke off. Seeking help from the other parties to the treaty would not just be an admission of failure; it would be to end the possibility of an equal alliance.

No, Smith thought, knowing that Captain Fitzroy felt the same. This was their mess.

'Ships on the lidar,' Carveth said. 'I've got an ID. . . three decoy blimps. Two net mines – must've come out of the *Chimera*. Bloody hell! I've got four enemy ships on the scope.'

'Have they seen us?'

'I don't think so.'

'Alright. Slow us down. Let's go in quietly.'

'Wilco.'

Sedderik said, 'Withdraw, Captain Fitzroy. The *Wisdom of the Thirsting Blade* will keep the enemy at bay while you contain the damage.'

'Thanks heaps, newt-chappie,' Captain Fitzroy replied. 'It shouldn't take long to stabilise. We've got nanites in the hull.'

Carveth turned round in her seat. 'They're like little beetles, I think,' she hissed in a loud whisper. 'Friendly beetles.'

'Moving round to intercept,' Sedderik said. 'Fight well, friends!'

As Carveth closed the radio, Suruk leaped to his feet. 'Curse this inactivity! My brethren move to fight and I am sitting in this rusted tub. If I could make my way onto that stealthy craft, that submarine of shame, I would teach its vile crew the extent of my rage!'

'You're right, Suruk. If only we had some proper weaponry. Perhaps I could lean out the porthole with my rifle. . . No.' Smith looked around the room, seeking inspiration. Gerald stared back at him. 'This is a battle of wits, chaps, like poker or lotto. Space is our board, and the craft on it mere pieces in the game. But the enemy do not have a monopoly on cunning, men.' As he glared across space an idea stirred at the back of his mind. 'Only by luring the enemy into a mousetrap will we mastermind their downfall. And then they'll cop it.'

'Real world calling. . .' Carveth put in. 'They're hiding, boss. This isn't a game of battleships. They're in cover.'

'Then I'll make them pop up, pilot!' Abruptly, the idea awoke. 'Oh my God!' Smith whispered. 'I know what we must do.' He looked away from her, away from space, and turned slowly to peer over his shoulder. For a moment he faced Suruk, but he did not meet the alien's eyes.

'Oh, no,' Carveth said behind him, 'you have got to be bloody kidding...'

Suruk chuckled, his laughter rising as Carveth's protests became more frantic. Together, all three of them looked into the corridor.

Rhianna put her head out of her room. 'Do you mind not doing that, guys? It's really weirding me out. And shouldn't you be fighting a space battle?' Then, realising that she was not the object of their attention, she looked down towards the hold. 'The mirror?' she said. 'Heavy.'

Smith activated the radio. '*Chimera*, are you there?'

'Still here,' Nathalie Fitzroy replied.

'I need to get inside you at once. I've got a plan.'

'One last hurrah, eh? Alright. I'll have the chaps look out for you.'

Smith switched the radio off. 'Carveth, prepare to dock. Suruk, is your spear sharp?'

The alien grinned. 'Does the pope cough pellets in the woods?'

*

The *Pale Horse* broke into realspace several hundred miles behind the Edenite battleline. 462 turned to Prong. 'Can we make another jump yet?'

One of Prong's Handymen dipped his robed head and

whispered to him. Prong nodded. 'The generators need to recharge,' he said. 'Thirty-eight minutes. By then the rest of our ships will be in range.'

'Have your vessels adopt a defensive position,' the Ghast replied. 'As soon as we're ready, make the jump and finish off the human dreadnought from behind.'

One of the technicians looked up, tugging his robe back to let him speak. 'Lord Prong, we have a new co-ordinate. It appears to be a Morlock ship, steeped in degeneracy and the wrong kind of wrathfulness.'

'Time to release the fighters,' 462 said.

Prong glared at his ally. 'I'll make that decision.'

At 462's feet, Assault Unit One laid his antennae back against his head and growled.

Prong looked down at the ant-wolf. 'I've decided to delegate that decision,' he said.

'Thank you,' 462 said, leaning into the communications array. 'Attention Ghast and Yullian fighter squadrons,' he barked into the commlink. 'Slaughter-Wing, do you read?'

'All hail Number One!' the loudspeaker snarled.

'Deathbolt Squadron?'

'Obedience is strength, Commander.'

'Gentle Patter of Spring Rain on the Temple Roof of Our Beloved and Entirely Non-Genocidal War-God Popacapinyo?'

'*Yullaaaaaiiiii! All glory to Popacapinyo!*'

462 drew back sharply as the squeal of mingled feedback and rodent fury screeched through the loudspeakers. 'Release the fighters!' he barked. 462 turned to Lord Prong, and found that the Edenite's smile matched his own.

*

The *Pym* swung into the *Chimera*'s hold and the great doors slammed silently behind it. Air howled through the vents, and as soon as the lights flashed green Smith spun the airlock and rushed down the steps.

A siren jangled in the steel rafters. Pilots ran in, heavy in their flight gear, followed by ground crews and technicians. They thundered past the *John Pym* to the rear of the hall where the Hellfires waited in a grim line like dogs straining at the same leash. 'Move it, you lazy bastard!' a voice yelled, and Smith realised that it was the autopilot of one of the fighters. 'Check my guns! Where's my pilot, eh?'

Captain Fitzroy ran in last. Ponytail bobbing, she bounded to his side as the rest of the *Pym*'s crew emerged into the hold.

'You all safe?' she demanded.

'Fine. How are you?'

'*I'm* fine. As to the rest of the ship, that's another matter.'

'Damage?'

'Yes. . . some – and some casualties. I'm just on my way to see for myself. The port railguns took a beating. One of our jamming programs caught a torpedo as it came in: the bomb still hit, but we redirected it onto the main armour. That's not the worst of it, though.'

'No?' Behind him, refuelling arms folded into the ceiling, hydraulics whining.

'Fetch me my blasted pilot, by God!' the Hellfire bellowed.

Felicity Fitzroy scowled. 'Shuttles took a bad'un to the noggin. They've got him down in sick bay, well out the game.' She shook her head. 'Now I've got twenty enemy fighters on the scope and four of our chaps against them. The Morlocks are putting six more into the fray, but our best player's sidelined and the match has hardly begun.' Her face hardened, the lips and eyes narrowing, and all the jauntiness was gone. 'Listen, Smith; if you can get me the bastards who did this, I'll take any plan you've got.'

'Alright,' he said. 'When we raided Deliverance, we picked up a piece of experimental tech. I can't go into much detail, but Carveth here knows how to start it up. We may be able to use it to access the controls of the stealth ship. Once that's taken out, it'll be a straight battle.'

'You think you can do that? Really?'

'I hope so. It's dangerous all right – but for the crew of the *John Pym*, danger is our middle name.'

'Not I,' Suruk put in. 'My middle name is the.'

'The overall result is much the same. We'll need Wainscott and his men too. This could get nasty.'

Captain Fitzroy shook her head. 'Damn, Smitty, you intelligence boys really are into some rum stuff. But what can I do? These are desperate times.' She turned to go. 'I'll tell Wainscott to get here.'

'Pilot!' the Hellfire roared. 'The bloody enemy are here and I'm sitting on my back wheel like a lemon pansy. Who's in charge of this shower?'

'Sounds like he's missing Shuttles,' Smith said.

Captain Fitzroy stopped and looked at him. 'Want to break it to him?'

Something rose up in Smith then: a mixture of pride, determination and wild enthusiasm. 'Dammit, I'll fly the Hellfire,' he said. 'Carveth, the *Pym* is yours. Do a good job.'

'But—'

'*You?*' Captain Fitzroy looked as if Smith had just announced that he was pregnant. 'You know how to fly a Hellfire?'

'Absolutely. I've got an annual about it and everything.'

Rhianna said, 'Um, Isambard. . . that's very brave, but, er. . . no.'

'Nonsense,' Smith replied. 'You're all for following one's dreams, Rhianna. Well, since I built my first model of one, I've dreamed of following my dream of flying a Hellfire Space Fighter—'

'Straight into a storm of lead,' Carveth put in. 'Boss, there's a reason that the only space fighters you've ever handled say 'recommended 12 and up' on the side.'

Captain Fitzroy glanced down the length of the hall, then shook her head. 'Sorry, Smitty, Polly Pilot here is right. I need someone with real flying experience.'

'Exactly,' Carveth said. 'You've got – what, three hours' actual flying time? You'd have to be seriously trained to work one of those. No offence, boss, but it's not for you.'

Suruk stepped forward. 'She is right, Mazuran. This calls for an expert. Captain Fitzroy, I will need a grappling hook and a chainsaw—'

'Where's my pilot?' the Hellfire bellowed. The fighter wing clambered up the sides of their ships, dropped into cockpits as the plastiglass canopies folded down. Slowly,

Shuttles's Hellfire rolled forward of its own accord, turning on its landing wheels. 'I need a bloody pilot!' it snarled. The arrogant nosecone turned to the *John Pym*. 'Hmm. . . who flies this rusty lunchbox?'

'Hey,' Carveth exclaimed, 'that's my ship!'

'Then hop on board, shortarse,' the Hellfire replied. 'If you can work that cranky old grid, you can ride with me.'

'Oh no.' Carveth took a step back from the pointed nose, the rows of gun barrels and the missiles jabbing at her from the upswept wings, the kill markings and the rearing lion breaking a massive ant in its jaws that someone much fiercer than her had painted on the fuselage. 'You've got to be kidding.'

'Do I look like I'm joking?'

'Me?' she squeaked. 'Me?'

'No,' said the Hellfire, 'the other pilot-class simulant standing right in front of me.' Its cannons swivelled down to lock onto her head. 'The one I'm pointing at.'

Smith stepped forward. 'Take me.'

'Bugger off,' the space fighter replied. 'I want the android. In the absence of my chief executive officer, *I* am my chief executive officer, and I'm telling you that I've made my choice.'

Smith turned to Carveth, controlling his anger with difficulty. 'Well, that's. . . you – you lucky cow!'

'Lucky?' Carveth's mouth went through fishlike movements. 'I'll—'

Thrusters rumbled around them, and her voice was lost in growling engines. She tried to make her point through gestures, many of which were not officially sanctioned signals of the fleet.

Rhianna cupped her hands around her mouth. 'We're right behind you, Polly!'

'I'd rather you were in front,' Carveth shouted, but by then the Hellfire was turning to her, flank on, cockpit open. She paused a second, wondering how in hell's name she was getting out of this, and then Suruk stepped in and shoved her buttocks-first up into the chair. And as the cockpit closed around her, she realised that she wasn't getting out of it at all.

Suddenly it was quiet and warm.

'Welcome aboard, girlie,' said the Hellfire. 'How many hours – wait a minute. . . where's your tie?'

'My what?' Carveth could not decide which was more frightening: the baffling rows of controls, or the easily understood awfulness of the view through the windscreen. Below her, Smith was waving like a piston, no doubt cursing her luck at getting to fly a space fighter, much as she herself was doing.

'Your *tie*, woman,' the spaceship said. 'This unit fights smart because it flies smart.'

'Look,' Carveth said, 'this is a terrible mistake. Alright, I'm the only spare pilot, but really – *really* – I've never flown a fighter before.'

'Oh, I get it,' said the Hellfire. Its systems powered up around Carveth. She felt like a mouse hiding in a toaster that had just been switched on. 'You want to cut and run, eh? Flip the switch on the front, would you?'

'This one?'

'Next one down. Thanks.' A light appeared on the dashboard. It said: *Ejector seat now under autopilot control.* The panel next to it activated. It read: *Ejector seat control switch also now under autopilot control.* 'Your flying experience stops at chicken, eh? Want someone else to do your fighting for you?'

Wainscott's men ran past the nosecone, followed by Rick Dreckitt. They looked extremely competent and warlike in their body armour. Rhianna said something to Wainscott, and he grimaced.

'No,' Carveth protested. 'Well, not much.'

'So what *have* you flown?'

'Um. . . the *John Pym*. . . and a sun-dragon on Urn. Look, I've really got to—'

'Dragonrider of Urn, are you? I *like* it! Now listen. . . you and I are going to go out there and blast the living hell out of anything in our path. If I believed in defence, I'd tell you that the best form of defence is attack – but I don't, so let's attack anyway. When they see my colours coming at them, they'll regret the day they were born!'

'Maybe they'll run away, too.' Wainscott's team ran into the *John Pym*. Rick Dreckitt followed them, but paused at the airlock. He lifted his Panama hat and tipped it to Carveth, then waved. 'Knock 'em out, kid!' he yelled, and she could just make out his voice. Carveth waved back, and then Dreckitt saluted and disappeared into the *John Pym*. The airlock door swung shut. The *John Pym* began to activate its engines. This was it. No ducking out now.

I'm coming back from this, she thought. *And when I do, I will go on the biggest bender imaginable. Curry, wine, sex, more wine, more curry—*

'You ready for this?' the Hellfire demanded. 'We'll go in

together. I'll regulate the systems, you do the blasting. Because if you're not ready. . . you know who controls the ejector seat. Now then, pilot, get your hands on the controls, because here we go.'

A mechanical arm folded down from the cockpit roof. It ended in a tiny plug. 'Neural shunt,' the Hellfire said.

Carveth pushed her hair back. The little plug slid into the socket behind her ear.

At once she saw schematics: weapons layouts, datasheets of torque and weight ratios. Her consciousness seeped into the ship, and it partly into her, their nervous systems linked. She felt the ship: its cunning, its ferocity, an unbending determination that frightened and electrified her. She felt fast and dangerous. She could smell pipe-smoke.

'Your brain tastes of Prosecco,' the Hellfire said.

Lights strobed before them. The bay doors swung open and the docking clamps flipped back. The *John Pym* dropped out of the *Chimera* as if falling through a hole in the ground. The first of the Hellfires moved into line.

The intercom crackled. 'What-ho. This is Allie, Shuttles's wingman. Just follow us in, new girl. Your ship'll do the hard work, even if he says otherwise.'

'Thanks,' Carveth said. Her voice hardly worked. The Hellfire cycled through its weapons like a pianist stretching his fingers.

As the docking arm folded down from the roof, putting them last in line to leave the ship, Carveth reflected that it could have been worse. After all, nobody was shooting at her yet.

*

It was pitch black in the hold of the *John Pym*. The power was almost completely down, the engines off except for a slow retro-thruster to hold the ship out of the battlezone. Soon the *Pym* would register to scanners as nothing more than a lump of metal.

'Sounds like bloody madness to me,' Major Wainscott growled. 'Believe me, I know lunacy when I see it. Sometimes even when I don't,' he added, glancing around. 'It talks to me, you see.'

'So do I,' Susan said. She pointed at the major. 'He's right. This sounds mental. But if it works, I'm game. Better than sitting in that dreadnought waiting to get a rocket up the arse.'

Dreckitt helped Smith get the mirror up on end. 'What the hell,' he said. 'The whole deal's a jump ahead of the nut factory, but how does that change anything?' He stepped back, admiring the mirror. 'So how do we work it?'

'Smith knows,' Susan said. 'Is there an 'on' switch?'

Smith wore the Civiliser on his right hip and his sword on the left. His hunting rifle was slung across his back. 'Right chaps, here's the plan: The enemy have an engine powered by this mirror, somehow. It's obviously still working. So, we cross into this netherworld and make it part of the Empire. As soon as any headman appears, we grab him and find out how to nobble the stealth ship. Simple.'

'Great,' Wainscott replied. 'Let's go!'

Dreckitt said, 'Just one thing. If you're with us, Smith,

and Rhianna's doing her shielding thing, who's been driving this crate?'

A sinister laugh came from the front of the ship.

'It's alright,' Smith said. 'We're plotting a course away from the fighting. . . actually, I'll just check that.'

Suruk strode out of the cockpit as he approached. 'I am ready,' the alien announced. 'Let us test the new hunting grounds.'

They called in to wake Rhianna from her trance. She equipped herself with a satchel and a very scuffed pair of boots. It was the most practical gear Smith had ever seen her use. He kissed her while Suruk pulled a face and looked away.

'Let's go,' Rhianna said.

Together they returned to the hold. 'Right then,' Smith said, 'let's get cracking. Wainscott, could your chaps get out of the line of sight? We need to have the jump here.'

'Course,' the major said, and the soldiers drew back.

Smith bent down and got to work on the frame. He turned the dial as Carveth had shown him, the puzzle solving itself as he rotated the little symbols. The diamond clicked into place. He moved across to the clubs. The mechanism spun easily, as if luring him in.

Suruk gave a thoughtful little growl. 'The air has changed.'

'I can feel it,' Rhianna said. 'It's kinda chilled – in a bad way.'

'Nix, lady,' Dreckitt replied, 'Just your imagination,' but his pistol was in his hand.

Smith stood up and began to adjust the little spade in the top right corner, as if tuning a radio. He was unpleasantly aware that his groin was up against the glass. There would be nothing to prevent the nether regions of Hell having full access to the nether regions of Smith.

'One more,' he said. Susan checked the beam gun.

Smith turned the little pieces, rotated each quarter and clicked them together. He pushed the heart down the groove, into the corner. All four pieces were in place. He stepped aside. Rhianna stared at him from the edge of the room. The whites of her eyes looked huge.

They stood in the hold and waited for something to change. For ten seconds, the room was silent.

'Ah, bollocks,' Wainscott said. 'Bloody woman was talking rubbish. It's these androids, Smith. You ought to get her looked at – change her oil or whatever it is they do.'

Suruk stepped forward, levelled his spear, and calmly pushed the butt through the glass. It met with no resistance. He withdrew it, looked at the end and gestured to Rhianna. 'Ladies first.'

'I'll do this,' Smith said. 'Gentlemen, follow me!' He approached the mirror, took a deep breath and stepped into it.

There was a loud noise and Smith staggered back, clutching his head. Rhianna ran to his side. 'It must be psychic feedback,' she said, pressing her hand over his. 'Ummm. . . has anyone got any aloe vera? Raw kelp?'

'I hit my head on the frame,' Smith said. 'Come on, men! This way!'

He drew his pistol, bent low and walked into – and through – his reflection. A wave of cold passed over him, like fever, and then he was on the other side.

He stood in a stone hall, vast and empty. Sheet metal had been pinned to the rear wall, so as to mimic the hold of the *John Pym*. Smith turned around slowly, and took in the sheer size of the hall: an enormous nave, worthy of a cathedral; the floor a chequerboard of tiles. An alien creature had been stuffed and mounted fifty yards above his head amid the vaults; it looked rather like a walrus with wings. Staircases stretched across the ceiling as if the great chamber had been built upside-down. It smelled of dust and, faintly, of soup.

'Well, crikey!' he said.

Suruk emerged next to him. He looked about, nodded, and took a folded top hat from his side. Tapping it into shape, he placed it carefully on the crown of his head.

'You came equipped,' Smith said.

'When in Rome, one should do as the Romans would do,' the alien replied. 'Conquer everything for our empire!'

Rhianna was next. She gazed down the length of the vault and said, 'English perpendicular Gothic, essentially Germanic but with mid-Victorian influences. . . far out!'

Wainscott followed, then Susan, guarding the entrance until the rest of the raiding party were inside the hall.

'What now?' Dreckitt said.

Smith reached into his coat and removed a portable radio tripod. He unfolded the little legs at the end and pulled up the telescopic aerial.

'That won't work here,' Dreckitt said.

Smith took the clean Union Jack handkerchief from his back pocket and tied it to the top. 'It'll work now,' he said. He set the rig down on the tiles. 'I claim this dimension in the name of the British Space Empire. There. It's ours now.'

'This is madness,' Dreckitt whispered.

'No,' Smith replied. 'This is Britain.'

'Same difference.'

'And we are all mad here,' Suruk added.

Wainscott snorted. 'Compared to Sunnyvale Home for the Psychologically Uneven, it's pretty dull.' He checked the ammunition counter on the side of his Stanford gun. 'I bet they don't even have a pills trolley.'

Susan gave Wainscott a hard look. 'Mission first, pills later. Then cocoa.'

'Right. Let's explore this place, then get naked and blow it up. What say you, Smith?'

'Well,' said Smith, 'Seeing that we've claimed this place for Blighty, we ought to tell its inhabitants the good news. Let's go.'

Wainscott made a series of swift arm gestures and the Deepspace Operations Group split into two. They moved down the length of the hall, using the columns as cover, keeping to the shadowed walls. Their boots were almost silent on the stones.

'Where is everyone?' Rhianna whispered. 'You'd think they'd guard the portal, surely. Polly said that she saw horrible things in the mirror when she looked in it.'

'Perhaps they are waiting for us,' Suruk replied, and he smiled.

Craig, Wainscott's infiltration expert, beckoned from the far wall. They crossed the hall and regrouped. 'Found the way in,' he explained. 'I think you'd better look at this.'

It was a broad oak door, studded with iron and flanked

by knights carved into the stone. Across the lintel, a stone figure smiled down at them. Its head and body seemed to be an enormous egg. 'What a skull!' Suruk breathed.

'And that's not all,' Susan said, and she opened the door.

They looked into a castle's grounds. Stone steps led down into a garden: to the right, a maze of hedges; on the left, thick forest bristling with conifers. A high wall encompassed both and, outside it, a patchwork of fields stretched away to the horizon. On the far side of the wall, a wad of towers rose up towards the cloudless sky. The air smelled fresh. The snickering of shears floated up from the garden.

Dreckitt gasped. 'Are we – is this England?'

Smith held his hand out palm-up. He felt no rain. 'I doubt it.'

'My God!' Wainscott breathed. 'Another dimension. I really have gone doolally.'

Smith looked a little closer, and the details of the scene were like the onset of a hallucination. A bird flew too close to a cloud, and a white tendril shot out and dragged it inside. In the distance, men could be seen painting the bushes in the garden. Hedges slid back and forth within the maze like pieces in a Chinese puzzle. In the yard before the castle stood a dozen statues that looked like plasticine. The towers and buildings were subtly shaped like other things: a top hat, a house of cards. They were not quite still; they changed position as if they had wheels, drawing apart almost too slowly to notice. *It's a watch face*, Smith realised, *it's moving like a bloody watch face.*

'Let's get going,' he said. 'Wainscott, how about we split up and work our way towards the central tower– the one that's central right now, that is?'

'Good idea,' Wainscott said. 'The one with the heart on it?'

'That's the fellow.'

'Two-pronged attack, meeting in the middle. My chaps'll flank round the maze.'

Smith nodded. 'Then we'll head through that little forest. See you there, Wainscott.'

'Will do,' the major replied.

I hope this is right, Smith thought as he hurried down the steps. Suruk, Rhianna and Dreckitt followed. If the *John Pym* was damaged while they were away, they could be stuck here forever. Still, at least it wasn't raining.

*

The lift was a mass of twisted ironwork and sparks. Captain Fitzroy took the stairs, bounding down the steps three at a time. Emergency lights strobed in the near dark, and she was lucky to reach the bottom without falling end over end.

They were bringing up the wounded from the portside gun deck, wheeling them into the forward mess for triage. Captain Fitzroy flattened herself against the wall to let the gurneys go past. Castors squeaked: deep within the ship, something collapsed on itself with a slow metallic groan. A doctor called for the orderlies to bring up the resuscitating gear.

'Captain?'

She looked down, recognising the freckled young woman on the trolley. Ensign Driscoll, former right wing, would not be seeing the lacrosse pitch for a while.

'Tallulah,' said Captain Fitzroy, 'what have you been doing to yourself?'

Driscoll spoke through a mix of pain and sedatives. 'You know that big brass lion attached to the mess wall?'

The captain nodded.

'Yes. It fell on me. I can't—'

'Say no more, Ensign. Your captain is here. You'll be right as rain in no time.'

'I think – I think I've lost my leg.'

'Lost it? Nonsense, Tallulah.' She pointed down the corridor. 'Look, it's just over there. You see? There's nothing to be worried about. Just a quick spell in sickbay and you'll be on the pitch in no time. We'll be whacking balls at the Household Division before you can say. . . can say – surgeon!'

'She's fainted, ma'am,' the medic replied.

'Patch her up, dammit.'

She hurried to the port gun deck, ducked under a joist and surveyed the chaos within.

The vast chamber had always looked like a mixture of a cathedral and a pumping station. Now it was bombed out: several guns had been completely destroyed and the emergency systems had barely managed to contain the damage. Most of the fire had been blasted out the airlocks, but shockwaves had buckled the roof and strewn the floor with lidar computers and range-finding gear. Cogs stuck out from the far wall like throwing-stars, hurled there by the force of the blast. An electrical cable with a girth like a python sparked and crackled at her boots.

The chamber was full of people: the injured and those trying to keep them alive. Three technicians in hazard armour sprayed coolant foam onto a small fire. A pair of ratings carried one of their colleagues past her. A gunner hung dead in the rafters, tossed there by the explosion. Twenty yards away, First Lieutenant Collingwood stood beside the wreckage of a railgun, struggling to drag a fallen girder from off the barrel housing.

'Come on, you idle buggers, lend a hand here!' he yelled. 'Mr O'Hare!' He jabbed a finger at a round-faced ensign. 'Run to the engine room. . . tell the chief I want three more technicians and two more sparkies. My orders, tell him – no arguments!'

The lad rushed past the Captain, seeming not even to notice her. 'Status report, Mr Collingwood!'

He was covered in dirt, she saw. His left trouser leg was stiff with foam. 'Not looking clever, Captain.'

'How long 'til we can get back in the game?'

He shook his head.

'Well, how long 'til the remaining guns are functional at least? Come on, man.'

'Forty minutes, ma'am, maybe an hour.' He wiped sweat off his brow. 'It's not just that, ma'am. The crew are done in. And some of the lads think there's nowt can be done, neither – not against a ghost ship.'

'What? I won't have that sort of talk. Put me on the main speakers!'

'Aye aye, ma'am.' He stepped to the comms post,

activated the ship's address system and rang the large brass bell beside it.

'Pay attention, team!' Captain Fitzroy did not lean into the microphone; she just put her hands on her hips and raised her voice. 'The enemy have gone into the lead: they got the drop on us and dealt us a low blow. But we're not out of the game yet. Men, this ship is England – a particular playing field of England, where history tells us all battles are won. I know you have suffered, and I cannot blame you if you are downhearted. But as your captain I ask you this: would you see witches burned in Piccadilly? Would you call a gang of six-foot rodents your lords and masters? Would you have your children live in an ant farm?'

The shouts from the intercom were almost drowned out by those around her.

'Gather your strength, crew. Let those who cannot fight leave the field, and let those who still can fight refresh themselves on the orange slices of righteousness. Pull your socks up and grab your sticks, girls, for the game is far from over!'

Men cheered; someone called 'Huzzah!' Captain Fitzroy turned to Lieutenant Collingwood. 'Ready for action in twenty minutes?'

'Why, no! Ten'll be plenty, ma'am.'

'Good.' She flicked the intercom to the bridge. 'Mr Chumble, bring us around. We're going back in.'

*

Suruk took the lead, having the greatest experience as a

tracker. The little forest smelled of pine needles and sap. The air was thick and close. Every so often Smith glimpsed the high towers between the foliage and he was relieved that they remained on course.

In fact, this new dimension wasn't too different to being in the Chilterns, at least not this part of it. It was not unlike some of the trips Smith had been as a schoolboy, apart from the dragonflies with smouldering heads, the thing that had snarled at them from the undergrowth – looking like a cross between a badger and a corkscrew – and the unnerving suspicion that some of the flowers were watching them. At least they didn't even have to make soup from powder, this time.

The ground was thick with needles, springy underfoot, and Smith was glad that Rhianna had worn her boots, even though he couldn't see her ankles now when she hitched up her skirt. Strange, he thought, how erotic he found her ankles. Equally strange that you couldn't really *do* anything with them. Such poor design pointed to either evolution or a deity without the basic kindness to indulge his sexual peculiarities. It was all very—

'Look!' Rhianna said.

The trees parted, and in the centre of the clearing, next to a clump of the biggest mushrooms Smith had ever seen, stood a long table. It was heaped with crockery, as if it had been used as a canteen by a passing army. Plates, cake-trays, samovars, teapots and silver cutlery lay in piles. Some of the silver had begun to tarnish.

'Hell of a place to chow down,' Dreckitt said.

'Well,' Smith replied. 'They've got teapots. They can't be all bad.'

Suruk raised a hand. 'Wait.'

Smith knew that tone. He froze. Suruk had stopped in the shade of a tree, seemingly lost in thought. Dreckitt paused, his hand halfway to his pistol. Rhianna stood with her head tilted to one side, frowning, as if trying to get some water out of her ear.

'I heard something,' the M'Lak whispered. 'A burbling sound.'

'You sure it wasn't a brook?' Smith replied. 'Brooks burble.'

'I fear not, Mazuran. There was whiffling, too.'

'Whiffling and burbling? Sounds bad. Any thoughts, men?'

Dreckitt pulled down the brim of his hat. 'In my line of work, the only thing that whiffles and burbles at the same time is a wise-guy on a grift. And I'm not talking some bindle stiff pulling a scam behind the eight-ball. Hell, in this joint I'm just glad none of us is called Dorothy.'

'Thanks for that,' Smith replied. 'If you could just transla—'

He was drowned out by a roar from beyond the trees. Something huge ran behind the firs in great bounding hops, the saplings bending to let its massive body through. Each bouncing step pounded the earth, setting the trees shuddering. A great scaly back appeared above the conifers, lifted by flailing, undersized wings. A neck thicker than a man's waist snaked between the trunks, and Smith glimpsed a hideous face, all horns, buck teeth and glowing eyes. It saw them. It roared again.

'Wait, Rhianna,' Smith said. 'You could communicate with the sun dragons back on Urn. Tell it that we're friends.'

'Okay.' She pressed her fingertips to her temples. 'I can feel its mind, but it's all nonsense. Somebody wants to kill something – that's clear, at any rate.'

'Me,' Suruk said. He stepped past her, giving his spear an experimental swing. 'I shall deal with this being. This is a battle I must fight alone. And in case it isn't, I would prefer it if you let me have the first go.'

Smith shook his head. 'Sorry, old chap, but we're doing this together.'

The creature lumbered forward. It had short legs, but the wild flapping of its wings helped lessen their burden. Trailing whiskers like those of a catfish brushed the trees. The eyes burned red, the mouth gabbled and snarled.

Dreckitt checked his pistol. 'What a way to go out,' he growled. 'Twenty-five years on the mean streets, and I get blipped off by a turkey the size of a dinosaur.'

'Maybe it's karma,' Rhianna replied. 'You know, for like Thanksgiving or something. . .?'

The monster ran its huge hand down the table, scooping up a clattering heap of crockery, and hurled it at them. Rhianna threw her hand up, shielding the four explorers, and the air was full of exploding china. Its head – somewhere between a catfish and a bald rabbit – swung down on its python-like neck, and peered at them all.

Smith raised his Civiliser, looked down the barrel, and shot it between the eyes.

The beast stumbled back, shook its head as if to clear it, and lashed out. Smith ducked aside, but not quickly enough, and the hand knocked him onto the table, amid the three-tiered ruins of a massive cake-stand. Smith twisted, broken china crunching under his weight, and fired twice. The bullets disappeared into the monster's chest as if into porridge. It reached out for Smith's head—

And Suruk brought his spear down on the beast's fingers. It roared and backhanded him, and Suruk parted company with the ground. He flew briefly upwards before making loud contact with a tree. Dreckitt's gun banged once, twice, and the creature drew back to the far end of the long table.

'It's immune to my rod!' Dreckitt snarled.

The beast leaped onto the far end of the table. The table flipped up, the edge nearly hitting Smith under the chin, and a rain of saucers broke on the ground around it.

Suruk staggered out of the forest, rubbing his head.

'Suruk, be careful!' Rhianna called. The goggle-eyed head swung to face her.

To her credit, she did not scream. Less to her credit, she reached out and said, 'Hey, I can totally see its tonsils. Check it out, guys. . .'

Smith tore the tablecloth from the remains of the tea party. 'Over here!' he called, flapping the cloth. 'Look!'

He sidestepped, waving the cloth like a matador. The monster turned, quick and lithe for all its grotesqueness. 'Run, everyone!' Smith called. 'I'll distract it!'

'Then what'll you do?' Dreckitt demanded. 'Give it indigestion?'

Smith ignored him. The creature drew back and up, its little wings working as if to break off its back and fly away. It blocked out the sun; the trees and spires disappeared as it rose into the air. The long neck drew back, like a cobra's body.

The monster pounced. 'Run!' Smith yelled, and he

threw himself and Rhianna out of the way. Its claws, like two thrashing spider-crabs, shot past him, clenching on one of the huge mushrooms as if to throttle it. The beast's head darted forward, bit a steak-sized chunk out of the mushroom and spat it out in a cloud of spores.

Smith found himself on top of Rhianna in thick grass, which had been much better when he'd imagined it in private. He hauled himself upwards, grabbed his gun and helped Rhianna to her feet. Beside him Dreckitt raised his pistol. Suruk, still groggy, pulled his spear back to throw.

'Now then,' Smith said, lifting his rifle.

Rhianna touched his arm. 'Wait, Isambard. Look.'

The monster stood a little way off, one arm raised as if to strike. But it was still: the great eyes were fixed on its own talons, not on the humans below. Slowly, the monster moved its claw away from its face, gazing at it in awe, like a medieval artist discovering the wonders of perspective.

The shot was perfect, despite the cloud of fungal spores surrounding the creature's head. One good bullet and it would be ready to adorn the trophy wall, next to the stuffed praetorian. But there was something in its expression that made Smith pause, a mixture of wonder and confusion that seemed eerily familiar.

'It ate all the mushrooms,' Rhianna said.

'Weapons down, chaps,' Smith said. 'Our work here is done.'

Suruk swayed a little. 'Surely you jest. Think of the glorious trophies and the honour we would gain from slaying this beast! Not to mention that it threw me into a tree.'

Smith shook his head. 'No,' he said. 'I couldn't kill it.'

'Why not, Mazuran?'

The monster blinked and looked around, as if unsure how it had arrived. Smith turned to look at Rhianna. 'Because it made me think of you.'

'Um—' she replied. 'Is that because you remembered that I don't approve of slaughtering helpless animals?'

'Yes. And also because it's out of its face on mushrooms.'

Suruk peered at the beast, then at Rhianna. 'Actually, now you mention it, there is a certain resemblance—'

'It's just a dumb animal,' Smith added.

'Dumbest animal I ever saw,' Dreckitt said. 'Come on. Let's find the boss lady and hand out some chin music.'

*

The Hellfire shot out of the *Chimera* like a pip from a fruit, the loss of pressure hurling it into space as the engines fired. Suddenly, all comfort was gone: Carveth couldn't see the other fighters or even the *John Pym*; only the stars ahead, glittering like broken glass. The cockpit was tiny, the engine roared behind her, and she missed the others terribly – especially, she was surprised to find, Gerald.

'All systems go,' said the autopilot. 'Resetting the tonnage counter to zero. Let's get down to business.'

'I've never done this before,' she said. It came out in a rush.

'It's simple. Find the enemy. Blow him up. Repeat until victorious.'

'Right,' she said, her hopes that the Hellfire would fly

itself fading fast. She had to hold the stick, which meant that she wouldn't be able to spend the battle with her hands over her eyes.

It took eight minutes of hard flying to reach the enemy. Carveth watched the dials, checked the fighters around her and wondered if there was an android god and, if so, what the hell it was playing at by letting her get into this mess. She ran though the instrument panel and sensed the depth of control she had over the ship. What were Smith and Dreckitt doing now?

Objects leaped into view. Three spacecraft like chunks of grey stone and, behind them, a sleek black shape, a Ghast vessel. She could see the burning-world symbol of the Edenites painted on the nearest battleship – and then something shot past her line of sight.

'What was that?'

'Enemy,' said the Hellfire. 'Throttle back to combat speed. Don't want to miss the action, do we? Good plan, that, going in for the big fish first. I like your style.'

Panic bubbled up. 'I didn't see the little ones!'

'Well keep your eyes peeled, because here they come. Weapons armed. Ready to stuff a few rockets up the big fellow's jacksie?'

The radio crackled. 'New girl's gone straight in. Break and engage, chaps.'

The enemy rushed in like swooping flies, completely silent. Lights burst from a ship – missiles, and the Hellfire snapped, 'Countermeasures away. Got one turning on the rear.' Light flashed on the right side of the screen. 'First blood to Allie. Nice kill, Hellfire 3946. Pilot? Bandit, three o'clock.'

'Really? Where?' Carveth swung the ship – it moved so easily! And suddenly there was a light ahead, the engine of a Ghast fighter. *Got him!* she thought, and she pressed the left thumb-trigger. The lasers opened up, cutting quad stripes through the night before her. The Ghast jinked, twisted right and down, looping to come back at her. She turned left, yawed the ship ninety degrees and cut the main engine. The Hellfire kept on course, but spun on its axis – suddenly the Ghast was directly before her. 'Fire!' she yelled, clenching the controls in her fists. Chainguns, lasers and missiles streaked out. One of the missiles flew off, bewildered by chaff, but the second turned in and, like an iron filing to a magnet, smashed into the alien ship. It burst in a flurry of light, suddenly nothing but embers.

'I got him, I got him! Did you see that?'

'Nice work.' The tonnage counter whirled on the dashboard. 'Now, the warships.'

'Yes, right.' She shook with fear and wild, shameful glee. 'I got him, I bloody got him.' She pulled up, and the grey-white frigate dropped into her vision. The craft's hide was alive with turrets, whirling to provide defensive fire as the Hellfires made their pass. 'That's a lot of guns,' she said, realising how feeble her voice sounded.

'All the more ammo to explode,' the Hellfire replied.

'I'm not sure.' A panel came on beside her head: apart from two dozen winking lights, a pointless grid-picture of the enemy warship appeared spinning like a bauble on a Christmas tree.

'You'd better not be weeding out, my girl,' the ship growled. 'Because if you've got cold feet now, they'll be much colder when you're floating in space. Now, let's teach these alien bastards who *really* owns the galaxy. All weapons ready, pilot. Just locking us in with the others. . . nice.'

The radio burst into life, a horrible shrieking noise, and Carveth flinched. 'What the hell was that?'

'Nothing,' the ship replied. 'Ghast broadcast, trying to intimid—'

The delay was enough. A disruptor shell clipped the bottom of the left wing and ploughed through the underside of the Hellfire, hurling the fighter off course. They spun away, back towards the *Chimera*. A siren blared in the cockpit. Carveth screamed.

'Bloody malfunction!' the Hellfire yelled. The battle went end over end in the windscreen, ships chasing each other like clothes tossed in a washing machine. 'Bastards've hit the – arrg – *mit mein fliegender Zirkus* – bloody buggering processor – *un prince tres petit, sur un planet tout seul*—'

And as the Hellfire went dead, Carveth passed out.

＊

Smith burst out of the wood, Dreckitt and Rhianna just behind him. Rhianna paused to catch her breath, while Dreckitt fanned himself with his hat. 'Bloody forest,' Smith muttered. 'Why can't they have a path?'

'Yeah,' Dreckitt added, 'made out of bricks. Yellow ones.'

They stood at the base of a broad staircase, made of something that looked like both sandstone and nougat. Before them, the main mass of the castle rose up and moved slowly. Gawky birds circled the towers. Smith drew the Civiliser. Rhianna tapped his arm.

'That tower,' she said, pointing. 'It's in there.'

Each tile in the tower's roof was painted as a playing card. It was a roost for gargoyles, an imposing blend of castle and a cathedral. There were no guards. Far above them, a carpenter sat on a wooden gantry, looking at a plan. He reached under his paper hat to scratch his head, then turned the plan the other way up. A moment later he began to scratch his head again.

'I see no sign of Major Wainscott,' Suruk said.

Smith nodded. The sheer brightness of the place was unnerving. 'No, for one thing, the place is still standing. I'd have thought he would have blown part of it up by now.'

'He's probably gone to apply for a green card,' Dreckitt said. 'I say we bust this joint without him, flying monkeys or not.'

'Totally,' Rhianna said. 'It's time to smoke or get off the hookah.'

Smith walked up the steps. The palace doors were twice his height. The left one was ajar. 'With me,' he said, and as he stepped inside the lights came on.

They rose from beneath the floor, turning the chequer-board tiles into a grid. A reddish glow lit the walls, revealing letters scratched into the paintwork, as if with a blade: W Kt to R Q. It was as Carveth had said, Smith realised: the chains of cards, the paintings of queens and kings. But she had not mentioned the throne under the centre of the hollow tower or the immense candelabra that hung above them like a twisted anchor, playing cards impaled on its spikes. A woman sat on the throne. The place smelled of tallow and old cabbage.

The doors slammed shut.

The Queen of Hearts stood up. In silhouette her crown made her look like a horned demon: it was not much of a relief to realise that the crown was metal, given that it was nailed straight into her brain. She seemed to glide down from her throne, her face as pale as the moon.

'So,' she growled, 'the white queen sends her knight. And three more pawns.'

Smith glanced left and right. From the shadows, figures moved forward. They were the ones Carveth had described – the Grim Reaper ace of spades, the thuggish king of clubs, the sharp-faced knave of diamonds fingering its pointed chin mockingly. This was a nightmare, Smith thought. It took all of his moral fibre to look the queen in the eye: foreign she might be, but she was something very close to a deity.

'Madam,' he replied, 'we are not pawns.'

'Can it, lady,' Dreckitt said. 'I'm done with the crazy talk. We've banged gums long enough.'

'Oh no. . .' hissed the diamond-faced minion, 'the banging's hardly started.'

Suruk looked around the room. 'Interesting. Is that item on your head part of your skull?'

'Quiet, frog-creature!' The queen glared at Suruk. He glared back. 'I had thought the guardian would have killed you in the forest.'

Suruk shrugged. 'We defeated it, but we let it go. Some things are too beautiful to destroy, and history's largest dragon-turkey is one of them.'

The queen scowled at him, a bad policy for anything with a distinct head. She took a step forward. 'So, what do you want from me? A game of chess, perhaps? I can kick a bishop through a stained glass window. An under-ling like you would be no problem. I have a taste for pawn as well as the occasional queen.' She seemed to grow slightly, her face lit with a kind of hungry severity. 'I am the grandmistress of the chess board, the lady of the high stake. I'll mate you in so many different moves you'll be aching for months afterwards.'

'That's enough of that,' Smith said. 'I am Captain Isambard Smith of the British Space Empire and these are my comrades. We didn't come here to play chess with you.'

'Cards, then.' The queen raised her white hands and cracked the knuckles. 'How about a quick shuffle? No?'

'No way.' Rhianna glared straight back. 'Who died and made you queen?'

The queen smiled: the lights dropped and shuddered, and suddenly the room was full of pulsing shadow. 'Nobody's died – yet. I did not inherit this place: I am it. *I* am the ruler of this realm, lady of pleasure and games, mistress of the cards.'

Suruk looked her over. 'I have seen such cards in the telephone boxes of Earth.'

'Nonsense," said the queen. "My courtiers and I have always been here, seeking new. . . techniques of entertain-ment.' She reached into her dress and took out a little box. Its sides moved as her long fingers manipulated them. 'Like this Rubik's cube. Opiates, potions, croquet. . . what's your pleasure?'

'We want Prong,' Smith said.

To his right, steel hissed. The knave of diamonds held a hideous piece of apparatus, tapering to a wicked point. 'Right you are!' it said.

'*Lord* Prong,' Smith added. 'It's his name.'

'Aw,' said the knave, and its shoulders slumped. It put the spike away.

'Ah, Prong,' the queen said. 'Go on.'

'We need to pass through the mirror or whatever it is to reach him. He's an enemy of the British Space Empire. Which, by the way, you've joined. Congratulations.'

Rhianna added, 'He's the high priest of a cult of vicious lunatics. He has no respect for people's rights and wants to prevent the peoples of the galaxy forming an alliance to promote peace and unity.'

'The guy's a two-bit bum,' Dreckitt said.

'Most bums have two bits,' the queen said thoughtfully. 'But it sounds like the same man. Prong found a way to manipulate this place. Not just to pass into it, but to use it to flick an object between your world and mine.'

'We've seen the object of Prong's you refer to,' Smith said. 'And it is terrible indeed.'

'Every time Prong uses his machine, it damages us,' the queen said. 'It drains the life from this place, makes it more like your world.' She shuddered. 'More *logical*,' the queen said, as if it was a dirty word. She leaned forward, her crown looming up like a metal cliff. 'I blame him for the demise of my walrus.'

'Typical,' Rhianna said. 'No concern for the environment.'

'I see.' Smith glanced at the wall. The paint was mildewed in patches. He had previously thought that it was what estate agents called a 'feature' but perhaps the decay was attributable to Prong. 'So how does this machine work?'

'Don't ask me,' the queen said. 'I just rule here.'

'Fair enough,' Smith said. It reminded him of Carveth's attitude when he asked her about faster-than-light travel. She had explained that some things just worked because they jolly well did.

'Come with me,' the queen said. 'Although you may need more peons to take Prong.'

'We've got friends, back in the gardens.'

She frowned. 'Maybe no more. The guardian will re-appear and he will not be pleased—'

'Wrong,' a voice said from the doorway. Wainscott stepped into the hall in a clatter of armour. The major was smiling broadly: Susan and the rest of his team had a look of hard determination. 'A. P. Wainscott, Major, British army,' he declared. 'Sorry we're late. Stopped for tea. Madam, you seem to have a chess piece nailed to your head. Smith, update.'

'We're going into Prong's ship.'

'Now you're talking! Lead on!'

Former Ambassador Quetic lumbered around the throne. He carried an axe and wore a metal breastplate, painted red. Above curled whiskers, two pink eyes glared at the raiders like headlamps.

He fished a watch out of his armour and studied the dial. 'Not much time, offworlders. Go now, or I shall make you late!'

Suruk snarled. Dreckitt cocked his pistol. Wainscott lifted his gun. Smith said, 'The day I take orders from a dirty lemming. . .' and Rhianna tapped him on the arm.

'We ought to leave, Isambard. Think of Polly.'

'You're right. Former queen, your empire requires you to open the portal back to our world. Quickly, now.'

The queen gestured to the shadows. A door opened and two tubby men pushed out a large mirror in a heavy frame. It was similar to the one on the *John Pym*, although the frame had a smoother, more organic design. The fat twins saluted.

The queen pointed. 'And here it is. Prong has configured his end of the portal to work one way only – otherwise I would have visited him a long while ago. Once you are through, there is no going back.'

'We can live with that,' Smith replied.

'Then be my guests. When you see Prong, tell him that the game is up.' The queen turned to the portal, the hem of her gown hissing over the stones. 'Goodbye. And you, Captain Smith. . . if you decide to cross me, just remember that I've got your number.'

'Actually,' Rhianna said, 'he's already dating someone. Goodbye.'

'Let's get cracking,' Wainscott said. 'This place is so demented it makes me want to pull my trousers off.'

Smith nodded. The mirror showed only darkness. His reflection was gone. There was nothing left to do but step through. 'Madam,' he said, bowing slightly, 'if you'll excuse us all, we have a spaceship to catch.'

The queen nodded and the executioner drew back. 'You are all extremely curious,' she said, and she dropped wearily into her throne.

*

Carveth burst back into life to see a needle slide out of her thigh. She screamed, realised that the Hellfire's emergency systems had woken her, remembered that she was in a space battle and did some more screaming.

'Warning,' said the dashboard. It had a new voice, a synthetic woman's voice. 'Severe damage to under-carriage. Landing gear destroyed. Pseudo-neural feedback at maximum. Shutting down systems.'

Lights dimmed and vanished. With a low whine, the engines faded into nothing. Carveth sat up, frantic. The ship was dying around her. She was stuck here. Stuck in a metal coffin—

'No!' Carveth cried, 'no, wait!'

'All systems closing down—'

'Shut your bloody face, you stupid cow!' the Hellfire roared. The cockpit burst into life, the lights flickered and held. 'I'll stop when I say so, you hear? Right,' it barked. 'You alright, pilot?'

'You're alive!'

'Absolutely. Dammit, this hurts. I took a bad hit there. How's tricks?'

'Terrifying!'

The ship let out a fearsome laugh. 'That's what I like. Make a joke of it. Good girl. Now, the last time I checked this wasn't a meeting of the WI – unless that stands for Wanker Incineration – so I want to see thumbs out of posteriors and on the damned controls.'

'Er, you've lost your undercarriage.'

'Yes, and if you look really closely, you might see me give a damn. I don't need wheels to blow scumbags from the sky!'

'But doesn't it hurt? The feedback gauge says maximum—'

'In all honesty? Yes, this hurts. You wouldn't believe how much. But I won't stop, you hear? I will not stop until I'm done, not while there's a battle to win – and nor will you! Now let's get back out there, dammit!'

'I think we should go home.'

'Pilot, do you believe in fairies?'

'No.' Her voice quavered.

'Well I do, because I've got a live one sitting in my cockpit. Now, are you going to lay waste to space or be a waste of space?'

Her head swam. 'Lay space?'

'Good. Hands on the throttle and take us round. Nobody shoots us up and flies away. Nobody! Do you believe me?'

'I believe!' a tiny voice squeaked. For someone who didn't believe in fairies, Carveth sounded a lot like Tinkerbell.

'That's right. We own space, you and me. That fat Edenite crate belongs to you. You just need to take it. We're going to bag him.'

Carveth's eyes looked over the systems monitors. Her heart was pounding, her throat tight, but something in her hands and mind was ready and quick, as though the Hellfire's spirit had seeped into her. She pulled them around so slowly that the engines hardly fired, until the pale grey bulk of an Edenite frigate lay before her.

'Look,' she said. 'I'll do this. But we're out of missiles. We need something massive to get through that armour.'

'Perhaps we should ask around,' the Hellfire said, and she thought she heard an evil smirk in its voice.

The radio crackled into life. 'Morlock fellows, what's your status?' the Hellfire asked.

'We fight fiercely, taking nosecones for the Hangar of Victory,' a voice replied. 'Yet the *Blade of Wisdom* is hard-pressed by crazed lemming men, eager to end themselves on our armour.'

'Roger,' said the Hellfire, 'on our way. And there,' it added, as Carveth's shaking hand set the co-ordinates, 'are all the armour-piercers you could want.'

*

Smith checked the Civiliser and drew his sword. He faced the mirror, and a determined man in a red jacket looked back as if to challenge him. Then he took a deep breath and strode into his reflection.

He felt cold wash over him, and he was through, in a darkened room, surrounded by red-robed technicians. 'Hands up!' he shouted, and the Edenites went for their guns.

Smith closed one eye and put two shots into the chest of a stormtrooper, then blasted a Handyman as he raised his shotgun. A side door burst open and an Edenite lumbered forward as the rotary cannon he held whirred into life. A second later a spear flew out of the mirror and into his chest. Suruk bounded out after it.

Wainscott was next, then Susan and Dreckitt. The major kicked out the legs of a robed thug in a conical hat and punched him unconscious before the brute could even shout 'Unbelievers!'

'Right,' Smith said, 'let's head up and take the bridge.'

From the floor came a thin, hard laugh.

A Handyman lay at Rhianna's feet. His face was waxy in the bad light, his hair hung down like something dead. He smiled. 'You're damned, heathens. There are a hundred times your number on this ship. Even your precious moral fibre will be nothing against such odds. Your blasphemy will be wiped out.'

Susan said, 'He may have a point. Taking the control room might be possible, but if they rush the doors. . .' She shook her head. 'Whatever we do, we need to work fast. Once they know we're here, they'll blow the airlocks and suck us out.'

'So now what?' Dreckitt said.

'We open the portal,' Smith replied. 'The queen said that it was fixed to be one-way. What if we alter that?'

Suruk chuckled. 'And then all Hell will be released. Apt.'

Smith turned to Dreckitt. 'Could we do that?'

He shrugged. 'If I can get the codewords, easily. But without them, not a chance.'

Susan glanced at the Handyman. He sat before them, cradling his wounded arm. 'He knows.'

'Hands off me, woman!' the Edenite spat. 'You may torture my flesh, but I'll never talk.'

'No, we may not,' Smith said. 'I refuse to stoop to such levels. Rhianna, would you mind preparing some sort of herbal tincture—'

'No, not the herbal tincture! Keep that witchcraft away from me! Don't you know what that could do to me?'

Not very much, Smith thought.

' Annihilator curse you, I'll show you how it works.'

The man heaved himself slowly upright. On his own, without his comrades to make noise beside him, he was weak. No moral fibre, Smith realised. 'What shall I do with the portal?'

'Open it. And then it's up to you – although I'd suggest that you run like hell.'

*

'Attention, attention,' the scanner declared. 'Clumsy humans defile the sacred space of Yullia. Destroy the unrodents with noble self-sacrifice!'

'I hear and obey.' Wingman Thwekic Nonch yawed his fighter and twisted away from the M'Lak battleship. The puny frog-monkeys were defending their ship fiercely, for a bunch of offworlder weaklings. In the edge of the windscreen, another Yullian fighter exploded in a sudden blossom of fire. Popacapinyo favours him, thought Wingman Nonch, and then he realised that it was gunfire, not collision, that had destroyed his squadron-mate. 'You failed!' he yelled. 'A thousand curses on your cowardice!' He toggled the radio. 'Scanners detect approaching Hellfire. Moving to intercept with extreme proximity.'

'May you leap to glorious victory,' his squadron leader replied. 'All glory to the war god, brave Nonch. And don't come back.'

Nonch swung his ramship to face the human fighter. It rose into view with an almost lazy grace as if it did not expect to meet opposition. The Ghasts had clearly strafed it before, since the thing had been riddled with disruptor fire. *Stupid fat offworlders!* Nonch's snout twitched with contempt at the furless halfwits, so weak and complacent in the fact of Yullian greatness. How could a species be so stupidly arrogant?

The radio crackled and Nonch toggled it. He recognised the tone of an autopilot.

'What ho, lemming-feller!'

'Offworlder!' Nonch cried, 'Death to your cowardly vessel! In collision I seek immortality!'

'You'll have to catch us first, old boy. Come and get it, Whiskers.'

The radio cut.

*

462 was at the far end of the bridge when the rear doors burst open and a puny bearded human ran in. For half a second he assumed it was just another Edenite weakling, he recognised the bearded man's uniform. 'Hands up, loonies!' Major Wainscott shouted, and immediately the shooting began.

The guards went down in a second. A side door opened and a bevy of gene-doctored ogres like men crossed with hippos thundered in. One of them swung an axe over his head and managed to get it stuck in the ceiling. One of Wainscott's men, clean-shaven and darker-skinned than the major, slapped a charge on the giant's side and ducked away as the brute ripped his weapon free. 462 just had time to ponder how being huge was not a great advantage in cramped conditions before the blastwave threw him to the floor.

He opened his eye and found himself lying next to an

Edenite soldier. The man still wore his combat sunglasses; in death he looked like a dummy. 462 rolled over and saw his praetorian standing over him, blazing away with a disruptor. Assault Unit One bounded over and licked 462's hand. Disappointed to find him still alive, the ant-wolf snarled.

On the wall banks of monitors threw up crazy images. Mayhem had broken out across the entire ship. Figures like Earth chessmen were smashing the Edenites' sacrificial altar of the Annihilator. A huge beast had stormed into the barracks and was shovelling cultists into its buck-toothed maw. One of the monitors flashed up a woman's face, an enormous metal crown seemingly nailed to her head, a striped cat in her arms. Woman and cat smirked at 462 and the screen went dead.

On the far side of the bridge, a M'Lak savage held up a severed head and bellowed at the roof. A female human swung a laser cannon. The beam bisected a trio of lemming-men as they rushed into the room.

'Remove me from here!' 462 shouted from the floor, and the praetorian grabbed the nearest bit of him – his ankle – and dragged him towards the lifts, covering their retreat with disruptor fire. 462 scuffed along the carpet, his coat riding up behind him like the cape of a failed superhero, as he made a mental note to destroy all humans as soon as possible – Edenite and otherwise.

They stopped at the lifts. 462 clambered upright and hammered on the button. Gunfire raged behind him. His bodyguard dropped behind a statue of the Annihilator and fired off bursts to keep the attackers at bay. 462 watched the lights descend as the lift approached. Come on, come on! he thought. *Don't you realise how important I am?*

The lift didn't stop. 462 pounded the door with his small fists, put his working eye to the window, and saw a face: a sour, wrinkled face, seemingly crushed under the weight of an enormous buckled hat. With a rumble of engines, Lord Prong was whisked away.

'Prong!' 462 barked. 'Come back! Don't go – you could martyr yourself and give me the lift. You ungrateful little geriatric little. . . *ak, fak*!' said 462. He looked down at Assault Unit One and sighed. 'Just you and me, eh?' It growled at him.

A gun boomed and the praetorian fell. 462 looked up to see Isambard Smith lower his Civiliser. They looked straight at each other for a moment as if unsure what to do and then both exclaimed, 'You!'

What would Glorious Number One do now? What was the best thing for the Ghast Empire? No doubt, 462 realised, it would be to sacrifice himself. A praetorian would roar and charge forward in the hope of taking some scum with it. A drone would hide in the hope of biting their ankles as they passed.

Thousands of hours of propaganda flickered through 462's mind: endless images of other Ghasts heroically dying for their leader. In that moment, 462 realised that dying for the leader truly was something that other Ghasts did. The greatest service he could give to his species, and to himself in particular, was to stay alive.

'You there!' Smith called. '462! Step away from the dog-monster, you little bugger, and put all your hands up!'

462 thought, *What now?* As if in answer, the lift doors opened behind him.

*

The needle in the pseudo-neural feedback meter was trying to bash its way out of the dial. In human terms, that was agony. Carveth twisted the Hellfire away from the M'Lak warship and the lidar began to flash.

'You lunatic!' she said. 'The lemming men are on our tail now.' She drove the controls forward, yawed right and started to head back towards the *Chimera*, then decided that with the Yull close behind, that was a bad plan. 'What do we do now?'

'What do you think? Dodge, woman!'

'That's easy for you,' she said, twisting back towards the enemy fleet. On the scanner, a blip appeared, a ramship creeping towards the centre of the dial. She turned, swung out on a loose arc and yawed back on the ventral thrusters. The blip fell away for a moment, then resumed its crawl towards the middle of the scope.

'Incoming fire,' said the Hellfire. 'Releasing chaff.'

'What? You didn't tell me he had guns! He can't have guns and ram people – that's not fair!'

'Then let's get rid of him.' A green light flashed on the windscreen and a targeting box appeared in the top-right corner and slid into the centre as Carveth weaved. The crosshairs rotated with the Hellfire and the glowing dot within them grew. '*Angel of Massacre*, Edenite heavy frigate,' the autopilot said. 'Nutter behind, nutter in front. Seems only fair the twain should meet, eh pilot?'

She had an image of the lemming man, his yell of fury rising in pitch and volume as he drew closer, and an image of the Edenites, cackling as they detected her. 'I hope you're right.'

'Course I'm bloody right. Now, I'm squitting out chaff twenty to the bloody dozen, so let's get this bang-on, alright? Get ready for some flak, pilot.'

'Oh, great,' Carveth said, and then the frigate grew in the screen, swelling as if to swallow them. She banked hard and twisted the fighter, the front thrusters blazing on the wings. They look like tombstones, she thought, and the white bulk of the *Angel of Massacre* flashed with anti-spacecraft fire.

'Heavy lasers and ninety-cal flak,' the Hellfire snarled. 'Weave, girlie, weave!' The radio light flickered. 'You still with us, Beatrix Potter?'

'You must die!' the lemming man squeaked across their frequency. 'Die in flames, offworlder!'

Carveth gritted her teeth and pushed the Hellfire closer.

The side of the *Angel* was a blaze of defensive fire. 'That's it, that's it,' the Hellfire said. 'Two lemmings on our tail. It's getting hairy.'

'I know!' she said. She rocked the Hellfire ninety degrees, came in as if to scrape the frigate with her wingtip, the Yull howling over the intercom. 'Make it stop!' she gasped.

'Wilco, pilot. Diverting all power to brakes.'

'Brake!'

The front thrusters burst into life. The nosecone was a pillar of flame. The back of the Hellfire swung out, throwing them out on an arc, and suddenly they were not parallel with the Edenite ship but facing it. 'Chaff away!' the Hellfire called, and Carveth kicked the pedal.

They rushed straight at the enemy, two Yullian ramships following. The *Angel of Massacre* loomed up, a dirty-white cliff, and Carveth pushed the stick forward as hard as it would go. The Hellfire dropped, the mass of the frigate rushing by in the windscreen and the ship ejected the last of its countermeasures.

In the cockpit of the ramship, Pilot Nonch was almost one with the war god.'Brave Yullian warrior,' the onboard computer announced. 'Scans confirm the target vessel as human.'

'For Popacapinyo!' the Yullian pilot yelled. 'Offworlder warship, now you die!'

A new voice, human and terrified: 'You god-damned overgrown muskrat! We're on the same si—'

The ramship crashed straight into the *Angel of Massacre*.

For once, the explosion was audible. It roared over the intercom for five seconds, the voice of the Hellfire bellowing in triumph. 'Got you, you tinpot bastard.' On the dashboard, numbers whirled. 'Look at that tonnage counter, pilot. Jackpot!'

'Bloody hell,' Carveth managed.

'That wasn't bad,' the Hellfire said. 'For a new girl.' A minute passed. 'Message from home. They've got Shuttles up and running, thank God.'

Carveth flopped back in her seat. The thought of home made her want to cry.

'Back to the *Chimera*,' said the ship. 'I'll drop you off at your crate on the way.'

'Right,' she said, keeping her voice level. 'Wait a moment. What do you mean, you'll drop me off? You mean you can fly without a pilot? You could have flown this whole mission on your own!'

'Sorry, but I have to have a pilot on a mission. Just in case I short out. Health and safety, you know.'

'*Whose* health, and whose safety?'

They turned for home.

*

Felicity Fitzroy watched the *Angel of Massacre* explode. As its engines melted down, the other Edenite ships broke formation. Hellfires shot into the gaps, harrying the enemy. The Edenites set a course out of the system. It brought them within range of the *Chimera*.

The dreadnought's guns thundered, and one of the Edenite warships blew apart in a storm of railgun shells. It broke up in a flurry of little fires, chunks of fuselage spiralling from the body like fragments of pottery shattering in slow motion, and Felicity Fitzroy grinned at the scanners and applauded herself.

The last Edenite craft, *Hand of Dust*, shot forward to be crippled by a salvo from the Blade of Wisdom. Sedderik sent his demands over the radio and the Edenites agreed to any surrender that didn't involve a M'Lak boarding party. A Ghast vessel, smaller and faster than its allies, turned tail and fled. Nobody noticed the shuttle that shot into its hold a second before the engines flared, and it was not until much later than its name was recognised: *Systematic Destruction*, the vessel of 462.

The *Chimera* and *Blade of Wisdom* circled the *Pale Horse*, locked their targeters onto its hull and waited to find out what was inside, as if looking at a parcel that had started to tick.

*

'Well,' said the Hellfire as they pulled up beside the *John Pym*, 'here's your ship. I've seen sardines travel in more style, but each to their own, eh?'

'God, you're obnoxious,' Carveth replied. 'But you're also about the bravest and toughest self-aware machine I've ever met. And I've met some. Who do I ask to give you medals?'

'Thanks, pilot, but gongs just slow me down,' the Hellfire replied. It sighed. As ever, if it felt any pain, it showed nothing. 'Someday, this war will be over. You can retire to the country and live quietly and I'll get myself rebuilt as a big red racing car. In the meantime, whenever tyranny raises its ugly head, I'll be there to shoot it off. Remember, pilot: you may not be an expert, but anyone who flies with me and doesn't end up ejected or dead is exceptional.'

'Thank you,' Carveth replied. 'It's been an honour.'

'Likewise. Now naff off out of my cockpit.'

*

The bridge was secure, but the rest of the *Pale Horse* was in chaos. Smith checked the monitors: those few that still worked showed him things he wasn't sure he wanted to see. He looked across the bridge, at the wide array of dead enemies, and reflected that it was time to go.

'Isambard?'

He glanced round. Rhianna stood before him, dwarfed by an enormous man in armoured dungarees. The soldier carried a dead Yullian under one arm and patted it absently as he stared at the roof.

'I've got a prisoner,' Rhianna explained. 'This is Leniatus, Lord Prong's bodyguard. He's a bit – you know. . .'

'I got a lemming,' Leniatus said. 'You want a go?'

'Well, jolly good,' Smith said. 'So much for them fighting to the death, then.'

Rhianna shrugged. 'You've just got to offer people the right things.'

'I'm going to prison,' Leniatus said. 'They got a farm.'

'Super,' said Smith. 'Don't suppose they've got any escape pods, by any chance?'

Leniatus nodded several times, very quickly. 'Oh yeah. They don't let me use them since I wouldn't open the pod bay doors and they told me that was bad.' He looked down at Rhianna. Why is your hair like dead things?'

'They're dreadlocks,' Rhianna replied.

'My lemming has nice hair,' Leniatus opined.

Whooping laughter chattered through the intercom. 'All change!' a voice howled, and a woman answered: 'Off with it!'

Smith did not want to know what 'it' was. 'Wainscott, are you ready?'

On the far side of the room, the major was cutting the insignia from a praetorian's trenchcoat. He looked up and nodded.

The raiding party took the lift down through six levels of what sounded like mayhem. Leniatus kept trying to tug Rhianna's hair. She managed to dissuade him gently. Smith hoped that he wouldn't try it on Susan, who would probably throttle him with his own dungarees.

The doors slid open and there, under a huge picture of the Annihilator, stood the pod doors. The sight of the escape pods sent a wave of relief through Smith as if they were the entrance to a pub.

'Well,' Wainscott said, 'this is it. We'll take the prisoner. The pod on the left is yours.' He leaned in close and whispered, 'Thought you might want some time with your lady friend. I'm sure she'll be most grateful to escape with you, if you get my drift.' He seemed to spasm – he was in fact winking. 'I know all about the ways of woman, eh Susan? Saw it on a James Bond film. Now, time for me to get back to Captain Fitzroy and give her my report.'

*

Smith wanted to return to Wellington Prime in the John Pym: partly so that its role in the battle would be recognised and partly because he was not sure how to park anything else. The crew sat in the cockpit, drinking gin and discussing wonders they could barely comprehend, as had happened many times before.

Something flared on the scanners, a sudden blaze of blue light. Electricity raged over the *Pale Horse*'s hull, the chains flailed in the vacuum, and it was gone.

'It's disappeared,' Carveth said. 'The greatest discovery for two thousand years, lost for good. Thank God for that.'

Suruk sighed. 'I fear that they will not return. Given the choice of this reality or an eternity of chess and decapitation, I know which I would take.' He sipped his gin: as M'Lak custom dictated, he had not taken any tonic water. 'A game of chess is similar to a swordfight, for you must think carefully before you move. However, it is hard to saw through an enemy's neck with a little wooden knight. So, not that similar.'

Rhianna's eyes became both distant and slightly alarmed. 'Whoa, imagine being trapped in there, where logic and proportion are meaningless, shifting like crazy tides of existence. Thank goodness that's not happened to me for at least a fortnight.'

Sometimes Smith wondered whether she got off her tree a bit too often. He topped up the crew's glasses and poured himself another drink. It was going down well. 'So what happened to your fighter, Carveth?'

'The Hellfire went back to check on Shuttles and get welded up. They make those things tough.'

'You didn't do so badly yourself,' Smith said.

'To be honest, I didn't dare get killed.'

'You were damn lucky,' Smith said.

She looked hurt. 'It's all skill, boss, honestly.'

'Getting a ride in a Hellfire, I mean. All I got to do was go to another dimension. Come on,' he added, 'you've all done bloody well, crew. Let's lock the mirror up and go home.'

Together, they walked into the hold. The mirror stood where they left it. It looked absurdly harmless. Smith closed the hold door – just in case – and reached out to the glass.

'Not so fast,' a voice wheezed from the shadows.

Lord Prong stepped out, pistol in hand. The skull glinted on his Helm of Sanctity. He looked smaller and nastier than ever, as though viciousness had shrivelled him into the wicked raisin of a man that faced them now.

'Well, well,' the Grand Mandrill said. 'You forgot to close the other mirror.'

Smith shook his head. Interdimensional travel and gin did not make good headfellows. Or bedfellows. 'Gosh,' he said, 'I didn't expect you to use a portal to Hell.'

'Why not?' It makes perfect sense. And if it doesn't, then that's a doctrinal matter. And what does doctrine say? *Burn more witches!* So everybody's happy.'

'Except the witches,' Rhianna put in.

'You'd know about *that*,' Prong replied, which struck Smith as harsh. 'I suppose I could have escaped like that weasel 462, but no. Coming back here seemed rather more in line with my duties of faith. Especially since it will involve killing the unrighteous. Namely, *you*. Decadent, all of you,' Prong added, almost sadly. 'Your men are weaklings, your women strumpets. You all deserve a good sacred beating.'

'Look,' said Smith, 'I realise you're angry, old chap, but—'

'I'm not old! You keep calling me that and I'll plug you!' Prong's hand wobbled as he raised the gun. His finger had to be weak, Smith thought. Perhaps if he could keep Prong talking for long enough, the old bugger would have to run to the toilet or lose control of his weapon. Hopefully, not both at once.

Smith glanced at Suruk. The alien flexed his fingers and nodded.

'Right,' Prong rasped, 'Unlock the doors and take me to the cockpit. Then, you'll fly this piece of unholy junk back to New Eden and face divine justice. Because if you don't, I'll shoot one of your concubines.'

Everyone yelled and moved at once. Smith leaped aside and drew his Civiliser. Suruk flicked out a knife and threw it in the same motion. Rhianna ran for the door, and tripped on the edge of her skirt. Carveth shouted 'Tosser!'

Prong's bionics made him astonishingly quick. He ducked and lashed out. His bony hand caught Carveth's jacket and in a second he had shoved the end of his gun against her side. 'Nobody move!' Prong snarled. Then he added 'Ow, my knees.'

He stood up slowly, pulling Carveth with him. 'Nice try,' Prong said.

'I actually find the term 'concubine' really offensive,' Rhianna said.

Prong looked down. Suruk's knife had hit him in the chest, where the organs had given up long ago. He had bionics for that sort of thing. 'Just get the door open, or the harlot gets it.'

'He means it!' Carveth cried. 'Just in case you're wondering, he really means it!'

'Give up, Prong,' Smith said. 'It's over. I tell you what. . . once you've finished sewing mailbags, you can do the citizenship tests and, provided you're no longer carrying on like an idiot out of the Dark Ages, you could come and live in British space. Can't say fairer than that, can you?'

'Shut up,' said Prong.

'You'd qualify for a free bus pass. You could probably get new dentures on the NHS.'

'Shut up! Now open the door or I shoot this whore of Babylon!'

Smith shook his head. 'Very well. Carveth, open the door. We'll settle with Mr Prong later.'

Slowly, she took a step towards the hold door. Prong kept beside her, as if glued to her hip. 'Victory over the unbelievers,' he chuckled. 'And I got to stand close to a girl. Wonderful.'

Rhianna cleared her throat. 'Excuse me. Er, Polly?'

Carveth looked over.

'That's the wrong door.'

'No it's not,' Carveth said.

Smith wondered how Rhianna could have made such a basic mistake. Of course, women and maps, but really. . . The truth fell on him like a brick. 'She's right, Carveth.' He pointed. '*That* door.'

'Indeed, little woman.' If Suruk nodded any harder, Smith thought, his tusks would fall off.

'Oh!' Carveth said. 'Duh! What was I thinking?'

Prong shoved her. 'You people are so stupid you can't find your own cockpits. Is it any wonder you lose?' Smith could almost smell Prong's smile.

Carveth swallowed hard and pulled back the bolts. 'Here we go,' she said. 'I hope you're ready for this.'

She opened the door. Smith nodded to Suruk and they crept forward together.

Prong peered into the darkness. 'The lights are off. Wait – I can see things blinking at the back. What are those, stars?'

'Eyes, actually,' Suruk said, and he pushed Prong in.

The Grand Mandrill stumbled into the engine room. Suruk slammed the door and shot the bolts.

Prong let out one long scream. It rose up, twisted into the metal rafters, dropped and curled away into a death-rattle. For a moment the room was silent. Then, behind the door, a new voice said, '*Ribitt!*'

Other frogs took up the croaking. The four crew-members took in the sound of Suruk's young. 'Should we maybe. . . I don't know. . . go and see?' Carveth said.

Suruk shook his head. 'By now they will have stripped him to the bone.' He glanced at his watch. 'And by *now*, they will have eaten the bones as well.'

'I never thought,' Rhianna said, 'that I'd feel pity for a vicious homicidal maniac.'

'I do not want your pit – ah. . .' said Suruk. 'Yes, I see what you mean.'

Rhianna turned round. She looked lost, as if she had just woken. 'Isambard, did I do the right thing?'

'You most certainly did,' Smith replied. 'Your quick thinking saved us all, Rhianna.'

'But I violated my principles of non-violence. And in doing so I killed a man.'

'Maybe, but you can take solace in the knowledge that he was an absolute knob.'

She shook her head. 'So that's it? A man's life is worth less if he's a knob?'

'Well. . . yes.'

'Yup,' Carveth said. 'Sometimes you just have to choose the lesser of two evils. Do you eat horrible diet food or scoff cake and worry about being fat? Cake every time.

Tell me: who would you rather have around: me or genocidal, misogynist, knob-face Prong? If the answer isn't me, don't feel obliged to answer.'

'You, of course,' Rhianna said.

'So there you go.'

'She's right,' said Smith. 'You did a great job.' He put his arm around Rhianna's waist.

Carveth came forward and patted Rhianna's arm. 'Thanks. You just saved us all.'

'This calls for gin!' Smith said.

'Once again, Mazuran, victory is ours,' Suruk declared. 'Our enemies are fallen, my spawn have dined in style and now the females are touching one another like in that book about the finishing school that you keep under your bed. I think I shall leave you to it. Perhaps a hunting trip through the mirror would be diverting.'

He reached out, but his fingertips met only polished glass.

The Dotted Line

28th of August, 1863.

Today I closed the portal and concealed it in a wardrobe. The rest of the apparatus will be disguised as amateur photographic gear. It seems a shame to destroy the research notes, though: with some minor alteration they might be passed off as an entertainment for children. My cover story is perfect: I cannot see how anyone will ever suspect me of any wrongdoing.

Dodgson.

Smith opened the door and slipped into the conference room. 'Well, I've never seen anything like it,' C'Neth was saying, gesticulating grandly. 'An absolute disgrace it was, terribly messy. But then, not being solid, things just go straight through me.'
'Don't they just?' Sann'di added.
   Smith crept towards a chair at the back of the room. Captain Fitzroy waved, stood up and said 'Hullo, Smitty,' in a hoarse whisper. 'I saved you a seat.' She looked very pleased with herself, which was understandable given that they had just won a space battle.

A certain fuzziness surrounded C'Neth. Smith wondered whether this was a sort of force field until he realised that it surrounded the entire room and that he had consumed quite a lot of gin. This was confirmed as his knee made loud and violent contact with a waste-paper bin.

'Arse!' he hissed.

'Hallo there!' C'Neth called. Smith froze. With a soft rumble, heads and equivalent organs turned to him. 'Come in for the signing, have we? Always room for one more, as they say. Here, are you alright? You look terribly flushed.'

'Important fleet business,' Smith said, rubbing his knee. 'The Imperial Fleet never sleeps, you know.'

'Not when we're around!' Fitzroy added.

'I'll bet they don't,' said C'Neth. He formed eyebrows and raised them.

'I've been doing something very important, actually,' Smith said.

C'Neth said nothing. He seemed content to let Smith explain himself – which, now that the discussion had falled silent, was the last thing Smith wanted to do.

From their little tables, the representatives of the galaxy's powers stared at him. Was he a drunkard, a mental patient, a laser-shocked veteran smuggled in to demonstrate the Empire's devotion to the cause of liberty? The Yothian ambassador's speaking-cone began to strobe red; Smith wondered whether this represented laughter or a warning signal.

'Now look here,' he said, much louder than he had intended. It occurred to him that the delegates were already making a perfectly good job of looking at him. 'I can't tell you what I've been up to, because it's secret, but let me assure you that it's been very important for everyone.

'I think you should sign this treaty because there are sides here, don't you know, and it's time you all decided which one you're on. There's a war on, after all. The Ghasts and Yull don't care if you want to stand to one side. They'll come for us all, and they'd rather fight us one at a time. Believe me, no man is an island – except for the Isle of Man, which is an island near Ireland and not really a man although it's got men on it... but that's beside the point.'

Smith had hoped that this would clarify things, but the delegates continued to stare at him. Governor Barton leaned across and said something to Felicity Fitzroy, and she suddenly released a set of percussive snorts, like bullets being cranked through a gatling gun. Smith persisted. If she thought he was so blasted funny, she could damn well have a bit more.

'Look...' he said, easing a finger into his collar, which seemed to be trying to silence him like a boa constrictor, '... you may not like Britain. We may look a bit funny to you. We don't really do emotions, and I know some foreign types have cooked up the idiot notion that we're arrogant. But listen... if the world was a bit more like Britain there would be a damned sight less murdering and wife-beating and stupid nonsense going on because some tinpot dictator or made-up man in the sky says so. So there. If you stand for murder and tyranny, or if you look the other way when innocent people are getting done over, then the only thing I've got for you is a choice between hot lead or cold steel, by God!'

The translation machines did their work, perhaps a little too well, and there was a ripple of movement as a number of delegates prepared to vacate their seats. Smith decided to moderate his tone, so as not to worry them.

'Peoples of the galaxy,' he said, his voice softening a little, 'at the end of the day, what matters is tolerance. Tolerance is the key, because once we start tolerating arses, the whole thing'll go wrong. I've done over more evil buggers than you'd believe, and I'll do the whole lot if needs be. Why? Because I'm not in the market to take orders from gits, that's why. Common decency, dammit.'

He looked around, vaguely hoping that the room would break into applause and drown him out, or that he would at least faint and thus escape this mess. What the hell did all these people want from him, anyhow? A tap-dance routine? He wondered where he was, remembered that he had been talking about people he couldn't bloody stand, and found it quite easy to carry on.

'Do you know, the Edenites would murder my chaps because they weren't meek enough or some claptrap. Well, I mean to say, you can't have that. And the Ghasts and Yull are no better: they'd do in every one of us if they could. And that's why we need to stand firm on this. Hand in hand in tentacle, or whatever those things you're waving at me are, so sign the treaty and let's get cracking, eh?'

Someone tapped him on the shoulder. He turned to see Suruk behind him, smiling fiercely. Rhianna and Carveth were at the door. Behind him, the delegates began to mutter.

'Well, that's just about torn it,' Smith said, and he walked out.

*

'Well,' said Rhianna, 'you said what you believed. And isn't that the real truth?'

The crew of the *John Pym* sat on the benches outside the hall, as if expecting a doctor to emerge and break bad news.

'It certainly came from the heart,' Carveth added. 'As to which end it emerged from. . .'

'It was a bold speech,' Suruk said. 'Personally, I would have ended it by charging into battle, but each to his own.'

Ten minutes later, Captain Fitzroy opened the door and slipped out, closing it behind her.

She paused, looked down at them and let out her virulent laugh. 'Tolerance! Very good!'

'Yes,' Smith said, 'very funny. Ho ho.'

'They signed, you know.'

Smith jerked upright. 'Really? After all that?'

She shrugged. 'Well, truth be told, they signed up ten minutes before you arrived. I did mean to tell you, but it seemed a shame to cut you off. Besides, after your little talk, I doubt they'd dare change their minds.' She yawned and stretched. 'Well, my work here is done. See you soon, Smitty. Keep in trouble and don't do anyone I wouldn't do.' She saluted. 'God save the king. Cheery bye!'

*

'All the parties signed,' W said. On the screens before him, the leaders of the Service smiled and handed round the biscuits.

George Benson polished his glasses. 'Also, we have the device.'

'Excellent work,' said Hereward Khan. 'Really excellent.'

'It will need to be securely stored.'

'We'll put it in the warehouse. There's space next to the Ark.'

W switched off the link and watched the screens go dead.

Now, he thought, it really starts. The Empire would take the war to the enemy. He frowned for a moment, thinking of what that would entail. The Ghasts would be too stupid not to fight savagely for every yard they had captured. The lemming men would leap at the chance to die for Yullia, preferably from a great height. Even the Edenites would put up a vicious show.

But there was no soldier born, bred or engineered that could defeat the Imperial common man. They will have the numbers, he thought, but we will have the quality. And it will be us who do the civilising.

'Hello there!'

W turned as C'Neth slipped through the wall.

'Well, I'm glad that's over!' the Vorl declared, pointing its nose upward. 'All that chatter – and did you see those Yothians? Terribly naff. It's enough to turn you solid, it really is. No offence.'

341

'Glad to have you on board,' W said.

'Oh, me too.' C'Neth tapped him on the arm. 'I know people have questioned our motives, but don't you worry. When it's time for the big push, I'll be right behind you.'

'I can't wait.'

C'Neth tried to put his hands on his hips, discovered he had no hips, and folded his arms instead. 'The thing about galactic tyranny,' he said, 'is that it's all so awfully *vulgar*. There's something so obvious, so crass, so. . . *passé* about destroying Earth. But you humans, along with us – not to mention the M'Lak and the Voidani – well, we might actually make space rather fabulous again, don't you think?'

'You know,' W said, 'I think you're right.' And, breaking the habit of a lifetime, he smiled.

*

Smith stood in the main hall in the shadow of an aspidistra. He watched the delegates leave the chamber, chatting and nodding, and tried to make himself look respectable. It wasn't easy: his body felt as if he had spent the last few days squatting in a wind tunnel, while his brain seemed to have been re-arranged with an egg whisk before being jammed haphazardly back into his skull. A succession of revelations danced through his head. There were other dimensions, full of demonic beings obsessed with cards. Carveth had won a dogfight. The Voidani had decided not to destroy Earth. He would never look at someone with a chess piece nailed to their head in quite the same way again, assuming he met anyone like that.

Maybe it had all been a dream. Perhaps he had brought it on himself, through a combination of drink, overwork and playing board games with Rhianna while she was smoking her jazz cigarettes.

One of the Khlangari wobbled past, hooted something and waved goodbye.

'Jolly good,' Smith managed. 'See you at the next one, eh?'

He reached into his pocket, found no handkerchief and then remembered that he had used it for a flag when he had claimed 'Wonderland' as part of the Pax Britannicus Interstella. *No*, he thought, *it was not a dream*.

Weary, Smith walked down the length of the hall. A few delegates were making their goodbyes. He passed Governor Barton, who stood in conversation with Le Fantome.

'It was, as we say,' Le Fantome declared, '*Excellent.*'

'Yeah, it's been alright, really,' Barton said. 'United front against alien invasion, which is good, and I think the delegates have even left us a few sandwiches. We should invite them back sometime.'

Rhianna stood by the window, looking into space. Smith walked up beside her, and as she saw his reflection she turned and smiled.

'Well,' he said, 'we did it.'

'Yes we did,' Rhianna said.'Spiffingly.'

Smith always liked it when she talked proper to him. 'Would it be appropriate to celebrate having done it by doing it?'

'I think that's an awesome idea,' she said.

'Greetings!' They looked round. Suruk strolled into the

343

room, carrying Lord Prong's hat. He seemed to be trying to play the top of it like a bongo. 'Good news. Sedderik the Helmsman has agreed to take my spawn onto his ship. He will dump them on a suitably damp planet. As soon as I have rounded them up and subdued them, they will trouble us no more. At least, until they are old enough to demand pocket money with menaces. Farewell, parental responsibility!' He gave the hat a firm tap and a large toad fell out of it. 'Found you. There is no escaping the Slayer. So, friends, what next? And whose skull?'

'Next, we have a little rest, Suruk. I think we all deserve it.'

'Oh.'

'It's not obligatory. You get on with the slaying if you want. Just don't let anyone bother Rhianna and I for a little while, eh?'

A wallahbot rolled back across the hall. 'Captain Isambard Smith?' It opened a panel in its chest and took out a telephone. 'Anyone?'

'I shall do the honours,' Suruk said. He took the phone. 'Greetings. . . No, he is elsewhere, doing important things. I am his comrade in arms, Suruk the Slayer. . .' He chuckled. 'Yes, many heads. . . Once again, the Space Empire is not only safe but larger. . . Thank you. . . it was a notable victory. . .' Suruk's smile faded. 'What do you mean, for a colonial? How dare you?. . . Fat oaf, are you drunk?. . . Cease your crazed ravings, or it shall not be merely the heads of the enemy I reap. Choose your words more carefully next time we speak, for when your head flies from your shoulders, you toddler-shaped inebriate, you will know that it is I, Suruk the Slayer, who encompasses your doom!' He slammed the phone down, looked at the others and said, 'The Prime Minister says 'Hello'.'

'Oh, bugger,' said Smith. 'Did you get his number?'

Suruk shrugged. 'Ten?'

There was a brief pause. 'Well,' said Smith, 'leaving aside making a death threat to the leader of the free world, I think we've done very well.'

'Er,' Rhianna said, 'Maybe we should go.'

'Excellent plan, old girl. To space, and to adventure! And look,' he added, pointing down the hall, 'if it isn't our very own ace pilot.'

Carveth strode in wearing her flying jacket and a new white scarf. 'Hello Boss, how's tricks?'

'I like the scarf,' Rhianna said.

'Thanks.' Carveth struck what she clearly considered to be a heroic pose: legs braced, hands on hips. Smith had seen Rhianna do similar things when attempting Yoga. 'Shuttles is up and about, you'll be glad to know. This is his scarf. Apparently I get to wear it because I flew in his ship. And if I don't, the Hellfire says it'll use its new landing gear to kick my arse until I cough up my own buttocks. Now,' she said, lowering her voice and glancing over her shoulder, 'the other news is that there was some food left over from the summit. About a ton of it. So now that the hold is frog-free, the ship is available again for riotous drinking and space travel.'

'Hey, wait,' Rhianna said. 'What about the mirror?'

'It's in safe hands,' Smith replied. 'The Service have it. I'm sure that experts are looking into it right now.'

'Let's hope nothing looks back,' Carveth said.

'Well, quite. After all, I'm sure the secret service would never unleash something that bizarre and dangerous on the galaxy.'

Carveth looked at Suruk, then to Rhianna, and finally back at Smith. 'Oh no. Not at all, boss.'

Suruk rubbed his hands together. 'Come, friends,' he said. 'Let us go forward together, and put the kettle on.'

Acknowledgements

There are a lot of people without whom this book would never have been written. As ever, my parents, family and friends have been great, as have the members of Verulam Writers' Circle, in providing help, support and criticism. John, Ed, Ian and Owen did sterling work in helping to fine-tune the manuscript (I also 'borrowed' a joke on page 99 from Owen, although he doesn't know that yet). And, of course, I should thank everyone, both online and in the 'real world', who encouraged me to send Smith & Co on a fourth adventure. I hope you all enjoyed it. There will be another.

About the Author

Toby Frost studied law and was called to the bar in 2011. Since then he has worked as a private tutor, a court clerk and a legal advisor, amongst other things. He has also produced film reviews for the book *The DVD Stack* and articles for *Solander* magazine. The first of his Isambard Smith novels, *Space Captain Smith*, was published in 2008.

THE CHRONICLES OF ISAMBARD SMITH

by TOBY FROST

Space Captain Smith

In the 25nd Century the British Space Empire faces the gathering menace of the evil ant-soldiers of the Ghast Empire hive, hell-bent on galactic domination and the extermination of all humanoid life.

Isambard Smith is the square-jawed, courageous and somewhat asinine new commander of the clapped out and battle damaged light freighter *John Pym*, destined to take on the alien threat because nobody else is available. Together with his bold crew – a skull collecting alien lunatic, an android pilot who is actually a fugitive sex toy and a hamster called Gerald – he must collect new-age herbalist Rhianna Mitchell from the laid back New Francisco orbiter and bring her back to safety in the Empire.

Straightforward enough – except the Ghasts want her too. If he is to get back to Blighty alive, Smith must defeat void sharks, a universe-weary android assassin and John Gilead, psychopathic naval officer from the fanatically religious Republic of New Eden before facing his greatest enemy: a ruthless alien warlord with a very large behind. . .

'Gives the sacred cows of sci-fi a good kicking before racing home in time for tea.' Dirk Maggs, director of BBC Radio 4's *The Hitch Hiker's Guide to the Galaxy*.

£7.99   ISBN: 978-1-905802-13-5

God Emperor of Didcot

Tea. . . a beverage brewed from the fermented dried leaves of the shrub *Camellia sinensis* and imbibed by all the great civilisations in the galaxy's history; a source of refreshment, stimulation and, above all else, of *moral fibre* – without which the British Space Empire must surely crumble to leave Earth at the mercy of its enemies. Sixty per cent of the Empire's tea is grown on one world – Urn, principal planet of the Didcot system. If Earth is to keep fighting, the tea must flow!

When a crazed cult leader overthrows the government of Urn, Isambard Smith and his vaguely competent crew find themselves saddled with new allies: a legion of tea-obsessed nomads, an overly-civilised alien horde and a commando unit so elite that it only has five members. Only together can they defeat the self-proclaimed God Emperor of Didcot and confront the true power behind the coup: the sinister legions of the Ghast Empire and Smith's old enemy, Commander 462.

A storm is brewing!

More shootouts than Jane Austen, more laughs than Thomas Hardy, and much better aliens than that Trollope chappie!

£7.99   ISBN: 978-1-905802-24-1

Wrath of the Lemming Men

From the depths of Space a new foe rises to do battle with mankind: the British Space Empire is threatened by the lemming-people of Yull, ruthless enemies who attack without mercy, fear or any concept of self preservation. At the call of their war god, the Yull have turned on the Empire, hell bent on conquest and destruction in their rush towards the cliffs of destiny.

When the Yullian army is forced to retreat at the battle of the River Tam, the disgraced Colonel Vock swears revenge on the clan of Suruk the Slayer, Isambard Smith's homicidal alien friend. Now Smith and his crew must defend the Empire and civilise the stuffing out of a horde of bloodthirsty lemming-men – which would be easy were it not for a sinister robotics company, a Ghast general with a fondness for genetic engineering and an ancient brotherhood of Morris Dancers – who may yet hold the key to victory. . .

'. . .a rollicking good yarn told with wit, style, and lashings of moustache wax.' Henry Coningsby, Waterstones

£7.99   ISBN: 978-1-905802-35-7